Praise for

Hunting Midnight

"Sets the standards on erotica meets paranormal . . . will have you making a wish for a man with a little wolf in him."

—*Rendezvous*

"Amazing . . . red-hot to the wall." —*The Best Reviews*

"A roller coaster ride of hot passion, danger, magick, and true love." —*Historical Romance Club*

Catching Midnight

"A marvelously gripping mix of passion, sensuality, paranormal settings, betrayal, and triumph . . . Dazzling . . . A sensual feast." —*Midwest Book Review*

"Holly has outdone herself in this erotic tale . . . A must-read." —*Affaire de Coeur*

"A wonderfully passionate read." —*Escape to Romance*

The Demon's Daughter

"A sensually erotic novel, and one of Ms. Holly's most entertaining . . . she blends history, fantasy, and intrigue to keep readers engaged to the final page."

—*The Best Reviews*

"Entertaining historical romantic-suspense fantasy that never slows down . . . powerful." —*BookBrowser*

"Holly crafts a thoroughly engrossing tale, deftly melding an alternate Victorian London with a retro-futuristic flair. That alone would make this an exceptional book, but the deeply sensual and emotional nature of her work also makes this a must-have for fans of more erotic romance."

—*Booklist*

continued . . .

Strange Attractions

"A sizzling, erotic romance . . . readers will enjoy this wild tale."

—*The Best Reviews*

"A different kind of erotic story."

—*Sensual Romance Reviews*

Personal Assets

"Holly has two great strengths: great sex and wonderful sentimental stories—who ever thought that those two could be successfully combined?" —*Sensual Romance*

"For a sensual and sweeping examination of contemporary relationships, with the extra zing of some very hot erotic writing, you can't do better than *Personal Assets.*"

—*Reviews by Celia*

Fantasy: An Anthology

"Emma Holly's Luisa del Fiore takes sexual allure to new heights . . . A five-star winner . . . Will keep you reading under those covers late into the night." —*Affaire de Coeur*

Beyond Seduction

"This erotic Victorian romance . . . [brings] the era to life . . . Emma Holly, known for her torrid tales, treats her readers to an equatorial heated romance." —*BookBrowser*

"Holly brings a level of sensuality to her storytelling that may shock the uninitiated . . . Fans of Robin Schone and Thea Devine will adore the steamy love scenes here, which go beyond the usual set pieces. [A] combination of heady sexuality and intriguing characterization."

—*Publishers Weekly*

"Emma Holly once again pens an unforgettably erotic love story . . . A wonderful tale of creative genius and unbridled passion." —*Affaire de Coeur*

Beyond Innocence

"The love scenes were an excellent mixture of eroticism and romance and they are some of the best ones I have read this year." —*All About Romance*

"A complex plot, a dark and brooding hero, and [a] charming heroine . . . a winner in every way. Go out and grab a copy—it's a fabulous read . . . A treat."

—*Romance Reviews Today*

"Truly beautiful." —*Sensual Romance*

"A superb erotic Victorian romance. The exciting story line allows the three key cast players to fully develop before sex scenes are introduced, which are refreshingly later in the tale than usual." —*BookBrowser*

Books by Emma Holly

COURTING MIDNIGHT
THE DEMON'S DAUGHTER
STRANGE ATTRACTIONS
PERSONAL ASSETS
HUNTING MIDNIGHT
CATCHING MIDNIGHT
BEYOND SEDUCTION
BEYOND INNOCENCE

Courting Midnight

EMMA HOLLY

BERKLEY SENSATION, NEW YORK

THE BERKLEY PUBLISHING GROUP
Published by the Penguin Group
Penguin Group (USA) Inc.
375 Hudson Street, New York, New York 10014, USA
Penguin Group (Canada), 90 Eglinton Avenue East, Suite 700, Toronto, Ontario M4P 2Y3, Canada
(a division of Pearson Penguin Canada Inc.)
Penguin Books Ltd., 80 Strand, London WC2R 0RL, England
Penguin Group Ireland, 25 St. Stephen's Green, Dublin 2, Ireland (a division of Penguin Books Ltd.)
Penguin Group (Australia), 250 Camberwell Road, Camberwell, Victoria 3124, Australia
(a division of Pearson Australia Group Pty. Ltd.)
Penguin Books India Pvt. Ltd., 11 Community Centre, Panchsheel Park, New Delhi—110 017, India
Penguin Group (NZ), Cnr. Airborne and Rosedale Roads, Albany, Auckland 1310, New Zealand
(a division of Pearson New Zealand Ltd.)
Penguin Books (South Africa) (Pty.) Ltd., 24 Sturdee Avenue, Rosebank, Johannesburg 2196, South Africa

Penguin Books Ltd., Registered Offices: 80 Strand, London WC2R 0RL, England

COURTING MIDNIGHT

A Berkley Sensation Book / published by arrangement with the author

PRINTING HISTORY
Berkley Sensation edition / October 2005

Cover art by Franco Accornero.
Cover design by George Long.
Interior text design by Kristin del Rosario.

For information, address: The Berkley Publishing Group,
a division of Penguin Group (USA) Inc.,
375 Hudson Street, New York, New York 10014.

ISBN: 0-425-20632-7

BERKLEY® SENSATION
Berkley Sensation Books are published by The Berkley Publishing Group,
a division of Penguin Group (USA) Inc.,
375 Hudson Street, New York, New York 10014.
BERKLEY SENSATION and the "B" design are trademarks belonging to Penguin Group (USA) Inc.

PRINTED IN THE UNITED STATES OF AMERICA

10 9 8 7 6 5 4 3 2 1

To my writing buddies:
Michele Hauf and Nita Abrams,
whose company makes me smarter, happier,
and certainly better fed!

Chapter 1

NORTHERN ENGLAND, 1813

The rain poured down like God's own deluge. That this comparison was justified could only be known to Lucius White, the oldest living blood-drinker in the world.

Hard silver sheets pelted his swaying coach and turned the rutted Northumberland road to mud. Braced to keep his balance in the creaking carriage, Lucius pulled the shade from the window and peered out. He found little to admire. This was sparsely peopled land. No charming village of rose-strewn cottages met his gaze, no isolated country estate. One would never guess it was May, much less mid-afternoon. The sky was dark, and clouds as gray as Lucius's eyes piled up behind the sharp-ridged hills.

Lucius's companion saw none of it. Edmund was a shape-changing immortal just like himself. He slept with his shoulders wedged in the corner and his long legs stretched across the black leather seat, as insensible to his surroundings as one felled by drink. Even so, Edmund managed to look the very picture of a fair-haired medieval lord.

He had been traveling with Lucius since the elder changed

him more than four hundred years before. From that night forward, Edmund had made Lucius's comfort his central care. Because Edmund was unintrusive and quick of wit, Lucius had never wished to change the arrangement. He did, however, wonder how he had inspired it. It had been ages since he felt moved to obey anyone.

He was glad—so far as he was able to be glad—that they had come here for Edmund's sake. Edmund's human descendants still dwelled in the area, and every so often he liked to assure himself they were well. Had the younger *upyr* been awake, no doubt he would have felt the charm of home scenery. It was day, however, and he slept. Because there was not a scrap of sun to avoid, this was more from habit than need.

Ancient as he was, Lucius had few needs left: blood now and then, sleep, a run in his wolf form. Friends were a luxury he believed he could do without. They served a purpose, but what he felt for those he had was more the memory of affection than the thing itself.

Why should I live? he wondered so distantly the rain seemed to speak the words.

There had been a time when *upyr* needed no enemy but themselves to keep their numbers sparse. With the formation of the *Upyr* Council to maintain order, their survival was much increased. Others besides himself could carry the elder torch.

Lucius's only claim to importance was that he was the last of the first *upyr,* the sole member of his race who recalled any world but this. The planet of his birth had been wet and green, a jungle whose sun filled half the sky. More than that, he could not say. As for his life here, he did not remember much beyond the last thousand years. Still, was not the death of any unique creature a sad event? Would not Lucius be missed if he disappeared?

He tried to care, but the coachman's rain-drenched misery had more substance. When the carriage lurched to a halt halfway up a hill, the human's disgust cut through his thoughts.

"Stay," Lucius ordered Edmund, though the other barely stirred as Lucius shoved the windblown door open. Lucius's Hessians sank to their ankles when he stepped outside. Rain pummeled him in sheetlike gusts. The cold did not discomfit him. In truth, the drumming was a mild pleasure. He was a cold creature himself. For the moment, he was at one with his surroundings.

"Horses can't get up this slope," the coachman shouted when he judged Lucius near enough to hear.

Soaked through, the many capes of their driver's greatcoat wrapped slick and black around his hunched shoulders. Because Lucius and Edmund had forgone the usual complement of footmen for the sake of privacy, the coachman was the only human there. Judging him wet but well, Lucius turned his attention to the four wretched equines who were harnessed between the coach's shafts. His heart squeezed with unexpected pity. Not only their tails but their noses hung to the mud. They had no knowledge of inns and stables short miles away. They only knew they felt terrible.

"I will walk with them," he called to the coachman. "Spare them my weight. Maybe with encouragement, they will get on."

Ignoring the human's skeptical thoughts, Lucius touched each beast in turn, allowing his power to flow through their shivering hides. Had the atmosphere been less thick, the coachman would have seen a soft gold glow. Lucius excelled at weaving glamours and could appear as mortal as any man, but over the years, his strength had grown so great its use was difficult to hide. When he reached the lead horse, he put his mouth to one ear.

"There's a boy," he whispered, sending soothing images of stalls and hay. "I'll keep you warm until we reach the yard."

He clucked to get them going, taking the shaft in hand so

the only weight the horses had to drag was their own. With an exclamation of surprise, the coachman slapped the ribbons across their backs. Not hard, thankfully. The human might be unsentimental about his partners, but he was not cruel.

No worse than other humans, Lucius mused. *And better than plenty of* upyr.

This thought had barely left his mind when he heard a hail and, through the gloom, spied a frantically waving lantern.

Highwaymen, thought the coachman, *come to slit our throats.*

"Someone has overturned his carriage in the ditch," Lucius shouted before the frightened man could reach for his blunderbuss. "I think we shall have to carry him to the inn."

His sharp *upyr* eyes had seen the carriage's remains. Indeed, the carrier of the lantern soon splashed up. The solid appearance of Lucius's old-fashioned coach, along with his inescapable air of authority, seemed to reassure the man he'd found help.

"Thank the Lord," he panted, his plain servant's clothes soaked through. "I'm afraid my master is taken bad."

Taken bad implied something different from broken limbs. Not in the habit of wasting speech, Lucius followed the servant to the wreck. There he found a youngish human huddled beneath a makeshift oilcloth lean-to. Well-wrapped against the weather, the man's eyes glittered with some fever. He appeared not to understand what was happening. He moaned when Lucius scooped him up, his body as hot as fire against his rescuer's cooler skin. He did not smell particularly appealing, even to one who liked human scents. Lucius judged him very ill indeed.

"Follow us," he said to the servant. "And bring whatever possessions you think your master cannot do without."

The servant hastened to obey, and soon they were lifting the invalid into the coach to the accompaniment of the coachman's audible grumbles. Not unreasonably, he believed the horses could not handle the extra load. Edmund was sitting up inside, awake but bleary, able to muster little more than a wide-eyed stare.

"Accident," Lucius said. He passed the rest of the story straight to his mind, along with a warning to get his glamour in better order. North of England or not, no human could be as pale as an *upyr*. Caught unawares, Edmund's skin was close to glowing.

Lucius waved the servant into the coach. Edmund would not harm him, and nothing could be gained by him taking sick as well.

That settled, Lucius guided the team up the last rises, befuddling the minds of his mortal watchers to permit speeding their progress without remark. The inn they reached was small: stables, a tap room and parlor, a few humble rooms for guests. Its size did not matter. Any warm place would serve.

No sooner was their arrival spotted than they were met with all the bustle humans seemed unable to do without. Tea was brewed, and coal fires stoked, and much conflicting advice offered as to whether a doctor should be summoned. During the hubbub, the servant (his spirits recovered from drying off) revealed that his master was the son of old Squire Delavert—rest his soul—back from the Indies to claim his inheritance.

"Never thought he'd see a penny," the servant confided. "Him being the younger son, and hardly the favorite. Why, if that horse hadn't tossed his older brother on his head, my master would have been cut off. That's why he sailed to Antigua to make his fortune. But can't nobody make fortunes today, not with *Parleyment*"—this mispronounced with scorn—"abolishing people's right to buy slaves!"

This declaration inspired a mix of murmurs, the locals having thought little about the issue. Nearer injustices like the price of bread had a better chance of arousing them.

Lucius kept his own opinion to himself. Humans were stubborn creatures. Any immortal who aspired too passionately to change them soon found his heart broken.

In this instance, at least, it seemed a kind of justice would be served. To judge by the dull black spots in the sick man's aura, Lucius doubted he would enjoy his good fortune long.

The question of doctors exhausted, the new arrivals—minus the coachman—were shown to a snug chamber. The invalid was put in bed, the innkeeper having decided the apothecary would be called if the weather cleared. Lucius would have been content to ignore the newcomers then, but Edmund pulled him aside.

Lucius noticed his friend was fully alert. Had Edmund been in his wolf-form, his ears would have been pricked. As they stood together before the window, the rain cast shifting patterns across his inhumanly perfect face.

"Have you seen him?" Edmund demanded in a low murmur.

"Of course I saw him. I carried him inside."

"But have you *looked* at him?"

Lucius saw little point in examining anyone who was likely to be beyond all earthly intercourse within the hour, but apparently there *was* something to see, because the sick man's servant was eyeing him. When he caught Lucius staring back, he crossed himself. *Spitting image,* Lucius caught from his poorly shielded human mind.

"He resembles me?" Lucius asked.

"More than *resembles,*" Edmund said with a muffled laugh.

Interest aroused, Lucius moved to the bed. His pulse gave a tiny fillip at what he found. Seen without his head-wrapping garb, the similarity was striking. Though the ailing man had attained no more than his third decade, he had the same fully silver hair as himself, the same straight features and smooth high cheeks. Lucius lacked the man's air of dissipation, but had he been human and possessed of a bit more color and flesh, the two could have passed for mirror images.

"Lord above," breathed the manservant, looking from one to the other. "You and Master Lucas could be twins."

Lucius's interest thrummed again at the name—Fate plucking the strings of his ancient soul.

Edmund looked at him meaningfully. Rather than acknowledge this, Lucius sat by the sick man's hip. The coincidence could mean nothing. If a man lived as long as he had, he might well encounter a double. Even if Fate was spurring him to take action, who knew what that action was? The man appeared beyond healing, even by Lucius's power. Nor was healing humans an interference he performed lightly. Humans had their own gods, or at least their own destinies. Lucius did not have the hubris to set himself against that.

"Lucas," he said softly, placing one hand on the sick man's perspiring cheek.

The invalid had subsided into a doze, but at Lucius's touch, his eyes twitched and then opened. Though unfocused, they were the very color of Lucius's own, down to the tiny threads of blue only the strongest lights revealed.

"You," the man said hoarsely, the first word he had spoken.

"Yes," said Lucius. "I look like you."

The man was in a state beyond surprise. "Dying, aren't I?" he said as if amused. "Must have picked up a fever on the ship."

His servant made a sound of protest, but Lucius would not deny his prediction. Instead, he inclined his head.

"Hell," said the man, then stopped to cough. When it ended, he was breathless. "Guess I'll miss my chance to lord it over those fools in Bridesmere. I was looking forward to that."

Lucius handed him the madeira the innkeeper's girl had left. She had not wanted to quit the room afterward. Something in her, deeper than self-preservation, was drawn to the scent of the *upyr*'s power. Fearing Edmund might find her too attractive, and betray himself with signs of hunger, Lucius had been obliged to catch her eyes and order her to go.

Edmund always had liked feeding from females most.

The sick man was too weak to be troubled by urges so tied to life. He took the wine from Lucius's hand, swallowed painfully, then sagged back, the glass still clutched to his chest.

"You saved me," he said. "At least from dying in the ditch. I've half a mind to leave my worldly goods to you."

"That would be unnecessary," Lucius said. "I've worldly goods of my own."

"Yes, but you'd give those hypocrites a turn. Make them think they weren't quit of me. I'd look up from hell itself to laugh at that." His lungs rattled as he both laughed and coughed, a fit that seemed unlikely to cease before his final breath.

"Master!" exclaimed his servant, just as Lucius touched his chest to take away the pain.

As he thought, the pain was all he could remove. The spots in the sick man's aura swarmed about his fingers, like angry wasps forcing his touch away. The man's body, or perhaps his soul, would not allow Lucius to heal him even had he wished.

Perhaps the sick man knew his end was near. His humor fell away as his coughing eased, replaced by an unearthly intensity. "You witness it," he gasped with a sideways glance at his servant. "I make this man, whoever the hell he is, my lawful heir. Everything I have, including my debts, is his. If he is as rich as he claims, he should not have trouble settling them."

Lucius shook off a moment's shock. "Are you certain this is what you wish? A friend or relative might be more appropriate."

"Hate 'em all," said the man, subsiding with the ghost of an acerbic smile. "Luckily for you, I haven't known you long enough to take you in dislike."

Lucius exchanged glances with Edmund. It struck him as

a bit ridiculous that a human would make him his heir, and for no better reason than a chance resemblance. One might conclude the man was wishing he could leave his fortune to himself!

At his silent request for an opinion, Edmund shrugged. "You cannot doubt he means what he says."

"'s a deathbed request," the man said with a laughing rasp. "You cannot in good conscience refuse."

A tightening low in Lucius's gut told him refusal was exactly the course he should choose. Who knew what human nonsense this bequest might embroil them in? His kind lived best and safest in the shadows.

"I cannot die in peace unless you agree," the man added slyly.

"A churchman might do you better for that."

"Ha. I hate those prosing meddlers worst of all. Come then, you've the look of an honorable man. Walked with your horses, you did, and took a perfect stranger into your care. Surely you're not too finical to accept a bit of property in return. My gambling debts should ease your conscience easily enough. Racked up quite a few while I was waiting for the old man to die."

"Damnation," Lucius muttered in surrender, in response to which the man chuckled.

As it happened, Lucas Delavert lingered to midnight, the very hour *upyr* powers reached their height. Thinking him better, the servant left to find a meal. Lucius did not stop him, though he knew the sick man's quiet did not herald an improvement.

He reached for Lucius's hand. His grip was unexpectedly tight, and power flowed across the contact without Lucius willing it. Shored up a bit, the man grimaced at his own panic. "'Tis the fear that pains me most. Given how I've lived, I've no doubt I'm bound for the pit."

"I do not believe in Hell," Lucius said. "If there is a god, I believe He grants each man peace when he leaves this world. If there is not, nothingness is all man has to fear."

"Well, you're no prosing fool." The man laughed weakly. "Nor very comforting. Don't think I fancy the idea of nothing any better than the fire. Wish I didn't think I'd be forgotten. That'd comfort me most of all."

Lucius could not think what to say to this, and did not get a chance to try, for just then the man's spirit flared in a golden burst of light, swallowing Lucius's sense of anything beyond it. Lucius saw the dying man's life even as it left him, *lived* it as though it were his. Lucas Delavert's birthing cry. His childhood. A favorite pony named Mr. Bunch. The voice of his older brother, Daniel, lifted in scold. *Why, Lucas? Why must you disappoint our father?* With limbs like silk, his dark-skinned mistress rolled atop him in their gauze-draped bed, warm West Indian breezes tickling their skins. His manhood pulsed as she enveloped it. *Lucas,* she moaned in admiration. *You are so strong . . .*

Forgotten passions swamped Lucius. Love. Fear. Envy. Joy like a burst of sunshine. He had a mortal's feelings again, with every weakness and every strength that implied. He wept with it, unable to command his own emotions in the slightest way. For a space of time he could not count, he was utterly lost to himself.

Edmund brought him back by slapping his cheek. Lucas . . . *Lucius* realized his friend had dragged him to the window. The casement was open and the now-soft rain pattered on his face.

"What . . . happened?" he asked, his own voice foreign.

Edmund laughed breathlessly. "I was going to ask you the same. You would not respond to me. Nothing moved but your eyes—and they followed scenes known only to yourself."

Lucius pressed his hands to either side of his aching head. "He gave me his memories before he died." He glanced at the body on the bed—now no more than a husk—and could not help shuddering. "He said he did not want to be forgotten."

Edmund was staring at him, his features still as stone: a quirk *upyr* developed when in deep thought.

"What is it?" Lucius demanded. "What are you thinking?"

Edmund shook himself. "I am thinking you would not have asked me that an hour ago. I am thinking it would not have occurred to you to be curious. Most of all, I am thinking this is a sign."

"A sign!" Lucius's mouth twisted.

"Well, if not a sign, then an opportunity. Think, Lucius. You share this man's appearance and memories. No one here knows he's dead. Even if they found out, you could thrall them into believing whatever you like. You could *be* him, if you chose."

"Why would I want to be him?"

"Because for a century you have not been a part of life. You exist—needing little, feeling less. Everyone has noticed it. Aimery. Gillian. All the Council. But if they could see you now . . . Your hands shake, Lucius. Your eyes brim with emotion."

Lucius braced his shaking hands against the rain-damp sill. "Those symptoms will pass."

"Maybe you should not let them. Maybe you need to plunge into life, to let yourself care as humans do. None of us want you to die. Why do you think Aimery sent me to watch over you?"

Lucius's eyes widened. Aimery was Edmund's brother and head of the *Upyr* Council in Rome. If he had asked Edmund to do this, his fears were severe indeed.

"I assure you," Lucius said, "I have never had the slightest urge to embrace the sun."

"No urge, maybe, but some morning you might have done it out of ennui."

Edmund's eyes were the ones glittering now. Lucius had

underestimated the depth of his attachment. The discovery perplexed him even as he felt—he paused to put a name to the sensation—even as he felt oddly touched.

"My survival means that much to you?"

"Your happiness," Edmund corrected. "Your enjoyment of life's drama."

Lucius ran his fingers through his short, cool hair. The dead man's locks and sideburns had been longer. Lucius would have to spell his to grow. The recognition that he was considering Edmund's proposal gave him a shock. "We have no idea what dangers this might involve, what exposures we might risk."

Edmund smiled, baring slightly sharpened, dazzling teeth. His relish for the challenge was obvious. Perhaps Lucius was not the only *upyr* who had grown bored.

"It has been many years," Edmund said, "since a paltry bit of danger could put me off."

The death of Mr. Lucius White of an unknown fever was an event of interest for the countryside. It was lamented that the apothecary could not have been called in time, but all in all everyone considered it lucky that Mr. Lucas Delavert, son of the squire that was, had found the stranger on the road and saved him from the otherwise sad fate of dying in the rain.

More compliments were heaped for assigning his servant the task of escorting the body back to London. Mr. Delavert, a dignified, youngish man, seemed uncomfortable with the praise, but this was considered evidence of a commendable humility. Indeed, everyone was much more pleased with the gentleman than they expected, having heard through local rumor that he was wild.

Edmund struggled not to laugh at Lucius's reaction to this praise, but with every passing moment, the utter madness of their endeavor struck Lucius with greater force. He had stolen a man's identity. He was going to assume his place in the human realm.

Most infamous was his arranging to have Delavert's body—supposedly *his* body—buried in a place to which it had no ties, though he was glad the manservant had gone with it. He had no wish to be keeping company with anyone who'd known the real Delavert so well.

By the time he and Edmund settled into the carriage, Lucius was grim. The coachman, now convinced he had been driving the heroic Mr. Delavert all along, assured them they'd reach Hadleigh Hall within the hour.

Edmund looked smugly pleased sprawled in the forward-facing seat. He was garbed in midnight blue and blinding white. The fashions of this period suited his athletic frame, from the skintight pantaloons and frock coats to the starched cravats and high-top boots. Come to think of it, even encased in medieval armor, Edmund had been a bit of a peacock.

"Lord," Edmund marveled now, his hand pressed to his waistcoat. "I fed so well from the people at the inn I might sleep all night." He grinned at the look Lucius gave him. "You need not reproach me. You did not want to spell them, and I am not as powerful as you. I had to bite them to ensure my thrall would stick. We would not want anyone remembering anything to contradict your story."

"*My* story." Lucius stared darkly out the window. The moonlit landscape was transformed by the recent rain. These northern hills would never be soft, but they were romantic, their heather kissed with purple, their boulders sparkling as if sprinkled with fairy dust. Lucius's mouth tightened at his thoughts. His *upyr* vision allowed him to see color even in the dark. Seeing beauty, however, depended upon the mortal whose memories he now harbored.

"You must make me your steward," Edmund said. "Then I may order your staff about and have my quarters underground. I do hope this Hadleigh Hall is fine. I shall think it hard if the squire's estate turns out to be a cramped farmhouse."

"Hadleigh Hall is a good, large place with a handsome park," Lucius assured him with a mix of emotions not his own. "The gardeners alone could comprise a small regiment. You shall have sufficient underlings to satisfy even your vanity."

Edmund laughed. "Your wit returns. I am sure that is a good sign, too."

Lucius was sure of nothing except that he wished most heartily to turn back.

Chapter 2

Theo Becket had come to town on a secret mission. That being so, the last individual she wished to meet on the pavement in front of Black's was Lady Morris. The wife of Bridesmere's mayor was a woman who wouldn't have known the meaning of discretion if it had been painted in foot-high letters across her chest.

Given how stout she had grown within the comfort of her marriage, it very nearly would have fit.

"Why, Theodora!" Lady Morris exclaimed. Sybil Morris was an old schoolmate of their mama—though in truth "old school rival" might be a better term. Having moved up in the world since then, she considered herself beyond any need to call Theo or her sister "miss."

Theo tried not to clutch her bundle too guiltily. "Good day to you, Lady Morris. Have you come to take the air?"

Bridesmere's prosperous high street sparkled down to its cobbles beneath a rain-washed sky, but Lady Morris laughed as if this were the drollest comment she'd ever heard. "I hope I know better than to take the air in town. I have come to visit

Mrs. Black. She has been getting the most exquisite embroidered silks from Italy, and I confess I cannot bear for anyone to have a chance at them ahead of me . . . especially now."

"Especially now?" Theo repeated, precisely as Lady Morris wished.

Lady Morris's manner was all elation. "La, I wonder that you have not heard! It is such a matter of speculation in my circle. Mr. Delavert the younger is returned from the Indies. Hadleigh Hall is to be occupied again, and who knows what other fine gentlemen may come to visit. My dear Sir Mayor called on the man this morning, and found him quite agreeable. From the looks of the trunks being unloaded in the hall, he has his own fortune to add to the squire's. Such an admirable thing, I think, when rackety young men make something of themselves."

"He is unmarried, I take it."

"Marvelously single." Lady Morris smoothed the navy velvet sleeve of her spencer with a kid-gloved hand. She was entitled to at least one cause for her contentment. Stout or not, she knew how to dress her Junoesque figure to best effect. "Naturally, I think my Lily worth at least an earl, but it does not hurt to keep one's options open. If two young peoples' affections become attached, who is a mother to stand in their way? Mr. Delavert is engaged to dine with us Tuesday next, before anyone else in town, and I am determined Lily shall have a new gown."

"I am sure Lily will enjoy that," Theo forced herself to say, imagining too clearly what the new gown would be made of.

"Indeed. My Lily has exquisite taste. My only regret is that your dear mother and you cannot be among the party. But perhaps later some more general entertainment can be arranged. A ball at the assembly rooms, in which many levels may mix. Certainly, it is not my intention to keep the man locked up!"

"I could never think it," Theo lied with a gentle smile.

Lady Morris's hope to do precisely that was transparent. "You are far too gracious to wish any estimable person less than the broadest possible acquaintance. Only in variety, after all, can that which is truly superior be found."

"Quite," said Lady Morris, her eyes narrowing only slightly in suspicion. "But I am keeping you from your errands. How I admire you and your mama for doing with but three servants. I declare, I can hardly accomplish all I must with ten!"

"It is indeed a marvel," Theo acknowledged.

"Well, but my dear husband's position must be kept up and that, thankfully, is a burden your family is spared. I take leave of you then, Theodora. Please give your mama my best regards."

"I hope I can give her better than that," Theo muttered as Lady Morris disappeared into the shop she must now wait to enter, and perhaps would not be able to enter at all today. She had purposely come at an hour when most ladies were at home.

Her vexation caused her to grip her bundle too tightly. At the betraying crackle of the paper, she forced her fingers to relax. Resigned to putting off her errand, she tipped her head to the cloudless sky. *She* was not too proud to take the air in town. Hopefully, once she'd ambled down the street and back, her luck would have repaired itself.

The Becket family—now sadly reduced to two girls and their mother—lived in a narrow townhouse on the corner of King George Square. The square was as tidy and respectable as the merchants who lived there could make it, but the Becket house seemed added as an afterthought. Half the width of the other houses, its features—though also halved—managed to looked squashed, giving it the air of an apologetic servant squeezing through a crush. Because the Beckets lodged there on favorable terms, they did not complain, at least, not beyond the occasional sigh.

As the daughter of a rector and the widow of the vicar who had shared his living, Mrs. Becket—and her daughters—were unquestionably genteel. Just as unquestionably, they had never in their lives been rich. Comfortable, perhaps, while the father and husband lived, but once their use of the vicarage was lost, even simple comfort was in short supply. If the mother felt the sting of their conditions most, it was because she recalled better days. Her fear was that her daughters, through association with those who labored for their bread, would marry into a lesser sphere than that to which their birth entitled them.

Aware of this, her daughters refrained from admiring the merchants' sons in her presence.

At the moment, her younger daughter was far from unhappy with her lot. Her errand complete, she ran lightly up the steps to the front parlor. Her shawl she kept about her shoulders, their finances not allowing for extra fires unless the chill was keen. She ignored her reflection in the hall pier glass. She knew no one would call her pretty, dark and small as she was. In looks she resembled their Welsh father. As a result, the best she could hope was to be thought exotic—and perhaps passably witty.

Similarly attired, her older sister waited in the parlor on the settee. Caroline Becket was tall and fair, her sweeter nature making her the favorite among their acquaintances. Even when they were girls, she was well-behaved. "A little lady!" everyone would exclaim. Theo had arrived at being a lady by difficult, dragging steps, her favorite activity as a child being climbing over walls to see what lay on the other side. It was her punishment for this that led to the discovery of her gift, since her exasperated mother had set her to mending her own torn frocks.

With such differences between them, by rights Theo should have hated her sister. Fortunately, Caroline loved Theo every bit as much as everyone else loved her and was, on many an occasion, Theo's best ally. Now, as Caroline spied her sibling, she set her novel aside. *The Mysteries of Udolpho* would have to wait.

"Well?" she demanded in a hushed whisper.

Fighting a laugh, Theo skipped across the threadbare carpet to show her sister the jingling contents of her reticule.

Caroline's muffled squeal of pleasure, considering its cause, was not the least bit genteel. "So much, Theo! Oh, how pleased you must be. Mrs. Black is paying you well."

"She has sold every length," Theo confessed breathlessly. With her hand pressed to the high, rib-hugging waist of her frock, she sank onto the settee to better enjoy their tête-à-tête. "She is getting twice what we expected, and says everyone loves your fiction of the needleworking Italian nuns. Not a soul has guessed the silk comes from Spitalfield's. But, oh, what a terror I received this morning, for whom do you think I should meet on the doorstep but Mama's least favorite schoolfriend."

"Not Lady Morris," Caroline breathed, the horror infinitely more enjoyable for being shared.

"The very same. Worst of all, she had come to buy *my* embroidery for her daughter. If I did not know what she was paying, I would be bereft, for I meant to hold back the green silk with the butterflies for you. Now I fear if you wore it, Lady Morris or one of her friends would recognize my hand."

"We cannot risk that," Caroline agreed. "If Mama found out you'd been selling your needlework . . ."

The sisters exchanged a deeply understanding look. Their mother would be mortified.

"Thank goodness Mrs. Black is close-mouthed," Theo said. "And that Uncle has agreed to bank the money. If only I could stitch faster, our debts would be settled with great dispatch."

"If only I had a skill," Caroline sighed, "I should help you repair our fortunes."

Theo smoothed her sister's wheat-colored curls. "Your

beauty is your fortune, and your good nature. With luck, we shall ensure you never throw them away on some 'awful upstart lawyer.' "

She expected her sister to laugh at the repetition of their mother's favorite epithet, but she blushed and lowered her gaze. "You shan't be thrown away, either," Caroline said in a feeling tone. "After all your work, that would not be fair."

"I had my chance," Theo said, her own cheeks threatening to color. "The next turn must belong to you."

"Theo," her sister scolded, covering her hand.

Before Caroline could try to assuage the guilt for which there was no cure, their mother entered the room. In looks, Mrs. Becket resembled her older daughter, in the quickness of her temper, the younger one. Her figure was trim, her face but lightly lined. While her means dictated her taste more often than she liked—if not often enough to mend their finances—her mode of dress was elegant. Today, she seemed distracted. Her fingers fussed with the ruffles about her throat.

"There you are," she said to Theo. "I've been looking for you all morning."

"I've been to Mrs. Black's, to see if she had some ribbon to freshen up my bonnet."

"Well, you may put your bonnet back on. I am sending James to hire a carriage. We must go to my brother. I have heard the most aggravating news, and I swear I shall not draw one free breath until I set it right."

"What news?" Caroline asked sympathetically—even as Theo's mind raced to the likeliest cause.

"It is Mr. Delavert," she guessed. "You have heard Lady Morris means to entertain him."

Mrs. Becket dropped into a chair. Theo's work table sat beside it. The sampler she'd been pretending to stitch to cover up her paying work lay across the partitioned top.

"I heard it from Mrs. Connor," their mother said, "whose kitchen girl heard it from Lily Morris's lady's maid. They are saying he must have ten thousand pounds a year, in addition to what he inherits from the old squire. Worse, they claim he is even handsomer than his brother was, and that his time abroad has polished his rough edges."

"Oh, Mama." Caroline laughed. "How can that be worse?"

"Because Lily Morris will catch him," Mrs. Becket cried, sounding quite wild, "before he has a chance to lay eyes on you!"

"Mama, I think you give myself and Lily too much credit."

"I do not. You are the handsomest girls in town. As to that, Lily's personality is by far the inferior. She is a peculiar creature: virtually without conversation. When she does speak, one has the feeling only she knows what she means. It is no wonder her mother scarcely allows her to say a word. If Lily Morris did not dress so richly and play so well, no one would give her a second glance."

"She does play like an angel," Theo murmured with a touch of mischief. "If this Mr. Delavert is musical, all the matchmaking mamas may as well despair."

"Rubbish!" Mrs. Becket's cheeks quivered with outrage. "Why should your sister be so pretty and so good if not to marry well? You nearly managed. I don't see why she should not better you."

Theo gasped at this unthinking cruelty. To talk of "nearly managing" a marriage as if she had lost her Nathan through some careless error . . . Yes, she might have been wrong to pursue him, but she had loved him and he had died. More precious things had been ruined than a chance to be called "missus."

"Oh, Theo," said Mrs. Becket, gone contrite at the hurt in her daughter's face. "Forgive me. I should not have said that. It is this temper of mine. It makes me say things I do not mean."

That Theo had the same temper, yet did not express it thus, she found impossible to mention.

"Oh, perdition take it," said Mrs. Becket, casting off her

misstep with the little curse. "If my brother cannot get us an introduction, I shall throw myself off Old Bridge."

"*That* is your plan?" Theo's dismay caused her mother to frown again. "That Uncle shall arrange it? Mama, much as I love him, I do not think your brother can call on Mr. Delavert."

"He is the son of a gentleman," their mother said, the prim set of her mouth betraying that she knew she was in the wrong. "His manners are as fine as any man can boast."

"He is a grocer," Theo said as gently as she could. "I do not think the less of him for his trade, but the Delaverts are an old landed family, second only to the Fitz Clares. Uncle William would do better to call on his cook than on the man himself."

"It is true," Caroline seconded. "I do not believe this scheme will serve. Only think how Uncle would feel if he were rebuffed. I hope—" Caroline cleared her throat. "I hope you will forgive me for suggesting it, but if you really are determined to make this man's acquaintance, the most sensible course might be to ask Lady Morris to invite us to her dinner."

"I ask Lady Morris," their mother spluttered. "*I,* who married the second cousin to the second cousin of Lord Fitz Clare. I go groveling to a woman who is the daughter of nobody, whose husband is a mere knight bachelor, a man who received his knighthood—I might add—because he owned a public house our *honorable* regent used to get drunk in. I should be ashamed to claim such a title myself, and yet I think Sybil would carve it into his boot soles if she could, that he might forever be stamping 'K.B.' in his wake."

Theo bit her lip against a grin, this accusation probably truer than her mother knew.

"She has been kind to us in the past," Caroline said, as ever inclined to think the best even of those who deserved it least. "And she loves to play Lady Bountiful. If you ask her humbly—"

"If I ask her humbly," their mother burst out, "she will have won before we get to fight!"

"Not truly," Theo said, reinforcing her sister's plea. "It would be a stratagem, such as that Signor Machiavelli wrote about. You need only play on her vanity and she will agree. Surely, for Caroline's sake, you could bring yourself to do it."

"Oh, not for my sake," Caroline protested. "For yours, if you wish, or not at all."

"It does not matter for whom I would do it," sighed their mama, "because I refuse to give into Sybil Morris's power to turn me down. Oh, what an inconvenience not to have been born a man. I should call on every eligible young man I met. You should both be married three times over!"

Theo was the first to let out her laugh. Fortunately, her mother saw the humor, too. "I would drink port," she declared, her eyes twinkling. "I would spend all day hunting and block the fires with my big, fat rump."

"Oh, no, Mama," Caroline demurred. "Even as a man, you could not be fat."

With this foolery and that which followed, all was soon warm between them again—just as Theo liked. Despite the return of amity, Theo knew better than to think her mother was relinquishing her ambition to put them in the way of Mr. Delavert. Her daughters would have to watch her closely, lest she devise an even wilder scheme.

Caroline came to the same conclusion. Sweet she might be, but not completely blind. While Mrs. Becket left to dismiss the carriage, she drew Theo to the window seat. "Mama isn't going to give this up."

"Not when she has made it a battle for honor between her and Lady Morris."

"But it is so silly. I do not even wish to be married."

"Do you not?" Theo looked at her closely. "Not even to have a home of your own?"

Caroline ducked her head and fiddled with the window's latch. "I would not like having to part from you."

Theo smiled. "If that is your sole objection, you must take me with you. You may put me in the attic next to the schoolroom. I shall be 'Aunt Theo' and scold your many children . . . or spoil them, whichever you prefer not to do."

"Guess," Caroline said with a little laugh, but Theo did not have to. "Maybe *you* will marry Mr. Delavert."

"I? Oh, never. I am a dark little monkey compared to you."

"Maybe dark little monkeys are to his taste. Besides, you are pretty, Theo. Lieutenant Thomas thought you the prettiest girl he knew—and that was after coming to court me." Caroline folded her arms as she said this, daring Theo to contradict the simple, if shameful, truth. The stubborn pose was so unlike her and so kindly meant that Theo could not be hurt.

"He cared for you," Caroline said, her soft brown eyes shimmering with tears. "I know Mama didn't fully approve of him being a naval man, but Nathan Thomas was a good-hearted, worthy soul. Please believe you shall be loved just as well again."

There could be no response to this except to embrace her sister and blink hard.

As she did, it struck Theo that, given how kind and beautiful her sister was, should Mr. Delavert fall in love with her, he would be a very lucky man.

Chapter 3

Hadleigh's servants accepted their new master with little fuss. Lucius held each one's gaze in turn and they fell in line—or as much in line as human servants ever did. They were not suspicious, at least, and Lucius was glad to avoid enforcing his will with the added power of a bite. He preferred leaving the minds of the mortals he dealt with as untouched as possible. Respect was good enough for him. He had no liking for sycophants.

Recognizing the servants the real Delavert had known was strange. The thoughts of those with the noisiest minds told him young Mr. Lucas had been no favorite. The housekeeper in particular thought him wrong to have put off coming home when his brother died. Lucius had to hide a smile as Mrs. Green silently vowed to keep the female servants out of his way. Despite the glamour Lucius had wrapped around himself to pass for human, she thought him too attractive for safety.

The maids themselves seemed more interested in their new steward. More than one blushed hot as they surveyed the fit of his clothes. As far as Lucius was concerned, Edmund was welcome to their attentions. He preferred solitude to the company of bed partners.

His and Edmund's separate duties thus apportioned, Lucius spent his first night at Hadleigh acquainting himself (or reacquainting himself) with the house and grounds. His first morning, to his surprise, he spent receiving gentlemen callers in his study, all of whom, not coincidentally, possessed daughters of marriageable age. Because this alarmed him more than a bit, Lucius politely evaded all their invitations except for one.

Bridesmere's mayor was a genial man, neither so intelligent that he alarmed, nor so stupid that he annoyed. That he had not known the real Lucas was a plus. Best of all, he only had one daughter, a daughter he secretly thought had little chance of catching Lucas's presumably worldly eye. With such low expectations, he was the obvious choice to accept.

Considering this more than enough to have accomplished once the sun was up, Lucius pleaded a headache and retired for the afternoon. The staff thought him a freakish fellow, but he was too exhausted to care. Though Lucius could be active during the day, that did not mean he enjoyed it. He was very happily dead to the world as soon as his head hit the down pillow.

Had he known what he would dream, sleep might have been less welcome. He lay on his back within a glassy cylinder, one of many in the ship's large bay. This was the holding chamber for the repair crew, where they "slept" until their services were required. The milky walls of his container curved less than a hand span above his face.

He had never liked being enclosed. He fought panic, fought to breathe, then realized the automatic life support was doing it for him. He was not being wakened to perform a job; he had merely been roused from his coma so the ship could check his conscious brain functions. He could not move except to blink, and could not feel except where sweat rolled down the cords of his neck. His stress levels were too high not to register. Relaxants began to tick into his system, to slow the pounding of his heart.

Subject viable, announced the tiny monitor above his face. *Next check, one hundred cycles.*

The flow of drugs into his veins increased, but rather than falling back into stasis as he should have done, Lucius found he was no longer paralyzed. Helpless to stop himself, he thrashed against the tube's claustrophobic walls.

Alarms shrilled in his ears.

"Bastards," he cried as pain shot through one flailing kneecap. "Damn you, let me out!"

He was drenched in sweat when Edmund shook him from the dream. Lucius had taken the old squire's apartments, but when his eyes snapped open he did not see their grandeur. Instead, as if he had not truly awakened, the stasis pod still surrounded him.

To his relief, Edmund's voice tugged him back to the present.

"You were calling out in your sleep," he said. "I did not recognize the language."

Unsettled, Lucius levered himself upright. Though he had not consciously warmed himself, his skin was dry. The bed's gold velvet hangings, doubled for protection against the sun, were closely drawn. Beyond their barrier, he smelled the night, cool and rustling with promise. His invisible tremors eased.

Sensing Edmund's anxiety, he spoke. "I doubt *I* would have recognized the language. These days I remember only human tongues."

"You sounded . . . troubled. Were you dreaming of the ship that brought you here?"

Lucius was not surprised by his guess. They had spoken

of his origins now and then. Though the question did not anger him, he didn't know how to respond.

Edmund gripped the bed's mahogany post. "It must have been strange to travel through the stars."

Lucius swung from the bed and strode soundlessly across the carpet to the window. He folded the shutters open and took a breath. "It was strange—and terrifying and wonderful."

He felt the emotions as he named them, and saw in memory the earth's small sun glaring from the heavens like a baleful eye. That sun had changed his people, warping the basic codes that formed their being, transforming them into a race of previously unimagined power: a race of immortal blood-drinkers.

Before the change, Lucius had been the lowest order of servant. The adjustment to near-god had been challenging.

He shuddered the memories away. That time was gone. The rich civilization his people had encountered had long since faded from human remembrance. For all anyone knew of it today, the entire period might have never been.

Edmund's hand settled on his shoulder as Lucius stared out at Hadleigh's park. For one odd instant another picture rose: young Lucas Delavert galloping his black gelding across the rolling grass below, thinking this time he'd outrun his punishment.

"I suppose they're all gone now," Edmund said. "Those who came on the ship with you."

"The last of the first elders embraced the sun before you were born."

Motion stirred the air behind him as Edmund flinched. Young as he was, an hour spent in the sun would set him ablaze, and a minute would raise blisters. By contrast, *upyr* as old as Lucius took days to burn, suggesting that those who had left this world before him had been quite determined to.

"Do you miss them?"

Lucius turned to see the worry, clear as crystal, in Edmund's blue *upyr* eyes. Around Lucius's ribs, the weight of the past tightened like a vise. He doubted Edmund understood the strength it took to keep his memories from crushing him.

"I do not remember them enough to miss them," he said lightly.

This answer seemed not to satisfy. The younger man had always been more attached to family and friends, as witnessed by their current presence in Bridesmere.

"I went to the castle last night," he said, letting the matter drop. "Robin is well, though worried about Percy's sulks."

Robin was Edmund's son by blood, and Percy was the lately orphaned head of the now ancient Fitz Clare line. At only five, the diminutive baron was too young to be without a strong protector, at least to Edmund's thinking. Luckily, Edmund's son, also an *upyr,* had agreed to serve as his guardian.

"I am not surprised the boy is sulking," Lucius said. "For a human, losing one's parents is no easy thing."

"No, but Robin hopes his spirits will rally. I only speak of it because, when I went to visit Robin last night, my wolf smelled deer in your woods. I thought a hunt might be in order."

Lucius smiled. "I would think you'd be hunting maids."

"Had two already," Edmund admitted. The memory of how determined the pair had been to have him—and at the same time—flitted satisfyingly through his mind. "This hunt is to work off the stiffness from our long journey."

"Just be careful. The old squire's gamekeeper may have set traps. I wouldn't want your wolf to get caught."

Edmund hesitated. "You don't wish to join me?"

Lucius surprised them both by rasping out a laugh. "I have enough souls warring inside me tonight. I do not need to add my wolf 's as well."

Edmund nodded, still not leaving. Lucius brushed his

cheek with his fingertips. "I am well, Edmund. Enjoy the chase."

Edmund held his gaze. "Do not let yourself slip back. Four hundred years is long enough to tire even me of worrying."

"Four hundred . . ." Lucius could scarcely believe he'd been causing concern that long.

Edmund grinned at his shock. Then, in a blur of speed only an *upyr* could have achieved, he left Lucius alone. The door swung shut seconds later with a quiet creak. The room felt empty. If Lucius had not known better, he would have said it felt lonely.

I will walk to Bridesmere, he decided, *and visit the scenes Lucas knew*. Either he would exorcize the human's memories, or embrace them once and for all.

He took the servants' corridor to the back, thinking it a discreet choice for a night egress. He was mistaken. He passed two amorous couples on his way. The first had barred themselves in the laundry. The second, less concerned about discovery, occupied the dusty corner by the kitchen garden door.

Though both were dressed, such humping of hips and heaving of sighs could not be mistaken for anything but full coitus.

Lucius had been living apart from humans long enough that he had forgotten how intense their desires could be. His defenses proved unequal to shutting them out. In truth, he would have had to be carved of stone to have avoided a sympathetic reaction.

He did not have time to draw back before being spied.

"Sir!" gasped the footman, apparently too close to release to withdraw. Despite his audience, the motion of his hips increased.

The maid simply threw back her head and wailed. Lucius read from her mind that she had spent three times already and was looking forward to doubling that number in the hours ahead. The footman's equipment was wondrously vigorous. She could not remember enjoying a tupping more, nor wanting one so much. As soon as she finished needing him between her thighs, she was going to thank him in the way she'd learned men liked best.

The pictures she held for doing this were explicit.

Shaking off her borrowed awareness—which included no consciousness of him—Lucius touched her lover's bunched shoulder. The footman's eyes were glazed but they came up.

"You never saw me tonight," Lucius said in a low, penetrating tone. "And, er, carry on."

His final words must have exerted more influence than he meant, because both servants groaned and peaked. Nor was this the end of their activity. Before Lucius could close the door behind him, they had sunk to the floor and begun again.

He shook his head as he stepped through the low herb beds, hoping they would not injure themselves. Unlike *upyr,* humans weren't equipped to tup all night, though these were young and healthy. It was Lucius's bad luck that the contagion of their arousal surged through him like pulsing fire. Hungers gripped him: to feed, to mate, to damn any goal but satisfying his desires.

He tried to control himself. He could not afford to bite a human in his current state. Even as he struggled, another lustful soul brushed his. It was a gardener, lying on a narrow cot in an outbuilding. He was on his side facing the wall, hoping to keep his gasps from other sleepers as he tugged his aching hardness furiously fast. He had held off pleasuring himself for weeks, but could not bear more delay. His mind was filled with someone named Caroline—so good, so sweet, so far above his reach. Her skin was cream, her breasts rich and soft. He could not have her, should not think of her, but—oh—she was beautiful.

When the gardener expelled his seed in a searing rush, the power of his release—felt but not shared—sent Lucius to his knees. It was a moment before he could get to his feet again.

Minks, he thought, standing shakily. His house was overrun with bloody love-mad minks.

He licked his eyeteeth, now sharp as knives. With regret, he realized he should have accepted Edmund's invitation to hunt. It seemed he'd have more than memories to exorcize tonight.

Chapter 4

As often happened when events reminded Theo of her lost lieutenant, she could not sleep that night. Rather than wake her sister with her tossing, she crept down the cramped back stairs to their walled garden.

The little space was quiet. Bridesmere had not attained a size where it would make noise much past ten. She sat on the low stone bench that slanted across one corner. A spidery clump of lilies, just beginning to bud, tickled her calf like a lover playing childish games.

That was all it took for her eyes to well up with tears.

Three years had passed, but she still missed Nathan. At twenty, he had been a treasure. Despite those traits of reckless mischief few males escape, his goodness had shone clear. He'd resisted her seventeen-year-old flirtation until it became as obvious to him as it was to her that her temperament would, in the end, suit him better than Caroline's.

He had kissed her the night he confessed the change in his feelings, the first adult kiss of her life. She had loved him all the more for his hesitance.

She would not have traded those memories for a king's ransom, no matter how bittersweet they were now. They were all she had of her fiancé. In truth, given her dearth of feminine attractions, they might be all she'd ever know of love.

Sighing, she pulled her thin kid slippers onto the bench and wrapped her knees in her shawl. The stars were blurs in a soft black sky, the wind a whisper through the young ivy. She suspected she'd had better than she deserved, but that did not stop her from wanting more.

Lucius came to Bridesmere to find the true Lucas Delavert, to discover how taking on his memories might affect his own character. Memories he found, too many, around every corner and up every lane.

Here, in a churchyard, Lucas's twelve-year-old self had been beaten by a curate who caught him drawing naked people in the window dust. At fifteen, a determined tour of the public houses (which had followed a fight with his father) concluded with him in the gutter, sleeping off the effects of too much "blue ruin." At twenty, in the alley beside a glovemaker's shop, he had kissed the pretty wife of a clerk who'd refused to serve him. His hand beneath her skirt had given her the first pleasure of her life, his vengeance for her mate's rudeness. She'd begged Lucas to visit her again, but he had only laughed.

He had felt as disdainful of her as he was of everyone in this town. Since boyhood they had accused him—with and without cause—of laziness, low companions, and general worthlessness. Every cart man and maid had an opinion, which they seemed to think they ought to air to his face. Lucas was the son of a privileged family, a fallen local prince. They thought they owned him, though only to the extent of damning him as they pleased, never acknowledging their part in molding the man he became.

By his frequent public concurrence, Lucas's father had lent his blessing to their disrespect.

Not a soul seemed to have believed in Lucas Delavert. They did not have to. They'd had his older brother in which to repose their hopes. If Daniel had lived, no doubt he would have fulfilled them—which might have explained why Lucas had hated him most of all.

By the time Lucius ambled past the last remembered tavern, he understood Delavert better than the man had understood himself. More than that, he liked him. Despite Delavert's disregard for others, despite his self-destructive ways, Lucius liked him fully as well as anyone he had met in a hundred years. Had it been possible, he'd have stood the man to a drink.

Surely there was something wrong with that response.

Lucius did not know the answer, only that his skin seemed not to fit as well as before, crawling with awareness as he passed each scene of degradations past. Poor Lucas. Every rebellion against his tormentors had proved them right.

Finally, when his wandering feet led him onto the high street, a scent brought him alert. Here was a memory, but not Delavert's. Eager for once to reclaim his sense of himself, Lucius halted. With his hand braced on the wall of a shop called Black's, he took the delicate essence across his tongue, tasting it as the wolf who lived within him would have done.

Violets twined through the familiar fragrance, a woman's musk, clay warmed by the sun. He glimpsed a face, lost to him for who knew how long. Someone he had loved. *Mena.* The name sent a shiver through his cool-blooded frame. He had lost her long ago. He recollected that much, though not how or why.

He was trailing the scent before caution could stop him. But why should he stop? This could not be the woman he had just remembered. Her very dust would be gone by now. He was in no danger of remembering too much. This human would be a stranger.

His strides quickened until the buildings he passed bled together. A reckless energy fizzed in his veins.

He reached a square with a grassy park. A dog barked behind a shuttered window, then was stilled by a glimmer of dominance from his wolf.

There, behind that last narrow house on the corner, was the source of the tempting scent. Lucius slowed to a human pace. His teeth had sharpened, his body quickening with excitement. He forced both reactions back, though the effort required was unnerving. He must not frighten whoever lived here. He meant only to investigate.

He circled the house's back garden wall. When he wished, he could move in absolute silence. He did so now, pulling his weight up the bricks. The exertion was not what had his heart pulsing in his throat. That could only be called fear.

Cursing the foreign weakness, he pushed up onto his arms.

A smile spread across his face. On the other side, a female human sat on a stained stone bench, her knees clutched to her chest, her thin muslin gown clinging to her limbs. A more harmless creature could hardly have been conceived. Here was no femme fatale, but a skinny, gawky, barely twenty-year-old chit.

She was what her countrymen would have called "a pretty girl"—but strictly out of politeness. Her rough, black hair straggled down her back, a few crooked papers testifying to her efforts to make it curl. Her eyes were dark and large, set in moody hollows under slashing brows. Her cheekbones were further slants of shadow, and her mouth possessed an odd piquant shape, fuller in its upper lip than its lower. Her skin was clear and brown, either from the sun or naturally. Lucius liked her face very much; and liked it even more because he knew in his bones it did not resemble his lost Mena's. Despite its youth, this girl's countenance had character, though it was not a face anyone could mistake for an English rose.

He had to lift his hand to stifle an unexpected laugh. Thanks to Delavert, his emotions were as volatile as quicksilver.

I could speak to her, he thought with another surge of high spirits. The tiniest brush of thrall would overcome her caution. He could introduce her to Delavert.

Entertained by the idea, he opened his mouth as she turned.

She had the briefest instant to be afraid. A man was peering over their garden wall. A man had caught her alone at night.

His hair was a silver so bright it shone through the darkness with its own light. He was smiling broadly, and his teeth had a glow as well. On her feet, Theo pressed her hand to her pounding breast. Every fiber of her being prepared to flee.

Before she could, a wave of warmth rolled over her, sweet as treacle. She saw how beautiful the man was, how young despite his silver hair. Looking at his eyes made her feel sleepy. They were dark gray, slitted now with amusement but strangely comforting. He looked the sort of man who would tease a woman more than he should, but not the sort who would do her harm.

"Do not be afraid," he said, his smooth, cool voice flowing so pleasingly into her ear it seemed—alarmingly—to be sliding down to rather lower parts. "Your garden smelled delicious. I could not resist peering inside."

"It is the mint," she said, too breathless for the words to come evenly.

"The mint. Yes, that must be it." His smile suggested the opposite; suggested, in fact, that *she* was the deliciousness who drew him here.

Her knees had turned to water. Though she had jumped up at his appearance, she found herself unable to stir another step. She wanted to stand here staring at his face all night. Just barely, she managed to close her mouth.

"Might I climb over?" he asked politely.

"Climb over?" she squeaked as another wash of warmth swept her tingling limbs.

"It strikes me that a young woman alone in a garden might be in need of someone to talk to. I assure you, I mean no harm."

His eyes were gentle now, his teasing gone. His look seemed to promise he would understand whatever she might say. She could not doubt he meant this assurance . . . at least, she did not think she could.

"You might come in for a bit," she offered with a dream-like sense of being both under a compulsion and completely free. "Though I dare say you shall find my 'talk' tedious."

He grinned in thanks, vaulting neatly over the wall. Theo saw him more clearly than she expected. He appeared a gentleman though he wore no coat, only a clean white shirt and braces. His buckskin breeches were nicely snug. Their soft buff color made the back of him look unclothed.

She knew she ought to shift her gaze from his posterior, but even as she struggled, the intruder froze, his ribs expanding with a sudden breath. To her relief—given the object of her fascination—a moment later he turned around.

When he spoke, the slight huskiness of his voice made her wonder if he had guessed what she'd been staring at.

"We should sit," he said.

She joined him on the bench, though it was improper. The cold stone slab scarcely had room for two, and certainly not for two who weren't intimate. His thigh was faintly warm where it stretched beside hers. Theo looked down at it, then up at him. He smiled and lifted his hand toward her face. Like one entranced, she did not think to evade him. The back of his knuckles brushed like gossamer down her cheek, leaving a trail of heightened feeling behind. Theo found she could not breathe.

No man had touched her like this since her fiancé.

"Tell me," he said, the words another caress. "What brings these tears to your lovely eyes?"

"Nathan," she blurted out, to her own surprise.

The inquiring lift of his brows was an encouragement she felt unequal to withstand.

"Nathan was the man I was supposed to marry. The only man I've ever loved."

He seemed to look straight into her. Someone else might have assured her she would love again, that she was too young to think of Nathan as her last chance. This man spoke neither platitude aloud, and yet his gentle expression conveyed both.

"Tell me how you met," he said.

She told him: how she had fallen in love with Nathan the very day he'd come to court her sister, how she had pestered him into falling in love right back. She told him how his uniform had brought a lump of pride to her throat, and that she'd watched him sail off to defend their country bubbling with dreams of marrying when he returned. She even shared her secret anger that he had not kept his promise to come back. Theo loved her family, but Nathan had been her chance to build a life of her own.

The stranger appeared not to judge her. No one had ever been this easy to talk to. She barely had to speak and he nodded. She was almost calm when she described her disbelief at receiving the ominous black-edged letter from Nathan's captain. Never before had she visited that memory without trembling.

"He should not have died that way," she said, her knees turned toward the stranger. "Washed overboard in a storm. He had not even seen battle. He never got the chance to discover if he could be the hero he hoped. As important as the prize money for capturing enemy ships would have been, he wanted most to strike a blow against Napoleon."

"I am sure he did." In all this time, the stranger had not looked away, nor—oddly enough—had she wished him to. Now his gaze searched her face with an intensity that should have alarmed her. "You are not to blame," he said softly.

"His death was not a punishment for stealing him from your sister."

His discernment stole her powers of speech. "It feels like a punishment," she confessed once she recovered. "It feels as if I shall never be able to redress my crime!"

He smiled, but the smile was so kind she could not take offense. "You have a means of redress in mind. I see it in your expression."

"It is silly."

He laid his hand on hers. "Nothing is too silly to tell me."

She could not think with his touch upon her; it seemed impossible to resist or even be ashamed. Thus he had that story, too, complete with opinions of Lady Morris that were not at all nice to share. By the end of her relation, her hand had somehow moved to his thigh. He must have drawn it there unnoticed, for she did not think she would have put it there herself. Now he took her hand in both of his and slid his fingers caressingly along either side. Her palm was tingling, her nerves atwitch. Deep inside her, where she should not have felt anything, a liquid heat pooled too high to ignore.

She feared what she would do if he did not stop.

"You have put a spell on me," she whispered.

Perhaps it was a trick of uncertain light, but his eyes darkened at her words. Though his lips were closed, she saw him drag his tongue across his upper teeth. They were both respiring harder than they had any reason to.

He broke the suspended moment with a shaky laugh. Carrying her hand to his mouth, he kissed her longest fingertip. "Would you begrudge me a spell if I could help you obtain your desire?"

"My desire?" Though she did not wish it, her voice betrayed everything she felt. The stranger uttered a sound she didn't think she'd ever heard a man make before, an animal groan of pain.

Suddenly his lips were on hers, and his tongue was sliding inside her mouth. She could not move and did not want to. His hands—now hot as fire—ran hard up and down her back. They were the firmest hands she had ever felt. All rationality left her, as if his kiss had sucked it from her mouth. Dizzy, she gripped his arms, marveling at the stony hardness of his bunched muscles. She wanted things she barely understood: his body inside her, his teeth on her neck, his palm pressed tight to her naked breast.

"God," he breathed, breaking free.

He shook as he leaned his forehead against hers. Mesmerized by the idea that his mouth had been pressing hers, she touched his lips with her fingertips. Their surface was satiny.

"Don't," he warned, and gently pulled her hand away.

She was sorry he had stopped her, but she liked the way his gaze burned into hers.

"I did not do this," he said, low and fierce. "I did not kiss you."

Abruptly, she felt confused. "You didn't?"

He shook his head firmly. "I think you must have been dreaming, because you'd been remembering your lieutenant."

She touched her mouth and wondered why it was tender.

When the stranger stood, the front of his breeches was pushed out. She did not see how this response could have been caused by their talk, but her mind wasn't very clear. A fever flooded into her through her eyes. She had always avoided staring at the evidence of Nathan's desire, but the stranger's shape compelled her, seeming naked despite the cloth that shielded it. The head pressed hard enough to show its rim, and the shaft slanted right as if it had tried to shift upward but had not found room. The whole of his apparatus appeared so urgent that the buttons of his flaps seemed in danger of bursting free.

She licked her lips, shamefully close to hoping they would.

"Look at me," the stranger ordered hoarsely. "Into my eyes."

She shook herself and looked at him as he'd asked. Her lust still throbbed within her, but at least she could think a bit.

The stranger cleared his throat. "As it happens," he said, "I shall be attending Lady Morris's dinner for Mr. Delavert. I believe I can encourage her to include your family as well."

"She will not do it. She wants Mr. Delavert for her daughter."

"She will," the stranger insisted. "And then your sister shall have the chance you desire."

"Truly?"

"Truly."

She looked down at her lap, suddenly shy. "It is kind of you to involve yourself in our concerns."

She looked up in time to see him smile, the expression oddly fierce. "A friend of mine advised me to involve myself more in life. Let us consider this my first step."

He bowed, then turned to the wall, clearly preparing to scale it again. With one idle corner of her attention, she noticed the lilies that grew beneath it were in full bloom.

"Wait," she called. "You have not told me your name. I must know to whom I am indebted."

He hesitated, then spoke over his shoulder. His profile was as stern and clean as a Roman coin. "You may call me 'L' until we are properly introduced."

"L," she repeated, privately convinced that restoring propriety to their interaction was as likely as snow in June.

He leapt over the wall before she could say more. One instant he was there, and the next he was gone. The only sign she had not dreamed the whole encounter was the dark, soft rumble of his laughter.

Lucius's laugh died a good deal sooner than his desire. Assaulted almost immediately by second thoughts, he began to run toward the wooded border of Hadleigh Park. He was afraid to assume his wolf form, to let the animal side of him out.

He had acted the wolf enough as it was.

Convinced he must have gone mad, Lucius dropped to his knees beside a rain-swollen stream. He plunged his hands into the icy water, then pressed them to his face.

When he'd climbed the wall of that secret garden, he had thought only to amuse himself. It had seemed safe enough to coax the girl to talk. How deep, after all, could young emotions run?

Amazed by his own stupidity, he dropped his hands to his thighs. His temperature remained high—downright feverish for an *upyr.* He was erect as well, his arousal scarcely lessened by his exercise. He'd only just met her, and the girl was already under his skin.

He should have known better than to touch her. Human warmth was a strong seduction for his kind. Certainly, he should not have kissed her with Delavert's wildness coursing through his veins. He had been thralling her to keep her calm, reading her just a bit, and thus he knew how much she missed her lieutenant; knew, too, how much of that missing was simply a healthy human body feeling desire.

He could have satisfied it. He couldn't remember the last time he had taken pleasure in the human way. He wanted to maraud her, wanted to leave the mark of his teeth on every inch of her coltish limbs. Because this was so, he could not conceive of a single way to approach her again in safety. If he'd had any sense at all, he would forget they met.

Coward, mocked a voice that could have been Delavert's.

To silence it, Lucius dove into the dark water. The current was cold and strong, the bottom thick with plants his power moved automatically from his way. By the time he surfaced, his head was clear.

He had promised Theo an invitation, though for her own sake rather than her sister's. He suspected he'd been showing off, just as Delavert would have done. That, however, was no reason to renege. He did not want to. Even if tonight had thrown him off balance, even if he wasn't sure he could keep these borrowed passions under control, he wanted to see her again.

He was alive tonight. He sensed each drop of water sparkling on his face, knew the precise pressure in every vein. The stars sang in his ears as they wheeled above him. He smiled as a frog began to croak in the reeds. Lucius had fallen so still the creature had forgotten to be afraid.

I shall see her again, he told himself, not caring to whom such willfulness belonged.

In that moment, seeing her again seemed a fine prospect.

Chapter 5

When Theo rose the next morning, a little later than usual, she hardly knew what to make of the night before. She puzzled to herself as she helped their single maid sweep the upper rooms. Had the encounter been a dream? Did that explain why it seemed unreal?

A bit of breakfast taken with her sister convinced her this could not be. Though she still felt fevered when she thought back, she was not prone to hallucinations. She *had* spoken to a stranger in the garden. She *had* let him (most improperly!) hold her hand. And there had been something else as well, something both better and worse that slipped provokingly out of reach each time she tried to draw it near. Her intervening sleep must have confused her recall. Letting a stranger touch her naked hand was assuredly the limit of what she would allow.

Vaguely unsatisfied with this logic, Theo gazed into her teacup. The leaves at its bottom had formed themselves into an "L." She pushed the cup away so sharply it rattled in its saucer. Caroline looked up but did not ask what the matter was.

Fortunately, neither sister was talkative before noon.

"Where is Mama?" Theo asked to distract herself.

Caroline set down her cup and grimaced. "Gone to our uncle's, I'm afraid."

"Oh, no! I hope she isn't—"

Since they both knew what Theo hoped, it was just as well that the maid came in.

"Miss Morris is here," she announced, breathless from trotting up the stairs, "to inquire if either of you is at home."

"What can *she* want?" Theo asked with considerably less cordiality than she ought. She knew she would do better to follow Caroline's example. Being born to a mother like Lady Morris demanded sympathy at the least—even if Lily was the most uncomfortable person Theo knew.

"We shall see what she wants," Caroline said with an indulgent smile. "In the meantime, Gretchen, please bring more tea and ask Miss Morris to meet us here."

When Lily entered the parlor, she was—as usual—in excellent looks. Though slightly older than the Becket girls, she did not show it. Her skin was porcelain-fair, her hair a lovely auburn. Her gown, a sheer sprigged muslin with a single flounce, fell beautifully to her shoes. Her figure was as graceful as her mother's now was stout. Theo had never seen her with a blemish or even a drooping curl. To be just—which Theo did not always wish to do—her only apparent flaw was her odd, blank way of sometimes gazing at one without speaking, exactly as if one were not there. While it was impossible to guess what she was thinking, it was just as impossible to imagine that it was good.

As a child, Theo had been sensitive to that look. Whenever Lady Morris—then a bit less socially ambitious—had brought her daughter to the house to play, Theo would burst into tears and hide in the closet. Caroline herself had not been able to coax Theo out. Finally, except for the occasional stilted morning call, the mothers abandoned the idea of them being friends.

Though Theo was embarrassed by her childish fear, even now she could not bring herself to warm.

As befitted her elder-sister status, Caroline invited Lily to sit. With the very stare Theo found so disquieting, their visitor declined.

"I cannot stay," she said, her gaze roaming the tiny parlor as if toting up the value of its contents. Squinting in puzzlement, she stopped at a cream-colored lily in a vase. Theo could not guess why; the vase was not Wedgewood or any other expensive make. Shaking herself from whatever had caught her attention, Lily again regarded Caroline. "I have come to extend an invitation from my mama. She wishes you and your mother to join us for dinner tomorrow night. Mr. Delavert is coming, and she believes you would be glad to make his acquaintance."

Caroline merely blinked at this, but Theo was not able to contain her surprise.

"How can that be?" she exclaimed. "Your mother did not imply she wished us to be of the party when last we met."

Rather than oblige Lily to answer, Caroline placed her hand over Theo's, silently urging her to keep quiet. A stroke of fortune as good as this was best left alone.

"Please tell Lady Morris we would be delighted to attend," Caroline said, "and relay our thanks for her great kindness."

"Yes," Theo seconded. "Mama will be gratified."

Lily was smoothing the fit of her apparently brand new gloves, and did not notice Theo's wit. "Good," she said. "Please let us know if you'd like our carriage to collect you."

Caroline bowed her head and murmured her thanks for this as well, but Lily was already gone.

"Well," Caroline said, staring at the doorway through which Lily had disappeared. "That was odder than Lily's usual."

"Her offer to send the carriage was considerate. I wager Lady Morris did not put her up to that."

"No. Lady Morris would oblige us to hire one, then pretend to have forgotten and apologize."

The sisters looked at each other before breaking into matching grins. " 'Mama will be gratified,' " Caroline mimicked, teasing Theo with her own words.

"Mama will be delirious. Assuming, of course, that she has not convinced our uncle to smuggle us into Hadleigh with a crate of turnips."

"Strawberries," Caroline corrected. "Turnips aren't romantic enough by half."

Despite Theo's amusement, she could not help being baffled as to what had caused Lady Morris's change of heart. If it had been last night's stranger, he was even more persuasive than she thought.

"Perhaps," Caroline said, "Lily is trying to make friends. I have sometimes thought she would like that. You never saw it, but she used to look rather stricken when you ran away."

"She has friends, from the best families in Bridesmere. Girls who would not give us the time of day."

"Yes, but from what I have seen of them, I do not think they are very nice. Their conversation seems to consist entirely of being cruel and that, at least, you cannot accuse Lily of."

This was true. Lily might be proud, but Theo had never heard her insult anyone. Of course, she had never heard Lily say much at all. Certainly, she had never heard her scold her friends for their unkindness, nor did she acknowledge the Beckets beyond the barest politeness when in her friends' company. Theo doubted she felt ashamed for this snub, though she could not swear that was so. What Lily loved or feared was a mystery. Apart from her interest in music and clothes, she was a shuttered house into which she let no one peer. Theo didn't see how a normal person could be friends with someone like that.

"We could try to be nicer," Caroline said.

"We could," Theo agreed with her fondest smile. "And I know which of us has the better chance of succeeding!"

When she heard the news, their mama was indeed gratified. As soon as she recovered from her wonder, she began pacing the parlor.

"Theo must freshen up your blue gown," she said to Caroline, clearly compiling a list. "I have a length of lace I set aside. With that and a change of ribbons, no one will guess your dress isn't new. Mrs. Connor can lend us her upstairs girl—she is ever so good with hair—and both of you shall have new gloves."

While Theo was glad to be remembered, she knew the expense was not required. "Our gloves are fine, Mama. Besides which, this is a dinner. We shan't be wearing gloves all that long."

Their mother waved her hand as she walked. "Caroline, you must prepare a short piece of music. Lily will outshine you, but politeness requires them to ask one of you to play. I should not like you to appear too badly in comparison."

"I thank you for your confidence!" Caroline laughed. "But I shall only play if Theo sings."

"Oh, Lord," their mother moaned.

"Theo's voice is pretty," Caroline insisted as her sister blushed at the knowledge that her mother's apprehension was warranted. "I shall ensure she learns the notes in time."

"Must you do me such favors?" Theo hissed to the side, wishing she were still young enough to be excused for pinching her big sister. "Now we both shall have to practice like lunatics."

Caroline smiled angelically and answered in a similar undertone. "If I must suffer being paraded before the great Mr. Delavert, I see no reason for suffering alone."

Theo crossed her arms and glared as their mama stopped

before the window and tapped her chin. "If only I could be certain of the weather being mild, those silk shawls your Aunt Marjorie sent from Norwich would be ideal. They are thin, but they are lovely."

"Caroline doesn't mind shivering," Theo put in helpfully.

"Hm." Their mother rounded on them without warning. "I hear from London that bosoms are exposed this year. Theo, you must lower your sister's neckline by at least an inch."

"With relish!" Theo grinned at Caroline's horror. Of all her duties, that one she would enjoy. Caroline's bosom was much handsomer than Lily's.

Her grin broadened as another possibility occurred to her. If her mysterious "Mr. L" were truly to attend, perhaps she would alter her frock as well. A very little bit of harmless flirting could not hurt anyone.

Chapter 6

"I do not feel easy letting you attend this dinner alone."

Edmund had crossed his arms and propped his shoulder on the wall of Lucius's dressing room. Delavert's father, the squire that was, had obviously enjoyed the trappings that came with being one of two great families in the area. As large as the adjoining bed chamber, the dressing room was furnished to impress whichever guests were privileged to be asked within. Once there, should the Grecian couches fail to awe, they had only to look up. The crest the squire had commissioned for the ceiling would have done just as well for an earl.

Memories of staring up at it while Delavert's father kept him cooling his heels were sharp in Lucius's mind. He could not deny a twinge of satisfaction at having taken possession.

His satisfaction did, however, have limits. For the last ten minutes, he had been trying to arrange his cravat into a waterfall. The requisite creases were proving a hurdle, and he was not comfortable calling his valet to help.

"I wouldn't worry about 'letting' me go," Lucius said as he tried to aid the artistic crinkling with his fingertips, "considering I did not ask your permission."

"But to attend alone, when you are not used to interacting with humans—"

"I have Delavert's memories to guide me, and I can steal whatever else I need from my companions' thoughts. If you had not insisted on posing as my steward, you could have come yourself."

Lucius didn't really want Edmund there when he saw his garden girl again, but the complaint served his purpose. He hid a smile as Edmund looked abashed and tugged at his cuffs. The young *upyr* did love ordering others around.

"You should feed first," he said, unable to resist another chance to guide. "Or take one of the maids. Preferably both."

Since Lucius believed he had at least the evidence of his hungers under control, this suggestion took him aback. Perhaps Edmund was correct in urging him to sate his appetites before he left. He could not eat human food, and watching humans grow flushed and merry from eating theirs tended to make his kind sharp-set. Alas, Hadleigh's maids had none of the coltish charms that had stirred his hungers in the first place. He doubted he could bring himself to feed from them.

"I am fine," he said a trifle too crisply. "At my age, I am hardly a slave to my desires."

"Maybe before, but lately you've been different."

"You wanted me to be different."

As this could not be argued, Edmund let out a breath loud enough to hear. "Promise you will be careful."

"There is nothing to fear. It is only a meal with a few mortals."

Edmund glowered, looking very much the lord of the castle he had once been. He spoiled the effect by reaching for Lucius's limp neckcloth. "You must spell it," he said in exasperation, "or the power of your aura will smooth it flat. Keep a picture in your mind of the shape you want. After a minute, it will stay."

Lucius let him fuss. If the fall of his cravat would silence Edmund's interference, he would consider the time well spent.

~

The period allotted to the Beckets to prepare for the all-important dinner was made to seem even briefer by their mother's increasingly agitated state. Finally, though, Caroline's pale blue dress was altered, a necessarily short piece of music learned, and their Norwich shawls pressed free of wrinkles with minutes to spare before their hosts' smart barouche-landau rolled into King George Square.

Theo felt quite fluttered as the footman handed her in. In spite of herself, she had been infected by her mother's ambitions. She was glad to see her sister in fine looks. Whatever Mr. Delavert's preference, he would not find her any less worth a stare than Lily Morris.

Theo's own appearance was better than usual. Her best white muslin suited her, its softness camouflaging the angularity of her limbs. Her own hand had embroidered the bodice with curling vines, and though her bosom wasn't as fine as her older sister's, she'd had just enough time with her needle to put what she had on show.

Their mother nodded in satisfaction from the forward seat, thankfully restored to calm now that nothing further could be done. "You look lovely," she said. "Both of you."

The ride to the Morrises' was short, their residence one of Bridesmere's larger and newer homes. Set at the center of a handsome crescent, the symmetrical white facade was lit by lanterns which showed off the balconies' fancy iron work.

Lady Morris received them at the door herself.

"You must forgive me for not inviting you sooner," she said once the first civilities were past. "I had no idea you and Mr. Delavert were acquainted."

She was ushering them up the staircase, a cantilevered spiral of marble steps. Theo was too distracted by its beauty, and her own inner tumult, to question their hostess's words. Her heart sped in her breast as their steps approached the drawing room. It, too, was done in exquisite taste. Its walls were papered above the dado in stripes of pale and mint green, and its faintly Egyptian furnishings were upholstered in pink and cream. A large chandelier hung from the ceiling, gleaming with pendants and candle flames.

Theo spared it a dazzled glance before looking to the gentlemen who were rising then from their seats. They were only two and she saw no strangers, so presumably Mr. Delavert had not arrived. The others she recognized. The first was Bridesmere's amiable and rotund mayor. The second, far more magnetic, was her stranger.

Every part of him was beautiful: his shoulders, his hands, his long, strong thighs. Her cheeks blazed with her awareness of their previous encounter, but even so she could not look away. His very garments seemed in league against her. Surely that navy frock coat fit him better than any in history, and his linen shone a blinding white.

The advantage his appearance gave him over ordinary females struck her as unfair. She had to gasp for air when, rising from his bow, his eyes met hers and smiled warmly.

He looked as if he found her anything but ordinary.

Oh, Lord, she thought in dismay. She could happily lead him to the nearest bedroom and bar the door.

Such was the upheaval of her feelings that it took a moment for her to realize the others were speaking.

"Forgive me," her mother said. "I was not aware we were acquainted."

"Not directly," said Theo's stranger. "You could say we have mutual friends. Lady Morris was kind enough to provide us the opportunity to become friends ourselves."

Lady Morris's smile was strained. She could not have liked being thanked for this. Nonetheless, she carried the moment graciously, broadening the introductions to Caroline. Caroline bobbed a curtsey and murmured a pleasantry. Then, before Theo could begin to prepare herself, he was bowing over her hand.

"Wait," she gasped, finally registering the significance of his preceding speech. "You are he? *You* are Mr. Delavert?"

"Lucas Delavert," he said with a teasing emphasis on the L. "Perhaps you were expecting someone more impressive?"

"Hardly!" she exclaimed, which caused his eyes to twinkle. Incensed, she snatched her hand from his hold. "I thought you were someone *else*."

Sensing this should not continue, even if she did not know why, Mrs. Becket seized the nearest distraction. "There is Lily now," she cried. "My, what a lovely silk she's wearing!"

She *was* wearing a lovely silk, a lovely pink silk embroidered with a net of daisies Theo had spent many weeks stitching. She thought the entire room must hear her temper snap. She could not choose at whom to be angriest: Lily for being a privileged merchant princess, the stranger for playing her the fool, or herself for believing—even briefly—that she might deserve to be admired again.

Lily greeted the Beckets with a noncommittal nod. Apparently, if she did secretly long to be friends, she was not going to betray this in front of anyone she wished to impress. Theo hoped she hid her own feelings half so well as she watched the beautiful Miss Morris turn to Mr. Delavert.

Naturally, Lily's eyes widened at Mr. Delavert's good looks. Even she, so attractive herself, was not used to meeting men like him. Seen among a roomful of people, he seemed a member of a different species, one exempt from normal human flaws. Theo noticed he bowed just as deeply to Lily as he had to her, though Lily—in contrast to herself—kept her composure.

"It is a pleasure to meet you," she said, her tone so polite it was hard to tell if she meant it. "I trust your return to Bridesmere is all you hoped."

"All I hoped and more."

Mr. Delavert's tone was oddly dry, but Lady Morris chose to take this as a compliment to her daughter. With a flush of triumph, she wasted no time maneuvering her guest of honor into escorting her daughter to the dining room.

"We need not stand on ceremony here," she said. "My dear Sir Mayor shall see me to the table. The arms of handsome young gentlemen shouldn't be wasted on old women!"

Her airy chortle might as well have been a rasp scraping Theo's nerves. Sensing this perhaps, her mother hooked her arms through those of her daughters and steered them through the double doors. Four tall footmen in livery ranged about the walls.

"Look at that centerpiece," Mrs. Becket whispered in Theo's ear. "There isn't a single lily in the bunch, while our garden overflows. What would you wager Sybil Morris wished our situations reversed, that she might manufacture some allusion to her own fair flower?"

Normally Theo would have responded, if only to check her mother's competitive tendencies. Tonight, to her regret, she was too busy gritting her teeth.

Lucius could not remember having sat through a meal this interminable. The soup was supped by thimbles, the fishes by endless bites. Every dish the footmen carried off seemed to be replaced by two more. Stymied as to how to dispose of so much inedible stuff, Lucius pushed it around his plate. He found himself wishing that the wine—which *was* excellent—was capable of rendering an *upyr* drunk. Sadly, its effect on his kind was fleeting. All too sober, he was left to dwell on how much he wanted to take Theo Becket aside and apologize: more than apologize, but an apology would serve for a start.

He should have realized his misrepresentation of his

identity would not amuse her. That was a jest more appropriate to the real Lucas Delavert.

On one point alone was he grateful for his poor judgment. The Beckets' presence saved him from being the solitary guest, an honor he had not foreseen and probably would have suffered for had it been successfully bestowed. That Theo was suffering instead diminished his sense of reprieve, but not so much that he wished her away. He could not even wish Lady Morris had supplied a more appropriate complement of males. Their presence would have presented further obstacles between Theo and himself. Whatever their misunderstandings, Lucius was as hungry for her company as he'd been for anything in his life.

Hunger aside, all he could do was try to catch her eye while she stared determinedly at her plate. She was lovely tonight, endearingly grown up in her muslin gown. He wanted to tell her this, but conversation was out of the question. From either end of the stately table their hosts held forth. If the mayor wasn't droning on about improvement projects, his wife was congratulating herself on how fine a table she had set. The Viscount Pembley's chef could not cook a roast to this turn, nor had she, even in Paris, seen such lovely quails as her dear housekeeper had obtained.

Neither Sir John nor Lady Morris listened to each other, no doubt the secret to their happiness.

The only interruption in the flood came when their daughter, a beautiful but strangely cool-mannered girl, tried to serve herself a slice of the much-praised roast.

"Why, darling," her mother cried. "What are you thinking? You know you never eat red meat!"

Slowly, stiffly, as if she were a clockwork doll, Miss Morris returned the slice of beef to the serving plate. If she were angry, Lucius could not read it. Her mind was a tiny candle sunk in a well, too distant to make out. Would that her mother's thoughts were as elusive. Unlike her husband, who judged Delavert too earthy for his offspring, Lady Morris's mind proclaimed her sincere belief that Bridesmere's newest bachelor was well on the road to falling in love.

Evidently, her daughter's previous conquests had only to gaze upon her to succumb. It was his bad luck that none of them possessed his status. Lady Morris had driven off every one.

"My darling Lily is ever so delicate," she confided to Lucius now. "I sometimes marvel she does not blow away."

Delicate was not the word Lucius would have employed; icy and peculiar, perhaps, but not delicate.

"I would like some beef," Theo announced a mite too loudly. "I'm not delicate at all."

If she'd been looking in Lucius's direction, she would have seen him smile.

"Oh, do," Lady Morris urged. "So agreeable to be sturdy."

Theo's sister, Caroline, "darling Lily's" presumed rival, disguised a laugh by coughing in her napkin. Theo was hardly the strapping farm girl Lady Morris's words implied. Up until then, the elder Miss Becket had seemed another uninteresting, if pretty, girl. This unexpected evidence of humor, not to mention affection for her sibling, made Lucius decide he might like her, too.

"I imagine," Lady Morris simpered archly, her heavy silver utensils poised above her plate, "that living among the heathens as you lately were, you have grown rather starved for the sight of fair English maidens."

Lucius pretended to swallow a bite of lobster. "Heathens have their charms," he said. "After a time, one grows fond of dark eyes and hair."

To his delight, Theo did look up at this, though the glance she shot him held more suspicion than gratitude . . . suspicion at herself, as well. Her mind might not remember their kiss, but her body did. Her tiny squirm of arousal spurred a response that made him glad he was sitting down.

"How very open-minded of you," Lady Morris praised.

"My own dear Lily is a great believer in the beauty of all cultures."

Mrs. Becket's fork clinked to her plate. Lucius could see she was bursting to volley back a few well placed—and to her mind, more deserved—compliments to her own daughters. Unfortunately for her, her manners would not allow her to stoop to Lady Morris's trumpeting.

"Still," said Lady Morris as if someone else had been speaking. "I do think our own good island may claim the finest flower of womanhood."

"Indubitably," Lucius agreed, for otherwise she might have gone on. Something within him, perhaps the real Delavert's affection for his mistress, could not like this topic at all.

"Oh, quite," said the mayor, having for once attended his yokemate's words. "Nothing like buxom English girls bouncing about in a country dance."

"I dare say some of them bounce," Lady Morris laughed, "but I assure you, Mr. Delavert, the girls of our circle are considerably more elegant!"

Instinctively Lucius tensed, his body responding to a sudden gathering of her will.

"Oh!" she exclaimed, covering her bosom with one plump hand as if a thought had just then occurred to her. "What a delightful idea I have! Mr. Delavert, you must give a ball and judge for yourself the justness of my claim. What better way to announce your intention to take the reins of Hadleigh than to reintroduce yourself to local society in the proper state."

Lucius knew this was the opening she had been waiting for since the night began. Lady Morris was hoping to volunteer herself to help him organize the affair, as he had no well-born female in his household. By this means, she would aggrandize herself and throw Lily into his company. The images in her mind were so vivid they temporarily confused his thoughts. She was seeing herself at his side welcoming guests, her gown so brightly gold it gleamed like the sun. *Finally I shall shine as I ought,* her mind declared. *I shall shine until they all go blind.*

"Mr. Delavert," Caroline Becket murmured in concern. Along with her sister and mama, she was seated across from him. She could see how his hands had tightened on the table's edge.

He forced his fingers to unclaw and hoped he hadn't gouged the wood.

"A ball," he mused as if the idea were unfolding its delights to his inner eye. Freed from Lady Morris's visions, his mental gears began to turn. He turned his attention to Mrs. Becket. She was blinking at him with widened eyes, her breath held in suspense over whether he would fall prey to her rival's ploy. Smiling, he put the tiniest bit of thrall into his gaze and spoke in his most soothing tone. "I hope you can forgive my boldness, Mrs. Becket, but in light of the interesting possibility Lady Morris has raised, I find I must do more than allude to our connection."

"Yes?" Mrs. Becket said avidly.

"I have discovered that your family are distant relations to the Fitz Clares, who have long resided in these parts. My steward, Edmund Fitz Clare, is a twig from yet another branch. As he is like a brother to me, I am sure you could be counted as some sort of cousin. Consequently, I hope, I pray, I may presume on your kindness in this matter."

"I would gladly be of service in any way."

Mrs. Becket sounded dazed, but Lady Morris must have guessed where this was headed. Waves of frustration rolled toward him from her seat.

"Excellent," he said, doing his best to ignore them. "Then you shall serve as my hostess for the event, as a sister would were I fortunate enough to have one."

"Grandmother would be more like," Lady Morris muttered, unaware that Lucius could hear. When he smiled pleasantly in her direction, her answering grimace was brittle.

"What a marvelous solution," she declared aloud. "But

I fear—if you'll forgive my saying so—that you are likely to require more aid. A ball is an elaborate event, one Mrs. Becket has been unable to undertake except on the smallest scale. Given your position, your ball must have more consequence."

"You help 'em," Sir John threw in with apparent artlessness. "No one's so good at putting on a rout as my Sybil."

Lady Morris beamed at her spouse. "You would not mind?"

"Not at all," he assured, beaming back.

It was then Lucius realized his control of this situation had been lost as handily as he thought he'd won it back. His stomach sank as Lady Morris clapped in delight.

"How felicitous! We must make it a house party all together at Hadleigh Hall. There we can pool our resources and plan. Do say you shall allow it, Mr. Delavert. I promise that between us we shall see the thing done right."

"A house party," he repeated, wondering how on earth he could squirm out of that. Bad enough he and Edmund had to hide what they were from his servants. He supposed he could thrall Lady Morris out of the idea, but—given the effect of their recent contact—he was loathe to touch her mind again.

"My dear Sir Mayor shall be busy," Lady Morris added. "He does have so many duties, but you must include what male friends you like. I'm sure Caroline and Theo will enjoy meeting them."

"Yes," her daughter said, breaking her long silence. "I'm sure that would be pleasant for everyone."

Her mother shot her a narrow glance. It seemed her darling was not expected to speak for herself. Lucius could not be troubled to wonder why. The thought of other men pursuing Theo, and of him being expected to supply them, had his jaw clenching.

"Do not press Mr. Delavert for so much," Mrs. Becket said quietly. "Surely meeting once or twice will be enough."

"Once or twice!" Lady Morris laughed as at some terrible

naivete, unaware that Mrs. Becket was motivated, at least in part, by a genuine wish to spare her rebuff. "My dear, you've no concept how much there is to organize. The food alone could require a week!"

"You need not do it," Caroline said to him even lower than her mama. "You need not do any of it if you do not wish."

He glanced from her to her sister. For some time, Theo had been blushing furiously at her plate. She was thinking of dancing with him, was picturing his hand on hers with a level of tactile detail that caused his fingers to curl. Ashamed of herself for wanting him, a glowing pink climbed from her low neckline.

As charming as that display was, she could not have guessed the effect her embarrassed heat would have on her scent, the scent that had drawn him to her in the first place. At last, as if she felt his bewitched attention, she looked up. Her expression pleaded, but for such a tangle of different objects, he thought he might suit himself in choosing which to indulge.

Such was his pleasure at her reaction that it was almost too late by the time he thought to wrench his gaze away. To know she desired him increased his hunger beyond the bounds of what he could hide. His evening breeches were unnaturally tight, his fangs half sliding free. For one dangerous moment, all he could hear was her pulse, and all he could smell was her blood. He had to swallow before he could speak.

"A house party would be capital," he said. "I do not know if other guests will be available, but for my part I shall enjoy becoming better acquainted with all of you."

Theo would never know how she survived the rest of the evening. She could not sit still even to take coffee with the ladies in the drawing room. Though she had been trying not to watch her stranger during the meal, she couldn't help recalling how his throat had moved with each savoring swallow of wine, how his shapely hands had wielded his silver, how his eyes had burned into hers the few times they'd met.

Unless she very much mistook the matter, he was as interested in her as she was in him.

She paced to the curtained bay at the front of the room. The street outside was quiet, the moon gleaming like silver on the paving stones. Sensitive as always to other's feelings, her sister soon joined her.

"Mr. Delavert is handsome," she remarked.

"His looks are pleasing," Theo admitted.

Caroline smiled and brought her coffee cup to her lips. "I caught him staring at you more than once."

Theo tied a knot in the curtain fringe. "No doubt he was wondering how a girl so plain could be related to you."

"Theo."

Pulling a face at her sister's scold, Theo put her back to the wall and sighed.

"A ball might be pleasant," Caroline said, her lips still curved secretively. "Hadleigh is by all accounts an impressive place. I have been told—" Here the faintest rose crept up her cheek. "That is, I have heard that the gardens are very fine."

"Fine is as fine does," Theo snipped.

Caroline's expression turned curious. "Have you some complaint about the new squire's manners?"

Theo sighed again. She had no wish to turn Caroline against him, nor could she explain her objection without it reflecting badly on herself. All the same, considering what she knew of his duplicity, she had to wonder if he were worth pursuing by anyone.

"He is a stranger to us," was all she could think to say.

"He will not be for long," Caroline predicted with a gentle laugh. "Not if Lady Morris has her way."

"If Lady Morris has her way, neither of us will need to worry about his manners."

She looked back to where their mother and Lady Morris

were engaged in happy discussion. For once, they looked like women who could have been friends as girls. Next to their animation, Lily seemed a painted doll. She was staring into the distance as if the others were miles away. It was hard to believe her as interested as her mother in catching Mr. Delavert. Then again, maybe this was how she'd attracted the countless beaus Lady Morris was always prattling about. Theo had not been invited into their hallowed "circle" enough to know.

"Mama is enjoying this," Caroline said, following her gaze. "Even if Lady Morris will try to ride roughshod over her."

"Mr. Delavert will look after Mama," Theo said, then wondered from whence in Hades that belief had come.

She was wondering still when the gentlemen returned from the dining room. Somehow she knew Mr. Delavert would join her as soon as Caroline drifted off. Determinedly, she faced the window. Despite her attempt to discourage him, the heat of his body told her how close he stood.

"I owe you an apology," he said, after a tiny breath of hesitation, "though I suspect from your manner you will not accept."

"You misled me." She tried to make the accusation calm. "And that after I had shared my reasons for wanting to come tonight."

"Your sister."

"Yes, my sister."

His thumb and fingertips touched her neck, the former gliding up her nape while the latter stroked a long tendon. "I doubt your sister needs such matchmaking help."

His husky whisper slid through her body like warm honey. "My intentions are not your concern."

"Aren't they?" He laughed, and it made her shiver. If she'd believed her knees would obey her, she would have left. His head bent closer, and closer yet, until he was nuzzling the side of her neck, scraping it with the smooth front edge of his teeth. The caress was strangely delicious. She thought surely one of the others would see and put an end to it, but inexplicably they did not. Perhaps Mr. Delavert had put a spell on the entire room. Whatever the reason for their privacy, she feared she would melt into a puddle before he stopped.

When he did stop, she had to fight a sigh of relief.

"You have no idea," he breathed raggedly, "how being near to you tortures me."

It was too much to allow, but when she turned to confront him she lost her breath. He was fair-skinned—pale, really—but just then his face bore a hint of color. Regardless of what he'd done, this evidence that he, too, was affected made her wish they truly were alone.

"The others aren't looking at us," he said with uncanny acuity. He touched the green silk ribbon beneath her breast, causing muscles deep inside her to jump shamefully. When she shrank back, his jaw tightened. "You will come to this house party, Theo. Do not imagine you can stay away."

"You have no right to use my Christian name."

His gaze held hers. She knew he had heard the weakness in her voice, the yearning she could not hide.

"You will come," he repeated, his manner oddly intense. "If you prefer, you may tell yourself it is for your sister's sake. I think you know she will not attend if you are not there."

"I love my sister," she said, the only protest she could think to make.

His eyes softened with his smile, bringing a frightening beauty into his face. "Love her all you wish. I assure you I have no objection to that."

Theo would have been delighted to bid her adieus then and there. Regrettably, the musical portion of the evening was still to be gotten through. Resigned, she stepped to the harpsichord with her sister to perform their piece. When it was done, she had no idea if she had sung ill or well, but her mother seemed satisfied, and Caroline patted her hand.

Clapping politely, Lily glided forward to takc their place.

For no reason she could explain, Theo's feet led her to the chair beside Mr. Delavert.

He smiled as she sat, but no more than any well mannered gentleman might. That this annoyed her she would not have admitted on pain of death. At least Lily's playing was a distraction. The work she had chosen was full of crashing chords and complicated finger work. Theo's sister would have been lost at the first measure, but Lily did the piece justice. Her hands expressed a passion the rest of her denied. The contrast always made her interesting to watch. Never having seen this prodigy before, Mr. Delavert listened with his mouth agape.

"Good Lord," he murmured, clapping loudly as the music ceased. "What an extraordinarily angry young woman."

Theo was so startled by this comment that for a moment she could not speak. Lily might be eccentric, even disdainful, but Theo had never known her to be angry. Certainly, if Lady Morris had heard in her daughter's performance whatever Mr. Delavert purported to, she could not have appeared so pleased with herself. Though Theo did not like Lily, nor want her companion to, it seemed unfair to allow the remark to stand.

"You must be mistaken," she said. "I am certain it was only Mr. Beethoven's fury you heard."

Mr. Delavert had no chance to debate her, for Lady Morris claimed his attention, asking if he cared to accompany her dear Lily in a duet, or perhaps simply turn the pages?

"Alas," Mr. Delavert declined. "I have no accomplishments of that sort. I cannot read music, and I'm afraid my idea of singing is more like a howl."

A candle guttered at his words, the shifting of the shadows lending his grin an unexpectedly wolfish cast. The hair at the back of Theo's neck stood up. She found she could imagine him howling. In fact, self-flattery though it likely was, she found she could imagine him howling over her.

Chapter 7

Lucius was worn to a frazzle by the time the fateful day arrived.

How could he direct his housekeeper in seeing to the comfort of his guests when he knew so little of human needs? Delavert's memories were worse than useless. The brash young man had rarely considered anyone but himself. "What do *you* think?" became Lucius's helpless refrain. While this endeared him to his staff, it hardly ensured the proper choices were being made.

A sensible *upyr* would have excused himself from meeting guests before sunset. Sensible or not, this would have prevented him from seeing Theo at the first possible instant. Since any delay seemed unbearable, he heaved himself out of bed at noon.

The house was a flurry of activity, with servants scurrying to and fro. Lucius knew they had grown accustomed to his late hours, but surely their preparations should have been done!

Alarmed by the chaos, he went in search of Edmund.

He found him dead to the world in his dark cellar apartment. Edmund had painted the walls mummy red. Adding to the bordello atmosphere, two of the maids curled naked against him on either side. Lucius frowned. No wonder tasks weren't being finished if his servants were sleeping in!

"What are you doing?" he cried with both voice and mind. If he had not, he doubted Edmund would have woken.

"There a fire?" Edmund croaked, laying a protective hand on the maids' bare bums. They cooed in their sleep and squirmed closer. Lucius didn't need to ask how they'd been fatigued. The bed chamber reeked of sexual congress.

"No, there isn't, but there might as well be. Why aren't you overseeing the staff? Have you forgotten our guests come today?"

"I haven't forgotten. The servants can handle what needs to be done."

"The servants—the ones who aren't in your bed—are flapping around like headless chickens!"

Edmund looked as though he longed to laugh. "I bit the ones who mattered: housekeeper, butler"—his voice lowered to a purr—"Lydia, the upper maid." From the remembered sensations sliding through his mind, he had done more than bite that one.

Edmund's lechery wasn't what caused Lucius to suck in his breath. For one *upyr* to feed from another's servants was a serious breach of etiquette. Though Lucius had put them under his influence, he had only spelled them by eye. Edmund's bite had the potential to undermine his control. Had Edmund been an enemy, the danger to Lucius could have been great.

"You are fortunate that I trust you," Lucius said with some asperity. "There are those among us who would kill you for less."

Edmund yawned. "You are fortunate I plan ahead, or your house would not be as near to preparedness as it is." He settled back against the pillows and scratched his chest. "Really,

Lucius, there's little risk your lady guests will arrive early. To judge by the servants' gossip, they're all hell-bent on catching you. They'll be primping to the last minute. Oh, and if you miss your coach, it is because I sent it to the Beckets. Lydia mentioned they're too poor to have their own."

"I didn't think of that," Lucius said, horrified at himself.

"That's what happens when you let your mind get muddled with worrying. Not that you shouldn't worry. Having these women here is quite harebrained. I don't know what you hope to accomplish."

"They are helping me fit into local society. No matter what a rake Lucas used to be, that ball will assure my place."

Lucius sounded glum even to himself. Thus far, he had avoided those who'd known his predecessor. The real Delavert might have relished rubbing his detractors' noses in his return, but Lucius would rather be ignored. Were it not for his hope of dancing with Theo, he'd have run pell-mell from the whole tangle.

"Well," said Edmund, letting his eyes drift shut. "Wake me again if you need me before sunset. In the meantime, maybe you should let your wolf out. Work off some energy."

In spite of his annoyance, it seemed a good idea. His wolf-form did not mind the daylight, nor was it restricted to a liquid diet. Lucius could hunt a squirrel or two, maybe find a spot for a nap. A dose of animal rationality might be just the thing to settle his nerves.

Mr. Delavert's carriage was even grander than the Morrises'. A large six-seater coach, its body shone like jet in the sunny square. Every member of the Becket household, servants included, wandered out to gawk. The coachman affected not to see, a sign—Theo fancied—of better than common discipline.

"No arms," said Mrs. Becket, pointing to the bare black door. "I wonder if Mr. Delavert bought this coach before the old squire died. They used to fight a terrible lot, or so I've heard. I can scarcely credit it myself. He seemed an amiable gentleman."

Theo gnawed her lip. Her mother would have sung a different tune had she known Mr. Delavert's penchant for nuzzling necks.

"His horses look to be in good health," Caroline said. "He must take care of them."

Rather than dwell on all-too-ready images of what care Mr. Delavert might be willing to take of her, Theo reached for the latch. "I'm getting in. I'd like to reach Hadleigh before dark."

Despite her words, she did not succeed in entering as quickly as she'd meant. True, she hitched her boot onto the step easily enough, but as soon as she leaned in, the most marvelous scent whirled out. It smelled like snow melting in the spring: clean and sweet, with just a trace of green, growing things. The fragrance filled her with the most basic happiness. Before she could stop herself, she inhaled to take in more.

Caroline was right behind her. "Do you suppose," she inquired innocently, "that Mr. Delavert has left behind a whiff of cologne? Unless, perhaps, it is the scent of Mr. Delavert himself that pleases you so much . . ."

Shaken from her fugue, Theo flung herself inside. " 'Tis the leather I was smelling."

"Ah," Caroline hummed. "The leather. I should have guessed."

"I don't smell anything," said their mother. "Though I grant you, it's immaculate. I shouldn't be surprised if he'd had it cleaned as a special compliment to us—or rather, should I say, as a special compliment to *you*?"

She smiled significantly at Caroline. Because this made both her daughters uncomfortable, if for different reasons, the topic was effectively laid to rest.

Determined to forget it, Theo kept her mind on the

scenery. The distance from town to Hadleigh was about ten miles, just far enough to excuse Lady Morris for implying it was inconvenient to drive back and forth. Because the coachman drove at a pace suited for ladies, an hour and some quarters passed before they reached the wooded edge of Hadleigh's park.

Theo had never been to the estate before. Rolling through the iron gates was like entering an enchanted land. The air itself seemed more golden, and all the plantings were lush. Despite her tightening nerves, she decided banknotes must make superb manure. She could imagine no other explanation for the extravagant verdure.

Anything less like the moors outside was hard to conceive.

"How happily situated Hadleigh is!" Mrs. Becket exclaimed with a bit more exuberance than Theo approved. "Look at those walnuts beside that stream. How natural it all looks. How clever his gardener must be. Heavens!" She craned so far out the window Theo was tempted to grab her skirt. "I think there's some sort of folly around that bend. Oh, do stop," she cried to the coachman. "I'm sure Mr. Delavert will not mind if we have a look."

The folly was a faux Greek temple with thick green vines. Even as they stepped out to admire it, the nicked wooden door opened. From the glimpse Theo caught of the interior, this "temple" was someone's home.

"Oh!" Caroline exclaimed and covered her mouth.

The man who was exiting—the gardener, to judge by his muddy trowel—turned at the sound. He blushed as hard as Caroline.

"Oh," Theo's sister said again in dismay. "Please forgive us. We did not know anyone lived here."

"That's all right," said the man. "Lots of folks like to stop."

Theo could not blame her sister for gaping, even in the face of the gardener's embarrassment. If Theo had not seen Delavert first, she would have thought this man admirable.

His build was sturdy, his hair a cross between red and gold. Beneath his persistent flush, he had an open country face, distinguished—so far as such faces could be—by a stubborn jaw.

"Are you the gardener?" she asked, as no one else seemed inclined to speak. "If you are, we have been admiring the grounds. They are exceedingly well kept."

"Sheffield," said the man, which she took to be his name. "Head gardener. And we've had a good growing year."

"I'm sure that's due in part to your skill," Caroline objected breathlessly.

"Yes'm," said Sheffield. "Much obliged."

The gardener clutched his trowel as if it were a lifeline. Theo was awfully tempted to laugh. The only thing missing from the perfect picture of a country bumpkin was for him to scuff his feet in the dirt.

She was spared her struggle by an odd occurrence. A percussion just short of pain struck the bone between her brows. Her stomach swooped and she felt, quite inexplicably, as if she *were* the gardener. He was remembering another occasion on which he'd seen Caroline—in Bridesmere's circulating library. Caroline's golden head was bent over a volume she was considering whether to withdraw. The nape of her neck was beautifully arched, the curve of her bosom generous. When she bit her lip in indecision, the gardener ached so hard he could have wept.

He was harder now. Lately, she was all he could think about. Indeed, he thought about her so often he worried he might run mad. If he had, Theo didn't see it. The phantasm—if phantasm it was—vanished as abruptly as it had begun.

Heavens, she thought, her hand to her throat. Maybe she was running mad herself.

Madness did not explain the gardener's condition. A hump as big as a fist pushed out the front of his breeches. Recalling the last time she had seen a man in that state, Theo blushed as hotly as the gardener.

An unexpected sound caused her to stumble: a low growl like that of a dog. She saw nothing when she looked around, but the automatic rush of alarm brought her back to herself. She had been staring at a stranger's breeches . . . in front of her family. Oh, how very embarrassing! At that moment, she wanted nothing more than to depart as fast as she could.

Thankfully, her mama concurred.

"Come girls," she said, her tone telling Theo (and likely the gardener, too) that she thought this exchange had lasted long enough. "It isn't polite to keep a host waiting."

Sheffield stood there as they rode away.

Watching is all he has, Theo thought, then rubbed the lingering discomfort between her brows.

Despite being in his wolf-form, Lucius felt infinitely more himself. He had chased three squirrels, consumed a hare, and napped at least an hour beneath a cool thicket. Doing so was safe enough. The grounds at Hadleigh held few dangers. When Lucius's wolf first allowed their souls to be joined, the melding of *upyr* and animal nature had ensured that every trait was maximized. Though his wolf-form wasn't as strong as it would be at night, it was still superior to most threats.

Buoyed by this certainty, when he smelled Theo's arrival at the gate, he was happy rather than anxious. He raced across the park to see her, flitting from bush to bush with his tail wagging. His elation rose as he caught up to the lumbering coach.

One of the horses rolled an eye at him, but because it recognized his essence as that of the person who'd helped him during the rain, it did not shy. Lucius was feeling frightfully pleased with himself . . . until the carriage pulled up at the folly, and his gardener Sheffield stepped out.

He shrank behind a hedge with every muscle tensed. Clearly, his wolf-self disliked seeing Theo near another male. His hackles rose, and a growl threatened to rumble from his throat. Though he swallowed the reaction, he couldn't help thinking that she was his. Outraged beyond what was rational, he had to dig his wolf's nails into the dirt to keep from leaping onto Sheffield's back.

He reached for Theo's mind, instinctively needing to connect. The last thing he meant was to lend her his mental powers. It seemed, however, that he had. She was picking up thoughts from the gardener, erotic thoughts that Lucius realized were directed toward her sister. This was probably all that saved him. Had Sheffield been lusting after Theo, Lucius could not have vouched for his self-control.

He broke the three-way contact as soon as he could, but not before noting where Theo's eyes had strayed. For the first time he could remember, he literally saw red.

He knew she heard him growl because she stumbled, but he did not receive a single warning for what came next. The sight of her faltering called up a memory. Lucius saw Mena, though how he knew it was she, he could not have said. Perhaps his emotions told him. From the pit of his being rose a joy so terrible it could have been misery.

He sat at Mena's kitchen table by a spherical glass window. In the moonlight her face was clear. Though she did not resemble Theo, she had a similar, exotically odd beauty. She was carrying something to him—a bowl of broth thin and pure enough for him to drink. His Mena was rich, a human diplomat with many servants. He loved that she had made this soup herself. It would not afford him true sustenance, but her care for him was precious.

Something of his gratitude must have shown. She opened her mouth, about to tease, when suddenly her knees gave way. She went down, soup splashing across the tile. Winded, she could not rise on her own. Fear stabbed through him as he helped her up.

"Don't fuss," she scolded laughingly, each line around her eyes a knife he hadn't guessed was there. "I'm just clumsy."

He knew she was lying. Though she'd hid it deep in her mind, he knew in that moment that she was ill.

He'd been young then: two centuries, maybe three. He'd barely understood what being immortal meant. But she was his first deep love, the one who showed the others for trifles. He'd understood what he would lose if he lost her.

He snapped back to his normal awareness panting, his wolf-form shivering with terror. The carriage was rolling into the distance, with Sheffield staring after it. No doubt he wanted to whine with longing every bit as much as Lucius did.

I won't lose this one, he told himself as he forced the tremors to subside. No matter what, he wouldn't lose Theo.

As she sat silently by the window, Theo tried to breathe away her headache. The path led them clopping over a stream, through a meadow where sheep were tearing at the grass, and finally by another folly, this one shaped like a crumbling keep. Then, like a stage curtain pulling back, the trees cleared to reveal a smooth, green slope of lawn with a house rising from its top.

"My," Theo said in spite of herself.

Hadleigh Hall was an imposing mass of stone cornered by four square towers. It was solid in a way to which more modern houses did not aspire. Though less than a century old, it seemed rooted on its hill, never to move again.

"Heavens," said her mother, leaning forward to see. Her voice held a hint of unsureness, as if she were at last becoming aware that her ambition might have overreached.

"It is just a house," Caroline said reasonably. "Large, to be sure, but—"

A streak of motion caused Theo to miss the rest of her speech. A low, dark shape was racing around the shadowed side of the hall, almost too swift to see. She held her breath, able to make out a curling tail and a distinctive sharp-eared head with a grinning mouth.

"A wolf!" she cried, louder than she meant. Her pulse was pounding so quickly she could have sworn it beat it in her mouth.

"Don't be silly," her mother said. "I am sure Mr. Delavert keeps dogs."

"It was not a—" Theo cut herself off. Perhaps she was being silly. Certainly, she was not herself this afternoon.

Caroline reached from her side of the seat to cover Theo's hand. "It must have been a dog. Bridesmere is too civilized to have wolves."

Theo nodded, but in her heart she knew what she'd seen.

Mr. Delavert met them in the entry hall, a large columned room with one broad arch leading to a stair. Seen among this grandeur, their host looked as disheveled as Theo felt. Despite their arriving past the appointed hour, his waistcoat was misbuttoned. Theo sensed him trying to search her expression, but given the events of the recent drive, she was in no mood to oblige. Even with her face averted, her body tingled each time he spoke. She barely saw her surroundings as he led them up to their rooms, no more than dimly aware that her mother's praise of his house was too fulsome.

"I hope you will be comfortable," he said, reaching past Theo's bosom to open a door.

They were alone in the passage. Her mother's and sister's voices trailed out from a nearby room that might as well have been miles away. Startled, her gaze flew to his. His smile was faint, but it affected her all the same. Indeed, smiling or not, Mr. Delavert was so comely lesser women would have swooned.

"Theo," he said softly. His arm was braced on the wall beside her, his hand level with her ear. Before riding in his carriage she had not noticed he had a scent. Now she could smell nothing else. Nervously, she licked her lip.

Her gesture might have been a sign. His long, tall body inclined closer, his stone-gray gaze settling on her mouth. Though he did not touch her, his warmth increased. Abruptly, she was glad no one but her could see his breathing go this deep.

"Theo . . ."

"I told you not to call me that."

It came out a sultry whisper, an invitation but for the words. Mr. Delavert ran his tongue around his teeth as she'd seen him do once before. For some reason, the habit sent a swirl of heat to her core.

"I'll come to you tonight," he said, hoarse and low.

"No," she gasped, finding her breath a second too late.

He had spun away and was striding down the hall as if another second in her presence would spell disaster. In a trance, Theo watched him go. The rhythmic flap of his coat tails was a seduction all by itself.

She was still standing dumbstruck when her mama poked her head out a door. "Aren't these rooms lovely?" she marveled. "Mr. Delavert has been kind."

Kind was not the term Theo would have used, but she complied with her mother's urging to change out of her traveling frock. Though tea was definitely called for, it was going to have to perform miracles to set her right.

As she sat in her room beside the window, dragging a brush through her stubborn hair, voices drifted up from the grounds below.

"You will leave this to me," she heard Lady Morris say. "I am a better judge of what interests men."

A languid sigh, which Theo recognized as Lily's, followed in response, but Lady Morris was not put off.

"Do not try to make conversation. It is not your strength. If food is served, you must eat less than the Becket girls. Do not talk to them overmuch, but do not appear unfriendly. Though the Beckets are beneath us, men are not fond of cats."

A murmur Theo could not decipher answered this.

"Keep your hands folded in your lap," Lady Morris added, "and your eyes lowered. If Mr. Delavert speaks to you, you may glance at him, but *briefly*—otherwise he'll think you are fast. You have the face and body of a goddess. That is all the man needs to know."

"Yes, Mama," said the goddess with a lack of enthusiasm that made Theo smile.

"Don't 'yes, Mama' me," Lady Morris snapped. "You will be twenty and six this summer, more than old enough to have found a match. I trust you know how hopeless that would be without my help. I can only thank heaven your idiot father isn't here to bollocks things up."

The tartness of her tone, especially toward her "dear Sir Mayor" lifted Theo's brows.

It seemed the Beckets weren't alone in hiding things behind closed doors.

Chapter 8

Lady Morris and her daughter having arrived, everyone gathered in a pretty yellow parlor on the eastern side of the house. Theo imagined it was sunny during the day. Now that dusk had fallen, it made do with a blaze of beeswax tapers.

"Do enlighten us, Mr. Fitz Clare," Lady Morris was saying as she poured tea—an honor she really should have left to Theo's mama. Bent over the task, her turban looked quite stately. "What is your connection to the Fitz Clares of Bridesmere?"

Mr. Fitz Clare took the china cup. His smile was wry, as if he knew precisely what she was hoping to ascertain. "My branch of the family moved to Italy some time ago. While Percy's guardian is a relative, I'm afraid my connection to the founding tree is not so close that I may forego earning my living."

Lady Morris clucked in sympathy. "I suppose we must all bear the burdens Fate sends our way. Nonetheless, I am convinced you could not have a finer employer than Mr. Delavert."

"Not in a million years." Mr. Fitz Clare's smile tipped on one side. "Mr. Delavert has no equal."

The object of these commendations was fiddling with the candelabra on the mantelpiece, clearly less comfortable in company than his friend. It wasn't hard to see why Mr. Fitz Clare would be confident. Mrs. Becket had been struck speechless by his appearance, a complaint Theo didn't think she had ever seen her mother suffer from. Unfairly handsome as Mr. Delavert was, his friend was a tall, blond god.

Theo doubted any of the women wished to question what a steward was doing among them—besides providing an addition to their male numbers. Evidently, Mr. Delavert had not wished to include other men. Thinking too hard about why that was made her head ache, and thus she stopped. It did not matter, in any case. Mr. Fitz Clare might be an employee, but he certainly presented the perfect image of a gentleman.

Indeed, more than one lady was struggling not to gape.

Theo glanced back at Mr. Delavert, now safely facing away. If she were honest, she would admit to a preference for her own devil. With his silver hair and his limp neckcloth, Mr. Delavert seemed the more human of the two. She doubted she would ever be comfortable around a man as flawless as Edmund Fitz Clare.

Perhaps Mr. Delavert sensed her attention, because he turned his head. He couldn't have looked more slyly pleased if he had read her mind.

Embarrassed to have been caught staring, Theo looked away, and was thus able to hear the end of a comment from her sister.

"How is little Percy?" she was asking Mr. Fitz Clare. "We were exceedingly sorry for him when he lost his parents, but they kept so much to themselves, we were not sure we ought to visit."

"They *are* a private family," Mr. Fitz Clare confirmed.

Caroline turned to Theo. "Didn't you sew him a stuffed toy? A wolfhound, as I recall."

Theo smiled. "Yes. It was made of brown velvet with button eyes. Our uncle sent it over with a delivery of groceries."

Mr. Fitz Clare's elegant eyebrows rose. "I believe I have seen him play with it."

"Oh, good. It is hard to guess what boys that age will like. I confess I could not think how to sew a sword."

"Speaking of wolves," said Theo's mother, finally finding her tongue—though Theo might have preferred she did not. "You shall never guess what my youngest thought she saw as we rode in: a real wolf, running across your lawn."

"Really?" Mr. Fitz Clare cast a quick, unreadable glance toward his employer. "I am sure it was only one of the dogs. The old squire kept a large kennel."

"That is precisely what I told her, but I did not think myself half-believed. Young people do have such imaginations!"

"*Some* young people," Lady Morris qualified. "My darling Lily has always been very sensible for her age."

"I should like to see a wolf," said her darling. "I should like to see it chase down a meal."

Theo's eyes widened at this declaration. Per her mother's instructions, Lily's shining chestnut curls were bent over hands she had folded docilely in her lap. To look at her, one would conclude she was incapable of a single bloodthirsty thought.

But perhaps Mr. Delavert had been right about Lily's character. Mr. Fitz Clare was peering at her oddly, too. To Theo's surprise, Lily lifted her head to meet his look—as if challenging him to a dare.

Theo's mouth fell open as she watched the two lock gazes. Lily was truly lovely with that spark in her eye, nearly as lovely as Mr. Fitz Clare.

Interestingly, Mr. Fitz Clare looked away first.

"Of course you'd like to see a wolf," Lady Morris said with a hint of warning. Lily was, after all, attracting the wrong man's eye. "What true lady doesn't like a hunt?"

"What true gentleman as well," murmured Mr. Delavert.

Theo did not have to turn her head to know he was regarding her. If she'd had any doubt, the shift of Lady Morris's attention would have set it aside.

"Too true," Lily's mother said, her expression narrowing. "All real gentlemen love a hunt."

Gentlemen did love a hunt, especially gentlemen of Lucius's ilk. Because of this, he knew there wasn't the slightest chance he would sleep tonight. Though he had tried to adjust his natural patterns to suit his guests, his awareness that Theo was here, under his protection, woke every territorial impulse his wolf possessed.

Doing his best to skirt the various trysting places of his staff, Lucius slipped like a shadow down the guests' corridor. Though he needed no more goads, he could not pretend to be unmoved by the activity. Luckily for his servants, he was too concerned with his own gratification to interfere with theirs. Still, he would have to establish some sort of compulsion to prevent them from taking their pleasure where guests could see. Minimum civility required that.

Striving to ignore a footman's distant chuckle, Lucius paused outside Theo's room. He knew she usually shared with her sister, but for obvious reasons he had decided to change her custom when he set the room arrangements. His anticipation rose as his *upyr* senses quested through the door. She was awake behind it, tossing restlessly in her bed as she tried to convince herself he had not really meant—or perhaps had not even said—that he would come to her tonight.

Lucius smiled. No force in heaven could have kept him away.

He tapped so softly on the wood he knew no one else would hear. Theo sat up but did not move to admit him. Her scent mixed fear and excitement, her heart thumping hard enough to make his mouth water. He entered, knowing that—whatever her misgivings—her body would rather invite him in than bar the door.

"Mr. Delavert!" she whispered in protest.

Since this seemed more for form than horror, he took in his surroundings. His eyes needed no more illumination than a cat's.

His housekeeper had chosen a pretty room, plain but nice, with the human necessities of a washstand, dressing table, and a chair or two. Her bed was placed by the wall. Theo waited with the covers pulled to her chin and her gaze turned to the birds someone had painted on the paneling. She appeared to be under the impression that if she did not look at him, he would not see her. In this she was mistaken. His eyes drank in every inch of her, even the parts he had to imagine.

"Really!" she said, but not loudly. "I must insist you depart."

He smiled at her offended manner, noting she did not offer to scream. "I thought you might be shaken after your canine encounter. It would be impolite to leave a guest in fear."

"More impolite than entering my room?" Sighing, she turned from the wall to face him. Her color was high, her nipples hot, sharp points beneath the covers she had pulled up. If she had known how every breath betrayed her desire, she would not have bothered trying to hide. "Why are you doing this?"

"Because, whether you wish to admit it or not, I know it is what you want." He sat beside her, easing one of her hands from its death grip on the blanket. She shivered when he rubbed his thumb across her palm. "Let us be truthful about this at least."

"My sister . . ." she said, her objection trailing off as his gaze finally secured hers. Pressing his will inside her, subtly, deeply, was an inherently male triumph.

"Your sister won't hear a thing," he assured her, though

this was not precisely her concern. "Nor will anyone else. The walls in this house are too thick for that."

She moaned, low and helpless, images rising in her mind of a number of situations in which the pair of them might make noise. She was breathing shallowly, her lips parted and moist. His fangs began to lengthen without his will. His cock had been rigid before he tapped on her door, but this new sign of arousal proved how far she'd breached his control. Millennia of restraint were all that kept him from taking her. The result would have been rewarding for both, but he pressed her hand to his breast instead, letting her feel his own hurrying heartbeat.

"I *did* see a wolf," she said, apropos of he knew not what. She was—thanks to his thrall—in a half-dreaming state where logic might not rule. "He was running very fast."

"Was he? He must have been difficult to see."

Thinking this must satisfy her, he gave himself permission to inhale the scent of her neck. Her skin was satin beneath his nose, her warmth as catching as a fever. Had his temperature not been humanly warm already, it would have risen then. To his delight, without his giving her the least instruction, her hand—the same hand he had been pressing to his heart—slid up his shirtfront and into his hair. The caress made his teeth lengthen so rapidly they stung his gums. He struggled to think clearly. He had not yet decided how to proceed. An exchange of pleasure, without a doubt, but certain barriers—her virginity at the least—probably should not be crossed.

The *Upyr* Council frowned on such things—though he suspected they would never get those they ruled to give up preying on humans entirely. Aside from considerations of self-defense, thralling humans added spice to *upyr* life. Tonight Lucius was glad the political reality was what it was. He doubted he was capable of stepping back from this.

Theo, bless her heart, had her own concerns.

"I want to see evidence," she insisted throatily. "I want to search for paw prints."

Reluctantly, he eased away. Despite the flush that stained her cheeks, he saw she was in earnest. He had planned to stay here, but if leaving the house would soothe her, he was not averse. He knew very well no "evidence" existed, and he wanted to allow her to remain as much herself as he could. Taking pleasure with a puppet was not his goal.

"Very well," he said. "I will bring you outside."

When he promised to bring her outside, Theo never dreamed he would fling wide a third-story window and jump out. Shocked, she rushed to assure herself he was well, only to find he had landed silently and without harm—very much as if he had flown.

To her absolute astonishment, he put out his arms. He seemed to expect her to leap into them.

"Do not be afraid," he said. "I will catch you."

His eyes glowed up at her through the dark, and suddenly the idea of jumping seemed perfectly rational. She did not even worry about exposing her legs as she swung onto the sill in her sheer nightgown.

He grinned, then crooked his fingers to urge her on.

Well, why ever not? she thought, scooting forward and pushing off. The fall was exhilarating, a whoosh of cool night air and a feather-light catch-landing. Mr. Delavert slid her down his body to the grass, her gown rucking up until her thighs brushed his. Though she was no soft miss, his muscles were a good deal harder than hers.

His muscles were not the only part of him that was hard. She should have been embarrassed, but her discovery of his arousal made it impossible not to squirm. Far from being offended, he wrapped his hands around her bottom and hitched her close.

The ridge of his manhood pressed her suggestively.

"I deserve a kiss for this excursion," he said. "I'm not obliged to ever let you have your way."

"What way?" she murmured and tipped up her face.

His breath rushed out, and then he kissed her as deeply as she could have wished in her most wicked dream. His mouth was silken, his tongue a brazen temptation. Abruptly, she remembered they had done this before. He tasted as wonderful as he had in her garden, but his manner was fiercer now. This was his home, and he must feel he was master here. It was not long before he groaned, tightened his arms, and lifted her against the house's rough stone wall. There, with a solid barrier to shove against, he crushed their bodies together.

She was on her toes from the force with which he pressed her, and she had the impression of amazing strength held in check. The rhythm of his movements compelled her to rock forward, too, though he hardly needed her help. He seemed to know what she wanted before she did, a perplexing but very gratifying trick.

In the face of such experience, she had little hope of reining in her own urges. Her longing grew until she felt a stranger to herself. The sensations were too big for her. She did not know what to do, only that shc had to do something. Without quite meaning to, she gripped his back.

"Lord," he panted. "I cannot wait any more."

He might have been speaking for her. His hand moved beneath what coverage remained to her gown, rising up her inner thighs and between. She gulped for air as his fingers slid over her secret folds, an intimacy that simultaneously terrified and thrilled. His touch tickled higher . . . deeper . . . She lifted her knees—though they seemed to lift themselves. She felt as if she had to press them around his hips, as if she absolutely must open herself to whatever he wished to do.

His voice crooned in approval, but approval was not enough. She sighed as his caresses increased in strength. She had not known how much she wished to be cupped until he did it. The sensations were as powerful as they were strange. Her body bucked and her neck arched back. It was the most marvelous torture.

"Yes," he said, shifting his thumb to some impossibly sensitive spot. "Let me feel you go over."

She moaned, craving more, craving him inside her where she was hot. She could not even be ashamed, though she did not know how to voice her desire. Luckily, she did not have to. The tips of two of his fingers curled just within her, his hand snugly gripping her pubic bone.

"There," he said and lifted her a fraction more.

The change was magic. She gasped as the pressure he exerted magnified her feelings. Something tantalizing swelled inside her, a hunger as sweet as sunshine.

"Oh!" she cried as her tension broke in a fluttering spasm. *"Oh, oh, oh."*

"Again," he whispered hotly by her ear. "I want you to come again."

Her body could not disobey. He stirred another spasm and another, pleasure lapping pleasure until her limbs were limp. When he finally let her stand, her knees gave way.

He caught her under her elbows.

She looked up at him, stunned by what had just happened. The lines of his countenance were still, his beauty as clean as the moonlight. Did she thank him or slap his face? And why had slapping him not occurred to her earlier? Was she, perhaps, not as decent as she believed?

Such questions could not be answered, at least not by her. His closeness beat at her in waves of insistent heat, communicating some deep physical tension. She sensed he wanted—no, *needed*—to experience what she just had.

"Are you well?" he asked, searching her eyes.

"I—" She wet her lips and tried again, her throat sore from crying out. "I feel as if I should . . . I think I would like to do for you what you did for me."

Rather than answer, he kissed her as if they'd never kissed before, savoring and deep and slow. Her head was spinning by the time his lips released her. Like a sculptor smoothing his creation, he stroked her tingling mouth with his fingertips.

His tenderness weakened her most of all.

"I would like for you to please me," he said. "But for now, I've taken sufficient pleasure from pleasing you . . . unless you have forgotten why you wanted to leave the house?"

She hadn't forgotten. She simply had begun to wonder if searching for wolf prints was important.

"Come," he said, that little word she would never hear the same again. He took her hand with an ease that tightened her throat. "Show me where you saw this wolf. We shall see how his marks compare to my dogs' "

"Wolf paws are bigger than most dogs'," she said, "and when they run they leave a single line of tracks."

He seemed startled that she knew this. "Yes," he said, slow and thoughtful. "That is true of *canis lupus*."

Theo had a good memory. Eerily—at least to him—she led him along the very route his wolf had taken around the house, though not one blade of grass was broken, nor one inch of soil depressed. Many *upyr* had the ability to erase their footprints. The most powerful could do so during the day. As far as Lucius knew, he was the only one who left no trail at all, not even for an instant. He had often found the gift convenient when he wished to give his companions the slip, but as he watched Theo crouch down to pat the grass, exclaiming that she was certain she had seen *something,* he wondered if he ought to be taking advantage of it now.

Had he ever learned to love properly? If he had, he did not remember the lesson now. Maybe, though, he should not be providing the means by which a woman he cared about doubted her own judgment.

With a shake of his head, he pushed the pinch of guilt aside. He had to hide what he was. If he didn't, he'd be sure to lose her. The world Theo lived in had no room for beings like him. Honesty could not be the foundation on which their bond was built. The best he could hope for was an interval like this, with Theo under his partial thrall so that fewer truths needed concealing. As it was, he would have to steal back some of her memories when the night was through.

Theo rose, sighing, and swiped her hands on her gown. "I am sorry," she said. "I could have sworn this was the way he ran."

"It is no matter. I enjoy being out at night."

She smiled and looked about her, breathing deeply of the cool sweet air, which was but a tenth as alive to her as it was to him. "It is nice. The country is quiet, as if we had the world to ourselves. I will admit, though, I would be frightened to venture out alone."

"You need never be frightened with me."

She laughed. "No, I need only be frightened *of* you."

"Not even that. I would never do anything you do not want."

She bit her lip, and he felt her think that, if this was true, she need only be frightened of herself, because there seemed no limit to the things she wanted him to do. Rather than say this, she reached shyly to brush his cheek with her fingertips.

"May I—Would you show me how to do what *you* want, Mr. Delavert?"

Her question went through him in a hot shudder. "Lucius," he said. "Call me Lucius when we are alone."

"But I thought—"

"Please. As a special favor to me."

"As you wish . . . Lucius." Her touch trailed hesitantly down his linen shirt, past his thumping heart to the waist of his stretched breeches. "May I do what you want, Lucius?"

His breath soughed in and out like a human who had run a race. He did not even try to speak evenly. "I want you to touch me. I love the feel of your hands."

She was bolder than he expected, even with his thrall. She

moved her hand directly over his bulging groin. Though the touch was light, her human heat was magic. "Shall I touch you as you touched me?"

"Lie down with me," he said, the request coming out a rasp. His weakened knees were already sinking. "Lie down with me on the grass."

She came down with him and kissed him, sliding one slender thigh between both of his. He should have let her be, but his instincts would not allow it. He had to roll her beneath him in the age-old male superior pose. Groaning with pleasure, he pressed his ache into her softness. Though his wolf most definitely approved, after a few sighing kisses, she pushed his shoulder to shift him off.

"This cannot be as nice as what you did to me," she said. "I think you must open your clothing. I think you must allow me to touch your skin."

He was half afraid to do it. The caress of human hands was as addicting to his species as the taste of blood. His control hung by a thread as it was. He could tell she was still nervous. It would take no more than a firm refusal to discourage her.

His indecision lasted a breath too long.

"Lucius," she said, scolding, husky, and his resistance unraveled like a fraying thread.

He popped his breeches open on either side, pushed them down, and lifted his erection out. He felt as immense as her expression told him he looked. Her fingers flew to her lips.

"Oh," she said. "I think I shall need both hands."

He had to smile, though the state of his fangs dictated that it be close-mouthed. "I should not dream of complaining."

She made a face at him and sat up. "Stay," she said when he would have joined her. "I want to see what I'm doing—without you getting in the way."

He would not dream of doing that, either. Committed now, he stacked his hands behind his head, mutely demonstrating his harmlessness. Even with this, she hesitated. Her hand hovered over the crux of his impatience, close enough that he felt her heat, but too shy to touch him yet. Though he meant to be still, he was too hungry. His spine arched in longing.

At this, she bit her lip. "Er," she said. "Perhaps you should offer me some guidance."

He had sufficient sense not to laugh. "My guidance," he said gravely, "is for you to wrap your fist around my shaft."

"Just one?"

"Just one for now. Put it on the base and grip tight."

He should have been prepared, but he gasped when she gathered her will and obeyed. Oh, it had been too long since he'd felt this. Her fingers were damp and hot, tingling sharply with humanness. His erection jolted longer within her grasp, and the thoughts that raced through her head did nothing to calm his lust. She was marveling at the feel of him: the silk-wrapped hardness, the leaping pulses of excitement. He could not doubt he was the first man she'd touched this way.

He was gladder than any noncelibate immortal had a right to be.

"This tight?" she asked, the question broken with her breath.

He writhed a little against the grass, struggling for the modicum of politeness his greed would rather have ignored. "Tighter, if you would . . . a little more . . . yes, *yes,* like that." Without warning, he tasted blood, having inadvertently nicked his lip as he spoke. It dizzied him for a second, and he had to pant for control. "Now—" His voice shook and he swallowed. "Draw your hold toward the crown just that tightly."

She obeyed him so well his whole body coiled with pleasure. He could barely bring himself to keep his hands where they were. The circle of her fingers stopped beneath his rim. A tear of sexual fluid squeezed from his tip. When a breeze rippled across it, it was tickling cool.

"You are shining," she said in gentle wonderment.

"My excitement makes me wet."

"Yes, but you are *shining*."

He struggled up on his elbows. His skin was glowing like a firefly, the illusion of his humanness blown away by the extremity of his desire. He couldn't remember the last time he had lost his concentration enough to let his glamour fall.

"It is nothing," he said firmly, but the order had no effect. Theo had no intention of meeting his eyes. Her gaze was, to her mind, more pleasantly occupied.

"It is beautiful," she said, her focus all on his lambent cock. "If I stroke you again, will you get brighter?"

He surrendered to the moment with a groaning laugh. Her attention was not moving from where it was. He would have to thrall the memory from her later.

"You must answer that for yourself," he said more practically. "Use your other hand now. Drag this one all the way up and start again with the next. You will see what effect you have."

Even he was not ready for the results. Her hand-over-hand caress put him into a thrall as deep as hers, a thrall where he writhed and moaned and ground his teeth together in ecstasy. Happily, she recognized his reaction for what it was. Better still, his excitement excited her. He could hear her quickened heartbeat from where he lay, could feel it pulsing in her hands.

"Slower," he groaned as his balls began to knot up. "Do not rush the end."

"You are red," she said worriedly. "I am too rough . . ."

Before she could fulfill her intent of loosening her grip, he slapped one hand over hers. This, at last, startled her gaze to his. When he was certain she would heed him, he spoke. "You are perfect. You could be even rougher and it would not be too much. Keep going slow and hard. You will see what you are waiting for soon enough."

She blushed deeply enough to heat the surface of her hand.

Innocent she might be, but not entirely ignorant. Unable to resist, he pressed her fingers close to his cockstand's head. "Tighten here," he said gruffly. "On the crown where I feel it most. Make every stroke tight all the way up."

He could not speak when she obeyed him, not even to assure her she was doing it exactly right. He was delirious with pleasure, incoherent and assaulted. *Upyr* were able to bear rougher handling than humans, but they were also more sensitive, their capacity for enjoyment intensified in every way. It wasn't long before his lips drew back from his fangs, obeying a compulsion stronger than caution or will. He turned his head away but even that evasion seemed likely to fail him soon.

He would be thrashing in a minute. He'd be over the edge and gone.

"Watch," he gasped, the only stratagem he could think of, "watch my cock when I come."

He hoped she listened. He could not control himself anymore. The orgasm rose from his feet, a tendril of aching, twisting gold that drew a thousand more threads inward. His fingers prickled with anticipation as each pull of her hands increased the pressure. He swelled and shuddered, but at last the sensation burst. Groaning with the force of his release, he shot a lengthy fountain into the air, as if he'd been neglecting his needs for centuries instead of years. He was lucky she had no experience, for the spasm was as inhumanly violent as it was long. Wave after wave of pleasure blazed through his nerves, nearly blinding him with relief.

The only thing that could have made it better was if his teeth had been in her neck.

He moaned at the sharp frisson of pleasure that idea stirred.

When his mind cleared enough to be aware again, she was stroking him gently, almost thoughtfully against his thigh. Her palm was shockingly wet. The *upyr* version of sexual emissions tended to evaporate. That she was slippery indicated just how generous his flood had been.

"My," she said. "I'd no idea there would be so much."

"Isn't usually," he mumbled around his retracting fangs. "'S been a long time for me."

She smiled, flattered and amused and shy. She appeared so clearheaded then, so much *herself,* that he became alarmed. Only when he probed her mind for signs of his thrall did he relax. She was still dazzled. If she hadn't been, she would have been questioning what had passed.

Thralled or not, her next words took him by surprise.

"I hope you'll forgive my presumption," she said, her lashes lowering coyly, "but I would like to express a wish that you shall not, in the future, have to wait quite so long."

Chapter 9

Edmund's sole complaint about human lovers was that they were so easy to wear out. His partners for the evening slept in the tussled mess that was his bed. The clock had not yet struck midnight. He was sure to catch a second wind when it did. His *upyr* powers were always strongest then. Truth be told, he was nearly stiff enough right now. With the least encouragement, he could have been.

Sighing, he climbed out of bed. He could change into his wolf-form. Go for a run. His son, Robin, might be induced to leave his charge long enough to hunt. Sadly, hunting with a pack of two was not a terrible lot of fun.

As for Lucius, Edmund harbored little expectation of his company. His sire had gone daft, what with trying to really *be* Lucas Delavert. Edmund wasn't sure what to make of his new obsession, but since it had sprung from his own suggestion, he could not scold. With luck, as the novelty of playing human wore off, Lucius would settle back to something more like his normal self; not as apathetic, Edmund hoped, but at least more sensible.

A wisp of human presence disturbed his thoughts. Someone stood at his door: a woman with a mind so shielded he scarcely knew she was there. Edmund guessed immediately who it was; there were not many humans with a mental signature like that.

At the realization, a current of precisely the sort of excitement he had been wanting streaked through his veins. Concluding Dame Fortune was smiling on him tonight, he strode swiftly through his sitting room and opened the outer door.

Miss Morris stood there in a ruffled white dressing gown, a little wide-eyed at being admitted before she knocked. When her eyes drifted downward and widened more, he remembered he wore no clothes. When she licked her lips, he was grateful he'd forgotten.

She was the comeliest mortal he'd ever seen. Her curls were an auburn cloud about her shoulders, her figure as perfect as a budding flower. She joined the beauty of an *upyr* with the warmth and lifeblood of a human. The combination presented a temptation the strongest of his kind would have had trouble resisting.

Certainly, no *upyr* would have resisted if she were ogling him the way she was Edmund—as if he were a tea cake and she had not eaten sweets in days. Fighting not to let his jubilation show, he stretched one arm above his head to lean against the doorframe. From reading the minds of many women, he knew the casual pose showed the breadth of his chest to good effect.

"My," she said now. "You are certainly blessed in your various parts."

"Promise me you are not a virgin," he said, "and I'll let you have your wicked way with whichever part of me you like."

She met his eyes, her features oddly and fascinatingly still for one of her kind. "What if I like them all?"

"Then I shall pray to every saint in the Bible that you are no maid."

Her lashes fluttered down in fans, a smile playing faintly across her lips. "I have not been innocent for many years, Mr. Fitz Clare. I ask only one favor from you in return."

"Only one?"

He meant to tease, but she was serious. "I ask that you not spill your seed inside me. I have no wish to end up with child, at least until certain of my plans are further along."

"Hm," said Edmund, inwardly amused at the unlikelihood of her plans ever bearing fruit. Daft or not, Lucius wasn't apt to let anyone shackle him. "Some might say your being here risks your plans."

She shrugged delicately. "Some might say ambition and pleasure can coexist . . . if one is clever enough."

"I could betray you."

"Not if you want me in your bed more than once."

Oh, her confidence was priceless. And her directness. She truly might have been an *upyr.*

"It does seem likely I would," he conceded. "On one point; however, I must correct you. My carnal efforts—though they be as constant as the stars—shall not disturb your hopes. I am *incapable of fathering a child,* an unfortunate condition I'm afraid no physician has the power to cure."

Her hand closed the space between them, her slender fingers barely brushing the crest of his erection. Despite the lightness of the touch, he twanged like a plucked harp string.

"You are not incapable altogether," she said softly.

"No, indeed. Not incapable in other ways at all."

Happy with how this was proceeding, he drew her over the threshold, not much concerned with the slumbering maids. His sitting room had a comfortable chaise. He saw no reason for Miss Morris to discover she was not the first to visit him tonight.

"You are very beautiful," she observed, her hands smoothing over his belly. "I never met a man who looked quite like you."

"Met many naked ones?"

At his jest, she glanced up from her caresses, perfectly expressionless. "Remove my clothes," she said. "I have decided to let you admire me."

A new intensity had entered her manner. This, he thought, must be a personal pleasure ritual, and maybe a necessary one. What male had triggered this need to have her beauty worshipped? Who had fallen to his knees before her power? Most of all, was she as susceptible to Edmund's looks as others were to hers?

Intrigued, he leaned in to untie her gown. As he did, his head descended naturally to her neck. Her skin was thin and silken. When he brushed his lips across a vein, her shiver of pleasure delighted him.

"Don't," she said unexpectedly.

He straightened with both brows raised. "Don't?"

"If you mean to bite me, please do not. I would not be able to explain a mark."

He blinked at her, wondering for one unreal moment if she knew what he was. If she did, she should also know he could heal small injuries.

Taking a minute to consider, he drew his hand from her shoulder down to her breast. Her dressing gown had fallen open, and beneath it she was bare. Her nipple tightened under his palm. The weight of her breast was slight, an uptilted sphere of pink and cream. If she was worried about people seeing evidence of loveplay, perhaps she would prefer being bitten here.

His face must have betrayed his thoughts. "I do not fancy marks anywhere," she clarified.

"You don't want me to bite you at all."

She shook her head emphatically. With smooth, perfect flesh like hers, he supposed he could not blame her. Unfortunately, if he did not bite her, he could not put her under his thrall. He hadn't Lucius's gift for spelling people with his eyes alone.

This presented a dilemma. It was one thing to ignore

etiquette and feed from Lucius's servants, and quite another to disobey this girl when she'd explicitly refused his bite. That would mean breaking laws his brother Aimery, the head of the *Upyr* Council, had worked long and hard to have passed. Edmund had supported his brother's efforts, had argued for them many times. There would always be *upyr* who saw little worth in having any boundaries set on them. But even if Aimery never learned what he did tonight, Edmund would know he had let him down.

Once upon a time, when he was still human, Edmund had too often disappointed those he loved. After all these years, he liked to think he had changed.

"I like kissing," Miss Morris offered. "Anywhere at all. And a good, hard ride that leaves me feeling tired. My mother—" She swallowed as if she were uncomfortable bringing her up. "My mother says I am too highly strung. Perhaps that is why bedplay is the only occupation that relaxes me."

In spite of himself, Edmund smiled. "You might be surprised by how very well I comprehend that."

"Then you will tup me," she said, the suggestion oddly innocent in her mouth. "Since you cannot make me pregnant, I will not worry and shall thus enjoy it without constraint."

She had closed her hand on the bulb of his shuddering organ, using just enough pressure to tug it up. The lust he felt at this was dizzying, his blood surging hot through his swollen veins. Alarms should have been clamoring in his mind. He knew he was not thinking as clearly as he ought.

Apart from her narcissistic bent, this girl was as near to a cipher as any human could be. Without biting her, Edmund wasn't likely to learn more about her—at any rate, not in a manner that he could trust. He would have to guard his secrets as never before; would have to watch his glamour, and his behavior, constantly. The challenge was daunting, but it appealed.

Maybe he needed a challenge. Maybe, in his own way, he had grown as world-weary as Lucius.

"Please," she said with a humility he did not think she often showed. "I want to see us naked together."

He bent to kiss her lightly on her rosebud lips. "I believe I can oblige you, though whether you like my idea of a 'good, hard ride' only time will tell."

His visitor tossed her hair.

"You will find me up to it," she predicted, and to his pleasure she spoke true.

Chapter 10

Theo and Caroline spent the hour after dinner strolling the nearer reaches of Hadleigh Park.

Rather extraordinarily, Mr. Delavert remained in bed. Their mother was closeted with Lady Morris in planning the coming ball. At first this had been interesting to watch, but for Theo and Caroline, the charm had palled. Between them, the mothers had paced the portrait gallery many times and just as many times declared it perfectly adequate to accommodating three sets of dancers. The necessity of a supper was debated endlessly and approved, and rooms were selected for card players and ladies' wraps. Most important, of course, was the guest list.

To both the Becket daughters' dismay, their mother seemed no more inclined than Lady Morris to count friendship as high as prestige. If social ambition were a disease, Theo's mother had caught a bout from her old schoolmate. Acquaintances who would have been more than welcome in either of their homes were now found wanting for their host's. After all, with Mr. Delavert throwing the event, any worthy in the county might be invited.

Theo had a sneaking, and somewhat embarrassing suspicion that their Uncle William should not be watching the mail.

She kicked a stone from the path she and her sister were following, trying to decide whether to air her suspicion. Caroline did like to think the best of people. She might not want to believe their mother had been as seduced as that.

At least their surroundings were conducive to peaceful thoughts. This part of the park was soft and green—and thankfully gardener-free. For this Theo was relieved. She had no desire to revisit the peculiar visions that had accompanied their first meeting. She preferred being left to admire the fruits of his work: the manicured paths, the beds of wildflowers and grasses, all charmingly displayed between rolling hills. The air was warm enough to do without wraps, and horse-tail clouds brushed the sky. From the deepening of its blue, Theo knew the flames of sunset would soon appear. Lulled by these rural beauties, she felt pleasantly dozy as they ambled.

"You slept late today," Caroline said, breaking the long silence. "And yesterday as well. Is anything troubling you?"

This was a question for which Theo was not prepared. She saw no way to answer that would not worry, and yet she did not want to lie. Thinking hard, she twirled her parasol.

"I believe it is the strange surroundings," she said at last. "I am unaccustomed to being away from home. When I do sleep, I've been having dreams that tire me out."

She had been having dreams she could not describe in polite company: of long, wet kisses, of hands touching her all over, of a smooth, warm mouth drifting down her neck and moaning hungrily. The sensations these dreams inspired were so powerful they thrummed through her even when she woke. She could not sleep after she had them. She could only thrash beneath her covers and long for their return. None of this could be shared with her sister, especially not their host's leading role.

Shared or not, she should have known Caroline would listen to more than her words. "If your room is not comfortable," she said, "I am certain Mr. Delavert would change it."

"My room is beautiful. Mr. Delavert has provided everything I could wish."

She had spoken incautiously. From the corner of her eye, she spied Caroline's curving smile. Theo did not have to guess what it meant. She rounded on her on the path.

"Why don't you like him?" Theo demanded.

Caroline was startled to a halt. "Whatever gave you the idea that I don't like Mr. Delavert?"

"Oh, I know you *like* him, but you do not think of him as a beau. You never flirt with him, and when he talks to you, you mumble. You are not giving him a chance."

Caroline's fair brows lowered. "Perhaps I should not ask this, but do you truly want me to?"

Theo gnawed her lip. *Did* she want her to? Had she ever? Or was she secretly pleased her beautiful older sister did not seem to notice how devastatingly attractive Delavert was?

"If I don't," she muttered ill-temperedly, "it is only because he is not good enough for you."

Caroline laughed softly at her lack of logic. "Theo, he has been kindness itself to us."

Because this was true, Theo sighed. Apart from a few too-long glances, Mr. Delavert had been a gentleman. Not once since their arrival had he tried to kiss her. Not once had he come to her as he threatened. That being so, it was not fair to blame him for her fantasies—which did not stop her from wanting to.

His eyes were haunting her, his stone-gray, devil-in-the-bedroom eyes. Whenever she chanced to meet them, she'd feel a tug deep in her body, as if his soul were calling to hers. *Come to me,* it seemed to say. *Come to me and be mine.*

Maybe it was time to admit she wanted to say yes, that she was not at his house for Caroline's sake, and that she might as well have forgotten what happened the last time she put her own wishes first.

She shook her head, not ready for that. Her lieutenant deserved a better memorial than for her to repeat the past. Indecent dreams were simply that. Theo had done nothing from which she could not turn back.

Fortunately, Caroline was too considerate to press the issue.

"Shall we head for the knot garden?" she suggested, tilting her head in that direction. "Maybe rest on the bench beside the fountain before we walk back?"

"That sounds perfect," Theo said, and squeezed her sister's arm. Even if she couldn't tell Caroline her secrets, knowing her sister loved her made their weight easier to bear.

"There you are!" Lady Morris trilled as Lucius tried to slip unnoticed down the passage to the kitchen.

The woman had the ears of a bat. Having spent the better part of the previous night with Theo, he had only just risen from his bed. All he wanted was a weak cup of Indian tea before he faced his guests. It was just his luck that Lady Morris had been lying in wait behind the stairway in the entry hall.

Now she tapped his arm with the fan she always seemed to carry, a coquettishness her daughter—supposedly the one in search of a husband—never seemed to employ. But perhaps Lady Morris was remembering her own days as the belle of Bridesmere.

"I declare," she said, "you do keep the latest hours. You must be the veriest night owl."

For once she didn't add that her darling Lily was one, too.

"I hope you did not want for anything," he said politely.

"Only your company, Mr. Delavert! You will be pleased to hear we have decided on serving pineapple ice—so cooling for the dancers, I think. Regrettably, we must forswear those charming German waltzes. I do think young people can be trusted as far as that—how else can they get acquainted? But waltzing is not accepted in this country yet. We would not want to mark your return by setting off a scandal!"

Laughing, she pressed her gathered fan to one cheek. "Now that you mention it, though," she said, despite his having had no opportunity to mention anything at all, "there is one means by which you might compensate us for your absence."

He knew he need not prod her. She would tell him what she wanted no matter what. It was just as well. The best response he had to offer was stifling his sigh.

"If you wouldn't mind," she went blithely on, "Lily and I were positively longing for a ride in your darling park. Do you suppose you could take us out in your carriage? It would be the greatest treat after planning your ball all day."

He was ashamed to need the reminder. Never mind she had maneuvered herself uninvited into the task. She was exerting herself on his behalf. He owed her something for her efforts. Driving out with her and her daughter was hardly the worst remuneration he could conceive. He didn't even suggest the others be included. Restricting the treat might, if he was lucky, gratify Lady Morris enough to keep her off his back for a while.

He glanced at the fan glass above the door, judging from the light that the day was blessedly near its end.

"I shall get my hat," he said, "and my gloves. I hope you don't mind taking the coach. I fear my eyes are sensitive to the sun—an unfortunate family trait."

"I am sure we don't mind at all," Lady Morris cooed. "Neither Lily nor myself enjoys being blown about, as one must needs be in an open carriage. You shall save us those fearsome worries about our hair."

She bustled off to get her daughter. After a pause to let his breath gust out, Lucius left as well. They met back at the door just as the coachman drove the carriage up. Lucius's riding hat and gloves protected him enough to hand the women in without turning pink. Brief though it was, the dose of sun made him feel as if he had swallowed a dram of brandy. Wanting his wits about him, he pulled the shade on his side and settled back. He left the uncovered windows for Lady Morris and her daughter.

Miss Morris was, as always, serene and silent, as if catching a rich husband were her last object. He had to wonder at her strategy. To be fair, he supposed she could bring a suitor up to scratch if all he wanted was to stare at her lovely visage or listen to her play music. This evening she struck him as more distant than usual. Her greeting was inaudible, her eyes hooded . . . and perhaps a bit secretive. That piqued him enough to try to read her, but he could not. She was the opposite of her mother, whose noisy thoughts were best avoided.

Miss Morris looked at him as they rolled off. Finding his gaze on her, she held his eyes for a long moment—weighing him, he thought—before returning her attention to the scenery.

It was a confident thing to do, even intriguing, for it suggested an interior life Lady Morris did not control.

Such subtlety escaped her mother. The horses had not gone thirty paces before she exclaimed she had "forgotten" her sketchpad.

"I am such a dabbler," she said with a self-deprecating laugh, "but my dear Sir Mayor loves to see where I've been when he cannot be there himself. Do go on, you two. I shall cut across the lawn and catch up. I should never forgive myself if I caused you to miss the best of the light."

A "darling!" and a peck for her daughter's cheek (which Miss Morris accepted without response) sufficed for her leavetaking. Again the coach moved forward, this time in deep silence.

"You have a fine estate," Miss Morris said after some length of it had passed. "Your grounds are most capacious."

"My . . . father, the old squire, liked a lot of space."

"The privacy must be pleasant."

With a mother like hers, Lucius suspected she got little enough of that. He thought his companion might say more, but this, apparently, was all the conversation he was to have—though Miss Morris did shift her position in a manner that allowed him to better admire her profile.

Because this honor was wasted on him, he fought a smile as they clopped past the castle-folly and through a thin grove of beech. Miss Morris smoothed her elegant gown across her knees. Lucius adjusted the brim of his hat. Lady Morris did not reappear, across the lawn or otherwise, but he was reasonably certain neither of them expected that. Outside the coach, the sun sank until a ribbon of heated pink unfurled on the horizon.

He began to think Miss Morris's mother must have ordered her not to speak.

Amused by his own discomfort, he cleared his throat. "Would you care to see the knot garden? It is the sort of thing ladies like."

Miss Morris did not waste a word in reply, but only inclined her head—perhaps to increase her air of mystery. As they approached the area, Lucius saw that Theo and her sister were already there, strolling arm in arm between the patterned box hedges. He smiled to see them. Their sisterly closeness was a marvel he could only begin to appreciate. Miss Morris's gaze followed them as well. Though her expression (or lack thereof) remained as it was, he sensed something from her, an almost emotion that had not been present before.

"You are not friends with those girls," he observed, abruptly seeing this as something sad—rather a new idea for him.

Lily Morris shrugged. "The Beckets do not need friends. They have each other."

"And you?" he inquired, touched for the first time by this young woman's humanness. "Do you need friends?"

Whatever she might have said was cut short by a cry. It was Theo's cry. Lucius hurtled himself from the carriage before its wheels had a chance to stop. Theo was hurt. He was so alarmed he nearly covered the distance between them at *upyr* speed. Some angel of self-preservation was all that kept him in check.

"What happened?" he demanded, vaulting over two low hedges in order to reach the center of the shrubbery.

Theo sat on the path clutching her leg. At his panicked appearance, she laughed softly. "I merely tripped," she said, "on a paving stone. I may be a little bloodied, not to mention embarrassed, but I assure you my life and limb are in no danger!"

He heard no more than half the words. A burning beneath his incisors warned him to stop where he was. She was bleeding. Her gown and petticoat were pulled to her knee to expose the scrape, and a slow rivulet of scarlet trickled down her shin.

He had lost his hat in his rush to get here, but his face felt hotter than could be accounted for by the sun's last rays. She was bleeding. His groin began to tighten and he didn't know how to halt the response. If it had been anyone else's blood, he might have been able to, but it was hers. The trickle glistened rich and red. Riveted by the sight, he licked lips gone desert-dry.

"Lend us your cravat, Mr. Delavert," Caroline urged. "We must tie something around the wound."

He shook himself. "Yes," he said, tearing the requested article from his neck. He fell to his knees on the grass beside her younger sister, no longer able to stand. His face must have looked strange. Theo's eyes were wide and round on his.

"Lucius," she said, then blushed deeply. Not only was she calling him by his Christian name, she thought she was calling him by the wrong one. "Are you well, Mr. Delavert? You are flushed and out of breath."

"It is nothing," he lied, forcing himself to wrap the linen around her scrape. His hands were so unsteady he could scarcely manage the knot. "When I heard you cry, I ran."

A soft footfall told him Lily had followed him into the garden. Her voice was cool and considering. "I think Mr. Delavert does not like the sight of blood."

Theo touched his wrist in concern. He could not bear her kindness on top of everything else. He stumbled away to collapse on the bench by the small fountain, leaning over his knees as his body vibrated with a truly terrible bloodlust. Never in his long existence had he felt a hunger as deep as this. He wanted to shove his fingers in his mouth and suck. They were stained with her, sticky with her life essence. No matter how this unstrung him, he could not bring himself to wash her off.

If he'd wished, the power of his aura could have dissolved her blood. Instead, he held it to him as if it were a treasure.

"Leave me," he grated out, catching Caroline's and then Lily's eyes. "Return to the house. Leave me alone."

Because his thrall was behind the order, they obeyed.

"No," Theo said when he would have banished her as well. "You are upset. Someone must stay."

She did not understand that sending her away was for her own good. If he bit her, if he gave in to this grinding need, his hold on her would increase. His power was so great he wouldn't be able to help it. Afterward, she would be that much less than she was, that much less the woman who was—sure as sunrise—taking possession of his heart.

He could demand she do as he pleased, and she would not have the will to resist. He would never know her true feelings.

"I am not leaving," she said. "There is no need. Look: the bleeding has stopped."

It had—probably due to the healing nature of his touch. Unfortunately, the damage for him was done.

She rose, wincing a little, then knelt again at his feet—a pretty, feminine gesture. Both her hands settled on one of his knees, the butterfly touch enough make every inch of his skin feel tight. "Tell me why you look as if demons were chasing you."

"I am the demon," he said, helpless, not knowing whether to laugh or cry. "If you really knew me, you would see."

"I would see a good man, a considerate man, a former rake who has grown into something more."

He did laugh then at the irony of her forgiving him Lucas's past, when Lucas was the one who would not have hesitated to use any means to win her. Lucius gripped her wrists in his bloody palms. She did not resist. She did not even seem frightened.

"You obsess me, Theodora," he confessed. "Your scent, your skin, the way your blood races hot and sweet through your veins. If I cannot make you mine, I don't know how I shall bear it."

Her eyes went dark as her pupils swelled. She heard the sensuality of his words even if she missed their meaning. He did not think he had meant to thrall her, but from her reaction he knew he had. Memories rushed back to her, pleasures he only allowed her to remember when she was under his spell.

When she spoke, her voice held the quick throbbing of her pulse. "What do you desire that you have not already done?"

Did he say what he did next to block his last retreat? Or was his conscience trying to give her fair warning?

"I want to bind us together," he said, "with a kiss."

"You've kissed me before."

"Not like this." He searched her soulful, shadowed eyes,

her furrowed brow, the flush of interest on her cheeks. He shook his head. "If you were wise, you would refuse me."

She smiled enough to lift the corners of her mouth. As he had the night she leapt from her window into his arms, he had the eerie impression that she was herself, that his thrall had no more substance than a veil of smoke.

"I cannot refuse you," she admitted as if she wanted to laugh at herself. "I am sure I should, but I don't know how."

As if her words broke a spell, Lucius scooped her up in his arms and carried her from the garden. It seemed the most natural thing in the world to lay her head on his chest. She felt him glance down at her; felt his hold tighten and his muscles tense. Beneath her cheek, his heart beat a fraction faster than it had before.

His maleness excited her: the hardness of his body compared to hers, the determination of his strides. The grounds passed them in a blur, blue and shadowed now with twilight. Her hair streamed over his shoulder as in a wind.

"Where are we going?" she asked, enchanted by the strangeness.

"Somewhere private," he nearly growled.

She laughed against the warmth of his neck. This was better than the other nights, the ones she had mistakenly thought were dreams. This was—she could not help but believe—the first approach to a secret that would change her life, a secret her intuition told her he had been hiding all along. She could hardly wait to know what it was. No garden wall she'd climbed as a child had ever been as interesting as this.

The blurring of the landscape stopped when he did. Still holding her, he shouldered open an ivy-covered door. It was the door to the castle-folly down the hill from his house. Behind the entrance lay a rich but very dusty room—perfect, she imagined, for a widowed squire to meet a lover privately.

As Lucius stepped inside, the dust scattered away from them in clouds. In moments, the circle in which they stood was pristine.

"How did you do that?" she exclaimed in delight.

"Never you mind," he said. "It could not matter less."

He was breathing hard again, and she did not think it was from carrying her weight. That seemed not to fatigue him at all.

"Aren't you going to put me down?"

"I do not wish to," he said almost sullenly.

"You'll grow tired of holding me."

"Never. Never of holding you."

When he met her eyes with his, a silver ember flared deep within. Suddenly he groaned and took her mouth in a fiery kiss, swinging her body around until its full length pressed his. There he held her tightly, his kiss moving from her mouth to her cheek, then from her cheek to her jaw, each shift accompanied by a pained utterance. When at last he reached the racing pulse of her neck, the sound turned into a moan.

Theo could not suppress a shiver. She had heard this moan in every one of her dreams. His tongue licked her beating vein as if it were a sweet. His lips fastened over it. He drew her skin against the front of his teeth. Locked in this position, his body shuddered as if suffering the torments of hell. Theo doubted hell had anything to do with it. The jutting hardness of his arousal dug into her as firm as steel.

"Oh, do it!" she cried in sympathy for his need. "Whatever it is you wish, please go ahead."

Nothing could have prepared her for the moment of penetration. Two coal-hot points of pleasure pierced her neck, the sweetest, sharpest, most unexpectedly erotic hurt she had ever experienced. Her body tightened with longing and liquefied.

Then he began to suck.

Ecstasy exploded through every cell, an inhuman over-surfeit of bliss. *Coming* was not the word for this. She blazed with pleasure, the fire dancing circles around her nerves. The flesh between her legs quivered as if fingers were squeezing it. If Lucius had not been gripping her, she would have collapsed. As it was, her head fell back and her spine relaxed—only to coil again seconds later with fresh delight.

There seemed no room for more sensation and yet there was. Each time his mouth drew on her the pleasure peaked. He moaned and sighed as if he felt the same, as if he could feel not only his enjoyment but hers as well.

If that was true, she did not know how he kept his feet. Finally, he could not and sank with her onto a fainting couch. His weight settled atop her, his hips rocking forcefully between her thighs. He did not attempt to hide his need, nor to disguise the end to which his efforts must be leading. She sensed he would not stop, maybe could not even had he wished. Faster he rocked, and faster yet, until at last with one great grind his body held tight against her mound. His breath rushed out with the hard release. She felt moisture surge against his breeches, then ebb away.

His sucking slowed and gentled, the pleasure she took from this mellowing. She found the strength to slip her hands beneath his riding coat. He had sweated through his shirt and waistcoat, but even as she registered the dampness, it began to dry.

Whatever had pierced her neck slipped free. His tongue dragged lingeringly across the wound. Any pain she might have felt dissolved.

"Theo," he said as if he were drunk. "Oh, God. Theo."

He had shifted his body half to the side and his face was buried in her hair. His hand petted the tingling peak of her breast through her gown. She could not speak. She rubbed the muscles of his back—now loose and easy—and wished their clothes were gone. When she opened her eyes, the thick oak beams of the folly's ceiling swam in and out of focus.

They were illuminated by Lucius's glow, which tonight was not merely golden but edged with all the colors of a rainbow.

He lifted his head to look at her. "Are you well?"

His voice sounded different—richer, darker, layered in the manner of a chord.

"Theo?"

She blinked slowly. "I feel a little tired, but very, very relaxed." She lifted one heavy hand to stroke his hair. Like smooth cool satin, it slipped between her fingers. He must have liked the caress because his eyelids briefly drifted shut. "What was that, Lucius? What did you do?"

"I formed a blood-bond between us."

To judge by his grave expression, this explanation meant more to him than it did to her. She could not bring herself to mind. In truth, she could barely bring herself to think at all.

"You bit me."

"Yes," he said cautiously.

She closed her eyes and snuggled into his chest. "You could do it again, if you like. Maybe when I wake up."

He did not bite her again. He knew he had taken more than enough. Though it was natural for humans to be temporarily weakened by a feeding, she was insensible. If her pulse had not been so steady, he might have been concerned. Instead, he carried her to the house and then to her room, wrapping them both in his strongest glamour, rendering them invisible to human eyes.

Her acceptance frightened him as much as the depth of what he'd felt when he fed from her. Whatever had occurred between them, it was no ordinary blood-bond. Those were for the reinforcement of *upyr* thralls, their duration dependent on the particular immortal's power. They were not supposed to bind the *upyr* to the human, nor make him feel some part of himself would die without the woman he had drunk from.

Troubled, he tucked her in her bed and pulled up the covers. Her taste still gilded his tongue, as tart and bright as starshine. When he kissed her forehead, she smiled in her sleep. He did not want to wake her but knew he must.

He had too much at stake to let her keep this night's memories.

Chapter 11

Caroline returned to the house exactly as Mr. Delavert instructed, but when she reached the front steps, she stopped. Lily Morris continued up them, her back as erect and her step as measured as ever. Caroline knew she should have followed, but a nagging reluctance to go inside kept her where she was.

She had not seen her gardener tonight.

Allowing this to matter was highly inappropriate. Aidan Sheffield was a person to whom she should have been indifferent. To have noticed him staring at her in the library was harmless; many men admired her looks, and Sheffield had not behaved in a threatening way. To have exchanged a few words, while questionable, was not dangerous. But to *mind* that she had not seen him, to *regret* that they would not have another stilted conversation exceeded every limit of good sense.

In all her life Caroline had never done that.

She gazed toward the rear of the house where the kitchen garden lay behind sheltering walls. Her breast lifted on a sigh—just as Theo's would have had she been contemplating Mr. Delavert. Her sister's amazement notwithstanding, Caroline couldn't wonder that she failed to view their host as a beau. How could she when every fiber of her being yearned for another man?

Every time she saw the gardener she feared she'd melt. Sheffield's eyes were a puppy's, his body a pugilist's. To be held in his arms was her idea of heaven, to be kissed by him a concept so daring it stole her breath. If she were wise, she would not let herself think of that.

Still, no harm could come from lingering outside a few minutes longer. The night was pleasant and the moon rising. Finding a quiet place to sit would not mean she awaited him.

She allowed her feet to lead her down the length of the garden wall. Frogs were croaking and crickets chirped. She had begun to relax when, reaching the halfway point of the barrier, her eyes encountered an image they could not at first comprehend.

A man and woman in servants' dress were crouched on their hands and knees in the blooming rose bed at the base of the wall. The man was bent over the woman's back, his hips rocking behind hers in a peculiarly insistent rhythm. He appeared to be trying to push her into the wall.

"Yes," the woman moaned, pushing back just as strenuously. "Oh, yes, roger me harder."

This was when Caroline noticed the woman's skirts were around her waist. More shocking yet, the man had shoved his breeches to his hips. His stiff red organ plunged in and out between the woman's legs. He grunted at her request, thrusting forward with such force that Caroline saw his ball sack swing.

If she'd had her wits about her, she would have covered her eyes. Instead, she stood there gaping, her heart thumping like a rabbit's, her breath choking in her chest.

Inevitably, a gasp betrayed her and the man looked up. He grinned but did not stop moving. In fact, unless her eyes mistook her, he pulled himself out farther to give her a better view. The veins that girded his weapon made her face go hot.

"Hey there," he called, the words coming out in a laughing pant. "My pike's big enough for two if you want to join us."

This snapped her out of her paralysis. She did not stop to think where she was going; she simply ran away as quickly as she could. Her cheeks blazed with embarrassment as the couple's laughter trailed behind her. How could that servant have invited her to join them? The way she was staring, he must have believed she wanted to. But she didn't . . . she couldn't even imagine how joining them was possible!

With jumbled, horrified thoughts like these she stumbled into the night, only stopping when someone caught her arms.

"Whoa," said the voice she feared most of all. It, too, laughed . . . until Sheffield saw who he held. His strong, work-hardened hands slid to her shoulders. "Miss Becket! You are crying. What has happened? Who on earth would dare to hurt you?"

She swiped at her cheeks, unaware until then that tears were running down them. "I assure you, it is nothing."

"It is *not* nothing!"

His outrage steadied her as much as his hands. "I merely saw something which upset me, something I should not have been looking at anyway."

Sheffield's normally open face underwent a change. "Those stupid bas—" He shook his head to dismiss the word. "Forgive me. I am sorry you were upset. Won't you come inside and have a cup of tea? Once you are calm, I can walk you back."

Caroline stiffened. It seemed her flight had not been random. Behind Sheffield's shoulder—and a very broad shoulder it was—an oil lamp burned in a small window. She had run straight to his temple-folly house. He had caught her on his doorstep.

"Oh," she said, her hands pressed to her freshly burning cheeks. "I am sure I did not mean to come here."

"I am glad you did. Now and then my assistants stay overnight, but I tend to get more than my share of solitude."

He escorted her in so naturally she could not resist. His home was a single room with a loft above for his bed. A kettle hung on the open hearth. The remains of his supper, not yet tidied, sat on a plain table. He stopped when he saw the mess.

"I should go," she said, beginning to tug away.

"No . . . I . . . Sit, please. Here is a chair. I shall clear this away while we wait for your tea to brew."

She sat in his single upholstered chair in the flickering firelight, watching him move at his chores, smelling the scent of him and his work. His nervousness at having her here was like an oddly endearing song. Long before he finished, her body warmed, readying itself for things she dared not name. The presence of the sleeping loft above her hung like a weight in her mind.

They had only to climb the ladder and they would be there.

She had just glanced up at it when he cleared his throat. "Did you enjoy Mrs. Radcliffe's story?"

Caroline was too busy blushing to comprehend.

"The Mysteries of Udolpho," he said in the direction of the washing up. "The book you selected at the library."

"Oh. Yes. It was marvelously exciting."

She colored again, thinking perhaps she should not have mentioned excitement.

"You did not find the descriptive passages a little slow?"

"I skimmed them," Caroline confessed. "But . . . you must have read the book yourself."

He looked over his shoulder, his smile at her surprise gentle. "I do read, you know."

"Of course you do." At her words, he turned from the sink to face her. To Caroline's embarrassment, his hands seemed huge as he dried them on a cotton cloth. "I simply assumed . . . Most gentlemen are not partial to books like that."

"I admit I usually prefer biographies, but in this instance my interest was stirred. Someone I admire was reading it."

"Oh," she said stupidly. He meant her. She was the person he admired. He had read what he must have thought was a silly novel because of her. Robbed of any ability to speak, she bit her lip.

"Forgive me," he said, his awkwardness returning at the rise of hers. "I had no right to—" Cutting himself off, he poured her tea. "Here." He walked to her with the cup. "I hope it is not too strong."

Their fingers brushed as she took it, and a forceful tingle rushed up her arm. The cup was thick and chipped. She could not bring herself to look at him again. Hoping he did not notice how red she was, she sipped and lowered her eyes.

"Oh, God," he said, the words bursting from him in agitation. "You are so beautiful!"

She could not lift the cup a second time. It was suddenly too heavy for her shaking hands. The steam rising off it made her feel as if she might cry again.

"I am sorry," he said. "I should not have said that. It is just, I have never had the chance before."

With a deeply pleading expression, he knelt and wrapped his hands on the arm of her chair. Despite their recent washing, earth stained his fingernails. Caroline did not care. She craved his touch on her all the same.

Before he could speak again, she did herself. "Please take the cup. It is heavy and I fear I shall spill on you."

He set it on the floor, then laid his cheek on the back of her trembling hand. The effect was stronger than the brush of his fingertips. Waves of heat swept alarmingly to her core.

"I would do anything for you," he swore, his mouth turning far enough to press her knuckles with a fervent kiss. "Anything you wished. I would guard your honor as if it were my life, if only to be close to you now and then."

She knew she had let this go too far. Simply by being here, her honor had a cloud. Feeling the stings of conscience, she forced herself to rise. "This is not right," she said when he failed to free her hands. "Both of us know that."

He closed his eyes as if the reminder hurt, then rose as well, his movements stiff but dignified. He released her hands and squared his shoulders. "I will walk you back."

"No—"

"I will walk you back," he repeated, "and watch you safely inside the door. *My* honor demands that much."

She met his gaze, then nodded.

Somewhat to her dismay, she found herself believing he would not repeat his improprieties.

Chapter 12

Someone tried to shake her awake, but Theo did not want to surface even though she knew who it was. Her dream was too delicious.

She and Lucius lay in bed, a huge affair with a headboard of silver metal unlike any she'd ever seen. The sheets were sky-blue silk and the mattress buoyant. Conveniently, a small round lamp glowed in the air above them, seemingly floating without support. Best of all, neither of them wore a stitch.

A thin arrow of hair led down Lucius's rippling belly to his most interesting parts. As her eyes followed its suggestion, he began to stir. She could not help smiling at the power of her attention to conjure such miracles.

"You are perfect," she said, drawing one finger boldly up his shaft. "How peculiar it must feel sometimes to be you."

Outside the dream, he shook her again. "Theo," he said. "Dear, dear Theo. I regret to do this, but I must. Open your eyes. Let me speak to you before you rest."

Her eyelids rose heavily. "Tired," she said.

"I know, my love, and I am sorry, but I want you to forget what we did tonight. From the time your sister and Miss Morris left us, I want you to forget."

"No," she protested. "Tonight was lovely."

"Yes, but if you remember, we won't be able to do it again."

"Are you sure?"

"Very sure. You would be horrified if you remembered. What we did was quite forbidden."

She laid her hands on his chest, now covered by his gray waistcoat. Preferring him naked, she struggled not to pout. "I am not convinced I would be horrified."

He smiled and kissed her, his tongue sliding gently into her mouth. She loved when he did that. It was the loveliest, lovely thing. Only now, in this half-dreaming state, could she be honest: Nathan's kisses, nice though they were, had not affected her like this.

"Theo," Lucius said, forcing her eyes up again. "I do not understand why you argue, but you know it will not serve. You will forget what we did after the others left. You will remember fainting and perhaps being carried back to the house."

"I never faint."

"Nonetheless, you did tonight."

She frowned and stroked the tiny pucker between his brows. Strange. He was usually warm when he touched her, but now his skin was marble-cool.

"Theo."

"Oh, very well." Her own brow crinkled at the swooping inside her skull that accepting his orders seemed to inspire. Though the feeling did not hurt, it was so disconcerting she wished she could push it off. "I remember nothing from the time the others left. I very foolishly fainted, and you carried me back to the house—which was dashing of you, I might add."

He laughed through his nose. "I am glad you think so.

Now sleep, love, and heal. I want you strong when you next wake up."

She settled back into her pillows. "I shall be strong," she promised, adding on her own, "and I shall try to remember how nice you are. I am happier when I let myself like you."

She had just enough alertness left to feel him caress her cheek, after which she fell into the coolest, calmest sort of sleep. Dreams came and went like birds crossing the moon. Between was a sea of soft, blue light. She lay on her back inside a glassy tunnel, unable to move. She did not feel like herself, but as if she were Lucius. The ship was lulling her, the ship that had carried him far from home. She heard its voice. *Mena,* it murmured. *Mena, why did you choose to die?*

She opened her eyes and it was night. For a moment, she could not think where or even who she was. The candle burning on the bedside table looked very odd, and the mattress was too lumpy. Even the sheets were altered for the worse, as rough as rope against her skin.

"Thank goodness!" Caroline cried. "We thought you would never wake."

At the sound of her sister's voice, Theo woke in truth. Caroline sat in a chair pulled close to her bed, a novel lying open on her lap. Apparently, she had solved *The Mysteries of Udolpho* and was now exploring *The Castle of Wolfenbach.*

Amused by her sister's choice of entertainment, Theo rubbed her forehead. "I see you have been getting on with your reading. How long have you been sitting there?"

"Two days, Theo! Mama and I were beside ourselves."

"Two days!" Theo looked in confusion toward the window. The old-fashioned casement was slightly open, and the soft night breeze carried the scent of grass watered by a rain—a rain Theo could not recall. "How is that possible?"

"You must have needed to catch up from those dreams that tired you." Though Caroline's tone was teasing, her expression held real concern. "Mr. Delavert was not worried at first—which vexed Mama—but after you'd slept round the clock, he sent for Doctor Harris. *He* said you had a fever, possibly due to your scrape—though that was healed by the time he came."

"Mr. Delavert sent for a doctor?" Theo could not have said why that struck her as inappropriate, only that it did.

"I do not believe I have ever seen a man that anxious. You would have thought he'd caused your sickness himself." A smile tugged Caroline's mouth. "I think Lady Morris begins to worry her darling Lily may not win her prize after all."

"Don't be silly," Theo said, struggling to repress a flush of pleasure.

"No, no, far be it from me to be silly. Just because he pressed cool cloths to your forehead with his own two hands does not mean Mr. Delavert's regard has grown beyond the partiality any host might feel for an ailing guest."

"Indeed it does not." Theo squeezed her temples in puzzlement. She seemed to remember the touch of his hands . . . though her forehead was not the part of her they had pressed!

"What is it?" Caroline asked. "Do you have the headache?"

"I am fine," Theo assured her. Whatever had caused her unnatural sleep, she felt perfectly rested now. "I am muddled is all. I did have a dream, and a strange one. I was flying through the sky in a glass bubble, over a city that seemed to rise straight out of a lake. The view was lovely, and the buildings were the tallest I had ever seen, taller even than in London."

Caroline laughed. "I think you are dreaming still. You have never been to London."

Theo's mind must have been more addled than she realized. She decided she had better not mention the dream where she'd been running through the woods—on four legs, no less. If Caroline heard that, she truly would think her sister had grown deranged.

"I must go," Caroline said, touching Theo's arm as she rose. "The others will want to know you are up."

"I do think we might send out the invitations for three days hence," Lady Morris was saying. "Since many we ask will be anticipating the event, a longer period seems burdensome. Surely Theo will be on her feet by then."

The two mamas, Lucius, and Lily sat in the music room. Lily Morris was, for once, playing something soft. Lucius concluded music did indeed have charms to soothe the savage beast. At present, her skill was all that kept him from leaping out of his seat to strangle her mama. Even Mrs. Becket, lately distracted by the pleasure of planning a ball, was staring amazed at her callousness. Quite clearly, she was remembering the reasons they had ceased being friends.

"Oh, do not gawp at me," Lady Morris said. "You know Theo would abhor a delay as much as anyone."

"Not quite as much as some," Mrs. Becket returned.

"We will wait," Lucius said. "No doubt she shall recover soon, but until she does, we will not set a date."

He did his best to keep his temper out of his voice. He was not, after all, angriest at them. He did not even know what he had done wrong, though he had revisited every detail a thousand times. Bitten or not, Theo should have wakened. Despite having panicked enough to call the doctor, he sensed no sickness in her aura. Her energy was, if anything, stronger than before.

Frustrated, he pressed a knuckle to his teeth just as Caroline appeared at the door. He jumped to his feet, his heart athunder, but her brilliant smile told him everything he wished.

"She is up," she said, her cheeks gone pink from rushing through the corridors. "She is speaking and clearheaded."

"I must go to her," Lucius said, which caused both mothers

to turn. Even Lily stopped playing. For a moment, her eyes were as sharp as Lady Morris's.

"Go to her!" Lady Morris repeated in laughing shock. "Oh, Mr. Delavert, you cannot know women well if you think she will welcome that. She will be in poor looks and disarrayed. You must wait until tomorrow morning, or even the day after."

Lucius clenched his hands. She was correct, but it did not matter. He turned his eyes to Lady Morris's with a ruthlessness he usually avoided, taking care not to read any of the stupidities coursing through her mind. He would not put it past her to have finally noticed his romantic preference, and to be hoping Theo would be excluded from a hastened ball.

"I will go to her briefly," he said, his coolness causing her to flinch. "You can have no objection to that."

Lady Morris's hand fluttered to her throat. "No," she said, blinking rapidly. "No objection at all."

As he sat beside Theo's bed on the spindly chair, Lucius was careful not to meet her eyes. Tonight he needed honest answers. He did not want to thrall her by accident.

"You must forgive my impatience," he said, gently taking her hand. "I have left your mother in the passage in order to assure myself without delay that you are well."

She looked behind him to the door. Her manner was hesitant but not alarmed. She was thinking that if her mother had let him do this, it must be acceptable.

"I am sorry for the worry I caused," she said. "I think the dreams I've been having simply tired me out. Now that I am awake again, I feel strong."

Her words made him wonder if this was the missing key. He had told her he wanted her strong again when next she woke. Given the hours she had been keeping and the natural—if temporary—weakening effect of his bite, two days of sleep might have been required for her to obey.

He kissed her fingers in relief. "What dreams?" he asked indulgently.

"Foolish things." She tugged back her hand to wave it. "In one, I was flying over a city in a glass bubble."

"That sounds amusing enough."

"It *was* pleasant. In another, though, which I did not judge fit to relate to my sister, I turned into a wolf and chased down a deer. It was so real I swore I could taste its hide!"

This surprised him more than he wished to show. He stood and moved to the window, unease rising in his throat. In his desire to be close to her, had he unwittingly sent her his private thoughts? He had never done so before that he could remember, but his experience with Theo had been unique. Stymied, he gazed out at the grounds. "No doubt that dream was the result of having seen my hound race across the lawn."

"No doubt," she agreed amiably.

Despite her obvious good temper, he thought a change of topic desirable. "If you are up to it, Lady Morris believes we could have the ball in three days."

"I am sure I shall be, but Lu—" With pinkening cheeks, she caught her slip. "Mr. Delavert, I have been wondering, do you think Percy Fitz Clarc might like to come? He is all alone but for his guardian in that big castle. I know he is probably too young to care for dancing, but if my Uncle William were invited, he could bring his children as playmates. Though he is a grocer, I do not think he will embarrass you."

She seemed embarrassed to have made the request. Lucius returned to her side.

"I would be honored to welcome your uncle into my home. I hope you do not think otherwise."

"I do not believe . . . That is, I suspect my mother does not plan to invite him." Catching him unprepared, Theo's eyes pleaded with him not to judge. "She and Lady Morris are trying to be careful of your consequence."

"I see," he said, and he did. Turning his gaze more cautiously to the birds and ivy on the painted wall, he rubbed his chin. "Tell me, are there others you would invite, were my 'consequence' set aside?"

"A few. Old family friends. Humble people, I admit, but very good. And perhaps our nearest neighbors from the square. The Connors would enjoy seeing Hadleigh ever so much."

"Theo—" he began.

"Miss Becket," she corrected.

"Miss Becket." He smiled down at her, sensing her dearness in a whole new way, one that felt unbearably tender. "I cannot promise Percy's guardian will let him come, but if you and your sister would compose a list, I will see that your friends are asked."

Her beaming response struck him as headily as the sun. He could not help recalling her previous promise to remember how nice he was. "You have made me happy," she said.

He touched her hair where it wisped in front of her ear. The intimacy startled her, though in her dreams it would have been familiar. Not wishing to upset her, he dropped his hand. "I will call your mother so she may know there is naught to fear."

Theo's voice came as gently as his had. "Thank you, Mr. Delavert, for everything."

"You are extremely welcome. I could not be more pleased to see you recovering."

Wishing this to remain the case, he decided it would be best to suspend his nightly visits. She tempted him so fiercely he doubted he could trust himself. Theo was human, and thus fragile. He might have forgotten much of his past, but not that. Not for any amount of pleasure did he dare endanger her health.

From this night forward he would move slowly.

The three naked immortals lay sprawled in the rocky clearing, their appetite well sated. Nearby, blood soaked the earth between the roots of a tall Scotch fir. Nothing else lingered from their hunt. In their wolf-forms, they could consume every bit of an animal. Their *upyr* power converted everything to energy, giving new meaning to the term "clean kill." Their persons were clean as well, adding up to three strong, spotless males who were, at that moment, kings of all they surveyed.

"Christ," said Robin, Edmund's son. "I've been missing that. It's been ages since I hunted anything more dangerous than Percy's boots. Lord knows how he loses them where he does."

His father snorted. "You're the one who insisted on being his guardian."

"Well, I wasn't going to let you do it. Poor lad would never have any fun."

"Fun like that boar had when he charged you and you jumped aside?"

"We'd only just run him down. He deserved his chance to fight. How was I to know he'd bite your tail?"

Lucius smiled. He could feel as well as hear the love beneath their quarrel. He had changed the pair of them, but he would never be Robin's sire the way Edmund was, nor did he think he'd ever see Edmund as easy as he was now with family. Empires might rise and fall while they lived, but Robin would always be blood to Edmund. Robin would always be home.

Percy seemed in a fair way to becoming the same. Both father and son had grown attached to the boy. They would let him live out his human life, but when that ran its course, they would offer him the choice to be what they were. Lucius hoped for their sake Percy would agree. With Delavert's example of what a family *shouldn't* be in his head, he was beginning to see how valuable a good one was.

"What do you think?" Robin asked, knocking Lucius's shin with his foot. "Is my father better at chasing tail or having his tail chased?"

"I think I have a question about your charge."

"Lord," Robin moaned. "Just when I was relaxing. Oh, go on then. Ask away."

"As you know, I'm hosting a ball—"

"Yes, I had heard you'd gone daft."

"Be that as it may, one of my guests, who is a sort of distant cousin to Percy Fitz Clare, was wondering if the boy would like to come."

"The little fiend would love it, but he can't."

"Can't?"

"He's got the Fitz Clare eye. It's my father's fault, because he keeps visiting the castle every generation. Fitz Clare power rubs off on Fitz Clares and, after a while, some of the babes get born odd. Little Percy can see right through our glamour. Knew I was different the night we met. Asked why his face didn't glow like mine. Stick him in the middle of a bunch of humans, and I cannot swear he won't spill every bean he has."

"You could not thrall him to keep quiet?"

"I cannot thrall him to go to bed! He's as resistant to that as the rest. And the sulks—Lord—you can't imagine the power of one small boy until you've seen them. 'You're not my papa,' he says. It quite undoes one." Robin sighed and leaned forward over his knee. "I don't say Percy means to tell secrets, but he's only five. It's all I can do to keep track of which servant needs to forget what. Unless you want this cousin to know what you are, I would advise keeping them as far apart as you can."

"Hm," said Lucius, mulling this over. He hated disappointing Theo, but Robin's advice seemed wise. Theo would not accept what *upyr* were as readily as a five-year-old. Her rejection—or her horror—were possibilities he did not care to risk.

Nothing more was said on the topic until he and Edmund took leave of his son and donned their clothes for the journey home. As always, Edmund's cravat settled into place as if freshly starched. They walked slowly for them, almost human speed. Considering this change from custom, Lucius was not surprised to discover his friend had something on his mind.

"You're becoming serious about this girl," he said.

Lucius's first instinct was to bristle. In no way was Theo Edmund's business. Knowing he meant well, Lucius tried to answer calmly. "I am taking care not to cross the line of what the Council allows. She has not refused me, and she will suffer no permanent harm from anything I do."

"You fed from her deeply enough to make her ill."

"That was unintentional, and probably not altogether due to my bite. I have, however, resolved to be more cautious."

Edmund made a noise that could have been skepticism or acceptance. Lucius did not try to read which because he was not certain he wished to know.

"I respect your brother's authority," he assured Edmund instead. "I would not undermine it."

Edmund made the noise again. "Aimery knows you are too powerful to punish, even if you broke Council law."

Lucius stopped walking. "There are more ways to punish than with power. Your brother would no longer be my friend if I turned vicious. You, of all people, know what companions mean to our kind."

Edmund's eyes glowed blue with emotion, intense but mixed. "I do know, but it has been many years since I thought you did. By God, that Delavert has changed you, more than I dreamed he could."

If Edmund believed Delavert to be the cause of his transformation, Lucius would not argue—especially since Edmund's response was not completely approving. Lucius's awareness that Delavert was but one influence on his character seemed better kept to himself. This venture into the human realm was, for him, no lark.

If he was going to keep Theo safe from his bite; indeed, if he was going to keep her at all, he was going to have to court her—the real her, not the bold, thralled version who goaded him to distraction from his better sense. When every layer of her being was in love with him, from the most conscious to the least, perhaps he would reveal the truth. Until then, he was going to need time and patience and a great deal of self-control.

God help anyone, Edmund included, who tried to stand in his way.

Chapter 13

Lady Morris would have been happy to play general to Mr. Delavert's army of servants, but in this she was impeded by Mr. Fitz Clare, who insisted all orders for the ball go through himself. Finding the steward immovable, and his master unlikely to oppose him, Lady Morris gave way as graciously as necessity demanded she must.

To Theo's surprise, she was prevailed upon to take a task: that of overseeing the decorations. She could not guess by what means Mr. Delavert had divined that she had the most artistic bent, but she would admit to relishing the challenge. As help she had the gardener and Caroline. Though the choice gave her pause at first, it turned out to be providential.

Sheffield, of course, knew precisely which growing things could be used—though obtaining this intelligence required an effort. He was, she discovered, a man of few words, and those to be had were all to the point. He seemed determined not to step one inch beyond the bounds his position allowed—at least, not in front of her—a determination she took to mean he wished the opposite. She needed no strange visions to detect his *tendre* for Caroline. That she could read in every sidelong glance.

What surprised her—indeed, what filled her with pity—was his equal care for herself. No climbing of ladders fell Theo's way, no lifting of heavy things—as if he wished to fill the role of a protective older brother. This would certainly never come to pass. Sheffield was a servant. An upper maid he might aspire to win, but not a gentleman's daughter—howsoever poor she was. All the same, Theo could not help feeling that he was an estimable man. Yes, she was quite as sorry for him as she could be.

For her part, Caroline was so diligent in carrying out her duties that she could have been a servant herself. Though she stammered occasionally and dropped things (most often when the gardener was near) she seemed not to mind her younger sister being put in charge of her.

Because Theo would have minded, her awareness that Caroline deserved Mr. Delavert's good opinion far more than she did could not have been stronger.

As compensation, she devoted what time remained to fashioning Caroline's gown. Fortunately, she had none of her usual fits and starts, and was able to cobble together a flattering pattern on her first try. Her fingers fairly flew through the work, which made keeping it secret much easier.

Secret it must be, for she had decided she could not bear for Caroline to be dressed less finely than Lily Morris. To that end, she had packed her last unsold length of silk, a pale, pale green with butterflies. With luck, Lily and her mother would be too busy during the ball to examine the garment closely. If Theo could keep the cloth hidden under other things until the fateful night, its similarity to bolts sold at Black's should go unnoticed. If not, she would devise some lie. Come what may, one member of the Becket family would do them proud.

To her relief, considering all she had to accomplish, her mysterious illness failed to return. Theo had never had this much vitality in her life, and concluded the country air must have done her good. Her only complaint was small. Despite sleeping soundly, she would wake each morning feeling vaguely dissatisfied—a quibble which did not detract from a noticeable improvement in her looks. Even her hair was not as coarse. Twice in recent days her mother had complimented her.

"I like being useful," Theo said, amused by her mama's surprise and unable to resist baiting her. "Perhaps when this ball is over I shall seek a position as a housekeeper."

"Heaven forfend!" her mama exclaimed, then regarded her thoughtfully. "I begin to doubt, however, whether we will have to worry overmuch about your future."

Mrs. Becket said no more, and Theo felt too awkward to add anything herself. She knew what she *ought* to want regarding Mr. Delavert, and she was *beginning* to admit what she did—though these two positions were sufficiently divergent as to leave her in some turmoil. That Mr. Delavert wished for anything beyond flirtation she could not feel assured. He seemed to fancy her, but how many men in the history of the world had seemed to fancy women they were not serious about? Ironically, had his behavior been more rakish, she would have doubted less.

One point in favor of believing him interested was Lily Morris's restlessness. Theo had not spent much time with Lady Morris's daughter, but she doubted she was in the habit of playing a few short measures on a beautiful pianoforte only to rise again and pace the room. This evening, as they waited to be joined by their mothers and their host, Lily had been up and down half a dozen times.

"Would you like me to read aloud?" Caroline offered. "This chapter is interesting."

"No," Lily snapped, then blew out her breath. "I thank you, though." She strode across the room's fine carpet, stopping at the carved marble fireplace.

The music room, placed in one of Hadleigh's corner towers, had two walls of large windows. Light poured past their draperies, but it was the melancholy purple light of dusk. To offset the darkness, candles burned in sconces on either side of the mantlepiece, their light twinkling prettily off crystal drops. Theo watched Lily stare at her reflection in the mirror that hung between, her expression giving nothing of her thoughts away. The country air appeared to have improved her, too. Had Theo looked that exquisite, she doubted she could have concealed a touch of smugness.

Lily turned to her without warning. "I owe a friend a letter," she said just as brusquely as she had refused Caroline's kindness. "Might I borrow your writing desk?"

Since Theo was surreptitiously stitching the final details of her sister's gown, she waved Lily to where her portable desk sat on a table. A letter to Mrs. Connor's eldest daughter—a friend of herself and Caroline—lay inside, but it contained nothing Theo feared to have Lily see. Undecided as to what news she wished to share, she had not got to the gossipy part.

"There is plenty of paper and ink," she said, "though you might want to sharpen my quill."

All was quiet while Lily wrote, a peace for which Theo was grateful. Theo preferred a period to prepare her nerves when Mr. Delavert was expected, which he generally was not until the evening. His stares had grown so very focused of late, and though they seemed to fasten on her only when she looked away, Theo could not help feeling rattled in his presence.

Most troubling of all was that, because he never looked at her when she was looking at him, she had no opportunity to search his eyes. Were not the answers she sought hidden there? She let her stitching drop to her lap and frowned. Perhaps they weren't. Perhaps the answers were in her own heart, but she wasn't eager to look there, only to know with surety that he cared for her. Then, so she thought, her own sentiments would come clear.

Lily popped up without warning. "I will finish this in my room. I cannot work in this light."

Theo opened her mouth to offer the use of her lamp, but Lily was out the door. Restless herself, she stowed Caroline's gown beneath a half-trimmed straw hat and went to the desk, thinking to finish her own letter. To her surprise, she could not find it among the sheets of paper. She clucked in annoyance.

"She must have taken it by mistake."

"Taken what?" asked Caroline.

"My letter to Katie Connor. I shall have to start it again."

"I am sure Lily would return it."

Theo made a face. It was cowardly, but she would rather write the letter over than chase after Lady Morris's progeny.

She expected Caroline to say she was being silly, but her sister had set down her book and was staring out the window.

"Oh, dear," Caroline said, suddenly rising from her chair. "I think . . . I believe I left the previous volume to this novel out in the garden. I must retrieve it before it is damaged."

She looked to Theo as if waiting for permission, and naturally Theo waved her off.

"I won't be but a minute," Caroline promised.

"I am fine," Theo said. "Take whatever time you need."

She wondered at her sister's manner. It was true such absentmindedness was not like her; she was always careful of the circulating library's books, but she hardly needed to be this concerned about Theo. She was entirely recovered from her illness, and had never feared solitude. Truly, sometimes her sister was too considerate for her own good!

Caroline exited the room as quickly as she could. She had spotted Sheffield striding toward the house with a book tucked beneath his arm, and knew she must head him off before he used his decorating duties as a pretext to come to her.

It had been difficult enough working side by side, but if Theo saw them together without her responsibilities to distract her, she was bound to guess Caroline's feelings.

As to that, Theo had only to ask a direct question, and Caroline would spill all. She was terrible at lying. Her only hope was to evade Theo's interest.

She was so determined to stop her admirer she nearly bowled him over outside the back garden.

"Miss Becket!" he said as she skidded to a halt on the grass. "I was hoping I might run into . . . That is, I have a book I think you might enjoy."

"I am reading one already" was all she had breath to say.

He stepped back, hurt and trying to hide it. "Yes, of course. I shouldn't have—" His eyes lifted to hers in a silent plea. "It is about a family of five daughters whose mama tries to marry them off. I thought it would make you laugh."

"I can't," she said. "I wish I could, but I can't."

He heard what she dared not say. The plea left his eyes, and his features softened with understanding. He seemed not lesser than she then but more—at least, more true to himself. After a moment, he nodded and turned away.

"It was kind of you to think of me," she added, because she could not stand his walking away any more than his hurt.

He stopped and snorted softly with his head wagging. "I wish it were possible *not* to think of you."

A thrill swept through her at his admission. To her dismay, she found she could not wish the words away.

At last only one night was left before the ball. Not surprisingly, Theo's worries kept her from sleep. Giving up on what was pointless, she dragged a chair into her window embrasure. All was peaceful under the stars. The next night's moon would be full, ideal for night traveling—not that the prospect of a good attendance calmed Theo's nerves.

She wondered if the guests would admire her decorations,

or if she had fallen short of the elegance to which they were accustomed. She had little experience with fancy parties, nor would she know many guests. Would she sit on the side? Would her sister? Caroline's gown flattered her and fit well, but what if their mother—or someone else—asked where it had come from? She thought she had devised a reasonable lie, but Theo doubted her sister cared half as much as she did about how she looked.

"It is vanity," Theo murmured. "Vanity and guilt."

Notwithstanding her good intentions, she could not claim to have tried to attach her sister and their host. Theo wanted him for herself, just as she had wanted Nathan Thomas. Her single consolation was that she had not chased Mr. Delavert.

Well, that and the fact that he might not actually be hers.

A pale flash of motion brought her alert. A hare stood on its hind legs beside the carriage path, its long ears flicking as if seeking of the source of some alarming sound. It found it apparently, because a moment later it exploded into a run, followed by two equally quick canines. Their low, streaking shadows were impossible to mistake.

"They *are* wolves," she breathed. "I cannot be deceived this time." She had the oddest urge to leap out the window and give chase, only checking herself when she touched the latch.

More sensibly, but not by much, she grabbed her dressing gown and scrambled for the door. This time she would catch them. This time she would get proof.

As she ran down the stairs she felt no fear, only an excitement that was close to joy. Oh, men had the right of it. No one should restrain herself to mincing walks. Across the entryway and terrace she bounded in her bare feet, a last scrap of caution all that prevented her from laughing aloud.

Stone steps met her unprotected soles, then gravel, then dew-soaked grass. She could not credit having moved so quickly—perhaps the hare had doubled back—but when she reached the side of the house, the wolves still pursued the frantic creature across the lawn.

I'm coming, too, she thought—no doubt absurdly.

One of the wolves halted. She could tell it had spotted her. Its head turned to its companion, to whom it gave a quiet bark. At this both wolves stopped to stare and pant. Grabbing its chance, the hare disappeared into the undergrowth.

"I am not afraid of you," she said, though she was a bit. "I am too big for you to eat."

The wolves seemed to exchange a glance.

Since they did not move, she stepped closer. She was not certain what she intended by drawing near, but one wolf took off like a rocket toward the back of the house. The other lolled its tongue at her before trotting off.

I will follow it, she decided. *I shall mark precisely where it leaves its tracks.*

She did mean to do this, but in her eagerness not to lose her quarry, she became distracted. The wolf seemed almost to lead her on, letting her catch up before darting ahead again.

The very sight of it filled her with awe. The wolf was large for its breed, with dark gray markings and wonderfully silent grace. Each time it looked back, the intelligence in its gaze enthralled her. Animal though it was, she couldn't help thinking it more than beast. Had she known the right magical procedure, she might have turned it back to a man.

With such flights of fancy, who could wonder if she forgot where she'd been?

She stopped when she reached an area that had grown picturesquely wild. Riding paths crossed it, with obstacles for horses to jump. She realized she could no longer spy the house—though she thought she knew where it lay. If ever she were going to become alarmed, now was the time. Perhaps the clever creature had been luring her to her demise.

Ahead of her, the wolf plopped down in a bare spot to scratch its ear.

Theo laughed at this mundane end to her adventure. "You are a handsome beast," she said, "but if you knew what a lady was, you would show better manners."

A tussock of grass rustled behind her. Theo spun, assuming the second wolf had come back. To her astonishment, Mr. Delavert appeared instead.

He wore his frockcoat, shirt, and trousers, his lack of a waistcoat suggesting he'd dressed in a rush. Was he concerned for her, or did he wish to chide her for making free of his grounds? With some embarrassment, she acknowledged the latter would be just. He had a right to expect his female guests not to ramble around at all hours. But perhaps he was thinking to turn this into an assignation? Her confusion blazed in her face, causing her to hope he did not see well at night.

"Miss Becket!" he exclaimed. "I thought it was you I saw. What are you doing all the way out here?"

Naturally, when she turned back to the wolf to show him, the beast was gone. "It was right there!" she cried. "A wolf, I swear it. There were two of them to begin with, but one ran off."

"I am sorry I missed it," Mr. Delavert said soothingly.

"Oh, I know you think I have lost my wits, but I saw it and it was not the least like a dog. It was big and very beautiful."

"Beautiful, you say?"

"I have never seen so handsome a creature in my life."

At her declaration, he rubbed the groove beneath his lower lip, his expression oddly miffed. "Perhaps," he said, "you ought not to be walking this far alone. It is the middle of the night, and there are—as you have seen—wild things about."

"You are right," she sighed, "but I could not sleep, and I was so hoping to get proof this time. Do you think I ought to inform your gamekeeper? He would set traps, which would be sad, but you would not want those creatures preying on your sheep."

Mr. Delavert's eyes widened. "I shall . . . consider it. I am not a fan of traps myself. They do not distinguish between what must be caught and what might as well run free."

"True," Theo said, "and they did not appear vicious. Perhaps they are only eating your hares."

He muttered something that seemed to concern Hadleigh's maids, but when she looked at him, he shook himself. "Come." He offered his arm. "I shall take you back to the house."

They walked a distance in silence.

"I know why I cannot sleep," she was finally bold enough to say. "But why you are awake? Are you nervous about the ball?"

He seemed not to feel her question was intrusive. "I should be, I suppose. Many of my guests will attend hoping to find fault. When I last resided here, I was hardly a favorite son."

"People will see you have changed."

She had squeezed his elbow unconsciously. He looked down at her and smiled, brushing her—briefly—with the heat of his eyes. Coming as this did after a long absence, his gaze created such a burst of feeling she was obliged to look away herself.

"Perhaps they will," he said, sounding amused.

"I am sure of it. You are not a wild boy anymore."

"Oh, I expect I possess a little wildness yet." When she glanced back at him, he was smiling into the distance. She wondered what he was thinking: something to do with other women, she suspected, something she probably preferred not to know.

"Why were you awake?" he asked, breaking into her thoughts.

"I was hoping I would not sit on the side all night."

"Never," he said gallantly. "I am sure you'll be besieged with partners. In fact, I insist on engaging you for the first two dances myself."

This was a distinction she did not deserve. "You need not . . . I was not angling for you to—"

"You would honor me," he said, his manner too polished to be certain he meant what he said.

She caught her lip in her teeth, annoyed with herself for caring—and for being so grateful. If he danced with her first, she need not worry about looking pitiful.

"Truly," he said and gave her a little bow.

They had reached the curving drive in front of the house. To Theo's surprise, Mr. Delavert did not move to escort her in.

"I shall take a final turn around the grounds. To ensure your wolves did no harm. Sleep well, Miss Becket. You have nothing to fear for tomorrow night."

She left him with a last glance over her shoulder. He had been watching her, but when she looked back he dropped his eyes. The moonlight made him a statue, some trick of its illumination lending his skin an alabaster glow. She wished he would look up. That would have eased the tightness in her chest, though she could not have explained why. He seemed so solitary standing there, as if he had been alone since the dawn of time. Tears burned behind her eyes, but she blinked them rapidly away.

Mr. Delavert was interesting enough. She need not invent reasons to find him more romantic.

"Well, that was close," Edmund said. Dressed again, wearing human form again, he joined Lucius on the shadowed side of the house. "You realize that woman has more than her share of curiosity."

"Her reaction is understandable. Wolves are scarce in England these days. Besides which, it is our fault. We let our wolves' enthusiasm get the better of our judgment. We should not have run near the house."

"She followed us, Lucius. She told us she was too big for us to eat." Edmund chuckled at the memory, then studied his nails. "She told me I was handsome, in case you were wondering."

"She told your *wolf* he was handsome."

Edmund's sole response was a smirk. Lucius was ashamed to admit that it nettled him.

"Lord," he sighed, dragging both hands back through his hair. Keeping Theo in the dark while resisting the urge to thrall her was harder than he thought. He knew how right it felt to touch her mind, to touch any part of her. To be in her company and simply speak, to allow himself no more contact than the gentle weight of her hand, was misery. If he had not felt her resistance weakening, he would have been tempted to break his restraint. As it was, he wished he knew what precisely would prove she had fallen in love of her own free will.

Considering all his dealings with women, Edmund might have known, but Lucius was reluctant to ask his counsel. Edmund's advice was too likely to come with opinions.

"Someone is watching us," Edmund said.

Lucius stiffened and followed his gaze to an upper window. A woman in a pale nightgown was just then shrinking back from view. From this distance, he could not read who it was, though he didn't believe it was Theo.

"A maid?" he suggested at Edmund's frown. "I do not think you need to worry. No human could hear us speaking from up there."

"Yes," Edmund said slowly. "No doubt you are right."

All her life, Lily had made it her mission to know more than others and reveal less. This was how she kept her advantage. A new gown, a prettier hat, a finer carriage than those of her friends—none of these were beyond her reach. If she couldn't obtain what she wanted, her mother could. Her mother, God rot her soul, was the only person Lily knew who had the strength to stand in her way. Lily hated and admired her equally. Until now, she had never encountered a situation where their united wills could be foiled.

They should not have been foiled now. Lily was the prettiest girl in Bridesmere, the prettiest girl most men had ever met. She was rich and accomplished and always stylishly dressed, none of which Theo Becket could claim—Caroline, maybe, but not Theo.

In the past, Lily's mother had been obliged to chase away her beaus, even the ones Lily liked, because none had had appropriate fortunes or families. For the first time, Lily was grateful. She and Mr. Delavert would suit. He was odd, but he was wealthier than her father, and he seemed to have a mild temper. Though not as stunning as his steward, he was handsome enough for her pride. Once she'd produced the requisite heir and spare, she would be able to get around him and pursue her private interests. Most important, with Delavert for a spouse, she would be able to lord it over her mother for the rest of her life. No matter how her mother tried to rule her, Lily would be free.

It was in pursuit of freedom that she had come to this unused room. She needed distance from her mother in order to clear her thoughts. When Lady Morris was near, Lily never felt as if she could breathe; a change came over her which she hated as much as the woman who caused it. Her mother was a plague. Lily deserved to be quit of her.

She would be quit of her if she could push Theo from her way. Though it had embarrassed her as a girl, she regretted Theo no longer ran in terror at the sight of her. Had the youngest Becket spent this visit barred in a closet, Lily would have been able to leave her be.

You were wrong, Lily thought to her mother. *You do not know the best way to catch Delavert. Like it or not, you will have to leave the next move to me.*

The appearance of the men on the lawn below pulled her

from her fuming. They were up to something, with their heads together as thick as thieves. Why Edmund would leave the house at all, when he could have been waiting in his room for her, was puzzling. As a lover, he was unsurpassed, and he was certainly slow to tire. She had been counting on his continued presence to keep her entertained after the wedding.

She very much doubted Delavert would be as interesting in bed.

She drew back from sight the moment Edmund looked up. Though she did not anticipate a scold, she had learned it was best to keep her doings to herself. By concealing even her feelings, she left no weaknesses exposed.

Lady Morris, for one, knew how to drive a knife into those.

"I *shall* have a wedding," she declared to the empty chamber, the back of her head pressed hard to the wall. "The finest wedding Bridesmere has ever seen."

She would have the men's secrets, too, but that could wait until she needed them.

Chapter 14

Thanks to Mr. Delavert putting his staff at their disposal, for once Theo and Caroline did not have to share a maid. Even more extraordinary, it was Theo's toilette their mother was most interested in overseeing. She had summoned her daughters to her room, and each was now ensconced before a dressing table. Theo's maid was a girl named Lydia. Thus far, she had proved adept, but Mrs. Becket frowned as she reached for the curling tongs.

"Just brush it through and pin it up. Even you cannot curl my youngest daughter's hair."

The maid dipped her head saucily. "I am sure she shall enchant the gentlemen all the same. Sometimes a . . . certain glow is more important than fashion."

"Hmph," said Theo's mama, though she sounded pleased. As if to hide this, she turned to Caroline. "Where is your gown, dear? You cannot dance in your petticoat."

"I am working on a last few touches," Theo said before her sister could stammer out a reply. "It is meant to be a surprise."

"Just be sure to finish in good time," said their mama.

"You know Mr. Delavert wants you both greeting guests." She looked distractedly at the door, obviously formulating some decision. "I am going to find you something to eat before it is too late. You are so slender it will not matter, and I want you to have plenty of strength for dancing."

"I may not need it," Theo cautioned.

Her mother smiled at her and touched her cheek. "You will need it, and it will not hurt to remind certain parties you are in demand."

Theo was still gaping when she shut the door.

"Oh, Theo," Caroline said, low and troubled.

Theo knew why at once. "Do not worry. If Mama asks, we'll say Uncle sent the cloth as a gift. I doubt she will ask, in any case. She has too many other things on her mind."

To Lucius's relief, the night of the ball was fair—warm enough but not stifling. He was flanked in the entry by Mrs. Becket and Lady Morris, who joined him in receiving guests. This was a mixed blessing.

After all her scheming to get where she was, Lady Morris found herself not as exultant as she expected. A brown fog of dissatisfaction blew off her aura, strong enough that Lucius soon wished to move away. Alas, politeness demanded he stay, even if it made him feel like he was rubbing against cobwebs. By contrast, the less experienced Mrs. Becket welcomed everyone with warmth and ease. From an idle brush with his hostesses' thoughts, he concluded their differing moods had the same cause.

Lucius's true affection had been noticed.

Theo was shining tonight. His faith in her artistic gift had not been misplaced. In truth, he wondered if he had done it justice. The old squire's home was not cozy. Its public rooms comprised a circuit on the ground floor. Through massive mahogany doors, the entry hall led to the dining room and from thence to the gallery. This imposing space, now serving as the ballroom, extended the length of the house from front to back. Its further end opened onto drawing rooms dedicated to punch and cards.

They were all fine rooms, but Theo had transformed them. Beneath her whimsical decorations, Hadleigh looked more like a faerie forest than a residence. Huge ropes of greenery festooned the ceilings and walls. Everywhere he looked, arrangements overflowed with flowers. The scent of hyacinths was enough to make an *upyr* drunk, and the *oohs* and *ahs* of each new cluster of guests were as gratifying to him as they were to Theo's mama.

"Such a clever theme," she murmured to him between arrivals. "I shall never read *A Midsummer Night's Dream* without recalling this. And to make up those nosegays for the ladies! If I may compliment my own daughter, that was a happy idea, and so fortunate that the flowers are holding up!"

Lucius hummed in agreement, though an awareness was creeping on him that more than fortune lay behind the flowers' sprightly state. He glanced at the arch of greenery that framed the door, its leaves as crisp and fresh as if still rooted in the ground.

The sight sent a chill skipping down his neck. Entirely without intent, his *upyr* power was conserving the decorations. Indeed, it had seeped into every corner of the house.

Grimacing, he tugged his white waistcoat. He'd assumed the younger staff's desires were infecting him. Now, with some discomfort, he realized his presence was responsible. He hoped tonight's attendees, here only for a while, would prove immune. The Becket and Morris girls seemed to be unaffected—with the possible exception of Theo. Then again, Theo was the only of his guests whose lusts he was paying attention to.

Concerned, he looked around for her. She and her sister were handing out nosegays from a heaping table nearby. He frowned as one haughty miss took the offering with no more thanks than if the girls were servants—though their gentility was hard to miss. Theo was bright as hope in white with yellow ribbons, while her sister's pale green, embroidered gown was truly beautiful. Lucius admired it all the more for seeing Theo's handiwork in every stitch. She might not know it, but she had, quite literally, wrapped Caroline in love.

No one should have had the ill manners to dismiss such girls. As much trouble as Lady Morris's aid had saved him, he saw there were disadvantages to having let her set most of the guest list. Some of these people were too high in the instep by half.

Happily, Theo saw him watching and rolled her eyes as the girl swanned away, clearly more amused than offended. Lucius winked in return and was gratified to stir a blush.

This night posed challenges, but it also offered rewards.

For now, rewards would have to wait. A ghost from Delavert's past appeared among the next group of guests. Lucius recognized Daniel Delavert's best friend, James Poole. He had the look of an avid huntsman: tall, well-fed, and tanned. He was, Lucius recalled, one of Lucas's severest critics. A young and pretty woman trailed behind him—a wife, Lucius presumed—whom Lucas had not met. Reality split and shifted inside him while he struggled to keep his expression blank.

"Delavert," said the man, his face tight with disapproval.

"Poole," Lucius responded in a drawling voice that did not seem his own. "How good of you to condescend to come."

"I would introduce you to my wife, but I remember how well you used to respect the marriage bond."

Lucius inclined his head. "Caution can be the better part of valor, though I suspect I am not the person who should most inspire your concern." He leaned closer, pitching his voice so only Poole could hear. "Even now, your young bride's eyes search the room for someone with whom to flirt."

This was only the truth, as the man must have feared already in his heart. Poole dropped his guard long enough to look worried, a slip he hid a second later beneath a sneer. "Still the same old Lucas, whatever fools might claim about you having changed. You'll never stop trying to shovel your own dirt in decent people's way."

"Many 'decent people,' as you call them, have a vested interest in seeing me as the source and repository of all stains. They enjoy feeling cleaner by comparison."

Poole might not have grasped the nuances of this barb, but he understood enough to turn red. "Daniel should be standing here, you bastard, not you, smirking in his place. You might think you can erase the past with your money and your fine new clothes but, mark my words, most of the people here know your existence for the outrage it is. By God, had your brother lived—"

"Yes." Lucius cut him off with a coolness that had nothing to do with *upyr* blood. He did not mind the insult for his own sake but for Lucas's. "I am well aware that, had my older brother lived, my father would gladly have banished me from his sight until the end of time. That, however, might be considered a flaw in his compassion rather than in my character."

Poole widened his eyes. This crisp defense would have been impossible for the Lucas Delavert he knew.

"Daniel would have forgiven me," Lucius added with a confidence he suspected the real Delavert could not have mustered. "Had he become squire, he would have mended our breach in the end. Unlike some, he had a Christian heart."

"Bastard," was all the rejoinder Lucius received, after which the man—his *guest*—rudely showed him his back and led his pretty wife away. Though Theo and Caroline stood too far to have heard the exchange, Lucius noticed neither offered the wife her flowers. She had to take them from the heap herself.

"What a disagreeable man," Mrs. Becket observed.

"Yes," Lady Morris mused, watching Poole's slightly

balding head disappear. "I do notice, though, that his outrage is insufficient to snub you outright. He stays, Mr. Delavert, and I've no doubt he and his wife will eat and dance."

She allowed her smile to broaden as she turned to him. That she took a proprietary interest in this victory was obvious, and yet, in that moment, Lucius couldn't help liking her. She had hit the nail on the head, and quite as well as he could have himself.

A little shriek of pleasure from Theo announced that their next guests were more welcome.

"Katie!" she cried, running to hug a plump girl in sprigged muslin.

"Goodness," said Mrs. Becket. "I didn't know our neighbors were coming."

There was no time to explain even had he wished, because Mr. Connor, neighbor and attorney, was there.

Lucius thanked him for coming.

"It is our pleasure," said Mr. Connor, his arm clasping his wife's waist. "Our daughter has been in alt ever since we got your invitation, and I think even our boys are looking forward to dancing. Katie"—he nodded in the direction of the girl now having a tête-à-tête with Theo—"tells us we may soon have reason to wish you joy beyond the felicity of your safe return from the Indies."

A search of Delavert's memories revealed that being "wished joy" was a euphemism for an engagement. Lucius was astonished. If Theo was describing his attentions as leading to that end, it could not be unwelcome. Before his hopes could run wild, however, he read from Mr. Connor's very open mind that the hint had come from Caroline. She had written his daughter—no doubt without Theo's knowledge.

"Oh, Mr. Connor," Lady Morris laughed, saving Lucius the work of finding his tongue. "What odd freaks you legal gentlemen take into your heads. I assure you Mr. Delavert is no different from any comfortable male. No such hope of being wished joy enters their minds."

"I dare say it doesn't," Mr. Connor agreed jovially, "until they find themselves at the church. Happened to me and the missus. Scarcely knew I was going to ask her until I did. Never been sorry, either—not in twenty-one happy years."

"Twenty-two," his missus amended fondly, obliging Lady Morris to feign a smile.

Lucius's ears were sharp enough to hear her teeth grinding. His amusement would have lasted longer had he not caught one of the Connors' sons regarding Theo with salacious thoughts. His own jaw tightened in anger. He could have done without the reminder that he wasn't the only male who could appreciate Theo's charms.

To Theo's relief, Mr. Delavert did not forget their engagement for the first two dances. She had not thought he would, but the exalted nature of the gathering left her feeling more insecure than usual. Lady Morris and her mother really had invited everyone who was anyone—all the grandees from the neighborhood, even a viscount from York. Gentleman's daughter she might be, but next to those refined ladies she felt more like a scullery maid. She had thought Lady Morris's scorn for bouncing country girls overly snobbish, but now she prayed she wouldn't bounce herself.

The only sight that made her happier than seeing Katie Connor walk through the door was Mr. Delavert crossing the room to bow to her—even if it did make her the cynosure of all eyes. She actually heard whispers, as if some of the ladies took the favor shown to her as a personal insult to them.

Luckily, Mr. Delavert had other concerns.

"That boy fancies you," he said as he led her out to the top of the set. His tone was mild, but her scalp prickled the same as if one of Hadleigh's wolves had growled.

"Percy Fitz Clare?" she asked, for this was the only "boy" she could think of. As far as she knew, Bridesmere Castle's youthful baron had not arrived.

Mr. Delavert's voice sank even lower. "The younger Connor boy. He seems to view you as his personal property."

"Oh, Hammond Connor is an idiot." Theo was relieved to be able to laugh. "He has fallen in love with fully half of his sister's friends. He used to spy on me and Nathan when we were courting."

The words came easily, as if Nathan were no more important than a childhood picnic or a once-loved doll. Shocked at herself, she fell silent.

"Ah," said Mr. Delavert as the musicians, hired all the way from London, struck up a minuet.

Neither spoke as they wound through their portion of the pattern. Theo was grateful for the barrier of her gloves. She was too aware of her partner's hands. They were strong and sure, elegant yet masculine. Though Mr. Delavert did nothing he should not, his fingers seemed to caress her palms each time they moved together or apart. Delicious pulses of awareness slid up her arms, then to parts considerably lower. Her temperature began to rise. She felt him watching her, but refused to meet his eyes, certain she would make a display of herself if she did. She stared at her feet instead, in spite of which she twice nearly fumbled a simple step.

"You are graceful," he assured her when they finally reached the set's bottom, now to wait while the other couples took their turn. "No one could complain of your dancing."

She had to look at him then, and the sheer force of his beauty struck her like a storm, full of lightning and energy. His eyes were polished silver in the candlelight. The way he held himself—without even trying—was as proud as an emperor. No man here was anything next to him, maybe no man alive. She curled her fingers into her palms to prevent herself from reaching up to stroke his jaw. The urge to embrace him was almost irresistible.

"*You,*" she declared hoarsely, "are the best dancer in the room."

His face darkened, a faint wine flush overlaying the ivory

of his skin. He seemed as grateful as she when the next bit of the dance demanded they part. He had composed himself by the time they met to link arms and turn.

"You are too kind," he said. "I have the advantage of inspiration."

This was too smooth a piece of flattery for her to answer. Judging it best not to risk her voice, she remained silent until the set finished.

During the second of their dances, he tried again.

"You look lovely," he said. "You've no idea how many men wished they were in my shoes."

His crooked smile invited one in return. "You're a mind reader then? I thank you for your compliment, Mr. Delavert, but I think I know the limits of my allure."

"Whereas I am utterly convinced you do not."

The figures of the dance necessitated a pause. Theo gathered her courage. "Am I to take these pretty manners seriously?"

"They come from the heart."

She glanced at him skeptically, and he shook his head. "I would make you believe me if I could."

At that moment, he seemed genuine enough. Perhaps she was being churlish to doubt him. Considering the way some of his guests had behaved, he hardly deserved that.

"I have found," she said as lightly as she could, "that sincerity is a hard quality to judge when it comes from handsome men wearing evening dress. Faced with such splendor, we women risk making fools of ourselves by too great credulity."

His smile said he took this in the spirit she intended. "Perhaps you are right. Time alone can prove my words—though I do doubt that you, Miss Theodora, will ever be anybody's fool."

The end of the dance prevented her from making the denial honesty required. Theo could be a fool, and a very bad one. Of that she had not the slightest doubt.

Her heart seemed determined to prove it when, immediately following his dance with her, he led her sister out.

Theo was left on the side to watch, but she could not mind. This treatment indeed distinguished her family. Strictly speaking, if Mr. Delavert meant to thank his hostesses by dancing with their daughters, Lily Morris should have been next. Lily seemed to think so, too. Though her hand was claimed soon after, her gaze narrowed on Caroline every chance she got.

She was accustomed to being men's first choice.

Despite the slight, Lily's expression was more calculating than annoyed. When she whispered in the ear of the woman who stood next to her in the set, Theo's stomach sank. Lily's neighbor was the wife of the man named Poole, the one who had sneered at Mr. Delavert. Unlike Theo, Lily Morris knew most of their guests. They were, Theo realized, the same cruel-natured friends Caroline had once pitied her for having. The disadvantage this presented was abruptly clear. Mrs. Poole's gaze slid slyly to Caroline. Whatever Lily had told her, it had not been nice.

The hopeful approach of Hammond Connor distracted Theo from her foreboding. He was a bit of a clod, but that was no reason to be mean. Smiling in a manner she hoped would be taken for sisterly, she allowed that she would indeed enjoy a cool cup of punch.

Half an hour later, Theo flapped her fan in the quiet of a window seat, recovering her breath from a jig most of the finer ladies had sat out. She had too much pride to pretend to be better than she was—even if her toes were throbbing from Hammond tromping on her feet. Mr. Delavert had smiled at her in passing, not too proud to jig himself. Though her pleasure in his smile was perhaps too great, she was happy with herself tonight—a decided improvement on her usual response to a ball.

She spied her mother across the room, looking about her in a worried way, but was too contented to hail her. Chances were, Lady Morris had overturned some order concerning the coming supper, and Theo could not bestir herself to fret over that. Let Lady Morris do what she would; no one could undo the triumph she and Caroline had enjoyed.

She believed this without question until Katie Connor burst breathlessly in on her solitude. Her normally cheery face was distraught. "You must come," she said. "Caroline is crying in the cloak room. People have been saying the most awful things!"

Theo leapt to her feet. "What things? Who would dare be unkind to her?"

Katie shook her head and tugged at her arm. "Not here. The walls have ears, and I am trying to avoid a scene."

To Theo's consternation, their passage was enough to draw stares. She recognized too few faces, and saw too many heads leaning close as she and Katie pushed through the crowd. Her neck was tight when at last they reached the ladies' retiring room. What was usually the library was empty but for Caroline. She sat on a little footstool, weeping quietly into her shawl.

"Oh, sister," Theo crooned, immediately kneeling at her side. "What on earth can be wrong?"

Caroline's gasping answer was impossible to make out.

"People are talking about light fingers wandering at Black's," Katie answered more helpfully. She had her hand on Caroline's trembling shoulder. "They are saying Caroline stole her gown. That your family cannot afford such things."

"I shall strangle Lily Morris where she stands!" Theo declared. Her sister and Katie blinked in surprise. With a muffled growl, Theo pressed her fist to her mouth. "I would not have guessed she would spread this rumor. Her mother, maybe, but not her. If I had not witnessed her starting the thing myself . . . But it is done."

Sighing, she faced her sister. "I am not scolding you, but

why did you not tell the story we had agreed upon: that the gown was a gift from our uncle?"

"Because he is *here,*" Caroline said, her voice recovered but froggy. "What if someone asked him to confirm it? Only think how awkward that would be."

"Oh, Caroline." Theo could not contain a regretful laugh. "You are too considerate for your own good. Uncle William is a clever man. He would have been quick enough to play along."

"I am sorry," Caroline said glumly. "You know I am not good at lying. Keeping secrets, yes, but not lying."

"It cannot be true," Katie breathed in horror. "Neither of you would stoop to stealing."

"Not stealing," Theo said. "Just commerce. I embroidered that cloth. I am the Italian nuns who have been exporting their goods to Black's. I am trying to pay our debts."

"That isn't bad," Katie said. "If I were you, I would be proud. I suppose your mother does not like it, but—"

"Oh, Lord!" Theo pressed her palms to her cheeks. "Mama! She must have heard the rumor. That was why she looked worried."

Katie's forehead puckered in confusion.

"She doesn't know what I'm doing," Theo explained. "She would never allow it." She did not add that Mrs. Becket had a hard enough time accepting an attorney's daughter as their best friend, but Katie's pinkened cheeks said she was aware of this.

"Oh," she said. "But you cannot let people think your sister is a thief. Surely that is worse!"

"Yes," Theo said in resignation, though her mother might disagree. "Surely it is."

"My mama could help undo the damage. Maybe spread the story about your uncle? You know what a gossip she is."

Theo squeezed her arm in gratitude. "You are a good friend to offer. Unfortunately, I am not certain Mr. Delavert himself would be able to convince his guests. Those who do not know us judge him for showing our family too much honor. For this to have spread so quickly, they must *want* to believe the lies. I suspect the only explanation they will accept is one that makes us look just as bad." She sighed, the truth of what she had to do sinking in. "However good my intentions were, I am the one who put Caroline in this spot, and I am the one who must clear her name."

Theo would have welcomed a delay, but she did not find it. The dancers were between sets when she reached the ballroom again.

At a whispered word from her, the orchestra leader called for attention. Grimly, she stepped onto the musicians' platform, facing but not meeting the sea of eyes. Her palms were damp, her heart racing so rapidly she felt ill. What would her mother think of this spectacle? For that matter, what would Mr. Delavert? Any doubt she had about how highly she valued his good opinion was wiped out by her gloom at the prospect of losing it. She wished she could see another solution, but she had stolen enough from Caroline. She could not take her reputation, too. No matter what the cost, she had to set this right.

She twisted her hands together and took a deep breath for strength. She did not think she had ever spoken to a group this large, every one of whom was staring.

"Please forgive the interruption," she began, willing her jaw not to shake. "I would not presume upon your patience but for an unfortunate misunderstanding concerning my sister, Caroline. As I am sure those of you with sisters will understand, she is too good a person and too beloved for me to let it stand. The gown she wears—indeed the gowns I see a number of you wear tonight—were embroidered by myself. I have been selling my needlework to Black's under the pretense of it coming from Italian nuns. I am not ashamed of this, only of causing embarrassment to those I love, and

I sincerely hope you will acquit Caroline Becket of anything worse than protecting her sister's pride. Thank you for your attention. Please enjoy the rest of the night."

Though Theo's speech was brief, it might as well have lasted an hour. Her knees were almost too weak to carry her, but staying where she was would have required more courage than she possessed. Head down, wishing she could stop her ears to the rising murmurs, she moved as quickly as she was able to the exit.

As she did, she seemed to feel a strong, warm arm squeezing her shoulders; seemed to hear a soft voice saying it would be all right. *You have stolen nothing,* it said, *that your sister would not have given you.*

Alas, the voice was only in her head. It disappeared as soon as she reached the servants' corridor.

There her tears, too long held back, threatened to overflow.

I must get away, she thought, pressing the heels of her palms to her brow. She was going to embarrass herself even more unless she did.

~

From the back of the crowded ballroom, Lily watched Theo Becket disgrace herself on Caroline's behalf. The display—which she never would have indulged in a million years—satisfied her deeply, despite her face showing nothing but mild surprise. This night was turning out better than she'd hoped, and she could only conclude she should have taken the reins long ago. Whatever Theo's aim, her entire family was branded now, no better than their uncle the shopkeeper.

She repressed the tiny twinge of regret this caused. She had no personal complaint against the Beckets. They had simply gotten in her way. Now they were out of it, and the world could settle back into the pattern it was meant to hold.

She slid her hands down her narrow gown, savoring a tactile pleasure almost as sweet as stroking her own skin.

Then she remembered what she was wearing: a length of

"Italian" silk bought from Black's, which had until that moment been her favorite gown. She would have to discard it . . . maybe pawn it off on her maid in the hope that Theo would someday see the servant wearing it. A minute smile tugged her perfect lips. It would serve Theo right for presuming to climb so high.

Her mother nudged her shoulder as Theo rushed red-faced from the room. Lily fought not to scowl. This was *her* plan they were following tonight. Yes, her mother was helping, but Lily needed no reminder of what came next.

Chapter 15

Lucius thought he had reached Theo with his mind, but to judge by the way she ran from the ballroom, it seemed not. Perhaps it was just as well, because who knew what she would have thought if he had succeeded? He simply had not been able to bear watching her stand up there all alone, feeling ashamed of herself while he nearly burst with pride.

His Theo might not be perfect, but she was brave.

She was also quicker than he was getting through the crush. He wasted precious seconds being polite, only to end up being intercepted by a footman when he finally gained the servants' corridor. Theo's scent trailed through it, so knew she had come this way, but short of snarling at the hapless footman and shoving him aside, he was compelled to wait.

"Excuse me, sir," said the man, short of breath from his haste to catch his master. "A young lady gave me this for you."

This was a note on cream-colored stock. Lucius took it from the footman's white-gloved hand. The script that addressed it brought him alert. He recognized Theo's clear but tiny writing from the letters he'd occasionally watched her compose. Plainly, she liked to get her money's worth from each sheet. He wondered what could have driven her to write to him directly. By human standards, this was a serious impropriety.

Forgetting everything, he broke the seal and opened the folded sheet. A few spare lines were all it contained.

"My heart is torn," it said. "I cannot decide what to do. Please meet me at the castle-folly so we may speak."

A "T" and a postscript to "come alone" ended the note.

My heart is torn? Lucius rubbed one knuckle across his chin. What could she mean by that? Torn by her attraction to him because of the respect she thought she owed her dead fiancé? Torn because she'd wanted the match for her sister? Or torn for some reason which would bring him no joy at all?

He tried to get a sense of her meaning by pressing the page between his fingers, but her feelings had left no mark.

"How long ago did you receive this?" he asked the footman.

"Not but a minute."

Lucius considered his course of action for two heartbeats. He caught the footman's eyes. "You will tell no one about this."

"No, sir," he agreed. "Not a soul."

A triumph that had nothing to do with overpowering a servant pumped through his veins. His breeches strained with his cockstand before he reached the outdoors. The reaction was ridiculous. Lucius didn't know what Theo wanted, but his body was quickening as if she had invited him to her bed. He shook his head at himself. Lord, he wanted her. With a house full of people, with who knew what gossip beginning to swirl, all he could think about was getting between her legs.

Stroking inside her.

Licking his way up her neck until her pulse beat quick as raindrops beneath his tongue.

He shuddered at a surge of bloodlust, his eyeteeth buzzing at the images. His recent restraint had done nothing for his control, though he doubted Theo knew how inflaming he would find her instruction to "come alone." His shaft was so stiff inside his clothing that his strides were uncomfortable. Rather than let this slow him, he hid himself with a glamour and walked faster.

He should have cloaked himself from the start. If there was any chance she had lost her heart, that she might be wholly ready to give herself to him, he could not bear more delay.

At his present pace, the castle-folly soon rose before him, a single candle burning behind its Gothic window. He paused to stare at the glow, needing a moment to compose himself. The night felt charged with importance. Theo would be leaving Hadleigh, her family's reason for staying gone. He would have opportunities to see her, but perhaps not under his own roof. He might never again enjoy the freedom he had tonight.

Though he warned himself that desperate men made mistakes, his anticipation rose like a whirlwind. As he stepped into the folly, a shadow drew his eye to the gallery, built to allow visitors to enjoy the window's view. His face instantly went cold. The shadow did not need to step forward before he knew.

It wasn't Theo. He had already made a mistake. The note that brought him here had been forged.

Lily Morris was clad only in her chemise. A lacy strap fell down one shoulder, baring her breast to its peak. Had the cloth not been damped to cling, that would have fallen, too.

"Thank you for coming," she purred, her smile more victory than seduction.

It did not matter that he could not read her: Lucius saw how she expected this to unfold. He would ask her what in Hades she was doing. She would answer coyly. He would scold and try to put her off. All of which would give her mother time to get a search party here. Lily and he would be caught in a compromising position. He was a gentleman—

an honorable man, so they thought—one who hoped to assume his place in society. He would have to ask her to marry him. Otherwise, she would be ruined.

If he'd been anyone but who he was, he would have been caught.

Fury rose inside him as pitiless as a winter gale. By God, these Morrises were arrogant. They must not think he would mind being saddled with Lily. She was, after all, such a pretty honey trap. From Lily's expression, she hadn't the least idea that the loss of any chance to be with Theo was one he'd mourn. A stone rattled from the wall as his temper swelled. Lily grabbed for the gallery railing. The boards that comprised it had begun to shake.

It seemed that keeping flowers fresh was the least of what he had forgotten his powers could do.

"Come here," he grated out before his rage could bring down the tower. Oh, he recognized that dangerous midnight tone, though he had not heard it issue from his throat for many centuries.

Lily pattered down the spiral stairs, too pleased with herself to suspect she had cause to fear. While he trembled with anger, she came to a halt incautious inches away. As if she enjoyed the sight of her own caresses, she watched her palms slide up his chest.

He was struggling too hard with his temper to push them off.

"I am sorry I've been cool to you," she said. "I was acting on bad advice. I am sure you would have made different choices had you known that you could have me."

He choked in disbelief, but this, too, she disregarded.

"Do not fear," she went on with the same stunning self-confidence, "I know how to make men happy. In no time at all, you will forget you ever fancied *her*."

Her scorn for Theo broke his paralysis. Lucius put his hand to her throat. For one horrid instant, he wanted to kill her. He knew he could shake her bones apart with a thought.

Instead, he squeezed just hard enough to bring her eyes up.

He might not be able to pull thoughts out of her mind, but he could bloody well put them in.

"Return to the house," he said low and harsh. "You will not tell anyone you saw me. In fact, you will not walk if you can run. If you value your life, Miss Morris, you will go now."

Her mouth gaped with fear, and then she flew from his hold, stumbling over her feet as she rushed out the door. As she grew small, her chemise flapped behind her like a thin white flag.

Satisfied she would not return, Lucius looked at the sky, heavy now with clouds. Though his tremors of fury had subsided, his guard remained. His *upyr* senses registered others on the grounds. Lady Morris was approaching with her searchers, and Lily's current path would intersect with theirs.

Despite his thralling her not to speak, he knew Lady Morris was clever enough to salvage their plan on her own—especially if the girl ran past witnesses half dressed. By now, Lucius's absence would have been remarked. If one of Lady Morris's companions escaped to spread the story, all would be lost. With the best will in the world, he could not thrall a whole ballroom.

He had to prevent his would-be seductress from being seen.

He did not let himself think too hard. He needed powers that had been his at the height of his knowledge, and thinking might hinder his recall. Closing his eyes, he sent his awareness toward clouds he suspected his anger had drawn here. Curtains of mist began to stretch toward the ground. They dampened his skin as they thickened, cool and smelling of the moor.

Come, he thought to forces that knew no speech. He had learned spells to achieve this in one age or another, but spells were not as swift as simple will. He spread his arms in welcome. *Come.* Through his eyelids he envisioned a coastal fog, so thick humans would not be able to see the hands at the end of their arms, so enveloping that the light of a lantern would be swallowed up.

The air grew quiet around him. Night creatures stilled. Even to his keen hearing, the distant music of the orchestra was muffled. *Good,* he thought to the fog. *Now stay.*

He opened his eyes to a world of gray.

He smiled, for once pleased with the scope of his ancient gifts. When he glanced down, he could not see his shoes.

Luckily, he had subtler senses on which to rely. He would be able to find his way. He was debating whether to trail Lily, to ensure she reached his house safely, when another presence put all thoughts of her from his mind.

In that instant, he saw he had a choice to make.

To his chagrin, it was not as hard as it should have been.

Theo could not comprehend how the fog had come up so fast. Weather like this did not just materialize, even on the moor.

She turned in a befuddled circle. A moment before she had been lost in her misery; now she was simply lost. She could not see the lights of the house, the full moon was a blur, and her hands threatened to disappear if she reached too far. It was, she thought with a shiver she could not suppress, as if she had been transported to the afterlife.

"Nonsense," she scoffed aloud. This fog might seem uncanny, but Fate was hardly likely to release her from facing tonight's aftermath. Her mother, for one, would be wanting an accounting.

"Hellfire," she said on a pensive gust of breath.

This way, she thought with a modicum of confidence. She had been heading this way when the fog came up. She remembered glancing up and seeing the building shaped like a castle. She didn't think anyone lived there, not like the gardener's house, though she wasn't entirely sure how she knew. She had veered toward it, thinking she could wait out the night inside. The folly commanded a view of the drive. She would know when Mr. Delavert's guests had left.

I shall be safe there, she thought, though she was not certain why she believed that, either.

Well, walk then, she told herself. If she did not find the place in a few minutes, she would stop and sit down. The fog had to lift some time. No harm would come to her if she stayed still.

She braced herself to meet with failure, but as she walked she sensed she was crossing familiar ground. The slope of the land seemed right. She began, oddly enough, to enjoy herself. Certainly, no distraction had ever been more welcome. The mist swirled like smoke against her skin, cool and sensual. She knew she was not dreaming, and yet the state of her mind felt very like it. She half expected—maybe even wanted—another visit from Hadleigh's wolves.

On a night like this, she could believe they might come close enough to pet.

The fog ahead of her stirred. She held her breath, but Mr. Delavert's emergence from the cloud struck her as perfectly natural. Of course he would come to find her, and of course he would succeed. She did, however, feel a little shy when she remembered what she'd been running from.

"Oh," she cried with hands to her cheeks. "How you must despise me!"

"Never," he said, immediately pulling her close. Despite the hardness of his chest, this seemed the most comfortable place in the world. She was sorry when he set her back. "I was worried when you ran off. Come inside now, out of the wet."

The door to the folly was behind him. She knew she should not go with him, but his hand was sweet and warm on hers. He tugged her gently, and hesitantly she followed. No one would ever know they were here. In this weather, no one could.

Curious to see the place that had drawn her, she glanced around. The furnishings were strangely familiar, but perhaps her perception was confused by the single candle, whose wavering light caused the shadows to shrink and swell. Mr. Delavert pulled her close again. Though she was not chilled enough to require it, she had no urge to step back. Warmth ran through her in lovely waves. The way Mr. Delavert chafed the length of her arms made her feel both cherished and forgiven.

"You are not angry?" she asked the brocade buttons of his white waistcoat. "I made such a scene in front of your guests."

He pressed her cheek to his heart, sighing softly when she relaxed. "Theo," he chided, and for once she had no wish to correct him. "Please believe I do not share your mother's horror of trade. Younger sons cannot afford to be that fastidious. I am only sorry you were not able to enjoy the ball."

"I enjoyed some of it. You were very kind."

"I assure you, kindness had nothing to do with it."

The dryness of his answer made her tilt back her head. He met her gaze but only just, then winced as he looked away.

Instinct told her he was trying to hide something important: some feeling or desire he did not wish her to see. Her pulse quickened. She wanted to break through his barriers, to know the truth of his heart. In that moment, nothing mattered more.

"Why won't you look at me?" she asked.

He faced her then, his eyes resigned. "I want to kiss you."

The confession sounded as if it had been dragged from him, but she could think of none she would welcome more.

"Why don't you?" she asked breathlessly.

She did not understand the reason for his groaning laugh, but when he framed her face in his hands, she had no trouble guessing what came next. He tilted her head like a chalice and breathed her name. His lips were parted as they brushed hers, his tongue sliding slowly over and between their curves. Tiny sparks of sensation flew back and forth. His hands drifted down the sides of her neck, then over her shoulders and back. When he reached her waist, his hold tightened and her body swayed. She had to clutch his tail coat to keep her feet.

"Theo," he whispered, fusing their mouths together and drawing hard. His palms descended the slope of her lower back, his fingers pushing inward and down, molding her curves until her bottom was snugly cupped. He lifted her then—suddenly and precisely—over the swollen evidence of his desire.

No gesture could have been more indicative of wrong intent, but Theo regretted it not at all. The press of that hot, thick ridge against her own arousal felt so good it shocked. She was alive in every cell, tingling from scalp to toes. Continuing to kiss him seemed the most important thing in the world. She gripped the back of his head, her thumbs finding the bareness beneath his cravat. Even through her gloves, his skin was warm, and the feel of his jaw working to kiss her deeper made her insides melt.

"You want this?" He broke free to gasp. "You want this of your own free will?"

"Yes," she said, not understanding why he had to ask. "Please, do not stop kissing me."

He reclaimed her mouth as if he were starving, then her neck, and then he shoved her gathered bodice over her breast. The air told her she was bare, but the heat that lit his gaze kept her warm. When he thumbed her sharpened nipple, the ache streaked to her core.

He did not ask, and he did not have to. With a groan of longing, he fastened his lips on the blood-rouged bud. His hair was silkier than any man's ought to be, his mouth indecently clever. Even as he flicked and tugged, his teeth compressed the flesh of her peak. There was something odd about their conformation, but nothing wrong with the way they felt. That was all too natural and right. She had no wish to protest and, in any case, the toes of her dancing slippers barely brushed the ground. The best she could do was writhe in his hold and plunge her fingers into his hair.

She wished she could reach more of him. Her touch seemed to please him, enough that he stripped off her gloves and urged her palms to his skin. Every inch of him was hot and silky. It wasn't long before his body was shuddering.

"Lord," he whispered against her nipple, licking it even as he spoke. "I have never needed anyone like this. How shall I bear not tasting you?"

She did not get the chance to declare he should. The door slammed open like a thunderclap.

"Unhand my daughter this instant!"

The angel Gabriel could not have sounded a more righteous peal. When Theo collected enough of her wits to realize who the intruder was, she thought she would have preferred the avenging angel—though Lady Morris looked, if possible, more horrified to see *her*. A group of guests crowded up behind her, round-eyed and curious. Behind them, Theo saw the fog had dwindled to wisps.

"Theo!" Lady Morris exclaimed. "What are you doing here?"

"Er," was all Theo found to say, feeling more dumbstruck than she had ever been in her life. To make matters worse, she had not yet lost her dizziness from the kiss.

Gently, but with a deliberateness guaranteed to cause the others to take note, Mr. Delavert set her down and pulled her bodice over her breast.

Theo gasped, only then remembering to clap her hand over it.

"Look," one of the ladies murmured behind her fan. "He's left love bites up and down her neck."

The tinge of jealousy failed to make her feel better. The accusation was correct. The skin of her throat was throbbing in the soft night air, and she had no doubt the marks were as clear as any badge of infamy. She had taken an embarrassment that affected only her family and turned it into a huge scandal.

As proof of how dire their indiscretion was, Lucius was once again unable to meet her eyes.

"Well," he said and cleared his throat. "Considering the situation in which you find us, perhaps this would be an appropriate moment to announce Miss Becket's and my engagement?"

Theo and Lady Morris cried "No!" at the same time.

"Now, now," Mr. Delavert said as if Theo were the only one who had spoken. "I know you wanted to wait a little longer, but people will understand if we hurry things along. Everyone here was young once."

You do not have to do this, Theo tried to mouth, but he had already turned to face the crowd at the door.

"We anticipate a small wedding," he said. "Family only."

Lady Morris looked as if she had accidentally swallowed a toad. "Felicitations," she said faintly.

The others echoed her with more warmth, though they were probably only glad because of the story they'd have to tell.

"You will leave us now," Mr. Delavert said in the firmest possible tone.

Their audience left, but their absence—and the quiet—brought no relief to Theo's sense of disgrace.

"Oh, God!" she cried a second before she thought she'd burst. "Mr. Delavert, please accept my apology. What an abominable way to thank you for all you've done!"

He released his breath heavily. "Theo," he said, just that and then nothing. He squeezed her shoulder. When she dared to look at him, he seemed every bit as uncomfortable as she had feared. He was only showing her his profile.

"Trust me," he said after a moment. "You are the last person to blame for this. If you hate the idea, however, we will find some escape."

"What escape can there be? Our position was impossible to mistake. Oh, but to impose on you in this way—!"

He drew one finger down her flushing cheek. "*I* do not hate the idea."

His expression was unexpectedly vulnerable. He must care for her at least a little to wear that look. The last thing she meant by her protestations was to do his pride injury.

"I do not hate it, either," she assured him. "How could I? You are the sort of man girls dream of. But no one should be forced to marry like this. Only a beast could think it fair."

"A beast," he repeated with a bitter laugh. Then he cupped her face and kissed her brow.

"We shall make the best of it," he said, but she had to wonder who he hoped to convince.

Chapter 16

Lucius's news was not what Edmund expected when called to his dressing room. Having heard it, his stomach felt full of stones.

"You cannot be serious. Marry a human? What on earth for?"

"Because I love her."

Feeling unsteady, Edmund braced his hands on either side of the marble-topped washstand, surprised to see a film of dust scatter from his way. He had not thought his powers collected enough for that. "What about your promise to do no harm?"

"Theo will be harmed if I don't marry her. Her reputation—"

"As if you cared about humans' reputations!"

Lucius shot him a look that said he cared about this one's. Edmund could not believe this was happening. He had wanted Lucius to become more engaged in life. Now he would gladly have sent Delavert back to the ditch where they'd found him. Hell, he'd have tossed him in the mud himself.

"I did not thrall her," Lucius said. "I tricked her, and with a perfectly ordinary—if despicable—human ploy. If Theo truly wishes to squirm out of this, she can."

His eyes cut away from Edmund's. The fact that he was defensive spoke volumes about how changed he was.

"And if she doesn't wish to evade it?" Edmund asked. "This is a marriage. Till death do you part. Do you intend to hide what you are for the rest of her life?" Lucius winced at the reminder of his bride-to-be's mortality, but this was no time to be soft. "Don't you think she'll notice when her husband fails to age?"

"I shall cross that bridge when I come to it."

"You may cross it sooner than you think." Turning, Edmund leaned back on the washstand and crossed his arms. Rather than allow himself to be confronted, Lucius moved to the window. He knew he was in the wrong; that much was clear.

"No *upyr,*" Edmund continued, "no matter how powerful, can maintain a glamour for years at a time. What if you fall asleep before she does? What if she draws a curtain without warning and sees your skin start to burn? This girl may be willing to marry you to save her honor, but she believes you are human. How will she feel when the truth comes out?"

"Perhaps it will not matter."

"And perhaps it will."

"If she falls in love with me—"

"How can she love you when the face you show her is a lie?"

"I have to take that chance." Lucius had been running his hands along the shutter's edge. Now he turned, the look in his eyes both helpless and pleading. "I cannot give her up."

Edmund steeled himself to be blunt. "You cannot change her into one of us unless she is able to make the choice while in full command of her will. That is our first and most sacred law. If you thrall her, if you force her to accept you by unnatural means, so help me, I will bring the Council into this."

"I shall avoid clouding her mind as much as I can."

"As much as you can!"

"It is all I can promise. You know what my power is. Why do you think I have refrained from biting her since she was ill? I love her, Edmund, but I do not want a slave. I will protect who she is with all my strength."

Lucius held Edmund's gaze. He did not try to hide his emotions, but laid them bare. The sight was more than Edmund could withstand. He knew he could not comprehend how long his sire had been lonely, how long he had hid this longing for a heart's companion even from himself. Though Lucius's hopes seemed doomed, Edmund could not bring himself to say so. He did not want to think what would happen if the elder had to give up his dream.

"I see I cannot sway you," he said gruffly instead. "Just promise you will be careful. I do not want to see you hurt."

Lucius's crooked smile broke Edmund's heart. "At least you have the wisdom to know which one of us is most at risk of that."

On returning to his rooms, Edmund found Lily Morris sitting naked in his bed, her knees pulled girlishly to her chest. He had been busy tonight, and was pleased with how smoothly he had run the staff. Before Lucius had shared his tidings, he had been planning to treat himself to his favorite upper maid. That reward having been missed, Lily had a predictable effect on his various arousable parts. Interestingly enough, though he wished to bite her, refraining was not the hardship it seemed to be for Lucius.

Edmund could just as easily bite someone else.

"I thought you would be gone," he said to Lily, beginning to undo his stock.

"*Mother* is gone. I took a mare and rode back. It is not too long a trip if you gallop."

Edmund thought the mare might disagree, but all he said was, "Lady Morris won't miss you?"

"I doubt Mother is in the mood to check beds tonight. She'll be regaling Papa with her complaints until he nods off. In any case, my maid is used to covering for me."

Her eyes followed the progress of the buttons he was opening in his waistcoat, a rosiness in her cheeks all that gave away her interest. Edmund smiled, his cock pulsing higher at her flush. Lily kept her feelings locked up like the silver. Now she released her knees and leaned back to prop herself on her arms. Her breasts were a lovely sight even to jaded eyes like his. Legs extended, her slim bare feet wagged from side to side.

The casual manner in which she uttered her next words was very nearly convincing. "Your master is marrying Theo Becket."

Did she expect this to come as news? "I hope you are not counting on me to speak against the match."

"Why would I want you to do that?"

"Oh, maybe because you were hoping to catch him yourself."

She tossed her head. "There are plenty more fish like him in the sea."

Were there? Had Lily ever tried to reel in her catch before, or had they always been chased away before it came to that? From his observation of the human world, men were easier to get in bed than to the altar. He peeled his shirt over his head and swung onto the mattress on his hands and knees. Lily looked up at him but did not move. "If you are upset about my master's marriage, perhaps you should have tried harder to attract him."

She shrugged, but he thought he saw a hint of irritation in the tightening of her lips. "Mother convinced me to let her arrange things. She always gets what she wants."

"An interesting division of labor, if I may say so."

He knelt back and dropped the front of his trousers, pleased to see her gaze descend to what he'd revealed. One finger reached to touch his vibrating shaft. She was, as usual, fascinated by his hardness—no doubt considering it a compliment to herself.

"You are not insulted," she observed.

"And you are not heartbroken."

He suspected she was angry—for being thwarted, if nothing else—but she smiled with lowered eyelashes. Letting her thighs loll open, she stroked their creamy surface with her fingertips. "Happily, I am interested in more than one sort of prize."

This calm of hers unnerved him, suggesting she had another plan up her sleeve. "I hope you know *I* shall never marry you."

"You are a steward," she said. "Marriage is the last thing I want from you."

Her scorn inspired a prick of annoyance that made him want to laugh at himself. What a charming creature she became on opening her mouth. He began to wonder she had any admirers. But she was reaching for him, her arms urging his body over hers. Despite his readiness, he held back a bit longer.

"You leave within the hour," he said sternly, belatedly remembering his own advice about *upyr* trying to hide what they were. Curtailing this encounter left time to spare before dawn. Lily must not see the changes that overtook him then. "I have duties to perform tomorrow. I need a few hours to sleep."

She pretended to bite the tip of his chin. "You had better work fast then, for I am in powerful need of exercise tonight."

She did not lie. Twice he took her, and twice she remained

eager. Apparently, this was how she intended work through her marital frustration. Sympathetic to her fervor, if not its cause, Edmund enjoyed an hour and a half of hard and pleasurable riding before he could bring himself to send her home.

Theo barely had time to absorb the idea that she would be married before the terms were set. Even as the last few guests climbed into their carriages, Mr. Delavert (Lucas, she supposed she ought to say) met with her mother in the library.

Afterward, Mrs. Becket brought the report to her daughter's room. Theo was sitting dazedly on the bed, still dressed except for her hair. Caroline had visited her already, with little to say beyond her kind if unconvincing certainty that everything would be for the best.

The mattress creaked as her mother sat.

"Mama," Theo said wretchedly, doubting her mother could reassure her any better than Caroline.

As it happened, her mother had no inclination to try.

"Well," she said, patting Theo's knee, "it is done, and if anyone has reason to be sorry, it will not be due to Mr. Delavert. In return for my blessing, he has agreed to settle the family debts and provide a dowry for your sister, which—in light of tonight's events—she may require. Truly, he has been more generous than we have any right to expect."

"Settle our debts . . . and provide a dowry . . ." Theo should have been pleased. Instead, she felt oddly nettled. Considering her mama's opinion of people who were in trade, she had not expected to be thanked, but with a word, Mr. Delavert—*Lucas*—had rendered irrelevant her every sacrifice.

With an effort, she swallowed back her pride. The knowledge that her mother must have bargained for these concessions mortified her, but she was in no position to throw stones.

"That was kindly done of him," she said aloud.

"Kinder than you deserve!" her mother burst out, obviously done with holding in her own reproofs. "What were you thinking, to trick him this way? Did you not believe you could win him fairly? Lately, you have been looking almost as pretty as Caroline. Anyone could see you were on your way to attaching him. And to announce to the entire attendance of the ball that you were sewing gowns! Our debts would have waited, but at least you might have kept it quiet. You are lucky Mr. Delavert would have you, trick or no trick."

I did not trick him, Theo tried to say, but nothing came out. Her mother's assumption that she had stung her to the quick.

"Oh, never mind," her mama said, fluttering her hand impatiently. "None of that matters now. Perhaps Mr. Delavert has some nice rich friends who'll fancy Caroline. A title would be pleasant. My pride does not require it, but for her sake, I should like to hear her called 'Lady.' "

This last proof of where Theo stood in her mother's heart stole what remained of her powers of speech. She had been sold, perhaps with some shame, but without regret. Fortunately, her mama required no response. She rose, stroked Theo's fallen hair, and looked down at her resignedly.

"You shall find your way," she said. "You always do."

This was small comfort when she closed the door behind her. Then the tears Theo had contained in her mother's presence began to well. She had everything she hadn't dared confess she desired. Sadly, the *way* she had it was as bad as anyone could conceive.

In agreeing to marry her, Mr. Delavert was acting the gentleman. No doubt he had, as her mother put it, grown a bit attached, but Theo could not persuade herself his liking would increase. Caught as he had been, even if through no deliberate plot of hers, a lessening of his fondness would make more sense. Why, someday he might resent being forced to marry, which was the last thing she'd been dreaming of.

I want him to love me, she admitted to herself at last. *And I want to know it is safe for me to love him back.*

Chapter 17

*Though Lucius wished their marriage to be an occa-*sion, if only for Theo's sake, delay seemed unwise. However little religious rituals meant to him, they were important to her. Until she was his in the sight of the human god, he knew he would not relax.

Mrs. Becket, practical soul that she was, shared his opinion. In consequence, all was organized swiftly: a special licence, a new dress for Theo, flowers for the tiny chapel on Hadleigh's grounds. The Connors and Theo's uncle were invited, but no other guests. Though Edmund scowled through the vows, for the most part the sunset ceremony went off without a hitch.

Lucius would never forget how Theo's hand had trembled when he slid on the ring.

She had been pale, poor thing, in her plain pink silk from the now infamous Mrs. Black. She seemed more stunned than unhappy, though he'd had trouble reading her. With all that had passed, he supposed she was unconsciously guarding her thoughts. In time, he hoped she would grow easier with him as her husband.

The word made him feel a bit stunned himself. When he'd engineered this marriage, he had wanted more time to win her in truth. He had not realized how much offering those age-old human promises would mean to him. And when she returned them . . .

It had not mattered what pressure she was under then. His heart had leapt and his face had flushed. She was his—or at least she would be tonight. One act remained to insure that.

In light of this, Theo's mother had suggested Caroline stay on temporarily. Delavert's memories informed him the practice was not uncommon: that sisters sometimes accompanied a couple on their honeymoon. Whatever increased Theo's comfort he was happy to do. Caroline, however, was sleeping soundly in her room. Lucius had no compunction about ensuring that. Theo might not know it, but she was safe. Nothing could make him hurt her tonight. Her sister could stay as long as she pleased, but for the next twelve hours, he was damned if he'd risk even a kindly interruption.

He opened the door to his chamber without knocking.

His resting place was a ship of a bed, with heavily carved posts and a rolling sea of French linen. Both layers of the hangings were tied back, revealing the coltish form of the woman who sat within. Lucius experienced a moment's start. Theo clutched the covers under her arms, but beneath this shield, she was bare. Even more surprising, she had called for extra candelabra. An assortment was now scattered around his room, filling the space with the scent of beeswax and golden light.

With this quantity of illumination, a human would have found it easy to admire her charms.

Her bold lighting choice aside, his bride's wide eyes and contracted muscles told him she was tense. Feeling a bit like his wolf stalking timid prey, Lucius crossed the carpet cautiously. He stopped at one of the bed's lower posts. Despite his desire to be calm and calming, his breath caught in his throat.

He gestured at the nearest candles. "This is unexpected."

"Mama told me . . . men . . . like to see things. I hope she did not err."

Lucius laid his hand on her covered foot. Her chill was palpable through the bedclothes, and he rubbed her toes soothingly. "Men do like to see things, though they do not necessarily expect their brides to be this considerate."

Theo blushed and looked down. "I do not want you to feel you've made a bad bargain."

"Theo." He moved beside her, taking a seat on the soft mattress. It seemed premature to confess he loved her, but some reassurance she must have. "Sweetheart, Fate may have taken a hand in this match, but I wish you to know I am not displeased. You are precisely what I would have chosen in a mate."

Clearly doubting this, she bit the delicious cushion of her lower lip. Lucius swallowed his urge to groan.

"Do you wish to take off your clothes?" she asked politely.

He stroked her hair behind her shoulder, savoring the silken whisper of locks and skin. Her hair was glossier than he remembered. She must have been doing something to it: washing it in egg whites, or whatever concoctions women used.

Beneath his caresses, Theo shivered just a tiny bit.

"I would like to kiss you," he said, "since I know you enjoy that."

"Are you sure? Mama also said men like to be naked."

"I begin to have more respect for your mother. Would you like me to undress, Theo? Maybe get the shock over with?"

"Yes, please—though I do not really think you'll shock me."

He had not expected to come to this smiling, but that he

could was a deep pleasure. "You might help me," he suggested, "If you wouldn't mind letting that blanket fall."

She did not protest his suggestion, though the determination its fulfillment took was obvious. He restrained his amusement as, jaw clenched, she let the covers drop to her waist.

Oh, she did remind him how much he liked looking, especially by candlelight. Her inner glow resembled the nimbus of the flames, gold meeting gold at the fragile barrier of human skin.

"You are beautiful," he said, drinking in her lovely vulnerable curves, her slender muscles, her endearingly gawky limbs. Her heart beat hard behind her ribcage, every inch of her trembling—not just with nervousness but with life. Though she could not look at him, she did not try to conceal herself.

"Caroline insisted you would like my appearance."

"Enough," he laughed. "I know they meant well, but your family may keep their opinions. Only you and I matter tonight." He took her hand, wrapping her palm in his as he pressed its back to his chest. Feeling how cold she was, he sent energy through the contact that she might warm. "Only you and I will know what passes between us. No one else has the right to judge."

Her eyes came up. He watched this new idea fill her mind, apparently intriguing her. Meeting her gaze was risky; he did not want to thrall her, but for this moment he could not resist.

After considering, she spoke. "You are not afraid of anything."

"Only that you will not enjoy yourself as much as I wish."

She grinned, abruptly no more fearful than a mischief-making girl. "Oh, you *are* a nice man, the nicest I have ever met!"

"I am glad you think so, because I mean for you to enjoy yourself quite a lot."

She flushed at that, which he always liked to watch, but a second later they were kissing. He could not have said which one of them moved, only that her hunger was so lovely he could not hold back his moans. Together, they tore him out of his clothes, a far more awkward and less ceremonious process than he had planned. As soon as he was free of garments, she squirmed over him on the bed where he had fallen back, her kisses deep, her hands eager, her naked skin as wonderful rubbing against him as any fantasy he could spin. The speed with which this encounter was unfolding took him aback. He began to suspect everything was going to happen faster than he'd intended.

He was not, after all, inclined to ask her to stop.

"God," he said, arching beneath her, his body painfully hard. He slid his thigh up between hers to make them part.

"Wait," she gasped. "I want to see you. I did not take my chance to look."

He let her push back, her face glowing like sunrise, her heat beating strong in the scented air. Revealed among waves of dark fallen hair, her nipples were raspberry red. His mouth watered in longing. He had to curl his lips together to hide his teeth. "Please," he said, the word like sand. "Take pity and look your fill quickly."

She laughed at him and, somehow, it made them equal. Her hand slid light as feathers down his chest, drawing a circle around his navel, ghosting over his pubic thatch. Her eyes followed her fingers' progress every step of the way.

His cock began to jerk with anticipation. She had touched him here before, but never without his thrall. He could not remain unmoved at the thought of that.

"You are beautiful," she said. "Every bit as much as I dreamed."

Her exploration reached his hardness, and he couldn't help sucking in a breath. "Theo!"

"Lucas!" she laughed in return.

He grimaced at the name, but when she skimmed his

shuddering length with her fingers, when she wrapped him in her hand and squeezed, he couldn't have cared less. The pad of her thumb tickled up a vein. Everything he wanted burst out in one demand.

"Rub me," he said. "Kiss me. Put your legs around my waist."

"What, all at once?" she teased, but he could not restrain himself. He took her mouth and rolled her beneath him, letting her feel his fully aroused body against her skin.

She did not mind his domination. Her sighs of rising enjoyment assured him of that. Her thighs moved around him of her own volition. She was hot and wet, her soft folds clasping the rigid underside of his shaft. They writhed together in a mutual greed for more friction. He began to read her desires—though he wasn't trying to. She wanted his hardness inside her, his arms locked tight, his kisses leaving marks on her throat.

He flinched, the image too close to what he craved himself.

"Please," she whispered before he could think of gathering his control. "Please make me yours."

Her hand slid down his body to find him, his jerk of reaction far more dramatic than her gentle grasp. He had to pant for air before he could speak.

"Wait," he said. "I will help." He put his hand next to hers on his penis, the intimacy of their cooperation unexpectedly moving. Both their hands tipped his thickness down. The head of him touched her wet, slick heat.

She gasped as he nudged the barrier at her gate, but he could not stop. He shoved and the sting snapped through him as if it were his own. Knowing it was not forced him to pause.

"Please," she urged despite her discomfort. Her hands slid down his haunches, her hips rising to take more. "Do not stop."

Her words stole everything but the urge to penetrate. His heart thundered hard enough to make him dizzy. In he sank with his muscles bunched, into soft creamy slickness, into the center of her warmth. He gripped her bottom to tilt her higher, digging his knees into the mattress, hiding his face in her hair.

He could not look at her. His power burned in him like a forest fire. He would sear her with his intensity. He would send her soul up in flames.

He pushed the final fraction with a moan of dread.

He was inside her then all the way. She held him, in her body and in her arms. Her hands smoothed up and down his perspiring back, and for a moment he simply marveled at his own response. His kind did not sweat easily.

Her lips pressed the pulse that beat in his neck.

She licked the salt from his skin.

If she'd had any inkling how much he wished he could do the same, she would have run in terror. Instead, she squirmed around his intrusion.

"I was not certain you would fit," she said, which made him both groan and laugh.

"Not only do I fit, but I'm going to move. Brace yourself, love. I'm very hungry for this."

Despite his warning, he did not rush. He could not; his nerves were too enraptured with delight. Each sleek, slow surge through her constriction sent his pleasure higher, until he did not know how one body could contain so many sensations.

Wanting more nonetheless, he rose up on his arms to permit a fuller range of motion for his hips, and to gain some distance from her throat. The temptation to sink his teeth was fierce, and the way she gazed up at him—half awe, half enchantment—did not help. He was trying to keep his arousal within tolerable bounds, but when she arched her neck and whimpered, his erection swelled.

Her fingers gripped his lower back hard enough for her nails to bite into his skin. "Oh," she said, high and reedy. "Do that again."

Upyr, especially those who'd been in existence for centuries, had more control over their bodies than humans did. In spite of this, Lucius could not call his obedience to her order deliberate. At her words, his cock stretched longer, until he truly was a bit large for her. The tight clasp of her around him made him grit his teeth.

He would never have guessed this act could be as sweet as feeding, and yet—with her—he could not deny it was.

Unfortunately, the first pleasure made him want the second more. To feed while making love was an *upyr*'s ultimate desire. His hips surged faster in a futile quest for distraction.

Her quavering moan was the opposite of complaint. She was cresting even then. Her shudders began deep inside her, squeezing over his shaft in ripples from root to tip. She called a name his blood was roaring too loud to hear, but the images in her mind were clear. *More,* they begged, and *deeper,* and *please, do it hard enough to make me cry.*

He gave her what she wanted, working deeper, harder, until he feared he would lose his mind. She came again, her contractions stronger. He was too sensitive for this, too tightly wound from waiting, but he kept his cock pumping in and out as fast as he dared.

No human could have withstood the extremes of feeling he experienced then. The veins in his neck stood out like wires. They felt like wires, as if an electric current were running through him instead of blood: hot and snapping, the sparks waking drives so basic no force on earth could turn them back.

He was going to bite her. His fangs had run out like knives, throbbing rhythmically with hunger. His throat ached with it, even his soul. Though he knew the danger, though he'd sworn to do her no harm, he could not stave this off. His head fell back on a groan of deep erotic agony.

"Your face," she gasped, seeing a hint of something she should not.

"Close your eyes," he managed to grate out even as he

pumped desperately. He had been trying not to thrall her and did not know if she would obey. He couldn't shield her gaze himself; his hands were clenched in the sheets. "Darling, please close your eyes."

He struck the instant she did so, her blood flooding his mouth with orgasmic bliss. He came with blinding force, taking her into him even as his ecstasy roared out. His sense of whose pleasure was whose threatened to dissolve. Her hands clutched the back of his head to hold him closer. His feeding—thank the angels—felt good to her. She convulsed around him, her next climax spilling over and doubling his.

He moaned against her throat. Stopping was impossible. The best he could do was slow. This was too close to heaven. She was his. She was in him, just as he was in her. The circle of it bound his heart.

Theo, he thought. *My God, how I love you.*

Chapter 18

Light burst behind her tightly shut eyelids, each flare a shiver of pleasure. Her husband's body trembled in her arms. The image of his face stayed with her: his need, his dark excitement, as if ecstasy and torment were identical. He had thrust inside her until their hipbones met, and instinct told her what his jerking movements meant. His groans ran like honey from her ears to between her thighs. When the pull of his mouth increased, and she felt him spill a second time, she thought she'd die of delight.

Instead, the world around her dissolved.

She was at a glittering party, high in a tower in the crystal city that was her home. Windows stretched all around her, providing a full-circle view of Arris at night. This building was the terminus for three ley lines. Air traffic skimmed from its landing pads, riding the earth-power like lighted beads on strings. Jewels were nothing to the sight, though plenty sparkled here. The murmur of people chatting in a dozen languages filled her ears, her pleasure increased by the fact that she spoke them all—including the one that had traveled here from the stars.

Not that Mena needed to speak *upyri*. As multilingual as their visitors were, she had learned their language for fun.

No, her job was ensuring that humans and *upyr* rubbed along peacefully—and, of course, that humans kept the upper hand. It was easy to forget *upyr* had weaknesses at all. But that's what treaties were for: to balance differences in power. Mena was very good at maneuvering the ins and outs of that.

She was smiling to herself when a suspensor tray full of drinks glided past her shoulder. The flying toys were all the rage this year, despite their tendency to cause accidents. Happy for the convenience, she nabbed a glowing blue cocktail whose rim was crusted with salt. Its contents were so icy they trailed vapor. As always, the first swallow was the best.

Oh, it was good to be bright and influential and at least relatively young. Looks didn't hurt, though those could be enhanced easily enough. Her silver gown—if this skimpy scrap of material deserved the name—flowed sleek as water to her knees.

Mena had no doubt her selection would please the particular guest she was interested in.

Sadly, the hand that caught her elbow did not belong to him. "Glad you could make it," said her superior from the embassy.

"Don't I always?" Mena hid her dislike behind a brilliant smile, though she doubted he liked her any more than she liked him. He had the decency to know gifts like hers were hard to replace, but that didn't mean he couldn't screw up her career.

"Watch yourself tonight," he said. "Don't be spending all evening with that *upyr*. You know how it looks for one of my crack negotiators to be getting cozy with the neck biters."

Mena pretended not to notice the slur. "How can I be a crack negotiator if I don't become familiar with my opponent?"

"Just don't forget he *is* your opponent."

"I never do. Being on different sides is part of the fun."

She left him to watch her make a lazy saunter through the crowd. Her heels were too high for comfort, but they certainly improved the show. Each clack against the marble tiles sent her pulse higher. Seconds later, a tingle between her brows announced her quarry had spotted her. Human or not, she was sensitive enough to know when someone probed her mind. She saw him then, in all his glowing white glory.

He was smiling faintly as he lounged against the curving window in his evening clothes. Some *upyr* damped their looks with glamour so they could fit in, but she had never once seen Lucius bother. He was alien from head to toe, too beautiful, too graceful, too humming with energy. Even his arrogance called to her deeper reaches—maybe especially his arrogance.

The quip might have come better from him, but he looked good enough to eat.

His silver eyes glowed brighter as she approached, the only sign that her presence excited him. He did not straighten when she stopped a short foot away.

"Tell me, Mr. White," she said, her voice slightly husky, "how do your kind feel about getting a lady a drink?"

His gaze dipped to her glass. "You appear to have one."

She tossed back the rest and smiled.

"In that case," he said, meeting her smile with one of his own, "generally speaking, we feel good about keeping our women as happy as we can."

"Your women." She laughed despite the thrill skating down her spine, a thrill that reversed course when he leaned closer. His scent was as clean as a rainwashed star.

"Isn't that why you're here?" he purred. "Dressed in that delectable shred of tissue, which—incidentally—matches my eyes? Because you're thinking about becoming my woman?"

She grinned. She couldn't help it. She liked fencing with him too much. "I don't know, Mr. White. Perhaps I'm thinking about you becoming my man."

Lucius was out of the bed so swiftly that when his back hit the wall, the plaster cracked.

I don't know, Mr. White. Perhaps I'm thinking about you becoming my man.

Those were Mena's words, issuing from Theo's mouth. He gaped at her. She appeared to be sleeping soundly. Her neck was smooth. He could not remember healing the marks of his bite. He must have done it without thinking.

He wished he could stop thinking now. Thc night Mena decided to take their banter to the next stage had been the best night of his life until then. Seeing himself through her eyes, the cocky immortal he'd been back then, told him he and Delavert had more in common than he had guessed.

But how could Theo possess Mena's memories? Lucius knew she was not Mena reborn, had known it from the start. Unless . . .

He pressed one unsteady hand to his mouth.

Maybe these weren't Mena's memories. Maybe they were his. Maybe he had taken them from her the way he had Delavert's. Once upon a time, he must have wanted to cling to whatever he had of her. In the closeness of their consummation, maybc Theo had read the very moments he most wanted to forget.

Those piled-up centuries were too heavy to be carrying now. If Lucius let himself remember, he would break beneath the weight of the loss, before his marriage even had a chance. Theo had to stay separate—as did his past. Else, how could he steer their course to a different end?

God help him, he should not have bitten her again.

"Lucas?" she murmured, rousing sleepily. She dragged one hand through her tousled hair. "My goodness, I must have swooned. You would laugh if I told you the dream I had."

Hoping she would not, he returned to her cautiously.

"You left the bed," she said.

He tried to smile. "I wanted to clean up."

Satisfied with this evasion, she sagged back against the pillows. "Mm. You are the cleanest man I know. Mr. Brummel is right to recommend daily baths. You always smell heavenly."

He sat with her, stroking her fingers until she slept.

Then he rose, not because he wished to leave, but because he feared if they engaged in more of this sort of bedsport, she would unearth every memory he had worked so hard to entomb. Affection was not enough to guarantee their future, nor was desire. Theo's love had to be deep and unconditional. As yet, he had no guarantee of that.

Lucas's absence pulled Theo from their bed. To her surprise, she found him slumbering on the sofa in the dressing room. The hour was early. From cracks in the heavy curtains came a hazy light. Even this seemed too much for Lucas. Though the sofa's upholstered back blocked him from the windows, he had pulled both sheet and blanket over his head.

She stared at the shape his long body formed. Should she be hurt that he had left their bed? Her mother's instructions about her "duties" had not covered this. But perhaps she had been snoring, or maybe Lucas was unused to sharing a bed.

Ha, she thought, though the theory did improve her mood. She knelt beside the lump that was her new husband. They were married, *very* married to judge by last night. Surely she ought to feel she could touch him now.

Careful not to wake him, she drew the covers from his face. In the dimness, his skin looked pale as snow. His lashes were spun silver, his beautifully shaped mouth relaxed and still. Even when she stroked the hollow of his cheekbone, he did not stir.

As she grimaced at the ease with which he slept quietly, his chest lifted on a breath. Unaccountably startled, she watched a faint pink flush creep across his cheek.

"Sun," he complained, fumbling for the blanket in his sleep.

Before she could cover him, his eyelids fluttered groggily open. His pupils were eerily small.

"I am sorry," she said. "The bed was empty. I wondered where you had gone. Why are you sleeping here?"

Though she blushed for asking, he only blinked hard and slow. "Didn't want to bother you. You're still new to this."

"I was not—" *bothered,* she tried to say, but he had sunk into sleep again. At a loss, she covered his head and rose. Come to think of it, she was tired herself. Her limbs felt as if they were carved of stone. She debated putting a pillow on the floor beside him, then decided that would be too strange, especially if the maids came in and saw.

Whether she was entitled to be hurt or not, she knew she was as she climbed back into bed alone.

Despite its awkward beginning, the next week of her marriage unfolded smoothly enough. The events of the ball seemed to have frightened off potential callers, but Theo did receive friendly letters from Katie Connor and her uncle's wife. Because her husband appeared not to miss his former guests' attentions any more than she did, she had no regrets. Any social ambitions he had harbored on his return to Bridesmere seemed to have worn off. For this Theo was thankful. She doubted a churchman's daughter could have helped his prestige.

Given how quiet the house consequently was, Theo was glad for her sister's presence—though as a general source of comfort rather than a necessity. Despite their mama's instructions to watch over the newlyweds, Caroline was not in their company much, evidently determined to give them plenty of privacy. Caroline's behavior made Theo smile, for she almost seemed to be avoiding her. That she knew her sister would never do. No marriage, no matter how irregular, could ever come between them.

In her sister's relative absence, her husband was all consideration—too much consideration, Theo thought. Such careful manners could not better their knowledge of each other to any great degree. She did her best, however, to get used to her new role and to trust that—in time—her confidence would increase.

Her most immediate worry was an inexplicable increase in her appetite. When the table was set with food a few days later, she ate almost everything that was laid out: racks of toast and eggs and salmon, not to mention coffee and sausage.

Her husband barely touched the spread, and Caroline was, per recent habit, eating in her room. A "headache," her maid had said. A new novel, was Theo's guess.

Lucas smiled at the decimation, apparently unfamiliar with what ladies ought to consume.

"You will be a favorite," he said over his teacup. "Edmund and I rarely do Hadleigh's cook such a compliment."

They sat in the yellow drawing room with the shutters and curtains closed. It was five in the afternoon, well past the hour for breakfast, but ever since Lucas had explained his sensitivity to the sun, she had been trying to adjust her schedule to suit his. The change was easier than she expected, almost natural. This afternoon, she felt as sleepy as Lucas looked, though that might have been due to her gluttony.

"I shall grow fat," she exclaimed in dismay.

"Hardly—considering how busy you have been keeping."

Lucas's droll expression brought a pleased, shy heat to her cheeks. They *had* been busy, every night as soon as the sun went down, at least three or four times. She wished she could tell him he need not set this limit for her sake, but raising the topic seemed delicate. She was afraid she would sound as if she were complaining, when in fact the opposite was true. Lucas was so very good at the marital act that it was difficult not to be greedy. It frustrated her that whenever their lovemaking appeared to approach a genuine meeting of souls, he would stop, saying he did not want to impose.

He seemed to *want* to think she was frail. Maybe he was correct to do so. Maybe most women were. All she knew was he had yet to spend an entire night in bed with her.

The omission had her counting the minutes until each day's end. She really had not had a chance to sate herself with him.

"I could be busier," she said before realizing how it would sound.

Lucas's eyebrows rose.

"I mean, busy in the house. I am the mistress of Hadleigh. I know I have no experience with large establishments, but your steward need no longer manage everything."

"Edmund likes managing everything."

Theo saw she had misstepped. Lucas had set down his teacup and was regarding her with surprise. She dropped her gaze to her hands. "If you prefer the way Mr. Fitz Clare runs things, perhaps he could instruct me. I must do something, Lucas. I would not have you think your wife is afraid to work."

"And I would not have my wife think she must work—especially when we have been married barely a week!"

He had jumped to his feet in apparent anger. Theo's mouth fell open as a salt dish—probably placed too close to the table's edge—tumbled to the floor. Lucas dropped to one knee to catch it, the motion as neat as a pin. To her amazement, when he set the dish back on the table, not a grain had been spilled.

"My goodness," she said. "What a lucky catch."

Lucas struck her speechless with his muttered curse.

A second later, he pressed his palms to his eyes. "Forgive me. My frustration is not your fault. You are not accustomed to sitting about like a doll. It is only natural if you are bored."

Theo was at his side before she could worry if this was forward. She laid both hands on his taut forearms. "Of course I am not bored. How could I be with you for company? I merely want to be a part of this house instead of a guest. I will wait to assume any duties, if you think it right."

He stared at her, then looked away—something he did too frequently these days. "I want you to be happy."

"I am happy. Heavens, Mama would say I am happier than I deserve. Think of all you have given me, all you have given *us*."

This answer did not please him. Pulling slightly away, he slid his graceful fingers down an unused fork. "If you would like to visit your mother . . ."

"You are kind to offer, but I would rather not."

She had spoken more tersely than was proper. Hearing this, a smile warmed his stone-gray eyes. "I should have guessed you might be enjoying your respite from maternal care. I am aware she believed you tricked me into marrying."

The reminder pricked her feelings. "Mama should have known better, but I suppose it is just as well. Now I finally know what she thinks of me."

"Oh, I do not think you know that," her husband said gently. "She loves you, Theo, every bit as much as she loves your sister. You and your mother are simply too different for her to read what is in your heart."

"Everyone says our tempers are alike."

"Your tempers, maybe, but not your understanding. You are young, too young perhaps to believe what I say, but in many ways you are older than your mama. Your heart is more forgiving and your mind broader. You do not judge the world as she does. For this reason, it is you who must make allowances for her."

A tear ran unchecked down Theo's cheek. "How can you see this in me? How can you know?"

He looked down at her—grave somehow, despite his beautiful smile. "I see it because it is there."

She wanted to believe him, though she knew her character also held traits a good deal less flattering. "I was furious at her for haggling with you," she admitted, grateful to have the chance. "I thought I would die of shame when she told me the terms to which you'd agreed."

Lucas laughed at this, a low rumbling sound she knew she could grow to love. "I confess I admired her tenacity. Despite your mother's scorn for the merchant class, she is a formidable bargainer."

Theo could not help but smile in return. She did not know how he'd accomplished the miracle, but he had made her feel a hundred times better. Observing her change in mood, he lifted her for a hug she was all too pleased to return. When he set her down, he did not let go.

"Read to me," he murmured against her ear. "I have grown curious about those novels your sister always has her nose in. I want to watch the sun set listening to you. Since our marriage, I have come to think your voice the loveliest in the world."

Flattery such as this could not be unwelcome. "As long as you do not ask me to sing," she said, a grin curving her lips. "That truly would pose a threat to our happiness."

His arms were clasped playfully behind her waist. "We cannot have that. I believe in keeping my women happy."

Your women, Theo nearly repeated until a shiver stopped the words. She was almost certain the man from her dream, the one who looked like Lucas, had said the same. The coincidence was enough to make her wonder just how close married people got.

Unsettled, she searched for a distraction. "Perhaps tomorrow, if you do not have other plans, we might pay a call to Bridesmere Castle. Percy Fitz Clare is our nearest neighbor. If we keep our visit brief, we should not displease his guardian."

Lucas stiffened in her arms. It seemed he liked this idea no better than her managing his house.

"We shall see," he said. "I cannot promise it will be convenient."

Theo regretted having brought this distance into his manner, especially when they'd been having a pleasant coze, but, "He is just a boy," she felt bound to say, "and probably lonely. Surely we can spare some time from our own happiness to add to his."

"We'll see," Lucas repeated and pulled away.

Though Theo did not understand his reaction, she knew she was in the right. Even if this time did count as their honeymoon, the little baron deserved company.

Lucius's powers were not required to read Theo's disappointment. Her face, unlike his, was the proverbial open book. He wished he could have answered differently. The closeness they had been sharing was precisely what he needed to encourage if she was going to fall in love.

Given her expression, he was almost grateful when she turned her back and began stacking things for the maid to clear—as undoubtedly had been her habit at home. Alas, even her spine was eloquent, speaking to him of hurt and unsureness. Her stubbornness was writ there, too. She wasn't going to let the question of Percy drop. Why should she? Alone in the world but for his inhuman guardian, the boy would probably love nothing better than to meet his pretty, kind, and still mischievous cousin. From the stories Edmund's son had told, the two were destined to get on.

The devil of it was, they were just as likely to become confidantes. Lucius was not ready to have Theo know the truth about what he was, and most definitely not from a five-year-old.

He was tempted to tell her he would ask Robin's permission, but such prevarication was not worth the breath it would cost. All it could gain him was a delay. In the end, Theo was as likely to ignore Percy's guardian if she disagreed with him. To Lucius's dismay, the knowledge made him admire her more. The person Theo was, without supernatural influence, merited protection.

"I will leave you," he said, not knowing what else to do. "And return for you at sunset."

Her face was soft when she turned from straightening the table, as if she, too, could sense her spouse's doubts.

"I shall look forward to it," she said. "I always do."

He opened his mouth at her wistful tone, but could think of nothing helpful to say. He bowed instead, aware that between now and sunset he must contrive a concession—if not about Percy, then something else. If he did not, he was in serious danger of losing what ground he'd won.

Chapter 19

"I do not think those curtains block enough light," Theo said to the housekeeper. "Perhaps we could hang a shade beneath."

Left at loose ends by her husband, Theo and Mrs. Green were seeing to arrangements for an apartment of her own. Apparently, it had not occurred to Lucas that she might want one, but considering his reluctance to share his bed, she did not think he would mind. To her relief, Mrs. Green did not bat an eye. Indeed, she had guided her to rather grander chambers than Theo would have dared request.

"Mr. Perrin in town could special-fit some shades," Mrs. Green suggested now.

"Please send him an order then. I want Mr. Delavert to feel as comfortable here as he does in his own rooms."

Mrs. Green looked slyly amused but only said she was sure the master would be satisfied with the work.

"Shall I ask Mr. Fitz Clare to approve the expense?" Theo asked, belatedly remembering her husband's comments.

"For this?" Mrs. Green blew a scoffing noise. "This is

women's business. He'll only forget half the things you need. Besides, the master has plenty of money. If you had a mind to, you could furnish the whole place new."

"I knew this would go to your head sooner or later," said a gently teasing voice from the door.

"Caroline!"

Her sister appeared pleased by the exclamation. "The servants said you have been inquiring after me."

"Because I have not seen you in ages. Your maid claimed you had the headache so often, I began to wonder if it were true."

"I am well," Caroline said, though now that Theo looked at her, she seemed wan. As if she did not wish to be examined, she smiled at her kidskin boots. "From what I hear, you have not had much time to miss me."

"I have time now, assuming Mrs. Green can spare me. Why don't we take a walk around the garden?"

Theo could have sworn her sister blanched, but a moment later, she squared her shoulders. "A walk would be lovely. We can see what new flowers have come into bloom."

"It will be a short walk," Theo assured her, wondering if her sister really was unwell. "I'd like to be back by dusk."

"That," Caroline said, looking very much as if she wished to laugh, "is also what I have heard!"

"You asked for your own rooms," her husband said from the open door to his chamber. She could see this had taken him unawares.

"Yes," she said unsurely. "But they are not ready. I thought you would not mind my coming here again."

"Of course not. I—" He rubbed the groove between his mouth and chin. "I suppose most married couples have their own."

"I am fitting mine up so you may visit," she said, wondering if she understood his dismay. "They will have special shades and extra bed hangings."

He stepped inside, some of the tension leaving his face. Interestingly, he carried a black, book-sized box. "That is considerate. I am sure I shall enjoy visiting when I am asked."

She couldn't help laughing. His brows quirked at the sound.

"Forgive me," she said. "I am amused because I cannot imagine a visit from you being unwelcome."

"Good," he said, his approval shoring up her nerves.

"Is that for me?" she asked, nodding toward the box.

"Ah, this." Sobering, he set his burden on the bed. "I was wondering . . . hoping you wouldn't mind indulging me in a game."

His face was carefully composed, as if he were determined not to let her guess his feelings. That alone made her curious. Already stripped to her shift (for she was usually too impatient to waste a minute undressing once evening fell) she stepped to his side. The lid of the box lifted easily. She caught her breath at what it revealed. She had been expecting jewelry, but a set of wrist irons lay against the red velvet. A chain connected them, and the bracelet portion was lined in leather. Beneath this odd device lay a black blindfold. Neither bore signs of wear.

Theo pressed her fingertips to her mouth. Though the arousal she always felt when Lucas was near coursed through her, she was unable to hide her surprise. "Do you mean for me to wear these?"

He smoothed her hair from her face. "They are for me," he said, his tone as neutral as his expression. "I have observed—That is, it is my understanding that you would like to make love more often than we have. These restraints are my insurance that I cannot hurt you if we do."

"I never believed you would!"

"Not intentionally, but you are not accustomed to the appetites of a man as worldly as myself."

She could not like the reminder that he was worldly, though the fact that he had observed her disappointment and wished to address it did assure her he cared.

She looked from the manacles to him. "You would enjoy wearing these?"

He was watching her as closely as she watched him. "Being denied free movement can whet a man's desires. If you are too shocked, however . . ."

"No," she said as he trailed off. Truthfully, she was a little shocked, but the part of her that longed for him most also felt thick and hot. She spoke before he could worry.

"Have you—" The break in her voice forced her to start again. "Have you been wanting to make love more often, too?"

"I have been trying to strike a balance, but I confess I find it difficult to get enough of you."

His words were too husky for her to think he was uttering empty kindnesses. It was beginning to dawn on her that she had no idea what kind of man he was. Certainly, she never would have imagined he would ask this.

"I thought—" she said awkwardly, wanting to understand. "You always seem to enjoy being in control."

"I love being in control," he affirmed in a smoky growl. "That is part of what makes surrendering control exciting."

He was indeed more worldly than she was. This concept was one she would not have entertained on her own.

"And the blindfold?"

His body went still as stone. She found herself holding her breath until he moved again. "The eyes are the windows of the soul. Sometimes one feels naked baring them."

Just then, his eyes were molten silver hot from the forge. His gaze cut away, but the evasion could only hide so much. His hands were fisted at his sides, his normally pale color high. His erection, which she could not resist looking at, thrust hard against his trouser front. She imagined caressing it once she'd secured his hands, smoothing her fingers over the silken heat that had captivated her from the first. He would be her prisoner. She would be able to explore him, to pleasure him, to take him inside her just as she pleased. She could make certain neither of them finished this night one climax less than satisfied.

The prospect roughened her voice until she marveled she could speak at all. "I would like to make you happy."

The corners of his mouth tipped up. "And yourself?"

"And myself."

Her confirmation broadened his smile. As always, the whiteness of his teeth startled her. "You are a treasure," he said with an amusement so fond it resembled love. "Shall I show you how to lock me up?"

"Oh, yes," she said. "That would be most helpful."

Old as he was, Lucius did not fear the effect of the iron shackles, generally so deleterious to his kind. He was relying on it, in fact, to sap his strength enough to keep him bound. The leather padding would prevent the metal from leaving welts, but he would not be able to break free. Even more important, the blindfold guaranteed he would not thrall her.

For once, it would be safe for Theo to take her fill.

Looking forward to this, his body thrummed as she followed his instructions, running the chain behind the bed's upper posts while he stretched out on his back. The shackles held his wrists spread wide above his head. He shuddered briefly—though not without enjoyment—as Theo clicked the last bracelet closed.

"There," she said with a teasing smile. "Now you are at my mercy."

She had no conception how true this was. Had she known the weaknesses of his race, had she possessed an iron spike and a mallet to drive it home, being at her mercy would have had quite a different significance. Edmund would have been aghast but, oddly enough, Lucius's vulnerability excited him.

Catching a hint of this perhaps, his beautiful young wife peeled off her linen shift. His shirt she could only rip down the front and spread—a procedure she seemed to relish—but his lower body she bared entirely. His trousers gone, her hands smoothed upward in reverse course—ankles, shins, knees—sending shimmers of feeling throughout his thighs.

"Blindfold," he reminded before they forgot in the heat of things.

Theo bit her lip reluctantly.

"All or nothing," he said, despite his regret at losing the lovely picture her body made. "We cannot play this game halfway."

"You are right," she said, reaching for the black sleep mask. "I am not doing this to make you half-happy."

She secured the material snugly across his eyes, blocking most if not all the candlelight. He let out a sigh, his body relaxing and tightening at once. The deed was done. He had blinkered his superiority. He had put himself in her hands.

What he had not done was diminish his sensitivity. Without his sight, his other senses were heightened. Hairs stood up on parts of his body he had forgotten possessed them.

Theo had him more in her power than she guessed.

She kissed his eyes through the mask, crouching above him on hands and knees. The position woke desires he'd kept secret even from himself. *She* dominated now; *she* set the terms. His skin prickled with awareness as her aura fluttered over him like a breeze. She kissed his mouth, his nipples, then the hardness of his breastbone. She licked a tickling path around his navel that made his stomach muscles twitch. His thighs knotted with anticipation as her hands drifted between them to cup his stones.

She weighed them curiously in her palms.

"I think you want me to kiss you," she said, her breath

washing over his waiting cock. "I think you'd like me to suck you into my mouth."

He did not have to tell her she was correct. Her close, wet warmth slid over and down his crown, her laving tongue, her tugging lips . . .

"Oh, yes," he said, his buttocks tightening to push him deeper. "Oh, Theo, yes."

She hardly needed the encouragement. She sucked him without hesitation, with a fascination for his responses that flattered as much as it pleased. Her hands were all over him, on his pulse, his skin—as if she meant to memorize every throb and squirm. Out of the blue, he remembered how good Mena had been at this, how lightning had seemed to shoot from him when he came.

Theo was well on her way to getting just as striking results—and that was before she decided to swallow all of him.

Nerves that had missed this for far too long blazed like the sun. His spine arched off the bed as she sank down on him and pulled back. Her lips were tight, her suction strong. His reactions were running away from him, but this seemed to be what she wanted. When he began to thrash, she trapped his hips in her hands. As if she knew exactly which pleasure would agonize him most, she sucked the very tip of him, her tongue dragging deliciously back and forth. It was almost more stimulation than he could take in. His shaft stood perfectly upright without support, marble hard and human hot. A very particular pressure welled in his core.

"Ride me," he gasped before it was to late. "I want to spill inside you."

Her teeth tugged him in a manner that would have made a human do more than gasp. She was reminding him who ruled now.

"Oh, God," he begged, aroused beyond bearing. "Take me in."

Her slow slide up his body made him just as wild as her

mouth. Her firm little breasts brushed up his belly, warm and peaked. When they reached his chest, she rolled up, catlike, her knees squeezing his ribs. She was almost sitting on him, her heat hovering over his rigid cock. Pushed beyond his limits, he tugged at the irons until his hands went cold. His efforts were wasted. The metal's ache only made the rest sweeter.

"Careful," she said as his hips tried to rise to hers.

"Can't," he gasped, straining even harder.

She took pity on him, letting him push up as she sank down. His head slid into her, then his shaft. He felt huge, but her slickness eased him until the pleasure of being fully, deeply joined brought a groan of thankfulness from both their throats.

Her hands slid up and down his chest. "Oh," she purred. "I know why you love this. Every time we do it, I feel it more."

Her words plucked at something in his mind, a memory waving a distant flag. Before he could pinpoint what it was, she began to move, obliterating his train of thought in a wash of bliss.

She rode him as if she'd done it a thousand times, as if the chains and blindfold freed her as much as they freed him. She took him deep and then shallow, shallow and then deep, savoring the rub of him against her as if only his smoothness could soothe her itch. He gritted his teeth to hold on against such delectable thoroughness, loving every second of the suspense.

She loved it, too. She rode him until sweat rolled down her belly, until neither one could keep from cresting. Their release burst in a series of explosions that would not stop. Again they spilled, and again, each contraction spurring his need for the next. Her clasp was oiled and sweet, both reward and temptation. He could not soften for more than a few heartbeats.

Luckily, she did not tire any more than he did, but sighed with pleasure each time he stiffened up again.

If this was madness, he never wanted it to end.

"One more," she murmured, bending forward until her lips brushed his jaw. "One more will be enough."

Amazingly, he could not answer. He was panting too hard for breath.

She pushed up on her arms again, riding him fast this time, driving straight and hard to the end. This was the stroke he'd yearned for, the one that completely swamped him with ecstasy. He could tell how much she wanted the end herself. She was wet enough to drip down him, tight enough to squeeze like a fist.

He braced his shackled hands on the headboard as fireworks began to blossom behind his mask.

"Let go," she urged. "Don't hold back."

He scarcely believed he had been, but at her words some last restraint inside him snapped. The iron—so he thought—had been inhibiting the sharpening of his fangs. They slid out now, full length, and his neck arched violently. An odd little pain beneath his ear had his blinded eyes widening. Theo had nipped him. She could not break skin, but she was giving him the same sort of love bite as an *upyr.* The gesture, exquisitely timed to match his final rise, slammed him through the barrier of climax like a sledgehammer. He came as if he had not come all night—copiously and hard, with spasms so vehement they deserved notice even from him. He grunted, then stiffened even more as she came, too.

Lord, she was killing him. He was dying of sweet pleasure.

Long wrenching minutes later they collapsed, awash in a very human mantling of sweat.

"Oh, my," she sighed against his still pounding immortal heart. "Oh, my, my, *my.*"

Actually shaking, he kissed the parting of her hair. "If I had the strength to, I'd say the same."

Her head lifted unsteadily. "Was that enough for you?" she had the humility—or perhaps simply the insanity—to ask.

He could not restrain a laugh. "Yes, love, that was enough."

She snuggled down again happily. "You don't have to call me that. I am aware you cannot truly love me yet."

"Would you like me to?"

He held his breath, surprised by his own audacity. He had not planned to press her so soon. Thankfully, she did not mind. He felt her smile against him, her fingers playing gently through his cloud of hair.

"I shall let you know," she said with an archness that should have been beyond her years, "as soon as my heart decides."

Hope caused his ribs to tighten even as he cautioned himself her teasing did not mean she loved him yet.

Theo lay against him, basking in contentment. This was how one should feel after making love to one's husband: cherished and sated and too exhausted to move. The feelings were so strong in her, she nearly drifted off without freeing him. Her wish that he would put his arms around her was all that reminded her.

"Oh!" she exclaimed, jolting up. "How could I have forgotten?"

She untied his blindfold and then his wrists. His hands had grown so cold they were tinged with blue.

"You are icy," she exclaimed, pressing the poor, neglected appendages between her breasts. "Oh, Lucas, I am sorry."

Her chafing must have felt good, because he closed his eyes and his spine arched a bit, the way it did when she hit on a caress he especially liked.

"I am fine," he said. "I probably lost circulation."

"But you are cold up to your elbows! I do not think this is right."

His eyes came open. When he sat up and pulled from her hold, his face wore the same guarded look it had earlier.

"I should leave," he said. "I do not want to disturb your rest."

She longed to tell him his leaving disturbed her, but he was swinging out of the bed, his torn shirt fluttering as he reached for the trousers she had so happily tossed away. Muscles moved in his legs and haunches as he stepped back into them. Sadly, not even the beauty of his body could distract her from her dismay.

She could not believe he would leave her after what they had shared. What was wrong with her that he would not spend the night? For that matter, what was wrong with him? She blinked at the furious tears that rose to her eyes but, as evasive as Lucas was being, he was in no danger of seeing them.

Then, unexpectedly, he turned to her, clasping her face in his hands for a quick, deep kiss. For one heart-stopping moment, his eyes locked and burned on hers.

"Thank you," he said. "Tonight was a gift I shall not forget."

The swiftness of his departure left her no chance to speak. She stared at the closing door, more confused than she had ever been in her life. What did he mean by this? Why did he keep leaving when, clearly, he cared for her?

Theo had to discuss this with Caroline, no matter how personal it seemed. Her sister might not know the answer, but she would listen sympathetically. Theo needed that so badly she hurt.

Chapter 20

Caroline wasn't sure her sister realized how strange her husband's household was. Perhaps Mr. Delavert's sensitivity to the sun explained why his servants woke late, but not why every housemaid she met was starry-eyed and dazed.

Today, she was more relieved than usual to leave the hall's sultry atmosphere. Her dreams of the night before had been heated, and—unlike the maids—she was not free to pursue even one. As had become her habit, she headed for the stables. The grooms, at least, rose at a reasonable hour. Theo was too young to remember the days when the Beckets had owned a horse, but Caroline's one unalloyed pleasure—aside from the knowledge that her sister was well settled—was rediscovering the joys of a decent mount.

At Mr. Delavert's behest, a mare named Clover was made available for her use. Caroline had fallen in love with her gentle manners, though she knew that forming a permanent attachment to the horse was unwise. Theo might be nervous in her new role, but Caroline doubted this would last long. She had always been the braver of the sisters, and Mr. Delavert—despite a certain awkwardness of manner—patently adored her. Caroline could foresee the day when a sibling's presence became not only unnecessary but undesirable.

With a heart as heavy as the weather, she turned Clover down the trail that followed a small trout stream. She wished her sister every happiness in the world, but in some ways leaving Hadleigh would make her life easier. She would not have to worry what Theo might see if she looked too closely; would not have to work to hide her blushes and restrain her sighs. As undeniable as these advantages would be, Caroline also knew going home without her sister would be lonely.

She was getting a taste of that loneliness today. The waters of the stream were dark, purling in near silence over mossy rocks. Caroline's mind began to drift as she clopped along.

In her imagination, she saw Aidan Sheffield climbing a ladder to help Theo decorate, saw him making tea in a thick chipped cup, saw his face as he tried to loan her a book. Dwelling on these memories was pointless, but she could not push them away. If she were truthful, she would admit to wanting more.

Even after she returned to Bridesmere, she was sure to be asked to call. She would—now and then—be able to see Sheffield. He might visit the library in town again. They would speak a little, as they had before. If she were very careful, no one would suspect what she felt. This was not much consolation, but it did give her something to cling to.

Lost as she was in her thoughts, Caroline could not have said what woke her to the fact that Clover had stopped walking: the sound of the mare slurping from a puddle perhaps, or the growing tightness in her own body, the one that demanded a restless squirm against the sidesaddle.

Whatever the reason, when she looked up, she saw the object of her fantasies a stone's throw ahead. Sheffield stood facing the water, his back shielded against watchers by a stand of trees. His eyes were closed, his expression strained. Caroline flushed with awareness even before she saw that his hands were on the front of his breeches, cupping a large swelling there.

"Oh, God," he moaned, clearly unaware of his audience. "Oh, Caroline."

The sound of her Christian name took her by surprise. Her involuntary exclamation had him spinning around, every bit as scarlet-faced as she.

"Miss—Miss Becket," Sheffield stammered, his hands now flying behind his back. "Forgive me. I . . . I did not know you were there."

"Forgive me," she said. "I did not mean to intrude on your solitude."

She had not fooled him by pretending not to have seen. He looked completely miserable, but she understood better than he thought. She knew the madness that had driven him to this spot. She had been fighting it ever since coming to Hadleigh, as if the air here conveyed some carnal infection. She did not consciously decide to slide off the mare. She only knew she could not in fairness let him think himself alone.

He did not expect her to do this. His jaw fell as her feet touched the ground, though other than this he seemed nailed in place. He watched her take two steps closer with widened eyes.

"I understand," she said, her hand going out. "I do not think you need to apologize."

"But I do," he whispered. "I have no right to think of you."

Their gazes held, burning with all the things they could not spell out but comprehended perfectly.

"Maybe," Caroline said, her voice low and soft, "I have no right to think of *you*."

It was the boldest thing she had ever said in her life. His lips shaped her name without sound, the name he had called in his fantasy. He shook his head, but she had had her fill of feeling guilty. She finished striding toward him and laid her hands on his chest.

The thudding of his heart shook her palms.

"Do not tempt me," he said once he'd caught his breath. "You know you will regret it."

In answer, she slid her hand to his shoulders.

"Caroline," he moaned as if her caresses hurt.

The corner of her soul that was not and would never be a lady thrilled with delight.

"I will kiss you," he warned, "and it won't be the kiss I would give a girl."

"Good," she said, surprised to find herself smiling. "A girl's kiss isn't the sort I want."

This was more than even he could resist. He cried out as he lifted her, crushing her to his front with shocking directness. His mouth was hot, his body hard. Caroline clung to him with all her strength, reveling in every liberty he took. His groans made her want to rub him; his hold ensured that she could. When she mustered the courage to kiss him back, the heat that flared between them should have seared them both. She didn't know what would have happened if she hadn't heard someone call her name.

It was her sister. She stood among the trees holding Clover's bridle. She must have seen the mare ambling unattended and worried for her rider.

Horrified, Caroline stumbled back from Sheffield. "Theo! We didn't—this is not what it looks like."

Except . . . it was what it looked like. Worse, it might have been more had her sister not turned up. Now a married woman, Theo knew this fact very well. Giving up, Caroline covered her mouth and moaned.

"I thought you had more respect for Lucas than this," Theo said. "He does not deserve to be embroiled in another scandal by our family."

Though Caroline wished Mr. Delavert was not her sister's

first concern, she could not argue. Nor could she recover her earlier daring. Theo's disappointment saw to that.

"I am sorry," she mumbled. "It will not happen again."

Sheffield squeezed her shoulder in silent support. She did not want to imagine how he felt, being treated like a source of shame. That he *was* a source of shame she could not deny. Knowing this, she thought she'd never felt so horrible in her life.

Theo looked at her, then shook her head. "You are my sister," she said, "not my child. It is not for me to say how you live. Just be careful, Caroline. You know how much I love you."

Tears had thickened Theo's voice. She had to turn and lead the horse away.

"Oh, Theo," Caroline whispered behind her hands.

With all the other changes in their lives, the last thing she wanted was to lose her sister when she needed her most.

Evidently, the unnatural shifting of Lucius's sleep pattern could only be sustained so long. He did not wake until well after the sun was down, and when he did, he was groggy. While a lessening of his powers might prevent him from thralling Theo, he disliked the thought of weakness. If he were not careful, he would lose abilities he needed.

Frowning, he rubbed his face and sent his senses questing through his rooms. To his dismay, no sign of Theo met his search.

It was, he supposed, a taste of his own medicine.

After a bit of wandering, he found his wife in the music room picking out a tune. Lucius recognized it as the piece her sister had played that night at the Morrises. How long ago that seemed! And how far he had been from guessing to what strange end his attraction to her would lead. He glanced at the tea things sitting on a nearby table. They looked as if they had been nibbled at, then ignored.

"How long have you been here?" he asked. "Did you not sleep?"

Theo looked up with circles beneath her eyes. "I was hoping to speak to Caroline today, but she was . . . occupied."

This seemed a source of unhappiness.

"I would be pleased to listen," he said, wondering what could put such amicable sisters at odds, "if you'd care to speak to me."

Her lower lip quivered a moment before she bit it.

"I see," he said. "You wanted to speak to her *about* me."

He was already stepping closer when the tears she had been holding back spilled down. In a trice, he had taken possession of the piano bench and was cuddling her on his lap. Her weight was a comfort he had not known he desired. He kissed her soft, shining hair. "Ah, Theo, if you only knew how I wished I could make you happy."

"You do," she said indistinctly against his neck. "Happier than anyone—though it shames me to admit."

"Why should it shame you?"

She pulled back to dry her cheeks. "I haven't thought about Nathan in weeks," she confessed. "I do not think I have truly missed him since I met you."

Lucius did his best to hide the way his heart picked up. "You were young when you knew him."

"Yes, but now I am not certain I ever loved him. What I felt for him was simply not as, as big as what I feel for you. My sister did something which upset me earlier, and the first thing I considered was how it would affect you."

Her eyes were huge and pleading, and Lucius struggled to think straight. This confession troubled Theo, however much he welcomed it. "I regret any hurt this has caused you, but if you are—" He paused, not wanting to misstep. "If you are trying to say you love me, that could not possibly displease me. I love you myself, and have done so for quite some time. If you knew how deeply my feelings ran, I fear you would be alarmed."

He had spoken as lightly as he could, but her mouth gaped all the same. She pressed her hand to her bosom, then laughed breathlessly. "I believe I *am* alarmed. My heart is racing like a rabbit's."

Lucius was quite aware of this. His body had hardened the moment her pulse sped up. Giving in to temptation, he bent to kiss the smooth, warm skin above her low bodice. "If I said it again, do you think you'd be terrified?"

"Well, I might," she said, matching his humorous tone, "but I suspect I would appreciate it even so."

Her fingers were combing his hair behind his ear with the most enchanting gentleness. He met her smiling, tear-washed eyes.

"I love you," he said. "More than you can conceive."

She sighed and rested her head on his shoulder. "Now *that,*" she said, "makes me happy."

Edmund was leaving. Though her eyes were shut, Lily heard the distinctive *shoosh* of him pulling on a silk dressing gown. He had slipped out like this before, but in the past Lily's exhaustion from their activities had dissuaded her from discovering where he went. By the time she woke, he was always back. Tonight her pride pricked her to bestir herself. It was time she ferret out what was pulling her lover from the pleasure her embrace bestowed.

She waited until she heard the sitting room door close behind him, then tiptoed silently after.

Hadleigh's lower level was a maze of narrow, lantern-lit corridors, most painted a dingy brown. She lost Edmund once and had to retrace her tracks, but at last she caught up to him outside the drying room.

She was genuinely shocked to see her lover was not alone. One of the upper maids, a buxom, curly-haired Scot whose coarseness was only emphasized by her airs, had been backed by him to the wall. She must have invited the treatment because her hands were slithering up and down his robe. Her voice carried clearly to the corner where Lily hid.

"Is milady sleeping?" the maid teased with a gurgling laugh.

"Like a baby," Edmund replied.

Lily had to press one hand to her mouth to muffle a gasp. She could not believe they had the audacity to be joking about her. She ground her teeth together as the maid's crafty expression intensified.

"I knew she could not tire you out. A real man could never get everything he needed from a juiceless stick like her."

"Certainly not every manner of thing I need."

Lily nearly bit her tongue with rage. How dare he? Edmund knew she was the best and most beautiful lover he'd ever had. He must be playing a game, lying to this stupid slattern for some reason she could not guess. That would explain why he made no move to take her, though the maid's hands had parted his robe and were now caressing him inside. Edmund hardly reacted. He seemed more interested in nuzzling her plump and probably unwashed neck.

"Oh, yes," sighed the maid, her head falling back. "Nip me the way you like."

She *would* like that, Lily thought scornfully, stroking her own unmarked skin. But then a change came over Edmund which made her want to rub her eyes. His lips pulled back and his teeth flashed white, some trick of light and distance making them look unusually sharp and long. They struck the maid's neck with an audible slapping sound.

This was followed by a mutual groan.

Tricks of the light aside, what Edmund was doing was more than a nip. He appeared positively locked to his partner's neck. His cheeks were hollowed, his Adam's apple working up and down. A rosy flush crept over his normally pale face and chest. Lily had to be mistaken, but it looked very much as if he were drinking blood from her vein. Even more peculiar, it looked as if the maid relished it. She had gone so limp with pleasure, Edmund had to hold her up. Lily could not doubt he was ready to swive her now. When he flung off his robe, his organ was as long and thick as Lily's beauty had ever made it.

With a grunt of impatience, he drew up the maid's plain frock and speared her to the wall.

More moans of pleasure met this assault. The maid wrapped both legs around him and drummed his buttocks with her heels. With all her thrashing, her cap fell quite unnoticed to the floor. It was hard to credit, but she seemed to be enjoying her ride even more than Lily had enjoyed hers.

This ride was certainly fast. Edmund's hips were a blur, his back hunched to keep his mouth fastened on her neck. Lily would have felt superior had this haste not suggested her own efforts had left him unsatisfied. Barely a minute passed before he thrust up hard and spilled.

With a sigh as musical as it was lengthy, Edmund let the maid slip down. Looking nearly as dazed as his partner, he lifted his head.

His lips were stained with blood all around.

Lily began to shake as he licked them savoringly clean. The maid's neck was bloody, too, with two dark puncture wounds. Lily feared she would be ill when Edmund bent to drag his tongue over them. The marks and the blood were gone by the time he stopped.

Lily did not know what to make of this. In truth, she wasn't sure she cared how the girl had healed. Her breath came ragged as she watched her lover clasp his current partner's jaw. The maid's eyes opened reluctantly. Like a mouse entranced by a cat, she fell still as his gaze probed hers.

Appropriately enough, Edmund's voice sounded like a purr. "This was a nice encounter, was it not? And you especially liked my love bite."

"Oh, yes," the maid concurred dreamily. "I always love that."

Edmund swatted her bottom as if amused. "Off with you then. Have a bite to eat in the larder and get some rest. I'll see you again tomorrow night."

The maid ran her hands across his collar bones. "Promise you are not going to someone else?"

The thought that he might still be greedy widened Lily's eyes.

Edmund kissed the maid's temple. "Not that it is your business, but I am taking some exercise—the kind I cannot get with pretty girls like you."

The maid's gratified simper was no better than Lily would expect. What Lily did not expect was how completely set she was on discovering where he went next. Never mind her fear: This depravity—and whatever else might follow—was the secret Edmund and Delavert had been hiding. She had to know its full extent before she could decide how to turn it to her advantage.

Of course, if no advantage was to be had, she would settle for revenge. Lily Morris would not play second fiddle to a lady's maid.

She slipped into a storeroom to let the girl go by. When she caught up to Edmund again, he was crossing the kitchen garden. He soon outpaced her, but that might have been just as well. His hearing seemed very sharp, his head turning alertly with every sound. This heightened her suspicions, every one of which seemed justified when he met Delavert in the grassy bottom of a wilderness.

The spy in her exulted. She'd known those two were conspirators.

She crouched on the slope above them, her presence hidden by a thorny bush. She was too high to hear what greeting they exchanged, but her brows shot up as both began to strip. Though she'd expected more degeneracy, it was not of this nature. To her surprise, they did not touch or embrace, merely stood side by side under the stars.

Despite her agitation, Lily couldn't help admiring their naked forms.

Her distraction ended when a candlelike glow began dancing—faintly at first and then more brightly—around each man. A soft ringing traveled to her ears, as if the rim of a crystal goblet were being stroked by a damp finger. Gooseflesh chilled her skin an instant before the glow flared like the sun. When she finished blinking, two large wolves stood in place of the men—no doubt the very wolves Theo Becket claimed to have seen.

One beast woofed quietly to the other, pointed his muzzle northward, and loped off. The other looked over its shoulder—almost in her direction—before following. Something about the attitude of its head, coupled with its sharp blue eyes, convinced her of what she would much rather have denied.

Crazy as it seemed, those wolves were Edmund and Delavert.

Lily sat back on her heels, the wind knocked out of her by the discovery. Those two were more than degenerate: They were horrors!

Delavert must have made some devil's bargain while he was living with the heathens in the West Indies, most likely trading his immortal soul for the power to run as a beast. Whether Edmund had joined him willingly she could not guess. She did know that when he bit the maid and drank her blood, the animal inside him had been rising up. Lily had not been able to satisfy him because his appetites were unnatural.

Her hand flew to her throat. She was lucky she had refused to let him bite her. Otherwise, she would have been as much under his spell as the stupid maid. He had used his infernal influence to convince the chit she liked the awful things he did.

No wonder Lily felt such fear of Delavert the night of the

ball. Her memory of what had happened in the folly was confused, but she must have sensed the monster he hid inside. Oh, it was the most infamous scheme she had encountered outside a novel! God must have been looking out for her when He inspired her to run.

Her mind reeling, she pushed unsteadily to her feet. This outrage could not be allowed to stand. She must do something, and cleverly. If those two fiends discovered she knew their secret, her life—maybe even her soul—would be at risk. Before this, she would not have said she valued her soul. Now the knowledge that she did braced her with righteousness.

She was also glad to have solved another mystery. She finally knew why Delavert preferred Theo Becket to herself. Apparently, one could not expect monstrous beings to have good taste.

Chapter 21

Theo dreamed she heard a man crying out in pain. A terrible brightness glared all around him, trapping him in his agony as surely as iron bars. Gasping for air, she thrashed her way from the nightmare. When she poked her head beyond the hangings of Lucas's bed, thin bars of midday sunlight pierced the room.

She rubbed her knee, which was aching as if she'd slept on it wrong. Her husband was gone, of course. No matter what avowals they exchanged, it seemed he could not be induced to stay. She might as well have removed herself to her now-finished rooms. But perhaps that impulse was childish. If she loved Lucas, shouldn't she accustom herself to his quirks? She simply wished she knew why he kept leaving.

In the cold light of day, without Lucas to hold her close, it was difficult to believe he really did love her.

Ordering herself not to act the ninny, she pushed out of bed to dress as well as she could without help. As she hooked her corset up the front, she remembered Lucas's face from the night before: shy, pleased, shining with hope that what he felt was shared. No one with a particle of judgment could think he lied.

"He does love me," she murmured. Lingering doubt notwithstanding, saying the words made her smile.

Hoping to share the feeling, she paused at the sofa where Lucas lay. Careful not to let the sun's rays reach him, she lifted his blanket and kissed his cheek. His skin was cool, and he did not move at her touch. He was the quietest sleeper she had ever met. Disappointed, she told herself he would sense she had been there—a bit of romanticism she had no wish to reason away.

It did not occur to her to wonder where she was going until she reached the front entry. She *was* a little hungry. In an ordinary house that kept ordinary hours, a maid would have woken her with a tray. As Hadleigh was hardly that, she was left to forage. She looked behind her toward the servants' corridor. Though the cook might not be up, some sort of edibles could be scrounged.

Despite her empty stomach, she frowned at the idea of staying inside. Her dream of the crying man echoed in her mind. What she needed was a dose of daylight, a benefit she had not gotten enough of recently. She was certain a walk outdoors would blow away the remnants of her nightmare.

As soon as her course was decided, she felt easier. She proceeded briskly down the gravel path that led to Hadleigh's woods. The sun was bright, the breeze warm and pleasant, and her niggle of worry about Caroline was shaken off. She would talk to her sister later, once she could speak calmly.

Strangely impatient with her pace, she left the path to hurry down a heathery slope, holding up her frock so as not to trip. She squinted against the sun. Had it been this bright when she came out? It was enough to give a person the headache. In fact, she thought she had the start of one. An odd throbbing pulse was beating between her brows.

Please, someone called. *Please, someone hear me.*

Theo looked about her in consternation. She was surrounded by empty pasture. No one was near enough to have spoken, not even a sheep. Her heart pounded with an inexplicable urgency. She had to run. She had to head for the trees.

Though she did not know why she did it, and would have been embarrassed had someone asked, she flew over the ground in her ankle boots. Over the next rise she went, through the little wilderness by the grove of firs. No matter how foolish she felt, she did not slow. She had to go faster. Someone needed her.

She was among the trees when a whine of pain came from behind her. She spun around so swiftly she nearly fell. One of Hadleigh's wolves lay panting in a patch of shade. His hind leg was caught in an iron trap, a huge one, half as large as his whole body. Theo's breath caught with pity. The traps's teeth were driven through his flesh. Blood oozed around the metal. The amount that had soaked the ground beneath him filled her with foreboding.

"Oh, poor thing!" she cried, moving toward it unthinkingly. Catching herself, she stopped and pressed her hands to her breast. Town girl though she was, she knew better than to approach a wounded predator. As if it sensed her fear, and despite what must have been a maddening amount of pain, the wolf thumped its tail in a weak greeting.

Theo couldn't help herself then. She fell to her knees to hold and pet the poor creature's head. The moment its pleading eyes met hers, the thought came to her that she ought to run for Lucas. With an effort, she shook the suggestion off. The house was too far, and this wolf appeared to be on death's door. Already, its beautiful blue eyes were clouding. She searched for a branch, anything to help her pry the trap open. Nothing she saw looked sturdy enough. Perhaps the wolf understood the futility of her hopes, because its muzzle sank to its forepaws.

"I am not giving up," she told it sternly. "You may be a

pest, eating rabbits and running off when you're supposed to prove you exist, but I am not going to let you die."

The wolf whined at this speech without opening its eyes. Desperate to make some attempt to help, Theo planted her boot on the lower jaw of the trap, weighing it down while she fought to force the upper half open.

Her shoulders screamed, but she did not stop any more than she heeded her awareness that no woman—and possibly no man—could budge this device alone. With a tool, she might have stood a chance, but as it was, all she could accomplish was pulling her arms out of their sockets.

Then she heard rusty metal creak. The iron hinges must have moved. Surely, if they had moved a little, they could move more. Heartened, she threw every ounce of strength she had into another heave. The trap popped open and lay flat, amazing her so thoroughly she fell on her bum.

"Goodness," she gasped, staring at the miracle. The wolf looked from the trap to her. With its tongue lolling out of its toothy mouth, its astonishment seemed to exceed hers.

"All right then," she said, struggling up. "Let's see if we can get you loose."

This was easier said than done. Wincing to herself, she freed the wolf 's leg from the spikes as gently as she could. Fortunately, the beast did not struggle or try to bite—as many animals would have done. This animal was stoic, not so much as yelping before she was done.

"That's a good fellow," she praised, daring to stroke its heaving side. In spite of the situation, she had to marvel at the softness of its fur. Then she realized she had a new dilemma. The wolf was too weak to walk and too injured to leave alone. If whoever had set the trap came back, it could not defend itself.

"I must carry you to help," she said, looking doubtfully down at it. The wolf was lean but nearly as big as a Saint Bernard. Then again, she had not expected to be able to unspring the trap. Maybe she could do this, too.

"I cannot know unless I try," she said, and bent her knees to slide her arms under it.

The wolf weighed a ton, but she managed to carry it back to Hadleigh in one go. Fearing she would never pick it up again if she set it down, she ignored the knocker and kicked the door for entry. Her boot heel made a satisfying hollow sound.

"Get the blazes out of bed," she yelled for good measure. "Your mistress is at the door!"

The wolf opened one eye.

"I am doing this for you," she told it. "If I cannot speak rudely now, when is it allowed?"

Fortunately, a sleepy footman with his shirt untucked soon admitted them. When he saw what she carried, his eyes showed white. He stopped in his tracks, but thankfully did not run. The wolf tensed in her hold at this new person's approach, then settled when she soothed it with her fingers.

"Get your master," she ordered, sounding uncannily like her mother in an angry mood. "I know he does not like sunshine, but bundle him up like one of Napoleon's mummies if you have to."

The footman hesitated. "Would you not like me to call someone to . . . take your burden?"

Her legs were trembling, but she locked her knees. "No one is touching this creature until my husband guarantees its safety."

She doubted the footman meant to mumble so loudly, but she distinctly heard him say the beast looked ruddy safe where he was. She supposed he did not notice its blood plopping to the floor.

"Sorry," she said to the wolf, trying not to joggle it in her arms. "We shall have you settled soon enough."

She hoped they would at least. Lucas had not seemed to bear the wolves any rancor when they spoke of them earlier.

Surely he would understand this one could not be left unguarded with God knew who setting traps.

"Good Lord," said her husband, looking completely staggered as he entered the hall. He had pulled on a pair of breeches, but had no shoes. Beneath the blanket he had clutched around him, he was as pale as blanched ivory.

"He is hurt," Theo said before he could ask if she had lost her mind. "We must take him somewhere safe. Perhaps the stable master can treat his wounds."

"Edmund," Lucas breathed, one hand going out to the wolf in shock. Then he seemed to recall himself. "We will carry him to Edmund's apartments. He has a knack for healing animals."

As soon as they reached the dimness of the lower corridors, Lucas gave her his blanket and eased the wolf from her shaking arms. To her relief, her husband seemed as worried for it as she. His hands stroked its fur just as hers had.

"Who could have done this?" he asked. "I gave no orders for traps to be set."

"Someone else must have seen the wolves and reported them to your gamekeeper. Perhaps he thought he did not need permission to act. I only hope the other wolf is well."

"The other wolf . . ." Lucas shook himself, looking grim. "Yes, let us hope he is safe. This one is far from it."

When they reached his steward's apartment, it was as dark as a cave and—once Theo lit a candle—as red as a brothel. Perhaps Lucas was considering the potential awkwardness of her intrusion, because he glanced from the closed inner door to her.

"I will see to waking Edmund," he said. "Perhaps you would be good enough to call for boiling water and clean towels?"

Theo didn't want to leave but saw the wisdom of his request.

"I will return quickly," she promised, taking a moment to press her lips to Lucas's cheek.

He looked at her in question, the big wolf hanging in his arms as trustingly as if they were old friends—though that might have been because the creature had no strength to fight. As singular a picture as this made, Lucas appeared to think he was doing nothing out of the ordinary. Theo's eyes teared with gratitude.

"Thank you," she said roughly. "Most husbands would not be this understanding."

"I—" he began, then cleared his throat. "I am sure if this creature could, he would be thanking you."

Lucius had the devil of a time barring Theo from Edmund's room once she returned with water and towels. Naturally enough, she wanted to see for herself that the "wolf" she had rescued was recovering. Lucius's plea that what he and Edmund had to do was unfit for feminine eyes did not satisfy her. He suspected her gratitude for his help was all that kept her from arguing more.

Uncomfortable as refusing her was, he had no choice but to keep her out. Edmund was a young *upyr,* and found changing forms during the day difficult, especially when weakened by loss of blood. Though the sun could not burn him while in wolf form, the iron of the trap had kept his wounds from closing. For as long as he had been caught in that unforgiving maw, his life had been dripping slowly out of him.

Lucius had intended to help him shift, which would have healed most of his injuries when he reformed. To his dismay, between trying to keep human hours, calling unnatural fogs, and spending his nights with Theo rather than feeding as his wolf desired, Lucius had let his power run down. The best he could do was prevent Edmund's condition from worsening until darkness fell, a process that involved letting his stronger aura flow into Edmund's. Had Theo seen him do this, she would have known his sensitivity to the sun was the least of his oddities.

At last, sunset arrived and Edmund was able to attempt a shift. The blink of an eye was usually sufficient, but tonight Edmund wavered between energy and matter for long minutes. The glow that was his essence faded in and out like a firefly. Alarmed, Lucius reached for Edmund's mind to help his consciousness reweave. His first brush with the fragile whisper that was Edmund's thoughts shocked him profoundly.

Though he could not read him clearly, Lucius sensed Edmund was drifting in the timeless void. This emptiness was their place of transition. All those who wished to change from man to wolf, or from human to *upyr,* had to pass here first. It was a place a weary spirit might want to rest. As the oldest of their kind, Lucius knew this better than anyone.

For centuries he had wandered with no wish to remember more than the moment he existed in. Joining a wolf pack, taking on an animal soul, had begun to change that. He had made one child before Edmund during the time he thought of as his "wakened" years, and after him, only Edmund's boy, Robin.

Of those three, Edmund alone felt like a son: a slight if blurred reflection of himself. For all his sensual indulgence, Edmund knew how to brood. Edmund knew what it was to have memories he would rather forget. Most of all, Edmund had a twin to the dark streak Lucius knew lived inside him.

Back in the days when Edmund was mortal, another elder had wanted to claim him, a ruthless female named Nim Wei. Though Edmund loved her, he had feared her darkness would damn his. He had begged Lucius to change him before she could.

"You are more powerful," he had pleaded. "And your spirit still shines with light."

At the time, Lucius had wondered whether his power or his light had been more important. Nim Wei was the sort of elder who might take revenge for a romantic slight. To be sired by a more ancient *upyr* would offer some protection against her wrath. Now Lucius did not care what Edmund's motivations had been. Edmund was his friend, flaws and all. Lucius did not want to lose him.

Recklessly pulling together what remained of his strength, he thrust his hands into Edmund's flickering, formless glow, letting his energy run into it like water. When his arms went icy, he ignored the pain. When his muscles trembled, he clenched his teeth. In his mind, he held clear the image of all Edmund was, of all Edmund cared about.

"Come back," he said hoarsely—ordered, he hoped. "You know you aren't finished with this earth yet."

The glow grew stronger, then threw back Lucius's hands. With a sound like a flint being struck, Edmund's tall, blond, Viking-descended body coalesced on the sheets.

He smiled weakly at Lucius's curse of relief. "Knew you'd miss me. You look almost as awful as I feel."

Speechless, Lucius clasped Edmund's hand, his own palms damp with fear. Despite what he had poured into his friend already, Edmund was frail. A cold blue fire sprang up where they touched.

"Don't," Edmund said. "I can tell I've drained you enough."

The wrench of guilt tightened Lucius's throat. "I should not have left you. We should have returned to the house together after our hunt. If Theo had not chanced to find you, you would have died."

"Yes," Edmund said in an odd, dry tone. "Her finding me was fortunate."

Seeing him shiver, Lucius pulled a blanket over him. As he straightened the wool across his legs, he saw that the wounds the wolf had taken, though lessened, still remained.

"My God," he gasped. "I've been so careless of my strength, I could not heal you completely!"

Edmund coughed out a laugh. "Do not be too hard on yourself. I doubt anyone but you could have brought me back from that brink. For a time there, I thought I was seeing angels. Contrary to expectations, this did not in the least please me."

Lucius shook off a shudder of lingering dread. "I am glad you came back, and I am truly sorry I did not know you were in danger."

"Lucius," Edmund said on a reluctant sigh. Though weary, he pushed himself higher on the pillows. "We have to talk about how Theo found me, because it was not by chance. As soon as I realized I wasn't going to free myself from the trap, I sent out a call. I expect the effect of the iron, and then the sun, prevented my mind-voice from reaching you, but I definitely felt it reach Theo."

When Lucius would have spoken, he held up his hand. "I know it sounds unlikely. I admit, it surprised me, too. Lately, I have not been sensing her emotions even by accident. I assumed I was learning to block her particular thought patterns, but now I think she may have developed an ability to shield, which only fell away when she slept. If that weren't noteworthy enough, she also freed me from a trap no human woman should have been able to open, after which she carried me at least a mile to your home. To carry a normal-sized wolf would have been impressive. To carry me, without a single rest, was nothing short of a feat."

Lucius's shoulders were as tight as if they wore iron straps. "Humans have been known to perform heroics."

"To save their children or loved ones, not to rescue wounded wolves. You have changed her, Lucius, and she does not seem at all aware that you have."

"If I have changed her, why is she walking out in the sun? Why has she been eating food enough for three mortals?"

"I do not know." Edmund's expression was frighteningly gentle. "Maybe you discovered a secret method for making her one of us. Maybe you thought to circumvent Council law."

This accusation, mild though it was, put Lucius's hackles up. "I assure you, I've done no such thing. I wanted, *want* her to remain who she is. Though it puts me through the *upyr* equivalent of hell, I am willing to wait until she is prepared to choose."

When Edmund probed his gaze, Lucius allowed it.

"What I say surprises you," Edmund said.

"Yes, it does."

"Then I beg pardon for the insult. The fact remains, however, that your wife is displaying definite nonhuman traits which may not be reversible. As I recall, when the wolf-queen Juliana was a human traveling with the head of your old pack, her proximity to his aura enhanced her strength. Perhaps a similar process is happening here."

Lucius gripped the bedpost to help him stand. Though the fall of night accelerated his recovery, his legs were wobbling. In truth, this whole conversation had put him off balance.

"Juliana and Ulric were soul mates," he said, "a one-in-a-million match."

Without lifting it from the pillows, Edmund cocked his head. "You are the one who is in love with Theo Becket. Are you telling me you cannot imagine she is your soul mate?"

Lucius could imagine it; he simply was afraid to. Over and over he had told himself Theo and Mena were not the same, but perhaps he had been protesting too much. The possibility disturbed him. He had been doing everything he could to court Theo, to keep her, and yet he did not want her to be the other half of his spirit. He did not want to admit she might be the love he could not live without.

The last time he had lost his soul mate had been bad enough.

Edmund pulled him back to the present by touching his arm. "I don't generally advocate exposing ourselves to humans, but you have to tell her what is happening. Whether you meant to do this or not, she must have a choice. If she leaves you—"

"—the changes may stop." Lucius sat again heavily.

"She will notice she is different, and sooner rather than

later. Humans are good at denying what does not suit their view of the world, but even they have limits. Most of all, though, telling her is the right thing to do."

"I know."

Lucius had answered calmly, but all at once his rage flared like a dying star. Theo was a hair's breadth away from loving him enough to stay. A few more months, perhaps a year, and she would be his. Now his blasted ancient power threatened to wreck all.

Without consciously willing it, he drove his fist through the carved headboard.

A second later, he forced himself to breathe. As he pulled free, mahogany splinters fell from his unmarked hand.

"Forgive me," he said to Edmund, who was eyeing him warily. "My temper is recovered. I will do what is fair. All I ask is a little time to decide how to break the truth."

Edmund opened his mouth, then shut it without speaking, apparently deciding further comment might be unwise. Lucius was thankful for his discretion. In his current mood, he was not certain what he'd want to run his fist through next.

"I must call a few maids to feed you," Lucius said. "Weak as you are, you will need more than one."

He turned away before Edmund could voice what was in his mind. As weak as Lucius was, he should be thinking of feeding, too, but even now he only wanted to drink from one cup. Given what he expected to hear, Edmund's next words surprised him.

"She is a kind woman," he said, the hesitance in his tone making Lucius turn back. "I felt her compassion as she carried me. She had no reason to help me and yet she did."

"It may be that, somewhere beneath her ordinary human awareness, she realized you were a man."

"Perhaps. And perhaps she would not willingly let a wolf suffer, either." Edmund shifted beneath the blanket as if he could not get comfortable. "I think I understand why you love her, why you want to protect who she is. Maybe, as difficult as this situation seems, you are luckier than you know."

He sounded wistful. Like Lucius, Edmund preferred to leave his past behind him. Though Nim Wei was not the demon Edmund's fears had made her, their relationship had not been a happy one.

"I pray you are correct," Lucius said. "At the moment, a little luck would be welcome."

Chapter 22

Theo was sorely tempted to put her fist through a wall. Lucas had no reason to treat her like a porcelain doll. Had she not kept her head when she found the wolf? Had she not rescued it by herself? All she wanted was to see the creature, not sew up its wounds—though, as to that, she wagered she had a tidier hand than Mr. Fitz Clare.

Alas, her husband was adamant. Her sole rebellion was not going to bed as he asked. Instead, she stood in a window in the yellow drawing room, a single candle for company. No matter what obedience she owed Lucas, she *had* to find a way to convince him that she was strong. Though she loved what they shared in bed, she knew she could offer more.

He deserved more. He deserved everything she had.

Sighing, she rested her forehead on the window, but a second later she straightened. A fat gray pony stood on the terrace, with a small barefoot boy on its back. The boy was staring up at her, proud as a little king, as if willing her to notice him.

She glanced behind her at the mantel clock. The golden hands said midnight, the very hour Lucas liked to commence their most energetic lovemaking bouts. Fighting a blush, she decided it was no hour for a child to be roaming the grounds alone.

She had better go down herself and confirm that he was not lost.

The butler stopped her before she could slip out, obliging her to wait while he retrieved her cloak. Luckily, when she reached the terrace, the boy was still waiting.

"Good," he said. "You can let me in. I was not sure the other servants would."

"Let you in?" Theo asked, nonplussed.

A footman had run after her, probably on the butler's orders. Hadleigh had to be the only house in England whose staff served one better at midnight than noon. Of course, she would not put it past Lucas to have asked them to keep watch. Perhaps he feared she would make a habit of rescuing wounded things. Seeing the footman, the boy slid down the pony's side and handed him the reins, clearly accustomed to being waited on.

"Servants are often suspicious of children," her small visitor said. "They might have thought I was a gypsy boy."

"You could have worn shoes," Theo suggested. "Or brought an adult."

The boy frowned at her as if he were puzzling her out. Considering how young he was, his self-possession was comical.

"My guardian is here already," he said after his pause to think. "Uncle Robin forbade me to come with him."

Theo was surprised. She hadn't heard guests arrive. But then a light flared in her head. "You are Percy Fitz Clare. How providential! I have been wanting to meet you for ages. Please do come in."

Despite his princely air, the little baron was agreeable to having his hand taken. If Theo had not believed it would offend his dignity, she would have carried him on her hip and spared his shoeless feet the walk inside.

"I do not mean to discommode you," Percy said, his tongue stumbling slightly over the formality. "I only wish to ascertain that my other uncle is well."

"Mr. Edmund Fitz Clare, you mean?" Once again, Theo was perplexed. "As far as I know, he is fine."

They sat side by side on a butter yellow settee, the boy's short legs forced straight by sliding back.

"I heard there was an accident." He leaned closer and lowered his voice. "I heard there was an *iron* trap."

"Oh, love, no!" Theo exclaimed, seeing at once that some servant must have been sent to Bridesmere Castle with a garbled version of events. "Your Uncle Edmund is perfectly hale. He was nowhere near the accident. A *wolf* was caught in the trap. Your uncle is helping my husband heal it."

For some reason this caused Percy to gape at her.

"But—" he said. "I thought you *knew*. I thought—your face shines just like theirs!"

"My face?" Confused, Theo put her hands to her cheeks.

"Er," said Percy, suddenly fascinated with his dirty toes. "I mean, your face shines with beauty."

This seemed so humorous a thing to say, especially for a five-year-old, that Theo had to laugh. No doubt some childish logic lay behind the words, even if she could not perceive it.

"Might I visit the injured wolf?" Percy asked earnestly. "Since I came all the way here?"

"Oh, I do not know," Theo hedged. "It might not be in a condition a young person ought to see."

Percy turned on the yellow seat. "Don't *you* want to see it?"

This was, had he but known it, the most persuasive question he could have asked. Theo did want to see the wolf. More to the point, she felt she had a right to.

"We shall both go," she decided and gave Percy her hand again.

Three maids in nightclothes were exiting the steward's outer door as Theo and Percy approached. Flushed and blowsy, they looked as if they had been providing services more intimate than water and towels. Theo stared at them in disbelief, but none of the maids, who seemed half-asleep, noticed their mistress.

All three caressed their own throats.

"He *must* be better," Percy said as he watched them go.

Theo shook her head. "I do not remotely want to know what you mean."

Percy giggled, which did not increase her faith in his guardian's good sense. Boys that age had no business noticing tumbled maids. Squaring her shoulders, she strode across the blood-red sitting room to the inner door. Having learned her lesson the last time, she did not pause to knock but pushed straight through.

The sight that greeted her made her blink.

In the bed, where she had fully expected to find the wolf, Mr. Fitz Clare sat naked but for a blanket bunched at his hips. He was unwinding a bloodied bandage from around his knee. Two other men, one of them her husband, leaned forward to examine what lay beneath.

"It is almost healed," said the one she did not recognize, presumably Percy's guardian.

Pieces began to assemble in Theo's mind, whether she wanted them to or not: the absence of the wolf, the raw, evenly-spaced wounds strung beneath Mr. Fitz Clare's knee. These were not bite marks. They were injuries made by spikes. Her face went cold, then hot, and her heart beat in quick, uneven flutters. Mr. Fitz Clare drew a startled breath and looked up. His eyes were as blue as the sky just before sunset. The back of them caught the light of her candle in a manner no human eyes should have done.

Her heart stopped fluttering to pound instead.

Mr. Fitz Clare's eyes were the same color as the wolf's. There was a reason, beyond miscommunication, that Percy had thought he was ill.

"Uncle Edmund!" Percy cried, yanking joyously free of the hand that had unwittingly clenched his. He ran to the bed and jumped on. "You are all right!"

"Theo—" said Lucas's low, shocked voice.

She turned toward the sound and nearly fainted when she saw him. The fact that her husband was instantly—literally, instantly—at her side did not soothe. He set her candle on a table, steadying her elbow even as she shrank back.

His appearance was—she had no word for it but terrifying. She had always thought him pale, but now he was white: snow-white, gleaming white, a white that made his face look more like marble than flesh. His perfectly carved bones pressed tight against poreless skin. His cheeks were hollow, his temples gaunt, as if in the space of hours he had undergone a month-long fast. His eyes were pure silver.

He could have passed for the angel of death himself.

"No, Theo," he said. "Don't pull away."

"Lucas." A broken whisper was all she could gasp out. She felt dizzy. His name sounded as unreal as this whole evening. She tried to tug her arms from his hold, but fear had drained her strength. All her muscles would do was twitch.

This white, shining creature was not her husband. This was not even a human being.

"I am sorry to have frightened you," he said, his hands still firm on her arms. "I have been helping Edmund. I do not have enough energy left to maintain my glamour."

"Your glamour." The word was mere noise to her. He still wore only breeches, and her palms were braced against bare white ribs. She did not want to touch him, but he was all that held her up. "What is all this? Why do you look so strange?"

She was so upset she began to cry.

"Sh," said her husband, pulling her to him to rub her

back. "I will tell you everything, love. I know it is a lot to ask, but please promise you will listen with an open mind."

His chest was cold and hard, but she clung to it anyway. "What is going on?" she demanded as forcefully as she could. "How did Mr. Fitz Clare turn into a wolf?"

It sounded worse when she said it aloud. She wanted Lucas to laugh at her. Instead, he kissed her temple with silken lips.

"I love you," he said, "more than life itself. Try to remember that while I explain."

Theo's thoughts flew across her face as if they had wings. Lucius had no trouble reading them. What explanation could there be? Why did he not tell her she had lost her mind?

He led her like an invalid to the outer room, sat her in a chair, and poured her a stiff brandy. Color came into her cheeks when she swallowed the drink, then ebbed away again.

Wondering where to start, he knelt at her feet and held her knees. When she looked at him, he did not shift his gaze away. He was too weak to accidentally thrall her. In any case, the truth was all he would tell tonight: the very truth her eyes were begging him to deny.

"I am not human," he said. "The face I usually show you is a glamour, an illusion to enable me to seem like you."

A tremor rippled through her frame. "If you are not human, what are you?"

"I am an immortal being called an *upyr,* as is Edmund and his son, Robin. When you saved Edmund, he was in his wolf-form. He could not change back until the sun went down."

"The sun is a danger to you."

"Yes."

"And the iron . . . Percy mentioned it as if it was important: that there had been an accident with an *iron* trap."

Lucius nodded, unsure if he were glad or worried that she was thinking clearly enough to reason this through. "The sun will burn us if we stand out in it too long. Iron weakens us, and would kill us if an implement fashioned of it were driven through our hearts."

"So when you had me put you in those shackles before we made love . . ."

"It checked my strength."

She stared at him, apparently too shocked to blush. "Should you be telling me this?"

He smiled, drew her hands to his mouth, and kissed her knuckles. "Most likely not."

She looked at the place he had kissed as if expecting to find a mark, then tugged her hands back to the chair arms. "Are you a demon?"

He tried not to flinch. "Some would say I am, but I do not believe so. I believe I am simply a different kind of man, as lions and tigers are different kinds of felines."

"More like lions and house cats," Theo muttered, which made him laugh. She looked up at the sound, her brows drawn together in concentration. "You must have been born human, unless the old squire fooled everyone as well."

"Ah," said Lucius, having momentarily forgotten the added complication of that lie. "I regret to inform you that I am not Lucas Delavert. I took his memories when he was dying of a fever. We looked alike, and he wished me to assume his place. He had a grudge against Bridesmere. Admitting he had died seemed like ceding a victory."

Theo had been leaning forward, but now she fell back in the chair. "If you are not Lucas Delavert, whom did I marry?"

She was breathless, her hand pressed to her bosom as if to contain her heart. Her shock—and the unspoken implication that she would not have married him had she known—caused him to speak stiffly. "I am called Lucius the White."

"Lucius," she said, emotions struggling for dominance in her face. "Lucius . . ." Suddenly, she snapped straight, one finger pointing accusingly. "You jumped out my window as if you could fly. And you kissed me in the garden behind our house the first night we met. And you bit me. You bit me on our wedding night!"

If he'd had the blood for it, he would have blushed, though her tone held more astonishment than outrage. He was rather astonished himself. He was unused to humans throwing off his mental persuasion.

"That is one of the ways we feed," he said carefully.

For obvious reasons, he did not want her to dwell on this, but she barely seemed to register what he had said.

"Oh!" she cried, covering her face in shame. "It is coming back to me. The things we did. The things *I* did before we wed."

"Theo." He pulled her hands gently down. "That is not your fault. I did not exactly force you, but you were under my thrall. You acted in ways you would not have in your proper mind."

"Your thrall," she repeated slowly. "You put me under it with your eyes. When I looked at you, I sometimes felt as if I were entranced."

"Yes."

"And afterward, you made me forget what we did."

"Yes," he said, grateful she was still saying *we*. He did not add that she should not be remembering those meetings now. Edmund's conviction that Lucius had altered her basic nature was a discussion for another time. "When I bit you, it increased my influence. That is why I tried not to take your blood too often. I wanted you, as much as possible, to be who you are, to decide freely what you feel and desire."

"But you—" She made a deliciously husky sound as she cleared her throat. "You *like* biting me, don't you?"

She was remembering their wedding night, when he had begged her to close her eyes because he knew he could not control his urges and was afraid she would see his fangs. She was remembering how his sucking had felt like an orgasm. Remembering this himself, his body tightened deep and low.

He should have tried harder to hide his reaction. As she watched her memory's reflection change his face, she made another mental leap. "Oh, Lord. You can read my mind. You know everything I have thought."

"Not everything. For me, the power to read minds is linked to the power to thrall. Of late, I have tried to avoid it."

"Of late . . ." She seemed as horrified by this as any revelation that had come before.

"I have seen civilizations rise and fall," he said. "And have touched many human minds. Believe me, yours contains nothing worse than any other, and much which is better."

Theo pinched her lower lip. "Can Mr. Fitz Clare read me, too?"

"No, love, he is a young *upyr* compared to me. In order to thrall someone, he first must bite them. The most he would have picked up from you is emotions."

"Well, that is a relief. I should not like the whole household inside my head!"

That she would rather he not be there, either, was clear.

"Lucius," she said, and this time she rubbed her lip instead of pinching it. "Exactly how old are you?"

His sigh could not be held back. "I do not know the full sum of years, but older than the flood of which your Christian Bible speaks."

"That *is* old. You must have seen many interesting sights."

"I am afraid I remember only a fraction. The weight of so much time is difficult to carry."

He let his gaze slide away. He did not want to speak of

this now, and maybe not ever. Theo's sigh echoed his own, but she was not sighing at him. "I cannot believe we are having this conversation. I cannot believe this is real."

"You have only to look at me and know it is."

She touched him for the first time since they had left Edmund's room, her fingertips skimming lightly down the side of his face. Her manner was so distant, she might have been caressing a statue. "You are still beautiful."

"But different."

"Yes."

Too different? he wanted to ask but turned his head to kiss her palm instead. "There is one more thing you need to know."

"Only one?" she said with a crooked smile.

There was more than that, but he doubted she was ready to hear it all. "Just one for now. You need to know I tricked you into marrying me. I arranged events so we would be caught in the folly. I wanted time to win your heart and did not think I'd have it otherwise. You and your family owe me nothing. What you decide to do from here on in need only be based on your own wishes."

He had startled her, and he wasn't sure he wanted to hear her response. He gripped the arms of her chair and rose. "You will need time to take this in. We can discuss this further once you've had a chance to think."

She followed him to her feet. They stood close enough to embrace, though they did not. His yearning to hold her was achingly strong.

"May I ask one question now?"

"Of course."

She hesitated. "I do not mean to suggest this is what I want, but would you let me go if I asked? Would you release me from our vows?"

He had never worked harder to keep his feelings hidden. "I would have to erase your memories of what I am, but, yes, if you wanted to leave, I would allow it."

She nodded, though she was trembling beneath her calm. He couldn't tell if he had made matters worse or better with his concession. She looked down at her feet—numb, he suspected, from too many shocks in too short a time.

"I will think then," she said, her eyes not meeting his. "I will . . . stay in my own rooms tonight."

Damnation, he thought as she left him.

He knew she did not intend for him to join her.

Chapter 23

Theo's mind rolled in circles as if chained to a water wheel. Her husband was not her husband. He was an immortal creature called an *upyr*. He drank blood . . . her blood. He could read her thoughts and erase them. He could turn into a wolf. He had tricked her into marrying him. He was not Lucas Delavert; he was Lucius the White.

She couldn't help thinking how uncannily right that name sounded, then paused at the head of the stairs. If he wasn't Lucas, were they really married? But maybe it didn't matter. It wasn't as if she knew what she wished the answer to be.

Her preference was no clearer when she reached her rooms. They were pretty now that they were finished. Furnishings had been collected from other parts of the house, elegant and feminine in pink and gold. Mrs. Green must have told the servants to keep things ready, because a coal fire burned in the grate. The glow reminded her of the moment Mr. Fitz Clare's eyes had caught her candle.

Lucius's steward had fed from those maids who had

stroked their necks. To judge by Lucius's half-starved look, he hadn't shared the meal. Considering that he might or might not be her husband, and that she might or might not want him to be, his probable abstention elicited more relief than it ought.

Stymied by her own confusion, she dropped to the end of the bed and moaned into her hands. Her head was bursting with questions—though she suspected she would have found more answers as befuddling as the ones she had.

Her husband was an ancient creature called an *upyr,* and she did not want him biting anyone but her.

After a period of staring blankly into the fire, she realized she was waiting for him to join her. Naturally, he did not do so; she had made it obvious she wished to be on her own. Made restless by his absence, however uncertain she was about his company, she paced back and forth until the windows grew light.

She had decided nothing except that she did not think he was lying. He was what he said he was, and he loved her. If she needed proof, she had only to recall that he had entrusted her with his deadliest secret.

She grabbed her cloak, never having put it away the previous night, and hastily left the house. This morning no servant delayed her. The day was overcast and cool, the sky the color of worn pewter. Perhaps later it would rain; for now it was merely damp. She walked until she reached the far side of the castle-folly. Satisfied she was out of sight of the house, she spread her cloak on the grass and sat down to hug her knees.

This was not the marriage she had dreamed of. It was not even the marriage she thought she had.

"Oh, Mama," she said, though she knew her mother would have been little help unraveling this knot. "What do I do now?"

Suddenly exhausted, she lay down and folded her hands beneath her cheek. Sparrows twittered peacefully in the folly's eaves. For the first time in her life, she fell asleep outside.

Some time later, a warmth radiating behind her brought her awake. Rolling onto her back, she found a silver-eyed wolf gazing down at her. His pose was that of a statue, a regal guard for a lost temple. Only his eyes glittered with life, and only they seemed a trifle shy. Though she was embarrassed to call him by name, she knew immediately who he was.

Tentatively, she put her hand in the creature's ruff. The silver eyes blinked slowly.

"Are you watching over me then?" she asked. "Making sure I am safe out here?"

The wolf bowed his head.

It seemed an invitation to pet him and so she did. The wolf whined softly, wriggling a little deeper into the grass. When she scratched him behind his ears, the extent of his enjoyment was clear from his wagging tail. Amused, Theo sat up and scratched his flanks. This, apparently, was wolf heaven. Had she not known who this canine was, she was certain he would have rolled over and put his feet in the air.

"Well," she said with a breathy laugh. "Now I know how to put you under my spell."

The wolf, her husband, sighed and laid his head on her knee. The gesture was unnervingly endearing.

"Oh, Lucius," she said, which caused him to turn one ear. "What am I going to do with you?"

He was close to falling asleep beneath her hands—the guarded rather the guard. Wanting him to rest, she made her strokes slower.

"I still love you," she said, finding this easier to confide to his beast. "I hope you do not doubt that."

The wolf licked her wrist delicately.

Theo suppressed a snort and let her head sag back against the folly wall. A husband who could wag his tail and lick her was going to take a while to get used to.

Lucius slept for half an hour before stretching hugely and trotting off. He woofed softly in response to her admonitions to be careful. He sent an image to her mind, showing he could change forms and free himself should he be trapped. He was more powerful than Edmund. The sun might weaken him, but it would not do lasting harm before he had time to get somewhere safe.

In spite of his reassurance, she felt anxious to watch him go. She wondered if she were capable of leaving him, if she would ever be able to stand not knowing he was well.

That, indeed, bore thinking on.

Aidan Sheffield had kissed Caroline again. In the greenhouse. With the smell of herbs and soil swirling like incense in the warm, close air.

Caroline touched her lips. They were bruised—in part from the force with which she had kissed him back. Now she fought the impulse to turn and see if he were watching her walk away. If he was, he would know she moved in a daze.

Other parts besides her lips felt bruised: her breasts, her arms, the tender spots between her legs where she rode his hard, muscled thigh. Her only comfort (if comfort it could be called) was that neither of them had meant this to happen. Nor had they followed the fire to its end. Aidan had torn himself away just as her desperation to give him everything reached fever pitch.

"No more," he had panted, his face dark with lust. "Lord God, Caroline, I want you too much."

He should have offended her. Instead, the memory of his grating voice made her liquefy. She did turn then, but the interior of the greenhouse was obscured by the reflection of the leaden sky on its panes. One more glance at Aidan's beauty was out of reach.

I cannot keep tempting Fate, she thought, worrying the

side of her thumb with her teeth. If she continued to see him, she would either ruin herself irrevocably or go mad.

One thing she knew for certain, Theo had no conception of how lucky she was to be married!

Theo did not return to the house. If Lucius was inside, he would be asleep. She was awake now, and had no inclination to confine herself within walls.

She would have welcomed meeting her sister, though she did not know what she'd say. Lucius had not given her leave to share his secret, and while it might be useful to discuss the gardener, Theo had hardly sorted out her feelings about that.

Theo was, after all, in no position to throw stones. Unbeknownst to her; prior to her marriage, she had behaved without a shred of modesty. Lucius blamed it on his thrall, but Theo was not so sure. She could remember bits and pieces of these encounters and—to her mind—they did not suggest a woman compelled. If Caroline had fallen for a man who was beneath her, at least she had fallen for a human being.

No, if Theo met Caroline, they could speak of the weather or when dinner would be served. Only that would be safe—not that such trivialities had no use. Theo could, without uttering one direct word, let Caroline know her love for her was unchanged.

Abruptly eager to achieve this, she turned toward Hadleigh's stables. If Caroline was riding her favorite mare, one of the grooms might know where she'd gone.

Theo found someone, but not the someone she was looking for. A small, glum figure stopped her in her tracks. Percy Fitz Clare sat slumped on a bale of hay behind the largest of the stone buildings. He kicked his heels against his makeshift seat while nearby a fat orange cat snoozed with her three kittens. Theo's recent experience led her to wonder, if only for an instant, whether the cats were more than that. If *upyr* could become wolves . . .

She shivered and pushed the thought away. Percy's presence probably meant his guardian remained at Hadleigh. She supposed Lucius's fellow immortals were equally interested in how his wife responded to her new knowledge.

"Hullo, Aunt Theo," Percy said, kicking the bale hard enough to send a dust cloud into the air.

"Hullo, Percy," Theo answered back, bemused that—despite the boy's low mood—she had become an aunt. Perhaps, having lost his parents, Percy was eager to claim family. He shifted now to the right. Perceiving the invitation, Theo dropped her cloak beside him and sat.

One of the kittens woke, stretched itself from whisker to tail, and began batting Percy's boot.

"No one will play with me," Percy complained. "They yelled at me for trying to ride Uncle Lucius's sheep."

"Your pony might have been a better choice."

"Not allowed," Percy said. "Uncle Robin is punishing me for tattling—which is not fair. How can I remember every secret I'm not supposed to tell? I am only five."

Theo rubbed his shoulder and strove to conceal her smile. She suspected Percy remembered he was five when it suited him.

The boy turned his face up to her. "Are you and Uncle Lucius finished fighting?"

"We were not fighting, merely discussing our situation."

Percy leaned over his knees and offered the kitten a finger to joust. "My mama and papa used to 'discuss.' "

"Did they?"

"Yes, especially about whether I ought to meet the old Fitz Clares. Papa said it was my birthright, but Mama did not want them giving me strange ideas."

Theo pulled a piece of hay from his hair. His locks were darker than those of his guardian and uncle, more gold than flax. All the same, she could see a family resemblance. Percy had their nose and jaw. For that matter, as a distant relation, Theo had a bit of their nose herself. Disconcerted, she rubbed its tip.

"Does your guardian treat you well?" she asked.

Percy treated her to a shrug. "Uncle Robin is all right. He yells at me sometimes, but usually he plays with me. Running around at night with a wolf is fun. He is big and strong and you know he can keep you safe."

Presumably safer than Percy's parents had been in their ill-fated curricle. She found it intriguing that the *upyr* had become the boy's guardians. That spoke of qualities one might not expect. Monsters to anyone else, to Percy they represented security.

"Thank you for my stuffed wolfhound," he added politely, calling her attention back. "I named him Bruce and he's very nice."

"It was my pleasure to make him, though at the time I had no idea you had real wolves with which to play."

Theo stroked his hair as she spoke, and Percy leaned into her side. He seemed as charmed by the petting as his "Uncle" Lucius's furrier self.

"I am glad you know the truth," he said. "I am terrible at keeping secrets. Plus, now I can ask you if you think I shall like it."

"Like it?"

"Being an *upyr.* Papa said they might ask me because I was born with the Fitz Clare eye. That means I can see through their glamour and am hard to thrall. They will have to wait until I am old, of course. That's what Papa said, anyway. They like you to live out your human life before they change you." Percy turned his head to eye her. "I suppose Uncle Lucius did not do that with you because he fell in love. You won't be really old for a few years yet."

"No," Theo said faintly. "Not for a few years yet." She had to swallow before she went on. "Tell me, Percy. The other night, when you said my face shone like theirs, did you mean it shone as brightly?"

"Oh, not as brightly," Percy said blithely, unaware that he was spilling yet another secret. "Yours just shines a bit, but that's probably because you're new."

"Newer than you might imagine," she murmured.

"So, do you think I shall like it?" Percy asked. "I know being old is a long ways off, but I could start deciding now."

"I cannot tell you," Theo said, her lips oddly numb. "As you say, I am new."

"You will tell me, though, when you make up your mind?" Clearly this issue troubled him. When he looked at her, his little brow was furrowed.

Theo brushed the creases and tried to smile. "I think you shall know just by watching. Those eyes of yours are sharp."

"I shall have to visit if I'm going to watch—at least now and then."

Percy's gaze had cut away slyly. Distracted from her shock at learning what else Lucius might have hidden, Theo laughed. Percy did not protest when she pulled him onto her lap, but snuggled into her as if he felt at home. Flattered by his trust, Theo bounced him on her knee.

"Why, Baron Fitz Clare," she teased, "could you be trying to cadge an invitation? If you are, I think I shall have to say yes!"

Lucius's fingers shook as he lit the tall white candles he had set around Theo's room. No doubt, he would have shown better manners to wait for an invitation, but his patience wasn't up to that. He had told Theo what he was, he had given her a night to think, and he had shown her his wolf up close. For the most part, she seemed to accept what he was. She claimed she still loved him, and this was a foundation on which he could build.

Build on it he would. Tonight he would show her the

fullness of the pleasures an *upyr* could offer in bed. If Edmund was correct about her taking on a portion of his power, there would be no need to hold back.

With the candles lit, her pink and gold chamber glimmered like a box for jewels. He had strewn white rose petals across the carpet and bed, which seemed a thing a suitor ought to do. The moon streamed through the windows, adding its own watery blue light. Uncustomarily hot, he stripped off his coat and reached for calm. He would not botch this. He would win her to him again.

He knew from the servants that she had spent the evening with Percy Fitz Clare, dining on sausages and seedcake and being regaled by Caroline Becket with a chapter from a story about a shipwrecked Swiss family. Between these two affectionate sisters, Lucius imagined the boy would never want to go home.

He was feeling quite in sympathy with that reluctance when the door latch turned. His wife had arrived at last. From her sudden start, she had not expected to find him here.

"Lucius," she said, stopping awkwardly inside the door. "You . . . you look much better."

"I let my wolf hunt this afternoon. I am not so hungry as I was before."

"Oh," she said and looked down, blushing. She knew the various forms his "hunger" could take.

"Theo—"

"Wait." She cut him off with a determination that could not bode well. "I am glad you are here. Percy revealed something to me today which I need you to confirm. He suggested you have already made me immortal. He said my face shone like yours, and there are other changes which I have noticed myself that make me think he might be correct."

Lucius had been standing at the end of her bed. Feeling in need of support, he gripped the footboard. "Tell me what changes you have noticed."

"My looks have improved to the point where my mother

said I was pretty. I have been eating more than usual and keeping hours which resemble yours. I am stronger than I should be and possibly quicker, too. And"—she gnawed her lower lip—"once I *saw* something that could only have come from inside another person's head. At the time, I thought my imagination had run away with me, but given what you have told me about your abilities, perhaps not."

"You saw what the gardener was thinking about your sister," Lucius guessed. "I was there, in my wolf form. I assumed I had accidentally sent you those images because I was linked to your mind, but since Edmund said you heard him when he called for help, this might have been an early sign."

"Then it is true. You have made me what you are."

"I do not know." When Theo pulled an impatient face, he crossed the distance between them to take her hands. "I am not being evasive. Truly, I am not certain what is happening, and whatever it is was unintentional on my part. You *are* still human. The sun does not burn you. You still desire human food. Sometimes when an *upyr* is very strong or particularly attuned to a lover, he lends her some of his powers."

"Lends?"

"The change can be permanent. Over the course of many years, the human becomes an *upyr.* It is not our usual method of transformation, but it has been known to happen occasionally."

"So the longer I stay with you . . ."

"Yes, the longer you stay with me, the greater the chance that you will become what I am."

She turned from him, her hand pressed to her forehead. "You knew this last night?"

"I thought it would be better to let you absorb the truth a bit at a time."

She nodded, accepting—he was relieved to see—that in this he had been honest. Limned by moonlight, her profile was as perfect as a cameo. Just faintly, he could see what

Percy had noticed before them all: a soft white shimmer of more-than-mortal energy.

The elation he felt at this, the sense of having stolen a wondrous prize, was too strong not to inspire an equal sense of shame. Intentionally or not, he had done enough without her knowledge. He could not steal her right to choose, no matter how much he wanted her.

"How long do you think I have until I cannot turn back?"

The question pierced him in his tenderest spot. "I do not know." He endeavored not to sound as if his very heart was hanging in the balance. "You may never become what I am. You might simply be an unusually strong human. Either way, though, the change will distance you from those you love. The safety of the *upyr* depends on secrecy. Humans are many and we are few. You would have to hide what you are even from your sister. If that seems too high a price to pay, the safest course would be to leave now. Leaving may be the only way to stop what is happening."

She turned to him, her eyes sparkling with tears that brought an answering burn to his own.

"I don't think I can do that," she whispered. "I am not sure I ever shall be able to."

His breath gusted out, the wash of relief and hope strong enough to dizzy him. Robbed of speech, he held out his arms.

Theo had never been so grateful to have someone hold her. Lucius was grateful, too—more than grateful. As he wrapped her tight, she could not miss the way his body pressed hers, the thickening of his most male part beneath his clothes. He was warm again, unlike the night before. The reason for the white rose petals was swiftly clear.

He had been hoping to seduce her. A bank of steam swelled inside her. Then and there, she knew she would not refuse him. In the clarity of the moment, she marveled that she could have considered it. Man or beast, his soul was true.

"I was wrong," she confessed before his embrace could distract her.

"Wrong?"

"When I saw you without your glamour, I told myself you could not be my husband. In my heart, though, in every way that matters, I know you are the man I promised myself to."

"Theo," he murmured against her hair. "You cannot know how glad I am to hear that. It may be selfish, but I hope you always feel this way."

She held him tighter, as eager and as frightened as if what was happening was her first time. Maybe in a way it would be. They had never been together without the barrier of some lie. She wondered if he sensed her desire to know him in truth, if he could feel how ready she was to forget caution.

But perhaps his own desires occupied him. His mouth trailed down the side of her neck with small sounds of longing. When he reached the pulse that beat at its base, he groaned. She realized his teeth were sharp when he dragged their curve with lingering slowness across her skin.

Unable to stop herself, her fingers dug into his waistcoat.

"You want to bite me," she whispered. "You want to feed."

His breath rushed in her ear. "I am sorry. You smell so good I cannot help but respond." He pulled back and met her gaze. "I do not have to do this. My wolf has fed."

She traced the shape of his upper lip, savoring its perfect curves before pressing it against the hardness of his teeth. As she did this, he sucked a breath. His canines suddenly extended longer, the tips now showing from his mouth. Their edges were gleaming sharp.

Her reaction to this surprised her. Deep inside, her body tightened and grew wet. She struggled to speak again. "You never let me see that before."

"I did not want to frighten you. Humans do not always relish the sight of fangs."

The display seemed to have done as much to him as it did

to her. His voice was hoarse. The strangeness of the moment, of him, excited her terribly. She found herself wanting to goad him, to see how far his needs could be pushed. Without quite deciding to, her nails scratched up and down his back.

"Could we kiss with your teeth like this? Would they cut me?"

"I would try not to let them."

"But if you drew blood, would I be thralled?"

He closed his eyes and shuddered. "I shall do everything I can not to use that power on you."

"Then do it. Kiss me until you cannot bear to refrain from more."

His hands gripped her arms like steel. "Would you have me stop then, or may I bite you as well?"

She let his silver gaze burn into hers, let him see how much she meant what she said. "I want you to feed from me. I want you to be as strong as you can. I want you to show me what you really desire in bed, as many times as you desire it . . . and I want to remember everything afterward."

He stared at her. She had never seen an expression so stark with lust. The thrill that went through her was deliciously sexual.

"God help you then," he rasped. "Because everything I desire is exactly what I shall do."

Chapter 24

A cry caught in his throat as he kissed her. She sensed he wanted more already, that they had begun this with him wishing he were driving in and out of her. His arms tightened almost painfully when he paused.

"Sorry," he panted against her lips. "The first time of the evening . . ." He shook his head as if she ought to understand what it meant to wait until he could have her. "With you in my arms, so warm and lovely, it is difficult not to rush."

He kissed her again before she could assure him she had no complaints. A flurry of motion brushed her skin, like giant wings beating up and down. She gasped into his mouth when she realized what he had done. He was indeed in a rush. She was naked, and in no more time than it took to blink half a dozen times. Her clothes lay in a shredded heap around her ankles.

Still fastened to her at the mouth, he chuckled at her surprise. "I promise to replace them," he said indistinctly, then pulled her quivering body to his front.

This time her surprise was, if possible, more welcome. His clothes were gone as well.

She had a second to appreciate the heat and smoothness of his skin before he was backing her toward the bed, his hands running over her back and bottom as if touching her fed other kinds of hunger. She clung to him as he lifted her, as he settled both their weight into the bed's softness. The strength required to do this reminded her that acquiring a nonhuman husband had benefits.

Prone now, their kisses slowed and deepened, but also grew more intense. He tasted different now that he was not concealing what he was: wilder, cleaner. She felt rather wild herself. Her body moved of its own accord, rolling against him, rubbing over him, trying to press every part of her against every part of him.

She found his skin as heavenly to touch as he appeared to find hers. The satin of his back enthralled her, the fluid, shifting strength of his legs. She followed the channel of his spine to the firm rounds of his rump. Here his flesh was almost too hard to give. It did give, though, his husky sigh attesting to his fondness for such pressure.

One sigh was not enough for her. She wanted thousands before the night was done. As if calling for its share of admiration, his cock throbbed thick and long. She wriggled her palm between them, her fingers curling to cup the updrawn bulge of his stones.

She did not expect the response she got. As if she had pressed some unbearable pleasure point, he bucked against her and broke their kiss.

"Yes," he groaned, up on his arms with his back arched hard. "Do that again."

Theo had no objection. She drew her hand up the ridge of his shaft, made a ring of her fingers, and pushed them down. When she reached his base, she cupped his sack once more. The tilt of his hips urged her farther. Behind the swell of his balls was a stretch of firmness she could not resist exploring. Apparently, this was worthwhile. His shoulders shivered in reaction.

"You like being petted," she observed, repeating the successful sequence, "as much as your wolf."

His body rocked in opposition to her gripping stroke. "I could not show you how much I liked it before—lest you think me peculiar—but my skin is extremely sensitive." He gasped and squirmed before going on, her caress having crossed his testicles again. "Every time you touch me, everywhere you touch me, the sensations are very strong."

Theo's cheeks felt as if they'd been painted in liquid fire. "Everywhere I touch you?"

He bent at the strangled question, drawing deeply, lusciously on her mouth. His tongue wet her upper lip when it withdrew, tempting her to chase it home.

"Everywhere," he confirmed, low and rumbling.

He seemed to know she needed kissing then, and seemed to know exactly how. Every move he made was bewitching: the weighted shifts of his body, the twitch and pulse of his erection within her hand. When she licked over and behind his fangs, his shaft swelled so dramatically it pushed her fingers apart.

"You like that," she breathed. "You like when I lick your fangs."

A helpless hum of enjoyment was all the answer he could give. He caught her lower lip in his teeth and tugged it out. Knowing he could nick her at any moment made the pool of warmth between her legs melt and run.

This was a reaction she could not hide. He grunted at the sudden wetness against his thigh. Releasing her lip, he cupped her most vulnerable softness in his hand.

"I am going to slip you inside my aura," he said. "You are going to feel my caresses as I do yours."

She did not know what he meant, only that the firm squeeze

of his palm made her arch and moan and spread her thighs. If his gaze had not darkened with masculine appreciation, she would have been embarrassed.

"I will give you what you need," he said and curved two fingers inside of her.

Though the intrusion made her groan with sensual bliss, it was not her true desire.

"I want you," she pleaded. "Your . . . manhood inside me."

His smile was a knowing curve that turned to molten silver when it reached his eyes. "Watch my glow, love. Feel it flow over you."

She had no choice. She watched it, felt it. His aura was not merely white but shot through with rainbow hues. Her skin began to tingle where the transparent wave rolled over her: her face, her scalp, her arms . . . Without warning, the tips of her breasts sprang sharply to life, as if someone were alternately pinching and releasing them.

"That is your blood," he said, his voice carnally thick and rough. "That is your pulse beating more quickly in the places your excitement draws it. Your lips are as red as cherries, but they are nothing compared to your nipples."

Her belly heated as if it, too, had flushed. She tensed, guessing what came next. Come it did. Her toes curled hard as the tingling wave of energy swept past her hips.

"Oh," she gasped, arching hard. Her little pearl of pleasure was a heated stone, beating out a rhythm so erotic, so forceful, it was all she could do not to beg him to rub it hard. Where his fingers had curled inside her felt much the same. She had always loved the feel of him there, but now he had awakened a cache of unsuspected nerves.

"There," he said. "That is how I feel when you touch me."

"Touch me more," she pleaded, writhing and wet. "Come inside me with your cock."

He smiled at her use of the word, but shook his head. "I want what I want tonight. That is the desire you gave me leave to fulfill."

She would not have guessed teasing her without mercy was what he wanted, but it was. With noises of deep enjoyment, he moved down her body, kissing her as he went, forcing her to cry out in equal parts frustration and delight. His fingers began to move between her legs in strong, slow strokes. Despite the very agreeable responses this elicited, it was his mouth that most tormented her. Small explosions of nearly culminated pleasure met each tug of his lips and tongue.

Though he did not break her skin, only dragged his fangs across it, she could sense him restraining his urge to bite her with every lick.

Her breasts ached from the treatment, her ribs, the taut, jumping muscles of her belly. Her senses drowned in want. As if he knew she needed something to bring her alert, he nipped one thigh hard enough to bruise.

Then, when she trembled, every inch of her focused on him, he sank his kisses into the softness of her secret folds. The first firm touch caused her to clutch his head. Here was the pressure she had wanted, the concentration of attention. He found her with his tongue, teased her deftly, sucked her between his lust-sharpened teeth . . .

It was more than human nerves could bear. She cried out as fire flared through her body, the very fire he had poured over it. She came in sweet pulsations, steadied in her thrashing only by his hands. The climax seemed to last forever, but at last he soothed her and murmured praise as her body calmed.

For a time, he laid his cheek on her hipbone and let her rest.

Once she had the breath for it, she said his name. This, apparently, was enough to suggest she'd welcome a renewal of his attentions. Her husband looked up her body, smiled, then slid his long, hard length slowly up her front.

Despite his indolent pace, he was not calm. Quickened respirations moved his chest, his heart pounding behind it as she had but rarely felt it do. His manhood brushed up her leg like heated metal—a caress he clearly wished to prolong. Finally he was stretched above her, his height and strength overpowering hers. If the slide of his body had not already rekindled her longing, one look at his face, at the uncustomary flush on his lips and cheeks, would have made her want him again.

Determined to have what she wanted, and soon, she gripped the muscles of his narrow waist with her knees.

"Bite me," she said.

His eyes darkened like a storm. "When I push inside you."

"Then push inside me now."

She reached for his erection, but he caught her hands, drawing them gently but inexorably above her head. There he held them outstretched and pinned. The sensation was oddly arousing, as if when imprisoned in this manner, her body's deepest desires were allowed free play.

He was not unmoved himself. His organ had scarcely needed enlarging, but in the time it took him to trap her, she could have sworn it swelled another inch. Lucius's awareness of this showed in a grimace and a slightly harder press of his hips. He did not, however, offer an apology.

"I want you at my mercy," he said, though his eyes suggested he was not completely confident of his right to make this demand. Theo had no such hesitation. He had, after all, once put himself in her power.

"I am not afraid," she said.

His expression narrowed. "Fear is not what I require."

"Then what is?"

Thoughts moved like clouds behind his beautiful, lambent eyes. He shook himself.

"Surrender," he said, appearing to find the answer even as he gave it. "Surrender of your own free will. I do not wish to rob you of the choices you will have to make, only to know that tonight, this minute, you are wholly mine."

A smile rose inside her, suffusing her with warmth and joy. How easy it sometimes was to give in!

"I am yours," she said. "You do not even have to ask."

Oh, she humbled him with her trust. He had not known how much he could love until this moment, nor how grateful her love could make him. Swiftly swamping this, though, running over his gratitude like an ocean wave, was the innundation of his need. He was aroused beyond measuring, almost beyond control—none of which he now had to hide.

It was a freedom for which he had dared not hope.

"Bare your throat for me," he ordered in a voice that held more than a hint of his beast. "I want you ready to be bitten by the time I thrust."

He could have performed this task, but that would not have provided half the pleasure of watching her do it. He released one wrist to let her pull her hair aside. She knew what this did to him. The knowledge was in the tremor of her fingers, in the consciously graceful arch of her smooth, warm neck.

"You are a vixen," he whispered, for the sheer delight of watching her blush.

His pulse was racing too fast to count, hers nearly the same. At the throb of one long blue vein, his mouth watered with desire. She was so beautiful, so sweet and trusting. His cock felt like an iron bar, his teeth like spears of fire. The feeling was similar to his wolf 's at the scent of game, but this response went deeper. Theo's baring of her throat triggered the deepest instincts of an *upyr*: to claim what he needed, to dominate a weaker race. She was more than a woman to him then; she was the drive for life itself.

A touch of dread gripped his nape. He wanted this too much. He feared he would hurt her. The way she stared at his fangs in fascination made him shudder too violently. When she broke the trance and met his eyes, his expression must have revealed he was considering pulling back.

"You have made me stronger," she said, each word slow and clear. "Don't you want to go as far as you can?"

Her free hand had fallen, curled against her lovely breast. Now she drew it upward, following the delectable line of her throat. Her thighs moved wider around his hips, then rose from the mattress until his hugely swollen tip nudged her gate.

Her slippery heat was the sweetest of siren songs.

"We both desire this," she said. "Do not make me ask again."

"Theo—"

"Do not make me ask."

The moan that rolled from his throat was pure surrender, then pure pleasure as the first push of his hips wedged his sensitive crown inside. To a certain extent, his body was capable of changing its natural size at will. Though deliberate will had not been at work tonight, he was nearly too broad and hard to slide in. He was certainly too aroused to force himself smaller. The knowledge excited him, probably more than it should. What was any male but a marauder? He bent to her throat, eager to fulfill both his pressing desires at once. Holding back a heartbeat longer, he licked her and tasted sweat.

Anticipation curled in his gut.

Then he pierced the blue stream and thrust.

Theo cried out, but not with pain. His shove of entry had reached its limit in tandem with his first suck. She was clamped around him like an angel's hand; she was pure ambrosia running down his throat. Even with these dual explosions of ecstasy, he was aware of her bone-deep tremors. The bliss all humans felt at being bitten washed over her.

That he sensed this so strongly came as a shock.

He had forgotten wrapping her in his aura. Now it brightened with pink and pearl, like the sun kissing the heather at break of day. Caught in this shared envelope of energy, their separate pleasures twined. When he drew back and thrust again, he could not be certain she was not thrusting into him. He knew his own shape: the press of it, the fullness, the way it bucked as her blood raced into him.

Such potent enjoyments could not last long. Three strokes had him riding the crest of climax. A dozen plunged him into its roaring flow. Fire could not have burned hotter, nor emptied him with such pleasurable thoroughness. He gasped at the force of it, shook with the length of it, then sighed with repletion.

I love you, he sent to her, unable to resist connecting in this final way. *Theo, I so love you.*

You, too, came her faint response.

He rocked her languorously in the aftermath, still hard but no longer needy, savoring the luxury of massaging well-sated nerves. When she arched in his arms and came again, he judged his happiness complete.

Mena lay in her bed, pillows piled behind her to ease her breathing. Her frosted, floating—and outrageously expensive—etched-glass lightglobe hovered to her right. It was set as low as possible to prevent it hurting her eyes. As long as she did not move, she was as comfortable as a person could be with bones that burned to their marrow with throbbing pain.

It was funny when you thought about it. Her world held so many marvelous inventions, and yet this illness that ate away at her was still able to find victims.

Despite the dimness, or perhaps because of it, the faintest halo surrounded everything she saw, as if she had one foot already in the otherworld. Ruefully, she smiled at her own refusal to accept pain treatments. Had she spent fifteen minutes with her doctor's crysto-electric cuffs, she would have slept—but slept to wake who knew where? Exhausted as she was, her pain was all that kept her awake.

She would miss too much if she spent her last hours unconscious. Her last sight of her beautiful penthouse apartment, fruit of her ambition and years of work. The city with its shining engineered canals. The aircars and hanging gardens and the simple hum of people in the street below.

Most of all, she would miss the man who sat by her bed, the lover she had never dreamed she would be lucky enough to meet. Lucius had become so much more than a source of pleasure and fun. He'd become the sweeter half of her heart.

At the moment, he looked like no one's sweeter half. He scowled at her stylish brushed metal floor, his forearms resting on his outspread knees, his hands clamped together like a supplicant about to plead. From the stubborn lowering of his brows, Mena suspected another argument was in the works.

This guess was wrong. When his despairing gray eyes met hers, they held something harder than any urge to debate. Her ribs tightened with sympathy and foreboding. He began in a low, measured tone.

"If you insist on doing this—"

"You can say the word, Lucius. If I insist on dying."

His beautiful pale lips thinned. "Very well, if you insist on dying when you know I could change you, when you know we could be together forever, I will walk out that door and never see you again. I swear on the ship that brought me, I will cut you out of my heart."

Oh, he stole her breath with the simple rawness of his hurt. She wondered if she should confess her belief that tonight would be her last on earth. Would he regret having lost what time they had to anger? Or would knowing how short that time was drive him to do something they both would be sorry for? She was certain of her decision. Immortality was not for her. Her faith might be vague, as so many people's were these days, but on that topic it was firm. If it were possible for him to make her immortal against her will, she did not want to tempt him.

"Since you insist on being dramatic," she said as lightly as she could, "I'll give you my own oath. Even if you do walk out that door, even if you curse my name and swear to forget we met, I will never, *ever* cut you out of my heart. Whatever existence I pass on to, you will live in my memory."

She reached for his hand, and he was unable to resist taking it.

She was grateful for this small favor, though he clasped her fingers a bit too hard.

"Mena, please," he begged, utterly humbled from the arrogant *upyr* she had fallen in love with two years ago. "I beg you, do not leave me alone."

"I will be with you—"

"You will not! That is a fairytale for priests and children, and even if you are correct and the soul survives, you will not be with me in a way that counts. I won't be able to hold you, to kiss you, to hear you sigh your pleasure in my ear. I love you, Mena, but I cannot stand by and watch you die."

A tear rolled down her cheek, but she did not waver. "You must do what you think best, as must I."

He rose, graceful even in his grief and anger. His gaze roved her face as if—despite his oath—he meant to imprint her image on his brain. Finally, he set her hand gently on the covers and let it go.

"I am sorry," he said, all his injured dignity intact. "You know how to reach me if you change your mind."

Theo choked on her breath as she came awake, the dream of the crystal city clearer in her recall than it had ever been. By comparison, her present surroundings seemed unreal. She half expected to find Mena's globelight floating above her head.

Instead, she saw Lucius. He sat on the edge of her bed facing away from her. He was bent over his knees with his face covered by his hands. The low sounds he was making, the hitching movements of his perfect back, told her he was crying.

Theo pressed her hands to her mouth. If he was crying, logic said he must have seen her dream, and if he had seen her dream, perhaps it was true. Their sensations had intermingled when they made love. Maybe, when she succumbed to her need to sleep, a vision of his past had slipped into her dreams.

Strange as the possibility was, it was no stranger than other things she had learned about her husband.

Wanting to comfort him, she laid her hand on his arm.

"Do not touch me!" he cried, flinching away. "I cannot bear to see any more."

Theo was startled to speechlessness. How could she make him see anything?

He rubbed his face and blew out his breath. "I am sorry," he said over his shoulder. "That is part of the past I wanted to stay lost."

"But why?" Theo asked. "I know the memory is sad, but obviously Mena was important to you. I wish—" When she hesitated, he turned on his hip and cupped her cheek. His touch gave her courage to continue. "I keep dreaming about her. I wish you would tell me who she was."

His thumb stroked the curve of her lower lip. She sensed him gathering his thoughts.

"Let me tell you what memories I do have first. They reach back to the turn of the last millennium, when William conquered this land. If pressed, I could tell you in detail what I did and saw on any of those days, though a good portion of that time I did not much care. It was not until I fell in with a pack of shape-changing *upyr* that my emotions began to wake. As I formed connections with them and their wolves, I realized I was older than I believed."

"Before, you said you were older than Noah's flood."

"Yes, but I only recollect fragments from that period: people I knew, events. I remember when Vesuvius erupted, and the sky caught fire over Pompeii as if hell had taken heaven's place. I remember—" His breath hitched, but he went on. "I remember the last of the children I made dying as a sacrifice to an Egyptian god—a successful sacrifice, as it happened; the Nile flooded hours after he burned. Today, I cannot dredge up his name."

"But—" Reluctant to push him when he looked this tired and sad, she swallowed back her words. His hand had fallen to her shoulder. She wrapped her fingers around his wrist, willing her warmth to penetrate his chill. It occurred to her that maybe she ought to push him. Maybe he had to face his past before he could move on.

"You remember Mena's name," she said softly. "Didn't you know her before you knew the Egyptians?"

"I knew Mena before any time history now writes about." He looked at her, weighing what he was about to say. "I come from another star, Theo. Though all the *upyr* alive today were once human, I was not, and I am the last who can make that claim. My ship, which I swore by in that dream, landed here when a civilization nearly as advanced as mine ruled most nations. Today Atlantis still exists in rumor. Mena's people lived even farther back than that."

Theo knew if she tried to speak, she would only stammer. A time before Atlantis? She could not conceive of that many years. She could barely conceive of Atlantis. Surely it was a myth, like the old Greek gods or St. George's dragon.

"It was real," he assured her. "As real as the life we are living now. Mena was a human I fell in love with when I was but a handful of centuries old."

"She was ill," Theo said, her sanity requiring that this be confirmed as well. "She would not let you heal her."

Lucius bowed his head. "I was not as powerful as I am now. I could not cure her except by making her an *upyr.* Mena did not want to be immortal. She believed all beings must rest and be born again—at least, that is what she said. I think . . . it is possible that in her heart she feared becoming a member of the race she had dedicated her life to keeping in check. She did not hate *upyr,* but in the end our people were rivals."

Theo ran her hand through his cool silver hair, trying to imagine how Mena's rejection must have felt. "Rivals or not, she loved you."

He lifted his head, his expression tortured. "She did not love me enough. That is why—" He closed his eyes, then opened them again. "That is why I wanted to forget. Especially now. Especially with you. I cannot be certain, but I think you and Mena share the same soul. When I met you, I kept telling myself it wasn't true, that if you were Mena reborn, my sense of recognition would have been unmistakable. I told myself what I wanted to hear, but after all the lives you must have lived in the interval, it is only natural that you'd seem different."

Theo squirmed a little in her seat. "Lucius, I do not think Christian people are allowed to have other lives."

She had amused him, though this had not been her intent.

"That is a discussion for another day," he said with a smile that soon faded. "What I wish you to know is that my belief that you and Mena share a soul led me to behave in an unjust manner. I hoped if I married you, I could make you love me. I hoped you would choose differently, but I had more time with Mena than I have had with you, years of time before the question of changing her arose. I know from your dream that she did love me, which would be comforting if I was not forced to conclude that love is not enough to make any woman wish to stay with me."

"Oh, Lucius!" Theo stroked his face. "What a terrible fear to have been living with all this time! I cannot speak of other lives. Apart from the experiences in those dreams, I feel as if I am myself and no one else. If it is true, however, and I used to be your Mena, by this point would I not just *seem* different but *be* so? Don't you think I would make my own decision?"

"Can you?" His gaze was piercingly intense. "Whether you become *upyr* in the course of time, or simply an unusually strong human, if you stay with me, you will be set apart from your kind. You will have to keep secrets from everyone you hold dear."

She looked into her heart, searching what she knew of him and what she guessed. In the end, the answer was clear. She was not afraid, just as she had not been afraid when she put her body in his hands.

His mind must have been a tangle of anxiety. He appeared

not to know what she was thinking, though undoubtedly he was trying to read her a bit.

"If you are not ready to decide," he said hastily, his own thoughts naked, "you need not answer now."

She smiled in spite of how concerned he looked.

"I love you," she said, "every bit as much as Mena did, but there is one important difference between us. She doubted you. I do not. You are giving me a choice, when we both know you could overpower me any time you please. You confessed the trick you played in order to marry me, when you could have left me believing I was in your debt. You are not the man you were with Mena any more than you are Lucas Delavert. I may not enjoy deceiving my family, and I might prefer to remain as human as I can, but whatever adjustments prove necessary, I choose to stay with you."

He could not speak. His breath caught and a tear rolled crookedly down his cheek.

"Truly," she said, circling him with her arms. "I choose to stay with you."

Chapter 25

Caroline did not even try to sleep, declining the maid's assistance when she offered to help her undress. She wanted no one fussing about her. Her thoughts were too full of Sheffield tonight.

"Ninny," she told herself, splashing her face with water from the pretty china washstand that graced her room. Every day women put inappropriate men from their minds. Every day they chose what was best for their families. Caroline was no rebel. There was no reason in the world for her to be acting in a way she had to hide from the people she cared about.

At the thought of Theo's reaction, Caroline groaned into her towel. All evening she'd been racked by the urge to confess. Little Percy Fitz Clare probably should be shielded from such matters, but Theo was her best friend.

Sadly, Caroline had no hope she would understand. Worse, given her second offense today, she could not promise she wouldn't repeat her sin. Theo had been her sweetest self tonight, both to Caroline and Percy, but the fact that she hadn't uttered another word about seeing her kiss the gardener had her sister on tenterhooks.

Caroline knew very well this did not mean she approved.

"Oh, God!" she exclaimed in exasperation at the muddle that was her life. "Please tell me what to do!"

The Almighty did not answer that she was aware of, though she was startled to look down and realize she had pulled her favorite green spencer over her gown. Apparently, without even knowing it, she was planning to go outside.

"I want to see him," she announced, since she was already talking to herself. "*We* should discuss this. *We* should decide if what we are feeling is worth fighting for."

Saying the words made her feel self-conscious, but also determined. She clenched her hands to strengthen her resolve. Was she going to spend the rest of her life more concerned with others' feelings than with her own? Virtuous though that path might be, it seemed highly unlikely to lead to personal happiness.

"I deserve to be happy," she murmured more softly.

She would not have been able to claim this even a month ago. Her time away from home had changed her. It wasn't simply the freedom from chores that Hadleigh offered, it was the freedom to arrange her days, to do what she wanted when she wanted to. Suddenly the pleasures to be had from ordering one's own life did not seem unattainable. Having had a taste of freedom, she began to imagine what she would do with more.

Aidan's heart leapt at the sight of Caroline Becket striding across Hadleigh's lawn. He had been thinking of her, had actually been on his way to stand beneath her window when, like a stroke of lightning, she had appeared. She was dressed for walking, the hem of her plain white gown soaked with dew. The hall loomed behind her, dark and solid, making her seem more ethereal than she was.

They gaped at each other in surprise. Aidan's skin tingled with an awareness he had not felt since he was a boy: an awareness of the power of Fate. His mother, God rest her, had followed the old ways—little offerings left at the spring, little charms tucked into his father's pocket to keep him safe. She had gone dutifully every Sunday to the village church, but Aidan had known where her true faith lay. Until that moment, however, he had not realized how much her superstitions had rubbed off on him.

"What . . . what are you doing here?" Caroline stammered.

Her hand had not merely flown to her bosom, it cupped one breast, as if she feared—or craved—another's caresses there. Aidan would have been happy to oblige her. Her spencer was as green as the grass she stood in, and its front buttons strained as she gasped for breath. Gentleman's daughter or not, Caroline Becket was as sturdy as a milkmaid.

"Aidan?" she said when he did not respond, then colored hotly for using his Christian name.

Her flush reinforced what his instincts already knew. Whether she had meant to find him or not, she had left the hall full of thoughts of him.

They *were* meant for each other, and the world's opinion be damned.

"I was coming for you," he said, because Dame Fortune favored the bold.

"For me?" she asked breathlessly.

A grin lifted his mouth which no amount of reasoning or propriety could suppress. "I was coming to gawp beneath your window like a mooncalf, and to imagine you in my arms."

She had reason to know what such imaginings did to him. Her eyes fell to the arch that pushed out his breeches. When she could not tear her gaze away, his erection strained all the more. No matter what happened next, the involuntary twitch of her fingers, as if she wished she were stroking him, was a thrill he would not have missed.

"Aidan," she said, or rather gasped. "I was . . ." She swallowed, still staring at his crotch. "I was just coming to see you!"

He laughed outright, suddenly free of doubt. "You love me, don't you?"

This, at last, wrenched her gaze to his. "Yes," she said unsurely, "but—"

Her hesitation mattered not a whit. Happiness washed through him in a rush of heat. "There are no buts. If you love me, you should marry me. I know your family will not approve, but—oof!"

As certain as he was, he had not expected her to catapult herself into his arms. She knocked his breath from him, not only because of the force with which she threw herself, but because of what she immediately began murmuring.

"Take me," she said, rising to him on tiptoe and pressing kisses to his jaw. "Oh, Aidan, take me now and make me yours!"

She might as well have waved a scarlet flag at a bull. His breeches felt as if they were strangling him, and his voice came out higher than it should. "Wouldn't you rather wait until we—"

"No!" she cried. "We shall not be able to marry for weeks and weeks."

Weeks did indeed seem long. She kissed his mouth, licking boldly between his lips until he could not hold back a groan. He wanted to swallow her whole, but held back for one last moment of sanity.

"Here?" he asked, thinking of the house and all its windows.

"Oh, yes," she said, stripping off her short green jacket and throwing it behind her. "I shall marry you, I promise, but I cannot wait anymore."

When her little hand cupped and squeezed his hugely swollen organ, all thought of argument flew.

"Here," he agreed, pressing her fingers tighter even as he

sank to his knees. "Oh, Lord, Caroline, don't let me go."

"Just for the buttons," she said between fervent kisses. "I shall get you free and then I'll hold you again."

She was willing, but not adept. He had to help her undo the flaps, and then her wondering hands were on his bare skin, stroking up and down in the most agreeable inquiry. Her touch felt so good, he had to grit his teeth so as not to spill then and there.

"You are so big," she marveled with only a hint of fear. "So hard and hot, but so silky, too. Oh, how I want to have you inside me!"

His lust flared higher at her frankness.

"Pull up your dress," he rasped, barely able to think straight. "Straddle my lap. I do not want to hurt you. I'm going to take you with you on top."

His announcement did not make her reconsider. With a moan of pleasure, she lifted her frock and scooted on her knees to hover eagerly above his thighs. She was open to him then, completely unprotected and immodest. Awed by her trust and almost unbearably aroused, he stroked one finger down her folds. He found heat and cream there, and tiny, tempting tremors of arousal. Her little swelling protruded dramatically. He had only to touch it and she cried out.

"Say it the way men do when they talk to each other," she said on a gasp for breath. "Say what you want to do."

The request sent jolts of feeling racing through his nerves—through hers as well, he suspected. This time, when she wrapped her hand around his shaft, her hold was not merely curious, it was tight. He had to fight to answer with any sense.

"Press my cock against your pussy and I shall say whatever you like."

He knew this was what she meant, because she shuddered and grew hotter. She pulled him forward until his crown found the same sweet welcome his finger had. She moved him then, up and down her softness, until a sound of tortured pleasure wrenched from his chest. Who would have thought she would do this? Who could have guessed she wanted to? But he could not doubt she did. With her gaze locked on his, she centered him at the entrance to her body.

He pulsed there like a wild and happily trapped thing.

"Say it," she said, bearing down so insistently that the first broad curve of him squeezed inside. "I want to be spoken to like a real woman. And I want you to take me like one, too."

She stunned him: this sweet, gently bred female who was giving him permission to be himself. Aidan hoped she was prepared for what she would get.

"Yes," he agreed, practically moaning it. "I shall fuck you. I shall fuck you until you cry."

Wet heat gushed against his crest as her head fell back. It would have run down him had her body not clasped him as closely as it did. For all her inexperience, she was ready.

"This is your last chance," he warned. "Tell me now if you have second thoughts."

Evidently, she did not. She pushed down as he pushed up, maybe even harder than he did. He could not bring himself to stop her. After all the waiting, after all the hopeless longing, he was blind with need.

The sounds she made, the energy she put into taking him inside her, told him her desperation was as fierce as his. Each small advance as he rocked back and forth, each new area of feeling reached and pressed against, multiplied both their pleasure and urgency. Caroline was so caught up in her mission to surround him that he was not certain she knew when her barrier was breached.

"More," she demanded, pushing still more forcefully over him. "Oh, God, that feels so *good*."

No man alive could have disobeyed such an order. With a grunt of effort, he drove himself fully into her.

Caroline had expected to feel like a woman when he took her, but not as if heaven itself had taken up residence between her legs. The sensation of engulfing him was exquisite—incredible warmth and pressure, a tingle that danced a sweet, quick caper at the tip of her pleasure bud. Had he been touching her there, she suspected her whole world would have flown apart.

Aidan seemed no less overwhelmed. He gripped her tightly, pushing up with his hips as if reluctant to lose one fraction of the penetration they had achieved. When at last he opened his eyes, they burned with feelings far more intense than lust.

She shivered with anticipation as he gathered her hair behind her neck and used it to tip her head. The hold made her his prisoner as much as his gaze, and the kiss he lowered onto her mouth surpassed any they had shared before. He sucked her tongue as if it was his prize, as if he would not allow himself to be refused. When he finally did release her, she could scarcely breathe. He shifted the hand that had held her hair to her breast.

"You are mine," he said, squeezing it possessively. "No other man shall have you."

Caroline had been dreaming of hearing those words all her life. She wanted to match them with an equal claim of her own, some gesture for the bold step she was taking. One glance at his heaving chest told her what it should be. She took hold of his shirt's open neck and tore the sweaty linen straight down the front.

The sight of his hard slabbed muscles and sharp nipples made her squirm on the stiffness that impaled her.

"No other woman," she declared on a gasp of sweet sensation, "shall ever have you."

Aidan had been goggling over her behavior, but at this he broke into a laugh. "I am sure I dare not disagree. And since we are stuck with each other"—here he pushed his hips in a manner that drew a moan—"we had better make the best of it."

"Yes," she agreed. "We had better."

He could not move well at first, their fit being rather tight. Happily, with each stroke her body eased, growing wetter and more responsive until at last his motions were perfectly smooth. His hands were firm and steadying on her waist.

"Now you feel the pleasure as you should," he said. "We will keep on like this, nice and slow."

"Not too slow." Her teeth gritted with sensation as his tip glided past her outermost reaches. She liked him there so much she could barely speak. "Remember, you promised to make me cry."

He did make her, and precisely when she was ready to beg him to. No woman, however innocent, could fail to guess what the increased tension in his body meant. With each thrust, he went faster, every muscle and tendon strained. His pleasure must have been riding hard upon his heels, whipped on by the long time they had waited. His efforts to wrestle back his culmination thrilled her. No matter how strong he was, she knew the end could not be far off.

Finally, he growled a frustrated surrender.

"Bite . . . my . . . shoulder," he said, the words propelled from him by the energy of his strokes. "I have to come. I'm going to push you over, too."

It did not occur to her to question him. As directed, she set her mouth against the clenching muscle. She tasted sweat, musk, and then—as soon as his hand worked between them—comprehended *why* he'd told her to do this. The instant he touched that tingling knot of flesh, her pleasure exploded. Only his brawny shoulder could have muffled her wailing cry, and never mind the ones that followed when his thumb began to rub.

"Yes," he praised, then lost his power of speech to a drawn-out moan.

Even in her extremity, she knew he was on the verge. With his free hand wrapped around her bottom, he thrust deeper inside her than she thought anything could go . . . until he drew out one last time to plunge deeper yet.

She gasped with pleasure and shock to feel it. As if he could not stop himself, he wrenched his second hand from between them to clamp that behind her, too. She could not mind. His pelvis ground against hers as if he could meld them into one body. She felt the pressure everywhere she needed to.

Her ribs lurched in time with his on a gulp for air.

Then his ecstasy let go, and he was lost to any awareness but the bliss of pouring out his long release. He groaned as he shot inside her, a deep, low rumble that shook her chest.

As she climaxed again herself, she thought it quite the nicest sound she had ever heard.

The grass was damp beneath her. Caroline still wore her gown, though hardly in the normal way. The hem was tangled up around her waist, and the bodice . . . well, that had been pushed downward along with the top of her corset until Aidan could suckle at her breasts. The pull of his lips and the tickle of his tongue felt lovely; peaceful at first, but that feeling soon became purposeful.

He smiled against her when he felt her slightly impatient wriggle, then pushed above her on impressively muscled arms. She was glad she had removed his shirt, though if she'd been truly wise, she would have torn off his breeches, too. The part of him with which she had finally begun to grow acquainted nudged hotly against her thigh. To her delight, it was as thick and hard as before.

She arched her back and, without quite meaning to, made

a sound like a purr. Fortunately, Aidan understood. "Shall we have a quick one then, love, to seal our bargain?"

"The first time was not quick?"

He flashed his teeth. "You cannot know 'quick' until you've been warmed up."

She stroked her hands up and down his arms. She loved this teasing confidence, so different from the deference he had shown before. "Will I like it that way?"

"Aye, love, now that your body knows what it's in for, I think you shall."

She did, as it happened, for he drove her to the lip-biting edge of bliss as swiftly as he drove himself. There they abandoned themselves to greed, grabbing the deep, hard pleasure that came as quickly as it was craved.

"One more," Aidan gasped, finding her with a shaking but still deft hand.

He watched her rise this time, watched her full breasts jiggle and her hips rock ever faster into his hold. Though this left her a bit embarrassed, his close attention seemed to heighten her final peak.

"Hm," he said, settling loose-limbed against her side, "I think I am beginning to discover what my Caroline likes."

She did not have the strength to answer, or even to shift her bottom off the stone she had just noticed was digging into it. She was too content to entertain more than the smallest worry about what would happen now. No matter what, they would be together.

She couldn't help thinking she should have ruined herself long ago.

The smell of smoke was what roused her from her happy dream. She pushed her head up off Aidan's chest. This was no hour for the staff to be burning rubbish.

Then she saw it: a faint silver trail rising against the predawn gray of the sky. It came not from a chimney, but from one of the upper floors of the house. Perhaps her eyes deceived her, but a flicker of more-than-smoke seemed to light the window nearest the plume.

"Heavens," she said, now sitting fully up. "I think Theo's rooms are burning!"

Aidan did not argue but jumped immediately to his feet and almost as immediately helped her to hers. Caroline tugged her gown to rights as best she could. They looked at each other, fear beginning to register in their minds.

"Perhaps she is not sleeping there," he said, his voice tight and tense, "but we must see."

Caroline did not wait for him to pull on his shirt. She ran toward the hall, hearing the fire now, seeing the flicker grow bright. Her breath came harder with fear than exertion. When she saw Theo's windows were indeed ablaze, she fell to her knees.

"I will alert the house," Aidan called, already changing direction toward the door. "They will not hear us from here."

Caroline scrambled up to follow him. She had to warn her sister. Oh, pray God she was staying with Delavert tonight.

This was the only thought her mind would hold. Her feet were not working as they should. She stumbled in Aidan's wake, up the stone front steps, across the entry. Aidan's booming hail to the household sounded as if it came from a strange distance.

"Fire!" he called. "Everyone out of bed!"

The entrance to Theo's apartments was up the stairs and down a corridor. A haze of smoke had begun to fill it, making her cough. Momentarily speechless, she could only point the way to Aidan. With a look of grim determination, he pulled his shirttail across his mouth and pounded on the door.

"Open it!" she cried. "That is only the sitting room."

When he touched the door knob, it was hot enough that he cursed.

He kicked the door open then. Billows of smoke poured out, stinging her eyes until tears ran down. Theo's pretty furniture was no more than shapes in the gloom. Fire licked like water across the ceiling, an undulating sheet of gold and brown that swallowed at least a third of the sitting room. Caroline stared in amazement. She had never seen or heard the like. The fire hissed and groaned like a living thing.

She did not see how any person could withstand it.

Then she saw two pairs of boots sitting by the door. One was Theo's, and one was Mr. Delavert's. They must have set them out to let the servants know they were there.

"Lord," Aidan said, seeing it, too. "They are both here."

"Theo!" Caroline wailed, choking on the acrid smoke as she tried to fill her lungs and scream again. "Theo, wake up!"

Her heart was breaking. She could feel the pain of it in her chest. She did not realize she was trying to leap for the bedroom until Aidan caught her shoulders.

"I shall get them," he said by her ear. "You return to the landing."

He shoved her, but she could go no farther than the door. She loved him, too. Though she wanted to call him back, the plea was locked in her throat. The staff was gathering. She heard the housekeeper shouting a sharp instruction in the corridor, not quite calm but not panicked. Mrs. Green would do what she could, and the others would obey her. Terrified it would not be enough, Caroline pressed her fists to her mouth and prayed.

A water-soaked sheet was thrown about her shoulders by a footman, the fabric heavy and blessedly cool. Aidan could have used one, but who was going to follow him? She looked around. She did not see Mr. Delavert's steward. Ridiculously handsome or not, he would have done anything to help his friend.

Instead, Caroline was being urged to come away.

"Get another sheet," she demanded. "I need one for the gardener."

The footman's eyes were white all around. He looked all of sixteen without his wig. She saw he was nearly too frightened to move. She would have to take control.

"Now!" she snapped, and to her relief he rushed off.

Chapter 26

*Lucius thought at first that the burning canopy col-*lapsing on their heads was part of a dream. The approach of dawn, not to mention the pleasant exertions that preceded it, had muddled his perceptions.

He had deliberately chosen to slumber at Theo's side, deciding he must trust her to accept the deathlike strangeness of an *upyr*'s rest. With all she had faced already, and with good grace, she deserved this last confidence. Now, ironically, it was she who slept like the dead.

As he batted sparks from his face and shook her, he gave thanks that he had wrapped her in the protection of his aura even before he roused. Apparently, his unconscious survival instinct now included her. Though the room burned down around them, not a hair on her head would be singed.

The air was a different matter. Lucius did not know if the amount he had trapped within the bubble of his power would be enough to sustain a human. Indeed, its insufficiency probably explained why she slept.

Resolved not to waste a second longer, he slung her over

his shoulder and strode from the smoldering bed. The room was not yet engulfed, but candles lay in blazing pools of wax on the carpet, remnants of his earlier romantic display. He stepped around them in puzzlement. He could not imagine how so many tapers had fallen over. As for that, he was certain he had snuffed all but two before they retired.

His step faltered as the truth struck him in an unexpectedly chill wave. This fire was not accidental. Someone had set it. Someone was trying to kill them. Worse, Lucius—the great and powerful ancient *upyr*—had slept through the whole attempt.

The threat his lapse posed to Theo's safety seemed so horrific that when the door burst open, he almost attacked the man behind it. Only at the last moment did he pull up short.

"Sheffield!" he exclaimed, recognizing the hulking figure beneath the sheet.

"Sir!" Sheffield exclaimed back—but with much more shock.

Lucius muttered a curse. His glamour was a memory, his aura pushed to a level a blind man could see. With Theo slung over his shoulder inside the glowing envelope of blue, he must have looked a sight.

"Sir," Sheffield said again, picking his way closer. "What the devil is—"

He shook his head, apparently deciding better of asking, reaching instead for his employer's arm. Lucius was too slow to stop him. The instant contact was made, his aura snapped out to surround the gardener as well.

Sheffield gasped at the abrupt cessation of heat and smoke.

"Go!" Lucius urged the man before his feet could take root. "There's only so much air."

Sheffield nodded and backed up. Lucius was grateful. Theo might be stronger than a normal human, but he did not like the limp way she hung, or her increasingly slow breathing. He sensed she was all right, only unconscious, but he damned well wanted her to stay that way. He was extremely glad to hurry through her sitting room to the end of the fire. Theo's sister was at the outer door, wrapped like Sheffield in a dripping sheet—or partially so. Her ability to hold it on was hampered by her acceptance of a sloshing bucket from the man behind her.

"Damnation," Lucius cursed, knowing he dared not damp his power. Without him to check the fire, its flames were too apt to flare. "The whole blessed staff is here!"

"Sir!" said Sheffield, reduced to this one stupefied word. He must not have thought the loyalty of Hadleigh's servants an appropriate cause for complaint.

Knowing better than to explain, Lucius gripped the gardener's jaw. He could only hope that in the smoke and confusion the others would not notice what he was doing.

"Get the women out of here," he said once the man's gaze was trapped. "Come back with as many loaded buckets as you can carry, and say nothing of what you have seen."

"Yes, sir!" Sheffield said crisply. He bent his knees to accept Theo's dangling form, fumbling only a little as he decided what was safe to hold. It was not every day he was asked to carry his master's stark naked wife.

"Have someone get Mrs. Delavert a blanket," Lucius added to the gardener's apparent relief, after which he returned to the task at hand.

His power held the fire at bay until the man returned, but this required more effort than he had foreseen. His energy and that of the flames were too much akin. They wanted to join forces, not stand opposed. He barely let out his breath until the gardener clunked half a dozen buckets down at his feet. Thankfully, they were wood rather than iron and would not interfere with what he meant to do.

"Place your hand on my back," he instructed Sheffield,

shouting to be heard above the fire's roar. As soon as the man obeyed, Lucius's aura rolled over him. That seen to, he spread his palms above the water.

The gesture was familiar: half instinct, half blurred memory. He had performed this magic before. He knew he could do it now. The last time, he recalled a city had been burning. This was only part of a house. As long as he created an intermediary between himself and the flame, he would succeed.

"Spread and bring peace," he commanded the water. "Spread and bring cool. Thou art strong water. Thou quenchest and do not boil."

The water glowed, then quivered, then exploded into a thick white cloud. Unlike the fog he had called the night of the ball, this cloud took the shape of a man. Hands of vapor reached for the fire, followed by a head with strangely lifelike silver eyes. For one considering moment, those eyes turned to regard him.

Lucius shivered. This, too, he had seen in the distant past. Though the impression of separate intelligence seemed new, he could imagine himself using this thought-form to intimidate an enemy. Swelled by Lucius's will and whatever primitive mind-sense was in the water, the mancloud grew until it had to crouch to fit the room. Leaving himself no time for doubt, Lucius fed it more of his energy.

The giant shook itself and spread its hands.

"Hush," said his creation in a soft, wet version of Lucius's thrall. "Hush and be still."

The fire screamed and raged, but could not win against the cloud giant. First a chair cushion sputtered out, then a set of drapes. The ceiling sighed in surrender and stopped burning. Finally, even Theo's bedroom went black. When it did, the cloud that had fought the battle lost its shape and dissolved. With it went Lucius's sense of the consciousness it had held. Purpose accomplished, the water had returned to its silent state, mere potential force once more.

The only sound then was plopping water and Sheffield

coughing out a prayer at Lucius's back. The reminder of the gardener's more exacting life requirements spurred Lucius to act. Grabbing a now-empty bucket, he flung it through a window with a crash, then directed the banks of smoke out the broken panes.

As fresh air gusted back, Sheffield collapsed to his knees.

"Sir," he gasped, the word an unspoken plea.

Lucius sensed his desire was more for denial than explanation. Few humans really wished to have an intimate encounter with the otherworld. With a sigh for being obliged to show him a small bit more, Lucius knelt in front of him.

"Do not be afraid," he said. "I know this has been confusing, but you will feel better when I am done."

As soon as he flattened one glowing hand on the stunned man's sternum, Sheffield drew a clear breath.

"Lord above," the gardener swore, the last of the smoke trailing out on his exhalation. "Sir, what was all that?"

Lucius gave him credit for having the nerve to ask, but he was spared the trouble of floundering for an answer when Caroline flung open the door. This time neither smoke nor confusion obscured her sight. Her mouth formed a startled O, but a second later she burst into tears.

"They are well," she cried over her shoulder. "Everyone is well!"

Lucius had half a heartbeat to pull on his glamour and damp his power. His entire human staff seemed to be trying to crowd through the door, eager to exclaim about blessings and bravery and how *very* worried they all had been.

Their voices were hardly louder than their thoughts.

To his surprise—and somewhat to his amusement—his housekeeper, Mrs. Green, had reversed her opinion sufficiently to be considering "Delavert" the "finest master that ever was." Still in the corridor, she had remained with "his lady" and was stroking Theo's cheek as she came around.

Lucius's gratitude for this very levelheaded kindness guaranteed the woman would be pleased with her next bonus.

"All right," he said, pushing to his feet to call the crowd to order. "It is over. Thanks to Sheffield's quick thinking and your help, the fire is out."

For some reason, this announcement rendered everyone speechless.

"Oh, *sir,*" one of the maids finally said in a considerably different tone.

The crowd had shifted, and the light from a handful of lanterns was now shining in from the hall, shining, in fact, straight on him. Alerted by the number of suddenly goggling eyes, Lucius glanced down to check his glamour. He saw at once that passing for human was not the problem.

Apparently, Theo was not the only one who'd left her bed naked.

Lucius had done his best to shoo Caroline Becket out of the half-charred sitting room, but Theo's sister refused to budge. He began to regret he had pulled on the clothes his much-neglected valet had tossed through the door. Had he stayed naked, he would have had a better chance of frightening her off.

Then again, maybe not. Though Caroline avoided looking directly at him—shirtsleeves still qualifying as underdressed—her countenance was unusually obstinate.

"I am sorry to disoblige you, Mr. Delavert," she said, "but Aidan and I really must speak with you."

"Aidan" seemed less sure of this assertion than she was, but since Theo's sister had the gardener firmly by the arm, his escape was blocked.

"Oh, God," Edmund moaned, only recently risen from his bed. He put Lucius in mind of a pale, sleepy drunkard after a night in his cups. In spite of this, he was—as ever—impeccably turned out, from his perfectly knotted cravat to his polished boots. "If those two are not leaving, I am sitting before I fall."

Since neither Caroline nor the gardener obliged him, he shuffled to an unburned chair in the darkest corner of the chamber, remembering—Lucius noticed—to flip out his coattails before he sat. Theo had lowered what remained of her custom-fitted shades, but patches of early morning sunshine still lit the blackened floor, and birdsong clamored through the broken panes. Of all those gathered in her room, her condition was the soundest. Both Caroline and Aidan were streaked with ash, but Theo had woken from her smoke-induced slumber with no consciousness of having been at risk. Lucius was glad for that, though he would have been gladder still had the others left them in peace.

His wife stood now by his side—her head on his shoulder, her arm around his waist—seeming to have lost all self-consciousness about displaying her affection in front of an audience.

Lucius grudgingly admitted that part was nice.

"What I have to say shall not take long," Caroline said. "I am sure it is in all our interests to reach an understanding."

"An understanding," Lucius repeated, resisting his temptation to glance at Theo. Even if this discussion turned out to be as uncomfortable as its opening suggested, he doubted Theo would allow him to escape by thralling her sister.

"Yes," Caroline confirmed, her arms now crossed beneath her breasts. She was trying to look determined, succeeded in looking prim, and undercut both with her obvious nervousness. "Aidan and I know something peculiar is going on. You were *glowing,* Mr. Delavert, and Theo escaped that horrid fire without a single burn. Aidan refuses to say what he witnessed when you were alone, though he insists he wishes to tell me."

"Is there a point to this?" Edmund asked, his head propped wearily in his hand. "If there isn't, I'm going back to bed."

Caroline did not give Lucius a chance to hush his friend. "The point is that Mr. Delavert obviously desires to keep quiet whatever explains these oddities. I am willing to go along with that, so long as certain conditions are met."

"Caroline!" her amour burst out. "The man saved my life!"

This clearly came as news, but Caroline recovered swiftly. "Mr. Delavert would not have had to save your life if you, if *we* had not been trying to save his. In any case, Mr. Delavert is not the person of whom I wish to ask the favor."

Theo's head lifted from his shoulder. "That would leave me, I suppose, though I cannot imagine why you think you need to resort to blackmail."

Caroline blushed but did not back down. "I want your help convincing Mama to give her blessing to my marriage to Mr. Sheffield. I know you believe it a misalliance, but I disagree. What's more, I think you are unfair to take that position. Some might say your husband bears a few black marks of his own—meaning no offense," she added hastily to him. "Whatever is wrong with you, you are an amiable man."

"Nothing is wrong with him!" Theo huffed.

"You are right, of course," Caroline immediately soothed. "Mr. Delavert is just different."

Theo had been glowering, but now she laughed at her sister's quick turnabout. "How can anyone argue with you? Even when you're angry, you are too nice!"

"No, no," Caroline protested in dismay. "I am not too nice. I am ruthless and determined to have my way."

"Well, you shall have it with me," Theo promised. "Though I cannot guarantee Mama will cooperate."

"*He* could guarantee it," Edmund murmured dryly, earning himself a warning look from Lucius. "Not that any of this delightful discussion matters, since there can be no question whatsoever of letting either of you lovebirds remember what you have seen."

"Letting us?" Caroline and Sheffield echoed as one.

Lucius knuckled his forehead in anticipation of Theo's

inevitable plea. He knew she didn't want to spend her life hiding the truth from her sister, but no *upyr* should have to face this sort of argument before dark.

Sure as sunrise, his wife caught his arm.

"Oh, Lucius," she said. "They will not tell. Caroline is wonderful at keeping secrets, and Sheffield has proven he is willing to risk his life for yours. Surely you could make an exception for them."

"I am afraid the exception is not mine to make. They are human. The first tenet of *upyr* survival is concealing what we are from them. Edmund's brother could grant a dispensation, but I cannot promise he would."

Theo glanced at his friend. "His brother?"

"Aimery Fitz Clare is head of the *Upyr* Council. It is our ruling body and court of law."

"This is nonsense," Caroline broke in. "Theo is human. She knows you are . . . whatever ooh-peer means."

"Er," said Theo. Evidently, telling her sister she was not human, or not quite, was a bigger hurdle than she cared to face just then. Lucius fought a smile as she neatly avoided further investigation by turning to him. "Could we not perhaps write Mr. Fitz Clare's brother for permission?"

Theo had been hoping to sidestep Caroline's questions, but because she was gazing toward Lucius and Mr. Fitz Clare, she witnessed the peculiar awareness that flickered across both men's faces at the same time. They looked as if they had remembered something important they meant to do.

Theo concluded they were communicating mind-to-mind.

"Actually"—Mr. Fitz Clare ran one uncomfortable finger beneath his starched white stock—"I do not believe a letter shall be required."

Lucius lifted a sardonic brow. "I suppose I do not need to ask who called Aimery here."

Mr. Fitz Clare's hands tightened on the arms of his chair.

"I sent a message about your marriage. I thought Aimery should be apprised. I did not expect him to come in person. I thought he would ask Gillian to look into it from Rome."

"Wonderful. You hoped the Council's Eye would spy on me without my knowledge. Edmund, I love you, but this time you truly have overstepped your bounds."

Though she did not understand this exchange, Theo could see that Lucius was deeply angry. His face was set like stone, and a wave of cold rolled off his arm where she had rubbed it instinctively. Sensing the tension, Aidan Sheffield pulled Caroline behind him.

Oh, dear, Theo thought. *They are going to fight.*

Mr. Fitz Clare seemed to think so, too. Slowly, stiffly, Lucius's steward pushed to his feet. To Theo's surprise, he was a little taller than her husband.

"I may serve you," he said with a dignity she had to admire, "but I am not your servant. My first loyalty must always be to our law. I wager even you have doubts about how well you have upheld that."

"You did this behind my back," Lucius said, "which suggests a rather insulting lack of faith in my willingness to act honorably."

"Enough," Theo broke in, the atmosphere so chill around her husband that her breath came out as a cloud of frost. The effect unnerved her, but she tried not to let it show. "People have been known to underestimate those they loved. It is an error, not a sin. I gather you are expecting guests. Perhaps it would be best if we prepared to greet them."

Lucius stared at Edmund a moment longer, then turned to her. *It is all right,* she thought to him, hoping he was listening. *We are together now. No one can part us.* She knew he heard when a gentle smile eased the stiffness of his face. He stroked the back of his fingers down her cheek.

"You are right, my love. I shall send the servants to their quarters. For these guests, we shall want privacy."

Their "guests" turned out to be quite a picture as seen from the shadowed safety of the entrance hall. First came a slim, fierce-looking woman dressed all in black. Everything she wore was made of leather, from her shockingly snug men's trousers to her thick falconer's gloves. Though her unearthly beauty declared her an *upyr,* her hood was thrown back defiantly, allowing a long mane of raven curls to spill to her hips. The sun did not seem to weaken her. She strode up the gravel path as vigorously as a man.

"That is Gillian," Lucius murmured in Theo's ear. "She is an elder and the Council's Eye. It is she who judges the true thoughts of an accused."

Another *upyr* followed her. His progress was slower but no less worthy of note. His black hood was fastened cowl-like around his face. The shadows it cast made him look a bit sinister—especially since he was even bigger than Sheffield. Theo assumed he was Edmund's brother, but his identity became secondary almost at once. He was holding Lily Morris thrust out before him, each huge hand gripping one of her arms. Though Theo did not feel like laughing, he looked like someone who had captured a smelly fish and was unable to put it down. Lily struggled wildly, both her legs swinging off the ground. Despite this, the arms that held her did not move at all. Her captor might as easily have been carrying a twig.

As they approached, Lily was shouting loud enough to be heard. "You cannot bite me," she declared furiously. "You cannot bite me! I refuse!"

"Good Lord," Mr. Fitz Clare burst out. "What is Lily doing with *him*?"

"Is there someone else with whom she should be?" Lucius inquired, thus causing his friend to wince. "Never mind. I can guess. In fact, I can guess a number of things. It occurs to me she must have told the gamekeeper to set traps. Certainly, she is the only human who could try to burn me in my bed without my noting her approach."

"But why?" Mr. Fitz Clare asked.

"That should be obvious, I would think. She has discovered what we are, Edmund, because neither of us is as good at keeping secrets as we thought."

"But I was *careful*."

Mr. Fitz Clare had no chance to defend his claim. His brother had reached the steps and was now ascending to the terrace.

"We found this one by your gate," he said, then tilted his head toward his leather-garbed companion. "Gillian says her mind was full of treachery."

Lucius seemed surprised. "Gillian was able to read her?"

"Who can't she read?" the man responded fondly. "Excepting, of course, yourself."

This was too much for Lily.

"They are monsters!" she cried, as if anyone there might be convinced to help. "I must tell my father to raise the town. They will not fail as I did. They will burn this place to the ground!"

"How medieval," Gillian said. She regarded Lily with cool distaste. "If I were you, however, I would not assume a hundred torch-wielding villagers would have better luck." She nodded at Lucius with such serenity Theo could not begin to guess what passed through her mind. "You are looking well, old friend, better than well. It seems dredging up forgotten powers suits you better than you used to think."

"When my old powers are called for," Lucius said. "I am quite content to employ them."

His hand was tight on Theo's, protectively tight. Despite the mildness of both their tones, Theo suspected a threat had just been exchanged.

The woman called Gillian dropped her gaze to her feet, not quite hiding her smile. "Shall we continue this reunion inside? Some of us prefer more shade."

"Please do come in," Theo said, judging it time she spoke up. Half-human or not, she was the mistress of this house. She pulled the open door wider. "I am delighted to welcome my husband's old friends. Shall I call you Gillian, or do you prefer more formality?"

"Gillian suits me," the woman said, her smile twitching upward on one side. "My husband here is Aimery, and I do believe you ought to stop thinking of his brother as Mr. Fitz Clare. Edmund is, after all, not a real steward. He is, in a manner of speaking, your family—at least until we discover precisely what has been done to you."

"He is a monster!" Lily shrieked, "And she is a monster for marrying Delavert!"

The head of the Council had heard enough. Aimery set Lily's feet on the marble tiles, hugged her wriggling body back against him, and covered her mouth with his hand.

Her objections muffled, he looked to his brother. "Please tell me this is not the human you were concerned about."

"No," Edmund said, sounding a little faint. "That one is my problem. I wrote of Theo, Lucius's wife."

Theo fought the urge to shrink back when Aimery turned to her.

"She does not appear unhappy," he said, "or particularly thralled."

"No," Edmund agreed. "She does not *appear* thralled, but Lucius's power has increased so much of late, I am not sure you or I would read the signs. One fact, however, remains certain. Though Lucius has not changed her in the usual way, she is no longer wholly human."

A muffled gasp told Theo her sister had heard this. Theo heaved a silent sigh. At least she no longer had to dread breaking the news herself.

"Gillian could read the girl," Aimery suggested. "Find out the truth."

Lucius's refusal was immediate. "No, I will not subject her to that."

"It would not hurt her," Gillian said soothingly.

"Her life is not your business, not even as the Council's Eye." Lucius pulled his shoulders straight. "I will let you read me instead."

Gillian's mouth fell open, an odd expression to see on an apparently unflappable *upyr.* "You would let me read you? You, who know what my gift involves? You, who could shut me out until Kingdom Come? Though I admit I would love to root around in your mind, it is likely you would relive your lost centuries. If Edmund's account of your recent activities is true, you have recovered more of your past. By the time I finished my examination, you might no longer forget anything."

"That does not matter," Lucius said staunchly.

Only Theo was close enough to feel the infinitesimal tremor that vibrated through his arm. He was frightened—terrified, if one allowed for the fact that he had more than a human's ability to hide his reactions. That being so, she was touched beyond measure to hear him offering to stand in her place.

"It *does* matter," she said, squeezing his fingers to warm them. "You have faced your worst memory. You do not have to face them all, not for me, not like this."

"Mena was my best memory," Lucius whispered down to her, his eyes welling up until they glittered like clear gray jewels.

"That is why she was the worst to face. Because you loved her so much."

"I love *you,*" he said. "Whether you are the same soul or different. I love you as I was not wise enough to love her."

His words moved her almost too much to speak.

"Gillian will not hurt me," she said, once she had swallowed the lump in her throat. "If she has read as many minds as her being the Council's Eye suggests, she will see nothing she has not before. Your friends will know you are innocent of coercing me. For that matter, so will you."

Lucius stroked her hair. "They do not have the power to force us to do anything we do not want. I . . . Theo, I am stronger than all of them put together."

Theo laughed softly at his clear reluctance to confess this. "They are your friends, love, and were they to shun you it would break your heart. That I will not allow when I can stop it."

Lucius's eyes glowed with gratitude and respect. Gentle as a moonbeam, he kissed her lips.

"Oh, *my*." The Council's Eye sighed with feminine amusement, her hand fluttering at her leather-covered breast. "With such demonstrations of love as these, I begin to wonder if this examination is required."

"It is," Theo said, turning toward her determinedly. "I will not have anyone left with doubts."

Chapter 27

*Gillian had settled on the picture gallery, where Lu-*cius had held his ball, as the spot for Theo's interrogation. Not yet waxed, the wooden floors still bore scuffmarks from the dancers' feet. The windows probably explained why the *upyr* had chosen the room. They were placed near the frescoed ceiling. Because they faced west and it was early in the day, what light shone through them petered out halfway down the wall. Had the bewigged portraits that hung from the paneling been alive, they would not have witnessed much.

Theo imagined this was just as well. She doubted the old squire's relatives would condone the use to which their family seat was being put.

"Will you have to bite me?" she asked nervously.

Gillian had finished setting two Sheraton sidechairs opposite each other in the center of the floor. Their arms were glossy, their upholstery striped brown silk. With a grace Theo concluded was inherent to the *upyr,* she gestured for Theo to sit in one.

"I do not have to bite you," she answered as she claimed the other. "Like Lucius, I am an elder. I can enter a person's mind without the aid of a blood-bond. For a deep reading, however, the process is easier if we touch."

They were almost touching now. The *upyr*'s scandalous black leather trousers were inches from Theo's knees.

"Skin to skin," Gillian qualified, offering her hand palm up.

The sight of it resting on the *upyr*'s thigh caused Theo to lick dry lips. Gillian was doing nothing to hide her nature. The faint white-gold glow of her tapered fingers was apparent in the murky gloom. Coupled with the silky surface of her skin, it formed quite an invitation. Even so, Theo could not bring herself to slip her hand into the *upyr*'s.

"You will read *all* of my life?" she asked.

"In order to ascertain the truth, I must. It is important that I weigh your capacity to judge what influence Lucius has imposed. If it eases your mind, I shall not speak of what I find to anyone, except as it relates directly to this matter or threatens the safety of my kind."

Theo searched the *upyr*'s face, but such alabaster perfection did not offer clues she knew how to interpret. This "judgment" sounded more like an art than a science. What if the Council's Eye misinterpreted what she saw, and Lucius were thereby hurt?

"You will find no evidence of wrongdoing," Theo said, unwilling to leave the result to chance. "I have recovered much of my memory from the nights my husband thralled me. Lucius lowered my inhibitions, but only enough that I did what I truly wished. Never did he force me. In truth"—Theo ignored the skin-warming blush that crept up her cheeks—"there were a few occasions when I urged him on."

"I am certain that shall be clear," Gillian said, a smile that should have been more reassuring curving her lips. "Give me your hand, Theo. This may be an art, but it is an art I have had centuries to master. I promise you, the truth will out."

Theo wished she were as confident as the *upyr*. She dried her sweaty palms on her gown.

"Very well," she said in resignation. "I am ready."

Lucius grimaced at the noisy ticking of the tall carved clock in the entryway. He could not fathom what was taking Gillian so long. Even a deep reading of someone's mind was not a lengthy process; time contracted to allow the images to flash by. If Theo did not return from the ballroom soon, he would be reduced to pacing the hall like a common human.

Not that the humans he had met recently qualified as common. He looked to the opposite bench where Caroline and Sheffield sat hand in hand. They could not know it, but their auras had begun to blend, mirroring each other in their play of color and light. Married or not, their spirits were in harmony. Lucius smiled to see it, then frowned when yet another muffled protest from Lily Morris disturbed the air.

She was wearing out what patience he had left. It was past time someone handled her. There was, after all, no chance she would be permitted to leave this house with her recall untouched.

"Shall I?" he said to Aimery, who had been restraining Lily all this time.

"Can you?" Aimery responded, his eyes widening with interest. "You do know that for an erasure of this sort you must *enter* her mind, not merely thrall her. That is the only way to ensure the proper memories are removed. Gillian said her barriers were extremely strong."

Lucius fought not to grind his teeth at this less-than-flattering implication. "If your wife can read her, I should be able to as well. I expect it is merely a matter of persisting long enough."

"Be my guest then. Her constant wriggling grows tiresome."

With the ghost of a grin to suggest he knew what would happen, Aimery let Lily go.

"Beast!" she cried, rushing straight for Lucius with her little nails curled into claws. "My papa will kill you all!"

Though Lucius admired her bravery, he was not going to let her attack. Thankfully, she had not figured out she should avoid his gaze. He caught her eye handily.

"Stop," he ordered in his firmest thrall.

Lily stopped as if her shoes were glued to the floor. A birdlike croak of horror stuck in her throat.

"You shall not bite me," she wailed as he approached. "I will not be marked!"

"No," Lucius agreed. "You shall not. Fortunately for both of us, my power does not require such aids." He grasped Lily's chin, bringing her eyes perfectly to his. "Open to me, Lily Morris. Let down your walls. It is your only hope of leaving this house alive."

She believed him. He could see that in the shudders which shook her frame. Her eyes had gone unfocused from his thrall, but her mental walls still resisted him.

"Let me in," he commanded. "I know you want me to save you."

"You saved her," she said in a small, hurt voice. "You saved her instead."

He knew she meant Theo, knew she had looked upon marrying Delavert as an escape.

"Now it is your turn," he soothed in a gentler tone. "I am sure you do not want this chance to slip through your hold."

"No," she agreed in a hoarse whisper. "I do not."

He was in her mind then, past all her guards. Thread by thread, he sorted through her memories: those he could leave her, those he must eradicate. He was proud of the delicacy with which he worked, the job as fine as any of Theo's embroideries. He doubted Lily would guess there were empty spaces in her picture of her recent life.

His satisfaction would have been perfect, had he not been

obliged to examine memories he knew she would rather have concealed, memories that unsettled even him.

In public, Lady Morris had sung her daughter's praises to one and all. In private, she had been haranguing Lily since she was a child, day and night sometimes, dictating how she must stand and speak, how she must smile and eat, and accompanying every instruction with a litany of shortcomings. Lily's indulgent papa did not possess the spine to stand against his wife, or have the perception to know he should. Left undefended, Lily's better emotions had been crushed by her own mother. The abuse had been effected in the name of guaranteeing her future, but had succeeded far better at robbing Lily of her truest self.

Considering the secret anger with which she lived, he could not wonder at her recent acts. The shock of discovering what he and Edmund were, coupled with the loss of her hoped-for escape, had caused her to snap.

Because he could not hate her, as he pulled free from the tangled shadows of her thoughts, Lucius decided to leave a small kindness behind.

"Your mother is only a mortal woman," he said, his thrall as soft and subtle as his own heartbeat. "And you are not a child anymore. She has no more power to make you unhappy than you cede to her in your mind. You need neither hate nor fear her so much. You can make your own decisions—without regard to her."

Lily blinked at him from her daze, with slow, sleepy descents of her fair lashes.

"Good," she slurred. "There are things I have wished to do."

Lucius knew enough to leave the matter there. When it came to changing human nature, a gentle push was the least likely to do harm.

"When I snap my fingers," he said, "you will sleep until the instructions I have given you become a natural part of your mind. When you wake, you will feel relaxed and calm."

He snapped his fingers and Lily collapsed in his arms. Catching her, Lucius looked to Sheffield. "Can you get her home without being seen coming from Hadleigh?"

The gardener's expression was dumbfounded. "I . . . I should be able to, but what explanation should I give her family?"

"Tell her you found her by the side of the road as you took the supply wagon into town, and that you assume she must have been sleepwalking."

Sheffield's gaze went from Lily's unconscious form to Lucius's face. He was not a stupid man, merely slowed by shock. Now he was reckoning up how easily what had been done to Lily could be done to him and Caroline.

"I can do it," Sheffield said. "I expect they will believe me. That sort never thinks a simple gardener can lie well enough to fool them."

"I shall vouch for your character, if required," Lucius said. "And I thank you. By this service, you put me in your debt."

The gardener understood perfectly. He nodded to Lucius as he accepted Lily's dangling weight, then carried her carefully out the door. As if Caroline also saw the importance of being useful, she jumped up to shut it behind him.

Lucius did not move after that, staring at the marble tile while he went over every detail of the last quarter hour. He did not see anything he had forgotten. Lily ought to slip back into her life without a ripple.

Everyone left him alone until Edmund stepped beside him.

"I am sorry about this," he said, low and rough. "If I had not been so sure of myself, if my judgment of Lily had been clearer, this might not have happened."

Seeing Edmund's remorse, Lucius shook his head. "It does not matter. As my wife was wise enough to say, anyone may misjudge. The important thing is that this has ended well."

"It will end well if Lily leaves the county and we never see her again. Lord, what taste I have in women!"

"Well, but you have plenty of time to improve it," Lucius pointed out.

"Ha ha," Edmund responded, a sign of humor Lucius welcomed.

With the first touch of Gillian's fingers, Theo's surroundings disappeared from sight. In their place, her life flew through her mind in a blur of color and sound, events she was astonished to know she had memories of. Her father and mother laughed over her cradle, so young and happy it wrenched her heart. Caroline roared like a monster while chasing Theo's toddler self around the old rectory garden. School lessons pelted by. Her father's death. Boys she had liked who had ignored her. Hurts she had taken and administered. Then Nathan's image rose from the day she had waved goodbye, scrubbed and handsome in his uniform.

Her sight was clearer now than it had been then, and it registered more than buttons and braids. She saw her feelings for her fiancé had been but a girl's: sweet, to be sure, but untried. The realization shamed her, yet somehow the wound did not sting.

Nathan would have forgiven her. Remembering who he was told her that. In whatever realm he existed now, he could not be hurt. Too, if Lucius's talk of other lives was true, perhaps when Nathan came back he would find the woman with whom he was meant to be. Theo prayed this would happen even as the pageant of her life rushed on.

She would have lingered on her memories of Lucius, but they raced by as well. She marveled at the difference in the love she felt for her husband—and at a far earlier date than she had realized. Her doubts seemed laughable when seen through her present eyes. Every step of the way, had she but known it, he had treated her as someone precious to his heart. She vowed she would never let him doubt hers again.

She returned to herself with a jolt. Her seat was beneath

her as suddenly as if she had been dropped into it. The *upyr* was watching her, no longer holding her hand. Seeing Gillian was a shock. Theo had been so engrossed with the panorama flashing through her mind that she had forgotten the other's presence.

"Is that it?" Theo asked, the words coming thick and slow.

Gillian sat back, her long dark curls spilling down her arms. She looked calm, but slightly dazed, as if she, too, had to consciously recall herself.

"That is it," she said. "I will inform the others that Lucius is innocent of all charges."

Considering Theo had just relived the events in question, the verdict came as no surprise.

"Thank you," she said. Her knees shook slightly as she pushed to her feet. She forced herself to breathe away her dizziness before she moved. Lucius would not be reassured unless she looked well.

Before she could leave, Gillian put a hand to her wrist. Her fingers were cool and smooth.

"Theo," she said, almost as if they were equals. "You have done all that is required, but if you would be kind enough to stay a moment longer, I would be grateful for a chance to speak."

"About Lucius."

"About Lucius and your future life with him." The *upyr* pulled her hand back to rub the arms of her chair. She seemed to be mulling over what to say. "Being his wife won't always be easy, though he is much changed from the man I knew even a year ago. Do you know—"

Gillian pressed her fingertips to her mouth. With some amazement, Theo saw her emotions were making it difficult for her to speak.

"Do you know," she went on, "for a long time Aimery and I were convinced he was going to embrace the sun, simply stand in it one day and burn. He barely cared enough to be sad for what he had lost. But you have brought him alive again."

"I am glad that pleases you," Theo said, unsure where this was leading.

"Pleasure is only part of it. Once upon a time, Lucius gave me my freedom and made it possible for me to find and keep the man I love. For the sake of what I owe him, I beg you, be strong for him. Do not give up if, for a while, 'better' becomes 'worse.' Do not take back the life you have given him. None of us want to lose Lucius."

Theo knew it cost this woman, this power among her kind, to beg anything of her. She thought carefully before she spoke. To Gillian's further credit, she waited patiently.

"I know Lucius would say you owe him nothing," Theo began, experiencing an odd need to be gentle. "And I would think that after what you have seen of my heart, you would not need to ask what you do. I have my flaws, but I am not weak. Lucius will always have my best, and would have had it without your plea."

"I am sorry," said the Council's Eye. "I have offended you."

"No. You are his friend. You felt you had to say what you did. What I wish you to know is that Lucius is no more weak than I am. If he had been as hopeless as you claim, he could not have *wanted* to live again. He could not have fallen in love with me. He would have given up long ago."

Gillian's hands were folded in her lap. It was to them she spoke her next low words. "Lucius would not survive losing you."

The statement held such certainty Theo wondered for a moment if it were true. Then she shook herself.

"He might not choose to, but I have no doubt he could. Nor do we have the right to judge. I suspect he has loved and lost more than any of us can comprehend. If he decides one day that he has had enough, I will cry, but I will not stand in his way. All beings, even those who are greatly loved, deserve their rest."

Mena might have been speaking then, so intimately did Theo in that moment understand her predecessor's heart. Maybe Theo *was* Mena reborn, and maybe, if it was true, she had reason to be proud.

Gillian looked up at her, her *upyr*-sharp eyes narrowed. "You are fiercer than I am in his defense."

She sounded jealous. Seriousness forgotten, Theo's lips twitched with the start of a grin. That this lovely woman could be jealous of her, for any reason, seemed humorous.

Then again, when one was capable of being friends for centuries, one might grow a touch possessive.

"I should be fierce," Theo said. "I am his wife."

The *upyr* stared at her, then broke into a smile. "Do not forget that, and you and I will get on."

One would think the Council's Eye would be satisfied to have this be the last word, but then she drew a quick breath.

"Oh," she said with a look of slight embarrassment. "I nearly forgot what occurred to me while I was reading you. My husband's three hundredth anniversary as Council Head is approaching, and I gather you have a fine hand with a needle. Now that your skills are likely to strengthen even more, do you suppose I might commission an embroidered tunic—fourteenth-century style—to give him for the occasion? You shall be invited, of course, as will Lucius."

Theo took a moment to close her mouth, this request requiring a number of unusual readjustments inside her head.

"I should be honored," she said, "and I am certain Lucius would like to attend."

"Excellent," said Gillian, her hands slapping her thighs. "You do not know how difficult it is to find a gift for a man who's seen everything!"

When Lucius opened his arms, Theo's last anxiety was swept away. Not caring in the least who saw, she rushed to him across the entry and pressed her cheek to his slowly beating heart. He was just warm enough to soothe her—perfect, she thought, for a wife who had a tendency to flush when her spouse was near.

"I love you," she whispered, holding him tight.

His palm stroked her unbound hair, its length now as silky as an *upyr*'s, if still unfashionably bereft of curls. Not caring two straws if it was, Theo hugged her husband until he laughed.

"I hope this means my name has been cleared."

"Yes," Theo said. "Completely."

She tilted her head back to meet his gaze. His eyes glowed with emotions deeper than words could express. She knew she had been right to let Gillian read her. Before he had believed she loved him voluntarily; now he had the comfort of knowing.

"Yes," Gillian agreed from the archway behind her. "It is my ruling as the Council's Eye that Theo Becket came to you of her own free will."

"Yea!" cried a young male voice that should not have been hiding on the stairs. Making enough noise for ten boys, Percy Fitz Clare clattered down the rest of the treads. "I am coming to visit! Every day as you promised! No more dusty, musty castle all the time!"

"Every day?" Edmund asked, sounding dubious but hopeful.

"I am convinced I did not promise that," Theo said to her husband's amused and inquiring look.

"You did!" Percy chortled, pulling Caroline across the tiles in an eccentric version of a jig, his motions consisting of more than the usual hopping up and down. "And on the days I am not here, I shall visit Aunt Caroline!"

"What about Robin?" Lucius put in. "Is your faithful guardian to be forgotten?"

Percy stopped jigging with a stricken look. As betokened his new optimism, it soon cleared. "I shall play with Uncle Robin at night."

"And what of sleep?" was Edmund's rejoinder.

Both Edmund and Lucius were smiling, clearly fond of their orphaned charge. Seeing their affection for Percy's antics gave Theo an unexpected sense of the family she would have from now on. Gillian would be a part of it, and Percy's presumably slumbering guardian. Lucius's friends would love her for his sake at first, but in time surely for her own. *Upyr* might sometimes be cold to touch, but she had learned their hearts were warm. She discovered she was looking forward to getting to know them all.

Her nerves thrilled suddenly at the idea. Who knew what other wonders she might encounter? This was, without a doubt, the best garden wall she had ever climbed!

"Must I sleep?" Percy asked, now hoisted onto Caroline's hip. "I want to play with everyone."

"I think you must sleep sometimes," Caroline said, "if you want to grow into a strong young man."

Rather than pout, Percy laid his head on her shoulder and closed his eyes. Theo had seen Caroline's sweetness perform such miracles before. Her older sister was definitely born to be a mama. Less familiar with Caroline's charms, Edmund gaped while Lucius chuckled.

"Who says humans have no magic?" he murmured in Theo's ear.

Theo kissed him and said, "Not I."

"You see?" Lucius turned to the others. "We must leave Caroline and Sheffield's memories intact. If Caroline is to help us with our little chatter-monster, I would forever be having to erase the new things he spilled to her."

"Am I your little monster?" Percy asked, just as Edmund groaned, "Oh, Lord, he is right."

Caroline and Theo smiled at each other in their old knowing way. Only one element was new: Theo's sister was beaming with happiness.

"Welcome to my family," Theo said.

"The pleasure is mine," Caroline assured her.

"Ours," Lucius corrected, snuggling Theo beneath his arm. "If I have anything to say about it, and I do, the pleasure we take in each other's company will be shared."

Despite the challenges—not to mention the adventures—Theo anticipated they would face, Lucius's joyously crinkling eyes convinced her his claim was true.

Married two months now, Theo thought nothing could be as splendid as lying naked on the lush cool lawns of Hadleigh with her handsome husband. Lucius's aura fended off any discomfort, and she was able to relax completely, her head pillowed on his arm, her body sated, her eyes dazzled by a firmament full of stars.

Though she remained by most measures human, with every night they spent together, her senses sharpened—until she could experience these nocturnal beauties almost as keenly as Lucius. The breeze ruffled over her, and the air was sweet with autumn scents. Tomorrow, Lucius's wolf would hunt with Edmund and Robin, but tonight he reserved for them.

"Mama seemed to enjoy supper," she commented lazily. "I think she is getting used to seeing Sheffield at the table."

Lucius chuckled into the dark. "I think she is working hard to convince herself he will be gentry, once I deed him and Caroline that land."

Theo rolled toward him and kissed his chest. "You are giving them a wonderful wedding present."

"I am giving them a practical wedding present. That property will keep them close. I have never seen Percy so manageable as he has been since Caroline took him in hand. Robin is ready to nominate her for sainthood."

"She deserves it. And so does Percy. I like having him around. I know he cannot be trusted alone with our uncle's brood, but hopefully Caroline and Sheffield will give him a few new playmates. By the time their children are old enough to comprehend what Percy says, he should be old enough to hold his tongue."

Lucius snorted softly and stroked her hair. Theo knew he considered this wish for playmates as likely of being fulfilled as she did. Lucius's marital contentment might have calmed the staff 's lustiness, but Caroline and Aidan were, from what Theo could see, too sharp-set to wait for their wedding vows. Theo was surprised to discover this simply pleased her. Her sister deserved a man who adored her in every way.

She was smiling to herself when Lucius shifted under her.

"I did hear some news which might interest you," he began. "Mind you, this comes from Edmund, who heard it from an upper maid, but I think it really must be true."

Something in his tone prompted Theo to prop her chin on her forearms to look at him.

His mouth twisted wryly as he met her gaze. "Lily Morris has run off with James Poole, the best friend of the real Delavert's dead brother."

"The man who snubbed you at the ball? But . . . he is married. Both of them will be ruined. What an embarrassment for Lady Morris, and, oh, how Mama will crow!"

"Yes, it is quite the scandal, made worse by Poole's gambling debts. Lily might not have known this, but they won't have much to live on. I gather the Morrises have been trying desperately to hush it up."

"Why do you have that strange look on your face?" Theo asked, smoothing her hand across the muscles of his chest.

"Because I suspect this is my doing. When I went into

Lily's mind to erase her knowledge of the *upyr,* I felt sorry for what I found. While I was still thralling her, I told her she need not think her mother all-powerful. I told her she could make her own decisions."

"Then she has made them, not you." Theo sank back down and hugged him. "Do not worry, love. Whether they are happy or unhappy will be their own doing—just as our happiness is ours."

"You *are* happy, aren't you."

His voice held too much male satisfaction for this to be a question, but Theo answered him all the same. She had learned one really could not give one's spouse too many compliments.

Grinning, she slid her hand down his side. "I believe I recently gave you reason to know how happy I am."

Beneath her cheek, she felt Lucius warm.

"Would you like to prove it again?"

Theo laughed and straddled his hips, delighted to find his body readying. The change was so swift that in seconds his hardness had lifted and was quivering like a tuning fork. She could hardly wait to kiss him to see if his teeth were sharp. For now, his lips were closed on his smile. His hands glided up her belly, reminding her just how admired his caresses could make her feel.

The only thing she liked better was driving him wild. She was growing fond of the beast in him.

"I know what you are thinking," he warned, flashing a hint of fang.

Theo gasped as his fingers tweaked the tips of her breasts.

"If you know what I am thinking," she said, "then I am the one who should have proof."

"Gladly," he growled, neatly rolling her beneath him.

To her immense gratification, he set about providing it at once.

Also available from

Emma Holly

Personal Assets

An Erotic Novel of Power and Pleasure

0-425-19931-2

Style and sensuality. Power and passion...there's something about the Parisian boutique *Meilleurs Amis* that provokes all who enter to blur the line between business and pleasure. And no one knows better than Beatrix Clouet, daughter of the founder, and her best friend Lela Turner.

Now these two friends will have to weigh their desires for professional success and personal satisfaction—while making their wildest fantasies come true...

"Holly brings a level of sensulaity to her storytelling that may shock the uninitiated."
—Publishers Weekly

Available wherever books are sold or at penguin.com

B141

Emma Holly

Beyond Innocence

0-515-13099-0

When her beloved father passes away, Florence Fairleigh finds herself alone in the world. All she wants is a man who will treat her kindly and support her financially—and she's come to London to find him…

Edward Burbrooke thinks marriage is the only way to save his brother Freddie—and their family—from scandalous ruin. As head of the family, Edward has vowed to find Freddie a bride—and fast.

Beyond Seduction

0-515-13308-6

To avoid marriage, Merry Vance has concocted a sinfully scandalous scheme: to pose for Nicolas Craven, London's most sought-after artist. No man in his right mind would marry a woman who posed nude for this notorious rogue.

But Nicolas has his own plans for the feisty young woman—and Merry has no idea how hot it can get in an artist's studio.

Available wherever books are sold or at penguin.com

B528